From Pat I...

There ... Valley with provisions. We are to start in two or three days and cache our goods here. There is amongst them some old mountainers. They say the snow will be here until June.

The next day Reed and three men hiked down to the lower end of the lake to the Donner camp. One of the rescuers, a man named Potter, had gone over the day before, and now he met them just outside the camp.

"You ain't ready for what you're about to see in this here camp," Potter told them.

In the spring of 1846, a wagon train of men, women, and children left Springfield, Illinois, bound for California and the promise of free land. But as they progressed westward, hardship met them at every step. . . . Battering storms and blazing desert heat ravaged their supplies and tried their spirits. Then they reached the Sierra Nevadas—and their nightmare truly began. . . . The true story of the Donner party lives on in history as one of the most astounding and unforgettable pioneer ordeals—a journey that began with hope—and then went so terribly wrong. . . .

Meet the men and women of
SURVIVAL
A Novel of the Donner Party

turn the page . . .

GEORGE DONNER—It was his advertisement in the *Illinois Vindicator* that promised free land in California to a willing and able wagon party. But when his dreams turned into a nightmare beyond imagining, all those who followed him paid the ultimate price . . .

JAMES REED—Proud, strong, and ambitious, the wealthy cabinet manufacturer was a surefooted group leader. But his insistence on taking the Hastings Cutoff, a rumored shortcut through the mountains, spread dissension and distrust—and made him enemies among his fellow travelers . . .

IKE BUFORD—An aspiring journalist, he dreamed of starting his own newspaper in California. His was the voice of reason amidst chaos—and of human compassion when man turned upon man. But it was the love of one woman that kept his hope alive . . .

HANNAH PRICE—Falling in love with Ike Buford was the last thing the pretty cousin of the Reed family had expected on her westward adventure. Now she carried in her heart a dream of their life together, of children and grandchildren—and the belief that love conquers all . . .

TAMSEN DONNER—A pillar of physical and emotional strength, George Donner's wife endured with a kindness of spirit and a commitment to her family. Even when James Reed's rescue party descended upon their lake camp, she refused to leave her dying husband's side . . .

COLONEL WILLIAM RUSSELL—He had led many successful wagon trains across to California, and he welcomed George Donner and his group when they joined Russell's massive company. But he refused to take the Hastings Cutoff that so many favored—and soon had no choice but to abandon them—and leave the Donner party to their own navigations . . .

PAT BREEN—Along the lake camp below the mountain pass, fear and hunger drove men to desperate acts. Breen's journal recorded it all with unflinching honesty—a document of horror.

LANSFORD HASTINGS—While some told the Donner party they began their journey too late to avoid snowfall in the Sierra Nevadas, his book, *The Emigrants' Guide to Oregon and California*, told of an enticing mountain pass, an alternative route that could save hundreds of miles and weeks of travel. For the Donner party, his promise was little more than dust in the wind. And by the time they realized they were misguided, it was too late to turn back . . .

SURVIVAL

A Novel of the Donner Party

K.C. McKenna

JOVE BOOKS, NEW YORK

SURVIVAL: A NOVEL OF THE DONNER PARTY

A Jove Book / published by arrangement with
the author

PRINTING HISTORY
Jove edition / July 1994

ISBN: 0-515-11405-7

A JOVE BOOK®
Jove Books are published by The Berkley Publishing Group,
200 Madison Avenue, New York, New York 10016.
JOVE and the "J" design
are trademarks belonging to Jove Publications, Inc.

PRINTED IN THE UNITED STATES OF AMERICA

10 9 8 7 6 5 4 3 2 1

PART ONE

*Maker of
Heaven and Earth*

July 3rd, 1931

From his wicker passenger seat on the left side of the plane, John Buford could see the engine hanging down from the high corrugated wing. The bottom of the wing, the wing strut and wheel assembly, the left engine nacelle, and the left front part of the fuselage of the Tri-Motor Ford had been turned to molten gold by the ambient light of the setting sun. Looking forward, through the spinning propeller, John could see the Sierra Nevadas, the range of mountains that separated Nevada from California. The airliner, belonging to Trans-Western Airlines, had departed Reno, Nevada, just a little over half an hour before. At just about dusk, they would be landing at the Sacramento airport. Right now they were passing over Donner Lake and Donner Pass. Their transit of the Sierra Nevadas would take about twenty minutes.

The stewardess came down the aisle, ducking her head slightly to be able to stand. She was wearing a blue uniform, complete with nurse's cape and cap.

"Are we going to be on time?" John asked. He had to shout to be heard above the noise of the three engines.

"Yes, I think so," the stewardess answered with a smile. "Would you like a stick of gum, sir? It will keep your ears from stopping up."

"Yes, thank you," John replied, taking the proffered piece.

There were nine other passengers in the plane besides John, and as the stewardess went on to attend to them, John

3

reached into his inside jacket pocket and pulled out the letter. The letter was from Miss Alice Reed, and it had invited John to Sacramento to speak with her great-great-aunt Patty. John hoped, sincerely, that Miss Reed's aunt Patty would be able to answer some questions for him.

Eighty-five years ago John's grandfather had come West by wagon train. A trip that had taken John only a matter of hours had taken his grandfather several months. Though he had asked his grandfather about that trip many times, the old man had talked very little about it. Then one day, when John's questions grew more persistent, his grandfather had answered him.

"I swore an oath to others never to speak of all the things that happened during that time," he had said. "I have kept that oath for all these years, and I intend to keep it until I am released from it, or until I go to my grave."

Learning about the oath made John even more curious. Curiosity was a part of John's nature. It was also a part of his trade, for like his father and his grandfather before him, John Buford was a newspaper man.

One month ago John's editor at the St. Louis newspaper where he worked had suggested that John do a piece on the opening of the West by wagon train. Remembering that his own grandfather had taken part in one of those great wagon-train treks, John had readily agreed. While doing the research he had come across some startling information about the fate of the Donner party. He had heard about the Donner party, but he had never paid that much attention to it. But some of the dates and names he saw in his research coincided with the little he knew about his grandfather's experience. Could it be that his grandfather was one of the members of the Donner party?

John had searched for more complete information, but he could find nothing to verify his hunch. Then he had learned that, incredibly, one of the members of the Donner party was still alive! She had been eight years old during the crossing.

She was ninety-three now, and she lived in Sacramento, California. John had decided to fly out to interview her.

The Next Day

When John went down into the hotel lobby the next morning, he was given a telegram from St. Louis. His editor wanted him to visit the Sacramento newspaper to make some arrangements for a syndicated column they were buying. As a result, it was early afternoon before John was able to telephone Alice Reed and ask if he could come out to speak with her. She told him to come ahead, her aunt Patty was looking forward to the visit.

The house was a large two-story brick home that sat well back on a spacious, tree-shaded lot. The grass was kept lush by sprinklers, which even now were working. Near the porch and along the fence were huge banks of flowers of every description and hue. John checked the return address on his letter against the big brass numbers he could see on the front of the house. Satisfied that he had the right place, he paid the taxi driver and sent him off, then walked up to the house and pulled on the rope to ring the bell.

An attractive young woman met him at the door.

"Mr. Buford?" she asked.

"Yes, I'm John Buford. Mrs. Reed?"

"It's Miss Reed. Please, call me Alice. Won't you come in, Mr. Buford? We've been expecting you."

John followed the young woman inside. The high ceilings, open windows, and overhead fans kept the house pleasantly cool. In the hallway, a very tall grandfather clock suddenly whirred, then gonged once, announcing the hour. As John looked at it, he couldn't help but be struck by how beautiful it was. The tall case was made of polished walnut, shining richly as if lit by some inner fire. The pendulum and the weights behind the glass front of the case were of gold, and the clock face was silver, with raised, black-enamel Roman numerals.

"What a beautiful clock," John said.

"Yes," Alice replied, touching it lovingly. "It has been in the family for four generations now. My great-grandfather James made it in his cabinetworks factory back in Illinois."

"You must be very proud of it."

"We are," Alice said. "Aunt Patty is in here." Alice showed him into a parlor where an old lady was sitting in a rocking chair. Her eyes were bright and clear, and as she looked at John, she smiled, almost as if she recognized him.

"You do look a lot like him, you know," she said.

"I beg your pardon?"

"Ike Buford. You are kin to Ike Buford, aren't you?"

"Yes, he was my grandfather," John answered. "Then you do know him? I was right, wasn't I? He was a part of the Donner party?"

"You mean you didn't know?"

"No, ma'am," John said. "I began to suspect it when I read about the Donner party. But my grandfather never spoke of it to me. I always resented that. I felt like he was denying me a part of my own past."

"Why wouldn't he speak of it?"

"He told me he had sworn an oath not to."

The old lady smiled. "Ah, yes, the oath," she said. "Of course, the oath was broken many, many years ago. And once one person broke it, the others felt that they were no longer bound by it."

"Evidently my grandfather didn't share that feeling. The oath was as binding to him on the day he died as it was on the day he took it."

"Your grandfather was an honorable man. You should be proud of him."

"Why did he take the oath in the first place? My grandfather was a journalist. A vow of silence on something like this must've been extremely difficult for him."

"Maybe it was his penance."

"His penance? What do you mean?"

"Everyone had to make their own peace with what happened. It drove some mad, it broke the spirit of others. But a few, like my father and your grandfather, found a great strength which they were able to call upon for the rest of their lives."

"You seem to have handled it all right," John said.

"Young man, that is very presumptuous of you. You don't know how I have handled it."

John flushed in embarrassment, then cleared his throat. "No, ma'am, I don't guess I do," he admitted. "I'm sorry. Please forgive my presumption."

The challenge left the old woman's face and her expression softened. She picked something up from beside the chair and held it tenderly, almost lovingly, in her lap. John saw that it was a doll.

"This is Penelope," she said when she saw him looking at it. She stroked the doll as she would a real child. "Penelope saw it all with me. And sometimes, on a cold breath of wind, or in the quiet of the night, just on the other side of a waking dream, I see it again. I am still there, in that terrible place, cold, hungry, and frightened. They tell me that those episodes are only memories. But those memories are as real as life. So where is the comfort in knowing that it is only an old woman's nightmares?"

For a moment the old woman's eyes were open windows to her soul, and as John looked into them he could see the deep scars. Then, as quickly as the windows had opened, they closed, and once again her eyes were so clear and so bright that John could not see through them.

"I know this is painful for you even now, after all these years," John said. "But would you tell me the story?"

"The story has been written many times. You can find it in all the old newspapers."

"The newspapers give only facts and figures. I need someone who can provide body and soul. I want to hear the story as my grandfather would have told it, had he been able."

"Perhaps your grandfather didn't want you to know."

"No, I don't believe that is true. I think he very much wanted to tell. But he was bound by his oath never to speak of it. You are now the only person living who can release him from that oath. Please do so. Share the story with me."

The old lady leaned back in her rocking chair and closed her eyes. For a long moment, which stretched almost into an entire minute, she was absolutely quiet. At first John waited patiently for some answer. Then he began to believe that she must've drifted off to sleep. He looked over at Alice Reed, questioning her with the expression on his face.

Alice held out her hand and nodded her head yes, as if saying, Wait a minute. It's all right.

Then the old lady began to talk.

"It all started in Springfield, Illinois," she began.

ONE |||

The long-legged man had been sitting on a trunk near the window while he pared the apple. When he was finished, he got up and ambled over to the little iron stove that squatted upon a pile of sand in a box in the middle of the room. He opened the door to the stove, then stretched out the apple peel, which was in one long piece.

"I'd make this near on to eighteen inches long, wouldn't you, Ike?" he asked the man who was busy with the printing press.

Isaac Buford locked the type in a form in the bed, then looked up. "I would say that's eighteen inches if it's an inch," he agreed.

The long-legged man tossed the peel into the fire, then closed the door. "You know, I once got into a contest with a friend of mine by the name of Joshua Speed. Now Mr. Speed was pretty much impressed with a few of his accomplishments, and he was convinced that he could pare a longer continuous peel from an apple than could any man living. He was so convinced, in fact, that he was willing to invest a two-cent wager to prove his point."

The man quartered the apple, then walked over and shoved a piece of it into Ike's mouth as Ike used a roller to apply ink to the type he had just set.

"Well, sir," he went on, returning to his trunk seat by the window. "It just so happens that I had carved a pretty mean

9

peel or two myself when I was runnin' the store back in Salem, and I fancied myself about as proficient in this peculiar skill as any man, so I offered to accept Speed's challenge. A time was set for the issue to be settled, and folks gathered from near and far to watch us go at one another." He chuckled. "You would've thought we were wrestlin' for the championship of Illinois."

"So what happened?" Ike asked. "Who won?" With the ink applied, Ike placed a sheet of paper on the hinged wooden tympan, folded it over the type, then slid the type-bed into position beneath the cloth-covered platen.

"Nobody won."

Ike pulled the printer's bar, causing the platen to press the paper against the type to produce an impression. "What do you mean, nobody won? What happened?"

The long-legged man held up his finger as if telling Ike there was more to the story. "I had thought I was pretty good, but Mr. Speed was a lot better than pretty good. It turns out he had his own orchard, you see, and pretty soon word reached me that he had set about practicing, day after day, until by the time the contest rolled around he was paring out peels twice as long as anything he had ever done before."

"So what did you do? Did you back out of the contest?" Ike asked. He removed the paper and held it up to look at it. It was the March 26, 1846, issue of the *Illinois Vindicator*. The *Vindicator,* like its rival newspaper, the *Sangamon Journal,* was published in Springfield, Illinois, and Ike was an employee of the paper.

"Well, now, you've done a mighty fine looking job there, Ike," the man said, examining the paper. "Yes, sir, I'd say the day you walked into this office was about the best day Jason Fielding ever had."

Jason Fielding was the publisher-owner of the *Vindicator,* and Isaac Buford was his printer's devil. As such, Ike opened the office in the morning, took advertisements and subscriptions from the customers, reported on the news, wrote feature articles, set type, and printed and often hand-delivered the papers. He also kept the office swept out, and frequently closed it up at night. Ike was twenty-eight years old. He stood just under six feet tall, and though he wasn't bunched with muscle, he did have a graceful strength about him. His eyes were a penetrating blue, and he wore his dark hair somewhat longer than normal.

Ike lay the printed sheet to one side, then proceeded to print the other flat sheets that waited in a pile alongside. "You didn't answer my question. Did you give up, or what?"

"Well, I didn't exactly give up. What I did was, I changed the contest somewhat. You see, on the day we were to settle the question, I brought an orange. And while Joshua Speed was peeling his apple, I was doing a pretty good job on that orange. Nearly everyone there saw what I was doing, and they commenced to laughing, but Mr. Speed was so busy concentrating on his apple that he had nary an idea of what was going on until it come time for us to compare our peels."

"What happened then?" Ike asked.

"Well, sir. The folks who were gathered around that day proclaimed Joshua Speed as the best apple peeler in the county, and Abraham Lincoln as the best orange peeler."

Ike laughed. "So tell me, Abe, has that talent served you well in Congress?"

"Not yet," Lincoln replied. "But there are a few honorable members of that august body that I wouldn't mind peelin' the way I peeled that orange." Finished with his apple, Lincoln walked back over to the stove and held his big hands over the top of it, warming them. "I have to tell you that being in Congress pleases me less than I thought it would. And I've been less effective than I would wish."

"I think you are a fine congressman."

"Do you really?" Lincoln replied. He laughed. "Or are you merely following the old maxim that 'one drop of honey catches more flies than a half gallon of gall'?"

"Maybe a little of both," Ike admitted. He had been working steadily all the while, and now he had a large stack of newspapers printed. When they were all printed on one side, he changed the type-bed and began printing on the back side.

"You are a lucky man, Ike," Lincoln said as he watched him.

"How so?"

"Because you have found a profession that you truly love."

Ike stopped his work and looked at Lincoln in surprise. The man was right. Ike did truly love the newspaper business, though he had never shared his feelings with anyone. He was surprised at Lincoln's perceptiveness.

In his short span of years Ike had worked in the lead mines over in Missouri, had been a flatboatman, a farmer, a carpenter, and a blacksmith's apprentice. He had also fought in the Black Hawk War, and it was there that he had first met Abraham Lincoln.

It wasn't until Ike walked into a newspaper office, however, that he found his true calling. When he saw the press turning out copy after copy, the letters dark, crisp, and clear on the page, he knew this was what he wanted to do for the rest of his life.

Though Ike had shared his plans with no one, it was his ambition to work for the *Illinois Vindicator* until he learned all there was to learn, then leave Springfield and start his own newspaper somewhere else. But that wouldn't be for a while. A hand press like this one cost $250. That was just about what Ike earned in one year.

He was about to reply to Lincoln's comment when Jason Fielding came in. A small bell tinkled on the door to announce his entry, but even if the bell hadn't sounded its warning, Ike would have known Fielding had entered. He could tell by the distinctive aroma of the publisher's pipe tobacco.

"Good afternoon, Mr. Fielding," Ike said.

"Hello, Jason," Lincoln added.

"Hello, Ike, Abe," Fielding replied. "Oh, Abe, I just saw Mrs. Lincoln over at the Emporium. She's looking for you, I believe."

"The Emporium? That means she'll be here next." Lincoln

unwound his legs from his position on the trunk. "I expect I'd better be going. That woman is uncommonly talented at finding things for other folks to do. Gentlemen, good day to you both."

"Good day, Abe," Ike called. The bell tinkled again as the congressman left.

"Do you think she'll find him?" Ike asked.

"I reckon Abe's been married long enough now to figure out how to avoid her when that's what he wants to do," Fielding replied with a chuckle. He looked over at the pile of papers. "Well, I see you have just about completed the job."

"Yes, sir," Ike replied. "Only about fifty or so more impressions and I'll be done."

Fielding picked up one of the papers. "Ah, good job, my boy, a very good job. Just the right amount of ink. It's dark, but not so heavy as to come off on the readers' hands and clothes, or to waste the ink. You're going to make a fine newspaperman someday."

Ike laughed. "I'm already a fine newspaperman, Mr. Fielding. I'm just not a newspaper owner."

Fielding laughed with him. "I'll give you that, my lad, I'll give you that. For in truth you are a much better newspaperman than the publisher of the *Journal,* or any of the publishers of a dozen or more other newspapers I could name." He looked at the paper for a few moments, then pointed to an ad in the middle of the page. "But I'm afraid you and I both missed a fine opportunity here. Folks all over town are talkin' about it."

"What is that?" Ike asked as he resumed the printing.

"Why, Ike, don't tell me you don't read our customers' ads? Don't you know that's a sacrilege? Especially when we say how everyone reads everything in our paper."

"I've read the paper backwards," Ike said, referring to the type. "I just haven't read it frontwards yet."

"My boy, a good newspaperman gets to the point that he can read faster backwards, and comprehend it better, than an ordinary person can by reading it frontwards," Fielding quipped. He turned the paper toward Ike. "I'm talking about this item."

WESTWARD HO!

For Oregon and California. Who wants to go to California without costing them anything? As many as eight young men, of good character, who can drive an ox team, will be accommodated by gentlemen who will leave this vicinity about the middle of April. Come on, boys. You can have as much land as you want without costing you anything. The Government of California gives large tracts of land to persons who move there. The first suitable persons who apply will be engaged.

George Donner and others

"I did see that," Ike said. "I guess I just didn't pay much attention to it."

"You should have. It would have made a fine story," Fielding replied. His pipe having gone out, Fielding walked over to the little iron stove, opened the door, then stuck a long stick down into the coals. Using the flame thus produced, he re-lit his pipe, talking around the puffs. "Of course"—puff, puff—"I can't hold it against you"—puff, puff—"seein' as how I let it get by me too." He tossed the flaming stick into the stove, then slammed the door shut. "But I don't mind tellin' you, it's about the only thing folks are talkin' about all over town."

"I know Mr. Donner," Ike said. "He's an old man. I wonder what would make him want to go to California?"

"Old man? He's only sixty-two," Fielding replied. "His brother Jacob is sixty-five, and he's goin' too. 'Course, I reckon I can see how that might seem old to a young whippersnapper like you, but to someone like me, it's not old at all. Besides, George Donner is as strong as an ox. There aren't half a dozen men in this town half his age who would be willin' to take him on."

Ike chuckled. "You won't find me in that number," he admitted.

"The age of the Donner brothers isn't what puzzles me," Fielding continued. "What puzzles me is why men of their means would want to pull up stakes and start all over. George and Jacob are wealthy men. As is James Reed, who is also going."

"James Reed? The man who owns the cabinet factory?"

"He *did* own it," Fielding said. "He sold out lock, stock, and barrel."

"I can see now why there is such interest among the townspeople," Ike said. "Most of the time when you think of men going West, you think of men who were hurt by the Panic, or who have lost their farm, or who have come upon hard times. The West beckons to such people, offering them a fresh start. But for men like the Donners and James Reed?" Ike shook his head. "It *is* curious. And it will be curious to see how they make out in the new country. Will they be able to repeat the success that they have enjoyed here? Or will the lack of civilization hold them back?"

Fielding stroked his chin and looked at Ike for a long moment.

"Tell me, Ike, now that you have posed that question, would you be interested in pursuing it?"

"I beg your pardon?"

"You said you would be curious to see how such men as the Donners and Reed make out in the new country. Just how curious are you? Enough to accept it as an assignment?"

Ike frowned in confusion. "How would you propose I undertake to do such a story?" he asked. "Once they leave Illinois, we may never hear from them again."

"We would if you go with them," Fielding suggested.

"You want me to go with them?"

Fielding pointed to the ad. "As you can see, they are looking for able-bodied men to assist them on the trip," he said. "You have had a wide range of experiences, all of which would serve you in good stead should you undertake such an adventure. All you have to do is answer the ad, then write a series of articles which you can send back from time to time as the opportunity presents itself."

Ike ran his hand through his hair and looked at the ad for a moment. "It *would* be an exciting adventure," he admitted. "Though it does seem a rather drastic length to go to for one story, don't you think?"

"Not if it is your last story," Fielding said. "If it is your last story for the *Vindicator,* you would want it to be something special, would you not?"

"Yes, of course I would," Ike said. "But I don't understand. Why should it be my last story for the *Vindicator*? Mr. Fielding, are you discharging me?"

Fielding laughed. "In a manner of speaking, I suppose I am," he replied. "Ike, do you think I don't know you have been dreaming of starting your own newspaper somewhere?"

Ike smiled sheepishly. "It must not be as much a secret as I supposed. First Mr. Lincoln saw through me, and now you. Am I wearing it printed upon my sleeve?"

"Not exactly, but I have seen you looking at the catalogue for presses."

"Yes, well, they are all much too expensive," Ike replied.

"Suppose I told you I know of a press, a used one to be sure, but very serviceable, that could be yours for only fifty dollars? You could buy that press and take it with you on the trip West. Then, once you are settled in California, you can start your own newspaper."

"This press you are talking about. Is it a good one?"

"It is a Washington Hand Press, my boy. That is the best they make."

"But such a press, even a used one, would sell for no less than one hundred and fifty dollars."

"Not if I choose to sell it to you for fifty," Fielding said. "It is the press I had before I got this one. And many is the time, I don't mind admitting, that I have been tempted to bring it out of the barn where it has been stored and put it back into service, for in many ways it is superior to the one I am using now."

"And you would sell it to me for fifty dollars?" Ike asked, excited now by the prospect.

"I will do even better than that," Fielding said. "I will give you one hundred and fifty dollars to write a series of stories about your journey. That means you can buy the press and have one hundred dollars remaining. If you are of a mind to accept the offer, that is."

"Yes!" Ike replied. He took off his printer's apron. "Yes, yes, I *do* accept the offer! Thank you, Mr. Fielding! Thank you very much!" He started for the door.

"Where are you going?"

"I am going to find George Donner! The ad says he will accept those who apply first. I intend to be first."

Hannah Price braced herself against the jerking motion of the coach and pulled the canvas curtain across the window to shut out the dust. She had begun her trip from Boston by train. She'd changed trains several times, then proceeded by riverboat, and finally by stagecoach. Thus far, the trip had taken two weeks.

Hannah glanced back inside at her fellow passengers. Sitting next to her was a woman who was perhaps five years older than she, traveling with her six-year-old son. The woman was pretty and friendly, but quiet. The boy was very active, as all six-year-old boys are on long trips, and he continually changed seats from one side of the coach to the other. Directly across from Hannah sat a fat, red-faced man. He wore a suit and vest, and carried a watch in his vest pocket secured by a gold chain. He took the watch out several times, opened it, then snapped the case shut, as if calling attention to his fine timepiece.

Hannah opened her purse and removed the letter sent to her by her aunt. Though she had already read it several times, she read it again.

My dere niece Hannah

I take pen in hand to rite this letter to you in hopes it finds you in good health. Tell yur mother who is my dere sister Ophelia that our mother suffers from advanced age and failing helth but remanes in good spirits all the same.

As you know her son Caden who is my brother and yur uncle removed himself some time preveous for an adventure in Oregon. Now my husband James Reed has decided that he to wishes to go west but not to Oregon but to California. To that end he and some other gentlemen of like spirit and adventure have undertaken to outfit wagons for the trip. Mother would not here of it but that she be allowed to go as well. I told her that she would not live through the whole journey but she said she didn't care she didn't want to remane behind in Springfield and die alone with her son and one dotter out west and the other dotter back in Boston. I ask James can she go and James said she culd and he has built a special place for her in our wagon.

James has also said that if I wish I culd hire someone to look after mother on our long journey to California so I am riting this letter to see if you would agree to do so. Ophelia told me in the last letter that you are a school teacher. There will be many children on the trip west and they will be in need of learning. James and Mr. George Donner have said they will pay all yur expenses if you will agree to teach the children during the trip to the west. They have also said that they will build a schoolhouse when we arive in California so you can have a place of your own. If you will agre to do this plese come at oncet as the time draws nye when we shall leve.

Plese give my love to my own swete sister Ophelia.

Yur affectionate aunt
Margaret Reed

The letter had come at just the right time for Hannah, for she was recovering from a period of grief over the loss at sea of her fiancé. She was certain that a change of scenery would be good for her. In addition, she was of an adventurous enough spirit to look forward to the endeavor ahead with enthusiasm.

A trumpet sounded from atop the coach, and Hannah folded her letter, then put it back in her handbag.

"Mama, why is he playing the trumpet?" the six-year-old asked.

"I don't know, dear. Maybe he just likes music," the mother answered.

"Why, son, that means we're comin' into Springfield," the red-faced man explained. He made a point of checking his watch again. "Right on schedule too."

The road smoothed somewhat as the coach entered the town, and Hannah pulled the canvas curtain aside so she could look through the window. How small and crude Springfield looked compared to Boston. And yet Hannah knew that this mean collection of buildings was a metropolis compared to what she would soon encounter. The stage rolled to a halt in front of the stage depot, and Hannah looked out at the people who had gathered to meet it. She had learned during her trip that the arrival of a train, boat, or stagecoach was quite an event in any town. That was because the conveyance, whatever it was, represented a connection to the outside world: travelers, news, letters, and often mail-order goods.

The young woman and her child stepped out first, to be met by the woman's husband. Though they gave no public display of affection, Hannah could see it in the look of intimacy they exchanged with their eyes. The husband took his wife's baggage from the boot of the coach and carried it over to a wagon. Even the overweight red-faced man was met by someone, a woman of near-equal girth.

Hannah stepped out of the coach hesitantly, then looked around. Although she had seen a tintype of her aunt Margaret, she had never actually met her. Nor had she met Margaret's husband, or any of her children. She had seen her grandmother once, some years ago, but she wasn't sure she would recognize her if she saw her again.

"Cousin Hannah?" a hesitant young voice asked.

Hannah looked toward the voice and saw a pretty young girl of thirteen or so. A dog was sitting patiently by her side.

"I am Hannah Price," she told the girl.

The girl smiled broadly, then rushed to her to embrace her. "Oh, welcome to Springfield!" she said excitedly. "I am your cousin, Virginia Reed!"

Hannah returned her cousin's enthusiastic hug. Though she had never met her before, she couldn't help but take an instant liking to her. The dog barked and wagged its tail enthusiastically.

"And who would this be?" Hannah asked, patting the affectionate animal on the head.

"That's our dog, Cash," Virginia said. "Don't mind him. He thinks he's people."

"Well, I'm very pleased to meet you, Cash," Hannah said. She held her hand out, and to her surprise, Cash held up his paw to shake hands. "Oh, my!" Hannah said,

"I taught him that trick," Virginia said proudly. "Come with me, Cousin Hannah. I'll introduce you to everyone."

"I must get my grip."

"Leave it here. Pa has hired some men to drive the wagons for us and help us on the train. One of them will collect your bag for you. Oh, just wait until you see the wagon Pa has built for us to travel in! It has an upstairs and a downstairs. It has bunks and chairs with cushions and springs. It has a beautiful clock. It even has an iron stove. They say it will take a team of eight oxen to pull it but, oh, it will be glorious! I have already named it the Prairie Palace Wagon."

Margaret Reed was lying on her bed with a wet towel wrapped around her head when young Virginia took Hannah into the house to meet her.

"Mama, here is Cousin Hannah, come just as she said she

would. Isn't she beautiful? Is your headache getting any better?"

Margaret laughed. "Yes, dear, she is beautiful, and my headache is some better." She sat up and took the towel from her head. "I suffer terribly from cruel headaches," she explained. "But the doctor tells me that a change of climate, such as they have in California, will be the cure for them." She took Hannah's hand in hers. "I am so happy you could come. You must tell me. How is my dear sister Ophelia?"

"She is fine, Aunt Margaret, and she sends her love," Hannah said.

"Well, you have met Virginia, I see."

"Yes. She is such a lovely girl, I am sure we are going to get along splendidly."

Another young girl came into the room. She was clutching a doll and she looked at Hannah through large, expressive eyes.

"Well, hello there," Hannah said to her. "And who are you?"

"My name is Patty," the girl said. She held up her doll. "And this is my doll. Her name is Penelope."

"How beautiful Penelope is. May I have a closer look at her?" Hannah asked.

Patty handed Hannah the doll, which was a small cloth figure with a porcelain face.

"Will Penelope be going with us to California?" Hannah asked.

"Yes," Patty said. "She wants to go where I go."

"You've now met Virginia and Patty," Margaret said. "There are also two boys, Jimmy and Tommy, who will be making the trip."

"Patty and Jimmy will be taking lessons from you, just like me," Virginia said. "Patty is eight and Jimmy is five. But Tommy is only three."

"What about the other children making the trip?" Hannah asked.

"With Mr. George Donner there are Elitha who is fourteen,

Leanna twelve, Frances six, Georgia four, and Eliza three. With Mr. Jacob Donner there are Solomon Hook fourteen, Will Hook twelve—those are Betsy Donner's children by her first husband—and George nine, Mary seven, Isaac five, Sam four, and Lewis three. Those are children of Betsy and Jacob Donner," Margaret explained.

"Oh, my, there are quite a few, aren't there?"

"Yes, and those are just the children of the Donners and our own family," Margaret said. "I am sure there will be more as the train grows."

Hannah smiled brightly. "Well, the more the merrier, I say. We'll have a fine school."

"Oh, Cousin Hannah, isn't it all just too exciting? Won't it be fun?"

Ike's application for employment was accepted, and though he thought he would be driving one of the wagons, he was given a different task. The emigrants were taking several cattle with them, and Ike was mounted on a horse with the specific job of keeping the cattle moving along with the wagons. For purposes of travel the herds had been merged, so Ike was in charge of them all though he was specifically employed by James Reed.

Ike appreciated the freedom of being on horseback, rather than driving one of the wagons, but he couldn't help but be a little concerned for the welfare of his press. It had been more difficult to find room for it than he had thought, and he felt that he had better keep a close eye on it lest it fall overboard during the trip.

There were several hundred people gathered on the sides of the street to watch as the wagon train took its leave of Springfield. The interest, Ike knew, was because of the unusual nature of the principals. These were no ordinary emigrants.

George Donner, whose wagon led out, was a well-to-do farmer. He had been married three times and had sired thirteen children. His third wife, Tamsen, was forty-five,

retty, petite, and—Ike believed—much stronger than she
ooked. George Donner had three wagons, twelve yoke of
xen, five saddle horses, and numerous milk and beef cattle.

Jacob Donner had an equal number of wagons and nearly
s many cattle and hired hands. Jacob's wagons were next in
ine.

But it was James Reed who made the most impressive exit.
His lead wagon was huge and heavy, though with its team of
ight oxen, it managed to keep up quite well with the others.
The built-in beds and stove had attracted the attention of
veryone, and for several hours before the train actually got
nder way, the townspeople had gathered around to look and
marvel at it. Mrs. Keyes, James Reed's mother-in-law, sat in
er rocking chair greeting all the sightseers with a friendly
mile. It was no secret that Mrs. Keyes, who in addition to her
dvanced years was in poor health, would probably not
urvive the long trip. She had been a popular, churchgoing
woman, and those who came to tell her good-bye knew that
hey were seeing her for the last time. Quite a few of them left
vith tears in their eyes, and one time Margaret Reed broke
lown and wept at the thought of leaving so many friends
ehind. Even James had tears in his eyes as he shook hands
vith old friends and business associates.

In addition to the wagon that young Virginia Reed, and
now all the others, called the Prairie Palace Wagon, Reed
aad two more, loaded with an assortment of fancy foods and
iquors. "A man of means need not have to go without the
better things of life just because he is out in the wilderness,"
Reed said, justifying not only the huge grandfather clock and
he other items of fine furniture he was taking, but the meats,
cheeses, and tins of vegetables and fruits that made up a
ignificant part of the cargo of his additional wagons.

Cash, who was part of the entourage, ran alongside the
wagons, snapping at the turning wheels. If he did that for two
housand miles, Ike thought, he was going to be one very tired
log by the time they reached California.

There was one young woman in the party that Ike had not

met before. She was an exceptionally pretty young woman with long auburn hair, green eyes, and flushed cheeks. When he asked about her, he was told that her name was Hannah Price and she was Margaret Reed's niece, come to look after Mrs. Keyes and to teach school to the children.

Hannah was pretty enough to elicit several long glances from Ike, and once, when she caught him looking at her, he had to look away in embarrassment. There was no need to be too forward about it. He would have plenty of time to meet her later. After all, this was going to be a long, long trip.

TWO |‖

WESTWARD HO
by
Isaac Buford

May 11th, 1846, from Independence, Missouri:

As many of you back in Springfield well know, the Donner Party, for that is how we now refer to ourselves, departed that fair city on the 16th ultimate, sent on our way by your joyous huzzahs and cheers. I have no hesitancy in telling you that many throats had lumps and but few eyes were unglazed with tears as we took our leave of you. Many of the travelers with this party have friends and relatives still in Springfield, and the unpleasant realization that our good-byes may have been final has intruded into our thoughts more than once.

Despite such periods of melancholy, however, spirits have been high as dreams of California are shared around the nightly campfires.

For those of you who wish to follow our journey, I will inform you that we departed Springfield via the Berlin Road. From Springfield we traveled due west to Quincy, whereupon we loaded the wagons onto the ferry to cross the Mississippi River. As the ferry could only accommodate a few wagons at a time, many hours were spent on either bank of the river, waiting for the train to be re-formed. We then traveled from the river town of Hannibal, Missouri, down to St. Louis, thence up the Missouri River valley, arriving in Independence, Missouri, on the tenth instant.

It is from this bustling city that so many emigrants have departed for the long trek Westward, as Independence is the last outpost of civilization. We shall take our leave of this place on the morrow, buoyed by the excitement of the adventure ahead, and confident in the trail skills our travel experience has thus far given us.

Of course, the more skeptical among you may point out that travel by wagon along well-established roads through cities, towns, and well-kept farms is no fair comparison with the ordeal of travel upon the great plains. I agree. However, it has had the beneficial effect of enabling everyone to grow used to living in a wagon, performing certain daily tasks, and determining what mechanical parts will require our greatest attention. It is my belief, therefore, that our travel from Springfield has made the Donner Party superior in many respects to those wagon trains that are first assembled here, and are introduced to the regimen of wagon travel for the first time as they go out into the great wilderness to the west of here.

This is but the first of what I hope to be many dispatches sent from this endeavor. By means of these articles you, the reader, will make the journey with us.

Finishing with his story, Ike folded it, put it in an envelope, then looked up at the campsite the Donner party had chosen. The wagons were drawn up in a line just outside town and the occupants, by now seasoned travelers, were engaged in the necessary business of the trail. A dozen or more fires had been started, and various meals were stewing, boiling, and frying in hanging kettles, pots, and iron skillets. More than one wagon was up on blocks with a wheel removed as repairs were being made.

Several children were on the ground near one of the Reed wagons, listening intently as Hannah Price read a story to them. The Reed dog, Cash, was sitting quietly with the children as if he too were learning. Ike nodded at Hannah as he walked by, and smiling shyly, she returned the nod.

It was a walk of about five hundred yards from the last wagon to the first building in town. The distance was necessitated by the need for grass for their stock. Previous wagon trains had cropped away all the grass nearer town.

Although Ike had portrayed Independence as the last outpost of civilization, he was, he believed, being generous in his assessment. Independence was a raucous community. Its streets were filled with mud from the spring rains, and were ankle-deep in the pungent droppings from the thousands of horses, oxen, and cattle that had come through so far.

The town owed its every existence to the wagon trains, and all its industrial energy and commercial enterprises were dedicated to serving them. Both sides of the street were lined with stores that offered everything one needed, and many things one didn't need, to outfit a wagon. Some stores specialized in cooking utensils, and as Ike picked his way gingerly down the foul-smelling street, he passed by piles of dutch ovens, kettles, skillets, reflector ovens, coffee grinders, coffeepots, knives, ladles, tin tableware, butter churns, and water kegs. There was a store that specialized in bedding and tent supplies, another in weapons and ammunition, and still another in tools and equipment—to include complete surgical and medical kits.

"Here, emigrant, get the hell out of the way!" a loud, angry voice shouted, and Ike looked around to see a large wagon bearing down on him. The wagon was without bows or canvas, or any of the other accoutrements that would indicate that it was a traveling wagon. In addition, it was being pulled by a team of mules, rather than oxen. The driver popped his whip over the team, keeping them moving in a brisk trot. Ike jumped back enough to avoid the wagon, but he couldn't avoid being splashed by the manure and mud that flew up from the rapidly turning wheels.

The wagon was loaded with large items of furniture: beds,

chairs, lounges, dressers, cabinets, and even a large stand-up clock.

"You'd best be gettin' out of the road, pilgrim," a friendly voice called to him. "The next scavenger might not be kind enough to give you a warning."

Ike stepped up onto the boardwalk that ran alongside the road.

"Thanks," he said.

"You with that bunch that come in last night?"

"Yes," Ike replied. "We're from Springfield, Illinois. My name is Ike Buford."

"Clay Berkley," the man said, offering his hand.

"What did you call that man? A scavenger?"

"A scavenger, aye, for that's what he is," Clay said.

"I don't understand."

"Didn't you see the goods on his wagon? The furniture and such?"

"Yes, I saw it."

"He scavenged it," Clay said. When he saw that Ike still didn't understand, he explained. "Wagons been comin' through here all summer. Lots of 'em are loaded down with stuff that they got no need in carryin' . . . things like dressers and tables and clocks and the like. Mostly it's fine items that folks want to hold on to. They figure if they made it this far, they can make it all the way to Oregon or California." Clay chuckled. "It don't take too long 'fore they see what a damnfool thing it was to try 'n' hang on, so they start throwin' things off . . . heavy things." Clay pointed to the wagon that had come by a moment before. "Folks like him take their wagons down the same trail a few days later just pickin' up the leavin's. They bring it all back an' sell it to the townfolk." Clay chuckled. "I tell you, we got some of the most grandly furnished houses in the country right here in Independence." Clay pulled a twist of chewing tobacco from his pocket and bit off a piece.

"I daresay you have," Ike said. He thought of his printing press. Was it destined to wind up on the trail like that?

"You lookin' to post a letter, pilgrim?" Clay asked, pointing to the rolled-up piece of paper.

Ike started to repeat his name, but decided it was no use. To men like this, strangers were either pilgrims or emigrants.

"Yes," Ike replied. "But it's not a letter. It's an article I'm sending back to the *Illinois Vindicator*."

"I see. Newspaperman, are you?"

"Yes."

"Well, I reckon there's need for newspapermen out in Oregon and California by now. Lord knows there's been enough folks go out there." Clay pointed across the street. "That's the stage depot over there," he said. "They handle the U.S. mail. I reckon they can get your article sent back to Illinois for you."

"Thanks," Ike said.

"But if you're as smart as I think you are, pilgrim, you'll be takin' that article back yourself 'stead of mailin' it."

"Why do you say that?"

"'Cause that there wagon company you come in with ain't goin' to make it."

Ike smiled. "I heard there have been over seven thousand wagons leave here this season. I see no reason why it should be any more difficult for us to make the journey than it is for them."

Clay leaned over and spit into the street. The expectorated quid swirled brown in a nearby mud puddle. He straightened up and wiped the back of his hand across his mouth.

"You ain't one of them seven thousand," he said. "You're a-gettin' started way too late. Like as not you'll get caught on this side of the mountains with the first winter snow."

"I thank you for your concern, Mr. Berkley, but we are an experienced company by now. Unlike so many other trains who make up here, we have already been on the trail for nearly a month. I think that experience will serve us well."

Clay fixed Ike with an expressionless stare, then spit again.

"Pilgrim, if you got anyone on that train you care about,

you mind what I say. You'd do better by goin' back to
wherever it is you come from, then startin' again next spring,
only get started somewhat earlier."

"Thank you," Ike said again. "I'll pass on your concern."

"Ain't no concern o' mine," Berkley said, taking another
chew.

Bidding him good-bye, Ike picked his way across the street
to the stage depot. There he made arrangements to send his
newspaper article back to Springfield. Then, his task completed, he decided to see a little of the city of Independence.

Ike noticed that there were nearly as many taverns as there
were commercial establishments, and all of them seemed to
be doing brisk business. From one he could hear loud singing,
from another, hearty laughter. At a third, two painted women
stood just outside, shouting and waving at the men who
passed by. One of them saw Ike looking at them.

"Hello, honey," she called. "Are you with the wagon
company that came in last night?"

"Yes, ma'am," Ike replied, a little embarrassed that he had
been singled out.

"Oooh," the harpy squealed. "Did you hear him, Emmalou? He said, 'Yes, ma'am.' A gentleman he is."

"He's too fine for the likes of you, Maribelle," the one
called Emmalou said. "Honey, I 'spect you'd best come with
me. This is the last chance you're ever goin' to have to see the
varmint."

"See the varmint?" Ike replied.

"Honey, you mean you ain't seen the varmint?" Emmalou
lifted her skirt all the way above her knees. "Well, you just
come with me, I'll show you the varmint."

Ike suddenly realized what she was talking about and he
blushed crimson.

"Thank you all the same, ma'am," he said. "But I'd better
not."

Seeing that they had lost their opportunity with him, the
two women immediately turned their attention to a couple of
other men who were walking by.

Ike chose one of the other taverns, then went inside. It was crowded and noisy and smelled of beer and whiskey. The floor was peppered with expectorated tobacco quids, and the air was thick with pipe smoke and body odor. Ike recognized some of the other hired men from the wagon train, so he walked over to join them.

"Hello, Ike," William Herron called.

"Ike, come and join us," Milt Elliot added. "We can have a bit of the creature."

"That is if you ain't feelin' that you're too good to keep company with the likes of workin' men," John Snyder said. Ike liked Milt Elliot and the Ohioan, William Herron. They were friendly men who were easy to get along with. Snyder, on the other hand, was a much more disagreeable person. One of the drivers, he had a tendency to abuse his team, and when Ike had once suggested that the oxen would respond as readily to gentle persuasion as to the whip, Snyder had told him to tend to his writing and let the men handle their own affairs. It was an obvious challenge, and Ike had been ready to accept it, but others had stepped in quickly to prevent the situation from getting out of hand.

Ike and Snyder had generally avoided each other since then. That was fairly easy to do, for during the day while the company was in travel, Ike's duties with the herd kept him busy. And at night, when the company was encamped, Ike wrote in his journal. That was what Snyder was referring to when he suggested that Ike might consider himself too good to mingle with the working men.

It was obvious that Snyder was still challenging Ike, and Ike considered accepting the challenge. But what purpose would it serve? Instead of taking the bait, Ike just smiled.

"Why, John, you don't look much like you're working now," he said.

Snyder bristled, but Elliot and Herron laughed.

"Come on, John, give it some slack here," Herron said. "We've a long way to travel together."

"I've no quarrel with Buford," Snyder finally said.

"Good, good, and I've no quarrel with you," Ike replied. He ordered a beer, then turned his back to the bar and looked out over the tavern at the others. Like the streets outside, the place was filled with fur trappers, buffalo hunters, adventurers, and opportunists.

"So tell me, lad, have the citizens of this fine community been bendin' your ear about how we're too late?" Milt asked.

"I've heard that suggestion advanced, yes," Ike replied. "You too?"

"Every chance they get."

"What do you think?" Ike asked.

"It isn't my job to think," Milt replied, taking another swallow of his beer. "I'm a hired hand, like the three of you. If the company goes on, I'll go on. If the company turns back, I'll turn back."

"I've heard there was a company that left here just two weeks ago," Ike said. "If we can catch up with them, we'd be no further behind than they."

"There's a way to get to California ahead of that company . . . ahead of all the trains that left a month ago," Herron suggested.

"There is?" Ike asked. "How?"

"By takin' the cutoff."

"Don't talk foolish, William," Milt said. "Even the mountain man said he wouldn't advise takin' it."

"What cutoff are you talking about?" Ike asked.

"It's the cutoff in Mr. Reed's guidebook," William said.

"You mean the Johnson and Winters Guidebook?" Ike asked. "I've seen it, but I don't recall any reference to a cutoff."

William shook his head. "That ain't the one I'm talkin' about. Mr. Reed bought him a new book this mornin'. This here one is called *The Emigrants' Guide to Oregon and California*. It was wrote by a man named Hastings."

"I haven't heard of that one," Ike admitted.

"I was readin' in it some," William continued. "It shows a new way to go, a cutoff that saves five hundred miles."

"I've never heard anything about that. Do you suppose it actually exists?" Ike asked.

"Accordin' to the mountain man, it does," Milt said.

"What mountain man?"

Wilt pointed to one of the mountain men sitting at a table in the back of the room.

"Is he saying this because of the book, or does he know about it for a fact?" Ike asked.

"He says he actually seen it oncet," Snyder said. "But he said we'd be plumb foolish to take it."

"Maybe I'll go over and have a talk with him," Ike said.

"Good luck."

"Why do you say that?" Ike asked. "Is there any reason I shouldn't?"

"That all depends on how long you can hold your breath," William suggested.

"Hold my breath?"

"I've run across skunks that smelled sweeter," William said, and everyone, including Snyder, laughed.

Ike, noticing that the mountain man's own beer was nearly gone, ordered another and carried it with him to the table. He set the beer down in front of the mountain man and, without so much as a word of thanks, the mountain man quaffed half of it down. Then, wiping the foam from his greasy, matted beard, he looked up at Ike.

"Sit you down, pilgrim," he invited.

William was right. The odor was terrific, but Ike managed to steel himself long enough to accept the invitation.

"Thanks," he said.

The mountain man studied Ike for a moment, staring at him with eyes that were more yellow than brown. Ike had no idea what the natural color of his hair might be because it was so matted and filthy. There were lines in his face . . . maybe more than just a few, though some of them may have been covered by dirt.

"I seen you was a-talkin' to them other pilgrims," the

mountain man said. "So I figure they must've told you about
the cutoff, and now you're wantin' to talk to me about it."

"Yes," Ike said. "I understand that there is a cutoff by
which we can save some time?"

"No, there ain't."

"Oh? I must have misunderstood. I thought you had
actually seen the cutoff."

"I have."

Ike looked at him in confusion. "But I just asked you if one
exists and you said no."

"That ain't what you ask me, pilgrim. What you ask was,
could you save some time, an' what I said was no. There is a
cutoff, but you can't use it."

"Why not? Is there a problem with Indians?"

"Nope."

"Then I don't understand. If one exists, and if there is no
Indian problem, why can't we use it?"

"It would be too hard for you to get your wagons through."

"But if it does, in fact, cut off five hundred miles, no matter
how arduous the travel might be, wouldn't it be better to use it?"

"Pilgrim, they's desert out there that a lizard can't cross.
And they's mountain passes that would stop a goat. Now
you're talkin' about crossin' it in wagons with women,
children, and old folks and such."

Ike waved his hand. "Disregard the difficulty for a moment. Is it physically possible for someone to get through?"

"It can be done, I reckon, if you're talkin' 'bout no more
than two or three men travelin' with mules," the mountain
man said. "Thing is, that damnfool Hastings claims that
wagons can use it."

"You're talking about the man who wrote the book? Where
is he, do you know? I would like to talk to him."

"Can't talk to him," the mountain man said. "He's out in
California."

Ike grew more encouraged. "He is? And he took wagons
through the cutoff?"

The mountain man shook his head. "You ask me, I don't

think the dumb son of a bitch ever even seen the cutoff, let alone took wagons or anything else through it. But he's wrote a book about it, tellin' all the emigrants that's the way they should come."

"Surely if he has written a book about it, it has been adequately researched. I mean, he wouldn't make such a claim in writing unless he knew for certain that it's true, would he?"

The mountain man glared at Ike. "Pilgrim, I don't know nothin' 'bout no book," he said. "I ain't never learned to read. But I do know that cutoff, 'cause I'm one of the few folks that's ever took it and lived to tell about it. And I'm tellin' you, book or no, that there cutoff is a killer. If you try an' take it, you goin' to leave lots of bones bleachin' in the sun."

"I see," Ike said, standing up. "Well, I thank you for your advice."

"Advice ain't worth a pitcher of warm piss, pilgrim, if you don't use it," the mountain man said.

"I'll keep that in mind." Ike walked back over to the bar to join the others.

"What do you think?" William asked.

"He was pretty adamant about not using it. Doesn't sound to me like the cutoff is anything we can plan on," Ike replied.

"Yeah, me an' John thought about the same," Milt said. "William's the only one still thinks we could use it."

"Why would you think such a thing, William?" Ike asked. "You heard him. He has actually seen the cutoff."

"He's not only seen it, he come through it," William said. "And the way I look at it, if he can make it across, I can too. I figure I'm as good a man as him."

"If just we four were going," Ike said, "I would agree with you. But we've got several wagons, women, children, and old people. Mrs. Reed's mother, Mrs. Keyes, for example. Surely you don't think she could make it through the cutoff?"

Snyder sneered. "What the hell you bringin' her up for? Hell, she don't matter none. She won't even make it across

the plains. Truth to tell, I figured she'd be dead long before
we even got this far."

"That's a rather cruel attitude to take, isn't it?" Ike said
icily.

"Easy, Ike," William said. "John's right. Mrs. Keyes isn't
going to live much longer and you know it. What's more, she
knows it herself."

Ike thought of the old lady who sometimes rode on the seat
of the wagon and other times lay in the special bed that had
been built for her. She was frail, and he was convinced that
she knew she wouldn't make the entire journey. Yet she
seemed so happy to be able to spend the remaining time with
her family that being around her wasn't at all depressing.

"Yeah, I guess you're right," Ike agreed. "But Mrs. Keyes
isn't the point. If the cutoff is anything at all like the mountain
man described it, we're better off forgetting all about it."

William finished his beer, then set his glass on the bar. "I
don't know, maybe you fellas are right," he said. "What do
you say? I figure it must be 'bout mealtime back in the
camp," he said. "And I don't know 'bout you fellas, but my
job says pay and found. That means I don't aim to miss airy
a feedin' time. Anyone comin' with me?"

"I am. You'll not find Milt Elliot missin' the call of the
dinner bell," the teamster said, finishing his own drink. Ike
and Snyder joined the other two as they took leave of the
tavern and picked their way back through the muddy streets
toward the wagons camped in the distance.

After supper that evening, James Reed called for a general
meeting and everyone—men, women, and children—
gathered around the large campfire that was built near the
Prairie Palace Wagon. Ike watched the proceedings from
the darkness, standing just outside the golden bubble of light
the fire produced. He searched the fire-lit faces of all the
others until he found Hannah Price. She was sitting on a box,
watching intently. Her auburn hair shimmered brightly in the
fire and her eyes, though reflecting the light, seemed to glow
from some inner illumination. From his position in the

darkness he was able to observe her closely, while he himself could not be seen. He appreciated the vantage point, but when he saw Hannah beginning to rub the back of her neck and look around, he knew that she knew she was being watched and was uncomfortable because of it. Not wanting to create any discomfort for her, he stopped staring and directed his attention instead to the man who had called the meeting, James Reed.

Reed held up his hands. "Ladies and gentlemen, I suppose you are wondering why we asked for a meeting tonight," he began. "But I have been speaking with both Mr. George and Mr. Jacob Donner, and we feel that a decision has to be made. It is a decision, however, which should be made by everyone, not just a few."

"What sort of decision, Jim?" someone asked.

"Simply put, the decision is whether we should turn around and go back to Springfield, hoping we can put everything together again for an earlier try next year . . . or whether we should go on."

"What do you mean?" Will Eddy asked. "Why is there any question as to whether we should go on? Isn't this what we have started out to do in the first place?"

"You haven't been into town yet, have you, Will?" Reed asked.

"No, can't say as I have," Will answered.

"Then maybe I had better explain it to you. According to many of the old hands in town, we have arrived here too late to begin our trip West. They say there is a strong possibility that we won't make it to the mountains before the first snow. If that is the case, we could get trapped on this side of the Sierra Nevadas."

"Nonsense. If we can average fifteen miles a day, we'll make California while summer is yet upon us," someone said. "I've got it all figured out."

"We may not average fifteen miles per day," someone else suggested.

"So what are you saying?" Will asked. "That we should turn around and head back to Springfield?"

"No, not that. I'm just trying to point out everything that should be considered, that's all."

"Mr. Reed," Tamsen Donner called. Ike wasn't surprised that she was the first woman to speak up, for Tamsen was clearly the headwoman of the party.

"Yes, Mrs. Donner?"

"Suppose we reach the mountains and the snow does come. What happens then?"

"We would just have to make camp and wait until the pass was clear."

"Why, that could take all winter, couldn't it?"

"Yes, ma'am, I suppose it could," Reed admitted.

"Have we provisions for such a long encampment?"

"I think I can answer that," George said, responding to his own wife's question, but knowing it was a question many would have asked. George stood up and walked over to stand beside Reed. Though shorter and more rotund, George did not give anything away to the younger man in the sheer dominance of his personality.

"My friends, I won't lie to you," he said. "We are provisioned for a journey of a specified time. If the journey goes beyond that, our provisions will run out. However, you can't help but have noticed by now that we are moving with a rather sizable herd of beef and milk cattle. It is my intention to increase the size of that herd once we raise California, but if need be, I am perfectly willing to use that cattle as a source of food."

"Well, now," Reed said, smiling broadly. "I guess you hear that, don't you, ladies and gentlemen? Mr. Donner has made a very generous offer, one that, I feel, will ensure that we reach our destination."

"Then I vote we go on," someone shouted.

"Me, too," said someone else.

Reed held up his hands.

"Wait a minute, wait a minute," he said. "Before we vote,

I have one more thing to say. I just learned today that Colonel William Russell left two weeks ago with a wagon party of substantial size. It is my belief that if we travel quickly, leaving by first light every morning and traveling until the light fails every evening, and if we apply the skills we have learned thus far . . . we will catch up to him. We can then join our wagon company with his and we will no longer be the last party, traveling at our own risk."

"Who is this Colonel Russell?"

"Jacob, you want to answer that?" Reed asked.

Jacob, who was a few years older but not quite as imposing a figure as his brother, stood. "Colonel Russell is a man of great experience," he said. "He has already taken several companies to California and Oregon."

"Well, then I say we join him," someone suggested.

"That's what I say as well," said someone else.

"Wait, not so fast," Reed said, holding up his hands. "There's one more thing you should know. Even if we do join them, they may decide not to accept us."

"Is that very likely, Jim?" one of the other men asked.

"I don't know," Reed answered. He stroked his chin whiskers. "It is possible, I suppose, though I don't think they would turn us out on our own out in the middle of nowhere. It would all depend upon whether or not they thought the addition of our party was an asset or a detriment to their well-being."

"If we catch up with them, that'll show them how well we can operate on the trail," someone said. "I think that would impress them enough."

"Me too!" another man shouted.

Reed smiled, his teeth gleaming in the light of the fire. "Those are my thoughts exactly," he said. "All in favor of leaving at first light tomorrow morning, and maintaining whatever pace is necessary to catch up with Colonel Russell, say aye."

The camp broke out with a resounding chorus of ayes.

"All against?"

Not one dissenting voice was raised.

"Very well, ladies and gentlemen, this wagon company shall get under way at first light tomorrow morning. Men, make certain your wagons and teams are ready to go. Ladies, have your coffee and biscuits ready and your cooking utensils struck. We're going to show these people in Independence, and those who are already on the trail, that we are not some ragtag bunch of emigrants. We're Illinoisians!"

Reed's final statement was greeted with a loud round of cheers, even though there were many in the party, including Ike himself, who were not native to Illinois.

"Come, we have much to do this night," a man said, and though he was speaking to his own family, it seemed to galvanize everyone into action. Ike saw Hannah start to lift a heavy box, and he hurried over to help her.

"Please, Miss Price, allow me," he said, picking up the box. It was heavier than he thought. "Oof, this would have been quite a load for you."

"It is my books," she said. "I thought we were going to be here long enough for me to hand them out to the children, but I suppose that must wait a while."

"Where shall I put them?"

"In this wagon, with my other things," she said, pointing.

Ike followed her to the wagon, then put the box of books in its proper place.

"Thank you," she said.

"Well, I suppose our adventure is about to begin," he suggested.

"Yes," she answered. "Will you be writing about it?"

"Yes."

"What a feeling that must be, to write words that will be read by the ages," Hannah said.

"You give me too much credit," Ike said. "I am writing for a newspaper only."

"Yes, but what we are doing is making history, are we not? Is our trek westward any less significant than that of the Pilgrims who came across the sea so many years ago?"

"No, I guess not," Ike answered.

"And is not everything written about the Pilgrims during their own time still read even today?"

"Yes, I suppose it is."

Hannah smiled. "Then what you write about us, Isaac Buford, will be read by our grandchildren's grandchildren."

"*Our* grandchildren?"

Hannah blushed. "I was speaking figuratively, Mr. Buford."

"Too bad," Ike said, smiling at her. "I must take my leave of you now. I have work to do. Good night to you, Miss Price."

"Good night to you, Mr. Buford."

As Ike walked away, she started toward the Prairie Palace Wagon to look in on Grandmother Keyes. Before Hannah climbed into the wagon, however, she looked back one more time at Ike, catching a glimpse of him just before he disappeared behind the last wagon. She had enjoyed her moment with him. Feelings that she had thought were dead, buried at sea when her fiancé went down with his ship, were beginning to stir anew.

Inside, Patty Reed was sitting on the floor of the wagon. Her doll was sitting at a toy table and Patty was serving it tea.

"My," Hannah said. "Are you and Penelope having a tea party?"

"Yes," Patty answered seriously. She nodded toward the doll. "But Penelope was the only one who could come. The others are busy packing the wagons."

"Well, I am sure you and Penelope will have a fine time," Hannah said.

The doll fell to one side, and Patty straightened her up.

"You must sit straight, Penelope," she scolded. "Sitting straight develops good posture."

Hannah laughed, for that was one of the things she had been stressing during her lessons. She turned her attention then to the old lady lying in bed.

"Good evening, Grandmother," Hannah said brightly. "How are you feeling this evening?"

"I'm feeling fine, thank you," Grandmother Keyes answered.

Among the voices that were calling and shouting outside, Hannah recognized Ike's, and she pulled the canvas flap to one side and looked through it to see if she could get another glimpse of him. Behind her the grandfather's clock struck nine times.

"Are you falling in love with him, child?" Grandmother Keyes asked when the clock stopped bonging.

"What?" Hannah replied, turning back quickly, surprised by her grandmother's words.

"You were looking to see if you could see Mr. Buford, weren't you?"

"I thought I heard him, that's all."

Grandmother Keyes chuckled. "You can't keep a secret from an old woman," she said. "I have seen you and Mr. Buford together."

"But we have never done more than exchange a few pleasantries," Hannah insisted.

"Perhaps with your lips you say a few words only. But with your eyes, you sing songs to each other."

Hannah laughed. "Grandmother, I'm sure I don't know what you are talking about." Hannah poured water into a basin and wet a cloth. "Here, let me bathe your forehead. I'm sure it will make you feel a lot better."

"Thank you, child," Grandmother Keyes said. "You are so good to me. It is wonderful to have someone as young as you pay attention to an old lady like me."

"When we get to California, I will come to visit you every day," Hannah promised.

"Bless you for your thought, child. But Hannah, I am not going to live to see this California we are all going toward."

"Of course you will," Hannah replied brightly. She looked quickly at Patty, to see if the little girl had been upset by her grandmother's words. Patty was busy with her doll.

"I am not going to live to see California. I know it, you know it, even little Patty knows it. But don't weep for me, for I will see it through your eyes, if you make it."

"If I make it?"

The old woman stretched out a bony hand to grasp Hannah by the arm. "The days ahead are going to be filled with trouble. You and your young man will have need of each other's strength."

"He is not my young man, Grandmother. He is a friend only."

"Listen to me. Don't let foolish customs and manners keep you apart. It will be much better if you are together."

"I . . . I will bear in mind what you have to say, Grandmother."

THREE |||

Hannah was awakened the next morning by Cash licking her in the face.

"Oh, Cash, go away," she mumbled sleepily.

Outside, she heard voices and whistles, and she sat up quickly, then poked her head through the tent flap and looked around. Though it was still dark she could see shadows and shapes as men worked to move the oxen into position to pull the wagons. Already, half a dozen campfires were blazing, and the smell of frying bacon and boiling coffee filled the air.

"Why, Cash, you good dog, you. You came to wake me, didn't you?" she said, patting the animal on the head. Cash wagged his tail in appreciation. "I had better hurry if I don't want to be left behind."

Quickly, Hannah pulled on her shoes and laced them up, then rolled up her bedding. Crawling out from her tent, she took it down, then put it and her bedding into one of the Reed wagons. "Come along, Cash," she said. The dog kept pace with her as she walked through the early morning darkness to the Prairie Palace Wagon. She peered in over the back gate. Virginia's excited voice came from the darkness inside.

"Cousin Hannah, is that you? I sent Cash to wake you up."

"Yes, and he did a good job too," Hannah answered. "How is our grandmother this morning?"

"I'm fine, child," Grandmother Keyes's voice answered. "I'm sure you have more things to do this day than to worry about me."

44

"Isn't it wonderful?" Virginia asked. "We're finally on our way."

Hannah chuckled. "We've been on our way for many days now."

"That wasn't the same. We were traveling through settled country before. But now, we have half a country behind us and half a country ahead. From here it is all new and exciting, and dreadfully wild."

Hannah laughed. "My dear young cousin. Practically everything I have seen and experienced since I left Boston has been new, exciting, and dreadfully wild. Would you like a cup of coffee, Grandmother?" she added.

"Yes, dear, that would be nice."

Hannah took the old lady's tin cup, then walked over to the Reeds' fire. Margaret Reed was bustling about preparing breakfast, not only for her own family, but for the hired hands who were working for them as well. A huge blue metal pot was suspended over the dancing flames, and a wisp of aromatic steam came from the spout.

"Good morning, Hannah. Is Mama awake?"

"Yes, Aunt Margaret."

"How does she feel?"

"She made no complaints this morning."

"I worried about her during the night," Margaret said. "She slept so fitfully."

Hannah poured the coffee and took the cup back to her grandmother. After that, she took the milk pail and stool, and started out through the predawn darkness to the rear of the train where the herd had spent the night. One of Hannah's tasks was to milk the cow every morning. Milking the cow wasn't difficult. Finding it in the midst of all the other animals was, for there were several score cattle accompanying the train, both of the milking and of the beef variety.

"Hannah, over here," a voice called from the darkness. "Excuse me, I mean Miss Price."

Hannah smiled, for she recognized Ike's voice.

"I don't mind you calling me Hannah if you don't do it in front of the children," she said.

"Thank you," Ike said, walking toward her from the darkness. He was leading something.

"What do you have there? Why, it's Twilleth," she said, recognizing the Reeds' milk cow.

"I figured you would be coming out to milk her," Ike explained. "So I brought her over here to wait for you."

"Why, thank you, Ike. I may call you Ike, mayn't I?"

"Yes, yes indeed," Ike said, pleased with the idea. "You want me to milk her too?"

"No," Hannah said. She put the stool down alongside the animal's flanks, then reached up and patted her gently. "Twilleth is used to me and doesn't mind giving up her milk. I'm afraid you would only upset her."

"I suppose you are right," Ike said, and he watched as Hannah began pulling on two of the cow's teats, sending two streams of milk swishing into the pail.

Hannah wasn't the only one coming for milk, and Ike's job was to keep all the animals together until the milking was done, then move the herd to a position behind or somewhere alongside the train. As the company moved out across the prairie, Ike would follow along, herding the cattle before him.

Some cows began wandering off in search of greener grass, so Ike had to leave to bring them back. But he no sooner got them in position than a few others wandered off and he had to go after them as well. By the time he had them all rounded up, Hannah, and most of the other women, had finished the morning milking. The sky had changed from black to gray, and now a tiny ribbon of red lay across the eastern horizon.

"Prepare to move out!" Reed shouted. Although the company referred to themselves as the Donner party, primarily because there were so many Donners and Donner employees, James Reed had assumed the role of leader of the group. It was a self-appointed role, and so far at least, no one had complained about it. Ike wondered, though, how long it would be before someone challenged Reed. Then he answered his own question. The challenge to Reed's authority would come at the first difficulty.

With the last milker hurrying back to the wagon carrying a pail of milk, Ike began herding the animals to the rear of the train. By now all the campfires had been extinguished, the cooking utensils loaded up, and the wagons brought in line. A piercing whistle broke the air, followed by the loud pop of a whip. The first wagon surged forward, then the next, then the next, until finally all the wagons were rolling. A few people were riding, but most were walking alongside the wagons. Actually, the children weren't walking. Full of boundless energy, they were running from wagon to wagon, then darting off to one side or another, finding some new and exciting thing to explore.

As Hannah walked alongside the Prairie Palace Wagon, she could scarcely believe the wonder that met her eyes. As if a rainbow had descended, the very ground itself was alive with wildflowers of all sizes, shapes, and hues. There were huge banks of blue cornflowers and yellow oxeye daisies. There were patches of purple lupin and silvery white rattlesnake master. Hannah's favorite, though, was the bright red Indian paintbrush, which dusted the prairie from horizon to horizon.

"Oh, how glorious it would be," she said to herself, though speaking aloud, "if the whole trip could be like this!"

The wagon train covered nearly twenty miles the first day. They made camp just before dark, ate their supper in the light of the campfire, made the few repairs that were necessitated by the day's travel, posted the guard, then turned in. By nine-thirty the entire campsite was rent with the snores of men, women, and children who were dead tired from the exertion of covering such a distance so quickly. They were proud of their accomplishment, however, and confident of their ability to master the distance before them.

On May 13th it warmed quickly, and with the heat came the clouds. Hannah watched the clouds build up into towering mountains of cream, growing higher and higher and turning darker and darker, until the sky in the west was nearly as black as night. The air stopped stirring, and it became very hushed, with only the sound of rhythmically plodding hooves, rolling wheels, and the occasional bang of a hanging pan or kettle interrupting the quiet.

There was a strange, heavy feeling in the air, and the men and women who were walking alongside their wagons spoke quietly, and kept a nervous eye on the sky before them. Even the animals seemed to sense that something was about to happen.

"Pa, look at the oxen. Why are they shaking their heads like that?" little Jimmy Reed asked.

"Because they can smell the sulphur."

"Smell the sulphur? What does that mean?"

"That means that the very gates of Hell are about to open."

"Mama, I'm frightened."

"James, there is no need to frighten the children like that," Margaret scolded.

"I'm not trying to frighten them, Margaret. I'm just trying to be truthful," Reed replied.

They could see the lightning first, rose-colored flashes buried deep in the clouds, followed several seconds later by distant thunder, low and rumbling. Then the lightning broke out of the clouds. No longer luminous flashes, the lightning now came as great, jagged streaks on the distant horizon, stretching from the clouds to the ground. The streaks were followed, more closely than the luminous flashes, by a louder thunder.

Then the wind came. At first it was no more than a gentle blowing, still hot and dry with the dust of the prairie. But the wind increased, and Hannah could feel a dampness on its breath.

"Hannah! Hannah, get all the kids in the wagon!" Margaret Reed shouted, and Hannah began scurrying about, finding the children and moving them back to their own family wagons.

The intensity of the lightning increased. Instead of one or

two flashes, there were ten or fifteen, and from each major
spear there came half a dozen more splitting off from it. The
thunder that followed was hard and sharp, and it came right
on the heels of the lightning. After each flash, the thunder
rolled over their heads with a long, deep-throated roar.

"Here it comes!" someone shouted.

The rains came then, sweeping down on them from the
west, moving toward them like a giant gray wall. The walkers
who weren't needed to keep the oxen moving climbed into
the wagons. Hannah settled down in the rear of the Prairie
Palace Wagon. The raindrops began slamming against the
canvas then, hitting hard and heavy, as if the canvas were
being pelted by great clods.

"Oh, Cousin Hannah! Isn't this a perfectly extraordinary
thunderstorm?" Virginia asked, her eyes shining with excitement. "It is wonderful."

"Wonderful?" Hannah replied. She laughed at her young
cousin. "I don't know that I would call it wonderful. But it is
extraordinary."

Hannah pulled the canvas aside slightly and peered through
the crack. Though the heavy curtain of rain made visibility
poor, she could see a solitary herdsman riding at the rear of
the train. Ike was taking the full brunt of the storm.

The rain was falling so hard that Ike could not even see the
front half of the train. It was all he could do to see all the
cattle in his charge, and he kept moving from one side to
the other to keep as close contact as he could. All about him
lightning streaked and thunder crashed, and water cascaded
down on him with as much ferocity as if he had been standing
under a waterfall. He was wearing a hat and an oiled-canvas
poncho, but that did very little to protect him. He was
drenched, and he felt wet clear through to the bone.

Suddenly one of the canvas wagon covers, caught by the
wind, tore loose from its bow fastenings and came flying
back toward the rear of the train. The cattle, already frightened by the thunder and lightning, saw something big and

white flapping toward them and became terrified. They broke into a gallop, and when the lead animal turned to the left, the others followed.

"Whoa!" Ike shouted. "Come back here!"

Ike knew that his shouts would have no effect, but he was taken by surprise at the sudden turn of events, and he couldn't just sit still and watch the cattle stampede, even if there were so few of them. Slapping his legs against the side of his horse, he started after them.

At first, Ike thought it might be best to just let the cows run until they could run no more. Then he could just get in front of them and turn them back. But as he looked ahead he saw that the herd was making a mad dash for the edge of a fairly deep ravine. The gully was little more than a rift in the prairie, perhaps cut by some ancient torrential rain like the one they were now experiencing. Nevertheless, it was several feet deep, certainly deep enough to inflict serious, probably fatal injury to any animal that might run into it at full speed.

Ike leaned over the withers of his horse, urging it to greater and greater speed. He drew even with the galloping herd, then slowly began to move to the front. The space between the lead animals and the edge of the ravine was rapidly narrowing.

Finally Ike was far enough ahead of the herd to put his horse between them and the gully. He did so, and taking off his poncho, waved it at the herd. He was assisted in this effort by a crashing thunderbolt that struck so close that the hair stood up on Ike's arms.

The cattle, originally frightened by the specter of a flying canvas, were threatened anew. They turned again, away from danger this time, and started galloping out across the prairie. Ike chased after them.

The cattle ran for at least three miles before exhaustion overtook them. They slowed. Then finally they stopped. Ike, who had kept pace with them, slowed his horse to a walk, then came up quietly beside them. By now the downpour had eased, and the thunder and lightning had passed through, flashing and rumbling far to the east. When he rode to the front of the small herd, talking quietly to them, they responded easily to his urging. Soon he had them all moving slowly and together, back toward the wagons.

By the time Ike returned to the wagon train, not only the rain but the wagons had come to a stop. In addition to the wagon whose cover had caused the cattle to stampede in the first place, two other wagons had lost their canvas as well, so those three were undergoing repair. Men, women, children, and cargo were soaking wet. After some discussion it was decided that, the sun having now reappeared, the company would stop long enough to allow things to be dried out.

Ike saw Hannah supervising the children in one of the drying projects, and he smiled and waved at her. She returned his greeting.

The next morning, which was the 14th of May, the travelers settled for a cold-camp breakfast, and got under way before daylight. Nothing remarkable happened during the day and they traveled nearly twenty miles, following quite easily the trail left by the thousands of wagons that had passed before them. The 15th and 16th were the same. The 17th was Sunday, and there was some discussion as to whether or not they should travel on this, the Lord's Day. A vote was taken, and because everyone was eager to catch up with the main wagon party ahead, the result of the vote was that they would travel.

The company made fourteen miles on Monday, the 18th of May. There was a great deal of excitement that evening, because one of the advance scouts reported seeing many campfires on the horizon to the west.

The Donner party caught up with Colonel Russell's wagon company at mid-morning on Tuesday, the 19th of May. The Russell company was camped alongside Soldier's Creek.

Compared to their own few wagons, the Russell company was enormous.

The Donner wagons stopped just short of the camp while James, George, and Jacob sought out Colonel Russell to seek permission to join. While they were seeking official permission, several of the women from the larger train hurried back to meet the women of the Donner party. As always, the first question was: "What news from back home?"

Actually there was little news the new arrivals could give, since they had left so soon after the Russell company. Nevertheless they told what they could, then both groups visited, exchanging stories and tales and examining relatives' names to establish, when possible, the existence of kinships.

Several of the children left to explore the new camp, and Patty Reed returned several minutes later to inform Hannah that she had counted almost eighty wagons, including their own.

"Why, it's like a whole city!" Hannah exclaimed.

"A city with its own governor," Margaret suggested. "One of the ladies told me that Governor Boggs is a part of the company."

"Governor Boggs?"

"Most recently the governor of Missouri," Margaret explained. "He is the one who ran the Mormons out of Missouri."

"Oh."

During the exchange of conversation, Ike heard that among the travelers of the Russell company was a journalist working for Horace Greeley. Making arrangements with Pat to keep an eye on the cattle, he hurried through the new company to find his fellow newspaperman.

Ike had once heard a wagon company compared to a city on the move. Until now, he had considered that to be little more than rhetoric. But the huge number of wagons in the Russell company, the enormous space taken up during the encampment, and the industry under way at this very moment made him reconsider. This truly was a city on the move. He

could hear the ringing clang of a blacksmith's hammer, the rip
of a carpenter's saw, the hammer and bang of mechanics at
work. Women were washing clothes and preparing meals,
children were playing, and men were hurrying to and fro on
one errand or another. The Russell company encampment
was nothing like the placid encampments the Donner party
had thus far enjoyed.

Ike asked a few people where he might find Mr. Jesse
Thornton and, as if being given directions in a city, was told
to walk a specific number of wagons around the huge circle
to where the Thorntons lived.

Jesse Thornton was a short and rotund man, bald, with a
bushy beard. When Ike found him, he was sitting on a camp
stool, spoon-feeding soup to a woman who was lying on a
canvas cot.

"Mr. Thornton?" Ike asked.

"Yes," Thornton replied. "I'm Jesse Thornton. What can I
do for you?"

Ike smiled, then rubbed his hand on his trouser leg before
he offered it.

"My name is Ike Buford, Mr. Thornton," he said, intro-
ducing himself. "Like you, I am a newspaperman."

"Ex-newspaperman," Thornton replied.

"I beg your pardon?"

"We are both ex-newspapermen," Thornton said again. He
took in the wagon-city with a wave of his hand. "Little need
for a newspaper here."

"Perhaps not," Ike agreed. "But when we get where we are
going there will be."

"You're going to look for a job, are you?"

"No, sir. I'm going to make my own job," Ike said. "I am
starting my own newspaper."

Thornton looked up in interest. "Do you have a press and
type?"

"A Washington Hand Press with a full complement of
type," Ike said proudly.

"And it hasn't been thrown over yet?"

"No, and it isn't going to be," Ike insisted. "Unless I go over with it."

Thornton laughed. "Good for you," he said. "Please excuse my manners, Mr. Buford. This is my wife, Mary."

"Mrs. Thornton," Ike said.

"As you can see, Mary is an invalid," Thornton explained. "It is our hope that the temperate climate of California will have a curing effect on her condition."

"I am sure that it will, ma'am," Ike said, touching the brim of his hat.

"You are with the wagons who just joined us?" Thornton asked.

"Yes. We started from Springfield, Illinois."

"Good, good, I'm glad to have the company of another newspaperman," Thornton said. "It is going to be a long trip. It will be good to talk with someone with like interests."

"Assuming we are permitted to join the company," Ike replied. "I understand we must be voted upon."

Thornton chuckled. "A formality only," he said. "No one is likely to turn you out in the wilderness. As a matter of fact, the more wagons we have, the better the chance for a successful journey."

Thornton's prediction proved to be correct, for when the men of the Russell company voted, they voted unanimously to allow the Donner party to join their company. Colonel Russell then stood to address all the men of the Donner party, including the hired hands. Colonel Russell was a tall man, with long, flowing yellow hair and beard. His hat had a low crown, but a wide brim, and he was wearing buckskins, with a fringed jacket and with pants that were stuffed down into high boots. He wore a brace of pistols on his belt.

"There are a few rules and regulations that you must keep in mind," Russell began. He looked right at James Reed and the Donners. "To begin with, this wagon company has only one master." He pointed to himself. "I am that master. I am the captain of the ship, the mayor of the town, and the general of the army. Any and all decisions made with regard to the progress of this company . . . or the safety thereof, shall be made by me. Will that be difficult for any of you?"

Both Donner brothers shook their head no, but James Reed spoke up.

"Colonel Russell, I am prepared to grant that in all matters dealing with the progress of the company you are the final authority," he said. "But I think there are certain aspects of day-to-day administration which I believe are best left to individual groups."

Colonel Russell stroked his beard and studied Reed for a moment. "Mr. Reed, I don't want to tell you what to have your wife prepare for dinner, nor do I wish to interfere with how you employ your hands," he said. "On the other hand if I should need the services of your hired hands for the good of the company, I shall expect them to be as obedient to me as if I am the one paying their salary. Is that understood?"

"Yes," Reed said hesitantly. "Yes, I suppose so."

"And you men," Colonel Russell said to the hired hands. "Do you understand that, in matters pertaining to the safety and progress of the company, I am in command?"

Without exception, all the hired men nodded in the affirmative.

Colonel Russell smiled. "Very good," he said. "Gentlemen, we are the last company making the crossing this year. Therefore we may sometimes have difficulty in finding enough grass for our stock. We may find the trail too deeply rutted by wagon wheels. There may even be an occasional scarcity of game. But if we all work together, I think we will have a safe and pleasant trip. We welcome you into our midst."

The men cheered.

James Reed delivered the acceptance speech for the new wagons. Then, as the men broke up the meeting to take care of their own business, Reed called Russell over for a consultation.

"Colonel Russell, I am in possession of a marvelous new

guidebook for the journey," he said. "Perhaps you would find it useful."

"Are you talking about the Johnson and Winters guide?"

"No, sir. I am speaking of the guidebook by Mr. Hastings. In it he tells of a cutoff by which a great number of miles and a great deal of time may be saved."

Russell snorted. "Yes, I've heard of that fool's book," he said.

"Fool's book, sir?"

"As far as I know there have never been any wagons go through that pass."

"Excuse me, Colonel. You say as far as you know. But is it possible that some wagons may have used the pass without you knowing about it?"

"I suppose so, but they're damn fools if they did."

"But surely, to save so many miles and so much time is not a foolish thing?"

"Mr. Reed, is it?"

"James Reed, at your service, sir."

"Mr. Reed, this here will be the third time I've made the journey. Fifth time if you count goin' and comin'. If there was a better way than the way I been goin', I do believe I would know about it. No, sir. My advice is to stay on the tried-and-true trail, and that, sir, is what I will do."

"I am not trying to undermine your authority, Colonel," Reed said. "I was merely making a suggestion."

"I thank you for your suggestion, Mr. Reed. But if you'll excuse me now, I have some things I must tend to."

"Yes, yes, and I must return to my wagons as well. Thank you again, Colonel, for accepting us as you have." Reed hurried back to his own wagons.

The mood was festive in camp that night, and the women went out of their way to make the meal reflect the mood. Ike shot a deer, and a few of the other men killed some sage hens. Several of the women made pies, and instead of individual family meals that evening, the tables were drawn together for communal meal—at least for the members of the Donner arty.

Most of the hired men ate together, but Ike managed to rrange his seating so that he was next to Hannah. His efforts ere helped by the fact that Hannah made no attempt to wart his plans. They spoke only in generalities during the eal. Then afterward, Hannah began putting another plate gether.

"Grandmother Keyes was sleeping earlier," she said. "Peraps now she will feel like eating."

"May I help take the meal to her?" Ike asked.

Hannah smiled. "Yes, if you would like."

With Hannah carrying the plate, and Ike carrying bread and offee, they left the others and walked back to the Prairie alace Wagon. It loomed large among the other wagons.

"That wagon has caused quite a sensation among the eople in the Russell company," Ike said.

"Yes, I know. Many have come to look at it."

"Everyone insists that it will have to be abandoned before he trip is over."

Hannah sighed. "Yes, they have told me as much also. But or now at least, it is serving its purpose well. It is making randmother comfortable."

"How is she doing?"

"She is growing weaker," Hannah said. "I don't think she ill be with us much longer. Of late she has had no appetite."

"Perhaps she will eat tonight. The food was exceptionally ood," Ike suggested.

Grandmother Keyes did not eat. Hannah was able to wake er, but the old lady pleaded that she was very tired and ould prefer to sleep. Hannah kissed her on the forehead, hen agreed to respect her wishes.

"Would you like to go for a walk?" Ike asked.

Hannah laughed.

"What is it?"

"I walk every day," she replied.

Ike laughed with her. "I didn't actually mean walk for the sake of walking," he said. "What I meant was . . ."

Hannah looked serious. "You want me to keep company with you."

"Yes, that is what I had in mind," Ike admitted.

Hannah smiled at him. "I believe I would enjoy that very much, Isaac Buford."

Ike led her away from the wagons toward a promontory about half a mile distant. From there they could see all the wagons and the trail over which they had come, as well as the trail, marked by the passage of earlier wagons, over which they would travel. A large, flat rock made a perfect place for them to sit. As they sat down, the clock struck eight.

"Listen," Hannah said. "You can hear the clock from up here."

Ike laughed. "You can hear the clock from all over the wagon train. I think everyone has begun to keep time by it."

"I hope it isn't damaged during the trip out."

"It's well packed and well padded," Ike said. "I think it will survive the trip."

"I'm sure everyone thinks it was very foolish of Uncle James to bring it, but it means so much to Aunt Margaret."

"Then Mr. Reed was quite right to bring it," Ike replied. He sighed. "Look at this, Hannah. Isn't this a sight to behold? An unbroken view of the horizon. I would like to write something that would make my readers understand what this is like, but it is indescribable. Magnificent, but indescribable."

"Yes, it is," Hannah agreed.

"Although being from Boston, of course, I'm sure you have seen many wondrous things."

Hannah chuckled. "Only houses and more houses. And buildings and more buildings. And then, of course, there are the ships at Long Wharf. Dozens and dozens of sailing ships whose masts rake the sky."

"That would be something to see," Ike said. "Did you know that I have never seen an ocean?"

"Then you shall have to see one when we reach California," Hannah said. "For it lies upon the Pacific."

"You have tobacco?" a voice grunted.

Startled by the sudden and unexpected voice, both Hannah and Ike jumped. They stood and turned to see an Indian standing there. He was holding out his hand.

"Tobacco," he said again.

"Oh, my!" Hannah said. She put her arms around Ike.

"Don't be frightened," Ike said. "He only wants a little tobacco." Ike reached into his shirt pocket and pulled out a little sack. He handed it to the Indian. "Tobacco," he said.

The Indian looked at the sack, pulled it open at the top, and sniffed. Then he grunted once, and without speaking another word, turned and walked away.

"You're welcome," Ike said sarcastically.

Hannah laughed, more from a sense of relief than from finding the situation funny. She continued to hold on to him.

"It's all right," Ike said. "I don't think he intended us any harm."

"He frightened me," Hannah said. "He came upon us so quietly."

"I know," Ike said. He smiled. "But under the circumstances, I can't say that his arrival was unwelcome."

Hannah suddenly realized that she still had her arms around him. With a little exclamation of surprise, she let him go and stepped away. "Oh!" she said. "Forgive me."

Ike put his arms out and pulled her back. "There is nothing to forgive," he said. "I am rather enjoying the experience."

"Please, Mr. Buford," Hannah said.

"I thought you were going to call me Ike."

"Ike, this is . . . unseemly," Hannah said.

Ike let her go. "You must tell me, Hannah. Are my advances rejected because my company is unwanted? Or do you dissuade them for the sake of propriety?"

Hannah smiled shyly. "Your company is not unwanted, Ike," she said.

Ike returned her smile, then offered her his arm. "Come," he said. "We should be getting back."

Wednesday was the first day of travel under the orders of Colonel Russell. There were some changes made. Prior to this, the Donner wagons had traveled single file. Colonel Russell preferred to move his wagons four abreast. This method made for a wider trail, but it had the advantage of greatly reducing the distance from the lead wagon to the last wagon. That enabled messages to be passed more quickly, and if it was necessary for a rider to move up or down the line, it was much easier to do.

James Reed did this frequently. Though George and Jacob Donner rode in their wagons, and others walked alongside theirs, Reed had thus far made the entire journey on horseback, riding his favorite horse, Glaucus. He actually had five saddle horses, and though he allowed the others to be ridden, nobody but he could ride Glaucus.

When the Donner party joined the Russell company, Colonel Russell had asked them to select a leader from among their own for their column.

"It will be much easier for me to transmit orders and information through one leader," he'd explained. "The leaders of each column will make up a council, and the recommendations of this council will provide me with guidance I need in governing the company."

The columns had the further responsibility, Colonel Russell had explained, of outfitting one wagon and one repair team to follow on behind the others.

"If one of the wagons in the column breaks down, the repair team will drop back and help make the repairs. If, at the end of the day, that particular wagon has still not rejoined the company, the other repair teams will return to the point of the breakdown and offer their own help. That way," he'd concluded, "there is little danger of leaving anyone stranded."

After some debate, the column had elected George Donner. It was fitting, someone had said, since they had been called the Donner party ever since they left Springfield. James Reed had been the first to offer his congratulations.

Ike had been instructed to move those animals that were under his watch in with the other livestock. The result was a rather sizable herd, and Ike had become one of the many herdsmen who had the responsibility of keeping the animals moving apace with the wagons. As before, however, the herd brought up the rear.

The great train continued its westward trek.

FOUR |||

ON THE WAY TO CALIFORNIA
by
Isaac Buford

We are no longer alone. The little party which so many of you watched leave Springfield has now joined up with a very large company. We are truly a city on the move as there are more than one hundred wagons and five hundred souls en route.

Except for an occasional drenching from the fierce thunderstorms, or a broken axle or wagon tongue, we have had very few unfortunate incidents. Indeed, the journey West has been more along the lines of a pleasant outing than an undertaking of difficulty.

Our nights on the prairie have been cool and pleasant, interspersed with song, campfires, and spirited conversation. We do not lack for surgical assistance, for Dr. Ed Bryant is among our number. Nor do we lack for any spiritual guidance, as the Reverend Mr. Cornwall conducts services on a regular basis.

It may interest our readers to know how a city on the move is able to feed itself. We did, of course, leave with a goodly amount of staples, to include 150 pounds of flour and 75 pounds of meat for each individual. We also laid in an ample supply of rice, beans, and cornmeal, all of which have proven to be good trail foods.

Those staples are further subsidized by such foodstuffs as we are able to acquire while en route. Thus far we have enjoyed the roasts and steaks of elk, antelope, and deer. We have also dined on rabbit, game birds of all variety, and sage hens. In addition, we have been fortunate in being able to catch fish in the various streams and rivers we have crossed.

Besides the meat, we often add wild peas, Russian asparagus, poke salad, and dandelion greens to our menu. The most popular addition for the children, however, is wild honey, for the women have been particularly adept at incorporating it into their recipes.

Water has been our most important consideration, and our route of travel is designed to take into account all possible watering points. To this end the Johnson and Winters guidebook has been invaluable. It is filled with such useful information as the number of miles a specific point is from Independence, as well as the number of miles these guideposts are from each other. Here is an example: "Large Marsh is identified as a place that is some 341 miles from Independence, and 14 miles from the previous landmark. About Large Marsh the guide says, "Here, immediately on the trail, the water is brackish and unacceptable, and there is little grass. However, there are several green spots to the right of the trail in the low hills and here, the grass is excellent and the water, from springs, is sweet and cool. The water and grass are some five hundred yards distant from the road. Great caution must be observed in approaching, however, to keep out of the sinks, which are numerous, dangerous, and deceptive. No wood."

To the readers who are comfortable with such modern conveniences of iron stoves and a ready supply of wood, there may be some wonder as to how a company as large as we can survive without firewood. Our fuel is, and for some time has been, "buffalo chips." This is a secret long known by the Plains Indians, for it is also their source of fuel. Buffalo chips kindle quickly and retain heat surprisingly well. Meat broiled over the chips has the same flavor as if it had been cooked over hickory coals.

As to the question of Indians, we have seen a few, mostly ragged and unimposing-looking specimens. Sometimes they come into camp to beg. Although the Indians favor horses, they have no use for oxen and little taste for beef. Thus our livestock grazes peacefully around the encampment without fear of molestation.

The most difficult part of our journey has been in crossing ravines and larger bodies of water. All obstacles thus far encountered have been negotiated, however, thanks to the ingenuity of our leader, Colonel Russell. He is most adept at contriving windlasses, rafts, or whatever device is required to get the job done.

I am sending this article back by way of Mr. Jesse Thornton. Mr. Thornton is a former newspaperman who has abandoned his plan to go to California due to the continued illness of his wife. I shall miss the companionship of a fellow newspaperman, but I am grateful to him for his offer to act as a mail and dispatch carrier for all who would use his services. All friends and relatives who may be concerned for the safety of their loved ones should be assured that, thus far, all is well.

On the afternoon of the 26th of May, Ike saw someone riding hard toward him, coming from the front of the train.

"Hold 'em up!" the man was shouting as he rode toward the herd. "Stop the herd! Hold 'em right here!"

As the rider got closer, Ike noticed that it was eighteen-year-old Billy Graves.

"What is it?" Ike asked. Some of the other herdsmen rode over as well to find out what was going on.

Billy wiped the sweat off his face with his bandanna, then pointed to the front of the wagon.

"Colonel Russell wants you fellas to stop the herd right here," he said. "We ain't goin' anywhere for a while."

"Why not?"

"The rivers," Billy explained. "This here is where we're supposed to ford. Leastwise, that's what the guidebook says, an' that's what the colonel says, him bein' here before. But on account of the spring freshet, they ain't nothin' goin' acrost there now, 'lessen it be a duck. That there river's gotta be more'n two hunnert yards wide."

"How long you reckon we'll be here?" one of the others asked.

"Beats me," Billy said. "I was only sent back here to tell you we wasn't goin' acrost right away."

"What do you think, Ike? You think we could take the herd up for water?"

Though Ike had not been elected as chief of the herdsmen, he was the oldest and the most educated of the group, so most deferred to him.

"I don't see why not," Ike replied. "Why don't the rest of you get the herd watered, then find a place where you can keep them quiet. I'm going to ride up to the front and see what's going on."

By the time Ike reached the river its bank was crowded with scores of people. Many of the men were standing around the lead wagons with Russell, obviously trying to determine the best way to tackle the problem. The women, and some of the men, were dipping buckets into the water to refill depleted water kegs. The children were running up and down, enjoying the water and the break in travel.

"There's no way around it. We're going to have to build a raft and ferry across," one man proposed.

"No need for that," another replied. "We could just lash a few logs onto the wagons and float them across."

"What about the oxen? How you goin' to get them across?"

"Yeah, I guess you're right."

"Oxen, hell. You ask me, it's that big damn wagon Reed has," another put in. "That's the one causin' us all the problems."

"You needn't worry about my wagon, sir," Reed replied. "I have managed to get it this far. I will get it across the river."

"You've gotten it this far using eight oxen," another said.

"Suppose I have. They are my oxen, bought and paid for."

"Is that so? How about the grass? You buyin' and payin' for that too? You have so damn many animals you're usin' up damn near as much grass as the rest of us combined."

"Gentlemen, gentlemen, please! It does no good for us to be arguin' amongst ourselves," Russell said. "That's just wastin' time. We need to figure us out a way to get across the river."

"There ain't no figurin' to it. We're goin' to have to build a raft."

Russell stood at the bank of the river with his arms folded across his chest, staring at the other side. Finally, with a sigh, he turned to the other men.

"A raft it is, then," he said. "All right, gentlemen, we'd best get started."

"There's a stand of trees over there," one of the men said. "I figure we can get the timber we need from that."

James Reed saw Ike standing just on the outside of the circle of men.

"How goes the herd, Ike?"

"Just fine, Mr. Reed," Ike answered. "We've moved them down for water and grass and they'll be content for a while. So if you don't mind, I'll bear a hand in building the raft."

"I don't mind at all," Reed said, waving his hand. "We must all pitch in to do whatever it takes to get us moving again."

Ike joined with a dozen or more men who, armed with axes, walked the quarter of a mile to the stand of trees. Quickly the men divided up the labor, each assuming the task for which he was best suited. Within a few minutes the axes were ringing, and soon trees came crashing down. As soon as a tree was felled, the trimmers would rush to it, chopping off the limbs so that one long pole could be produced. Others would then attach a team of oxen to the pole and pull it down to the bank of the river, where still others began fashioning a raft. Work continued on the raft for the rest of the day, stopping only when the men knocked off for supper.

After supper, the women announced that they had a treat in store.

"We are going to have a dance," Tamsen Donner said.

"A dance? That's nonsense. We've no time for such foolishness," George Donner replied.

"Mr. Donner, we have been on the trail now for five weeks. We have been getting up early every morning and trailing until dark every night. We have traveled on Sundays and we have traveled in thunderstorms and blazing heat. And not once have we complained. Now we are going to have a dance!"

George Donner looked around at several of the others in his column, and saw that they were following the discussion very closely. Finally he let out a sigh.

"Very well, Tamsen," he said. "If a dance is what you want, a dance is what you shall have."

"Yaahoo!" one of the men shouted, and there was an instant flurry of activity as everyone began to get ready.

Ike was amazed at the number of musicians the train was able to produce. Pat Dolan played the fiddle, but that was no surprise to Ike, because he had heard the young Irishman play before.

The music began then, with the fiddles loud and clear, the guitars carrying the rhythm, and the accordion providing the counterpoint. Men, women, and children began arriving from other columns within the train, and soon the dance under the stars was no different than a dance indoors.

Though Ike would have preferred dancing every dance with Hannah, he really couldn't do that. Proper etiquette required that he also dance with the other young women, and that Hannah accept the invitation to dance from any man who asked her. Though he was often on the floor with one of the other women, and Hannah with one of the other men, their eyes managed to meet frequently, and during those moments they exchanged smiles and pretended that they were dancing only with each other.

The dance provided a good way for all the bachelors and single women to meet each other, but a few, John Snyder among them, seemed to find more of an attraction in the keg of whiskey. The more Snyder drank, the more boisterous and obnoxious he became, and soon he began shouting insults to the young men from the other columns. At first he was doing it in jest, but as he became drunker, the jesting became more cruel. Once one of the young men started toward Snyder, but cooler heads prevailed and the ruckus was quickly settled.

Then, around ten-thirty, one of the butts of John Snyder's caustic comments decided he had had enough. The tall, broad-shouldered Swede knocked Snyder down with one well-placed blow to the chin. It happened quickly and unexpectedly, and when a couple of the women let out shrill cries of fear and surprise, the dancers stopped and the music came to a halt with a few ragged bars.

Though he was knocked down, Snyder was not knocked out, and he raised up as far as his elbows, glaring at the man who had hit him.

"You son of a bitch," Snyder growled. "You hit me."

"Yah, I hit you," the Swede answered. "And if you get up I vill hit you again."

"Come on, Johansen," one of the big Swede's friends said, putting his hand on his arm. "Come on, leave him be. We don't want any trouble from the likes of him."

"Mr. Snyder, you are intoxicated," Reed said. "I suggest you go pitch your bedroll somewhere and sleep it off."

"Just because you are a rich man, Reed, that don't mean you got any right to tell me what to do. You ain't the wagon master, you ain't the column master, and I ain't workin' for you," Snyder growled.

"Nevertheless, Mr. Snyder, I will not stand around and allow you to cause any more trouble," Reed said menacingly.

Snyder got up slowly, glared at the others for a moment, then walked away, disappearing into the darkness.

"All right, that's over, let's get the music going again!" someone called, and within moments the music had restarted.

Ike was the on the other side of the open area from where the ruckus happened, and he had watched, relieved that it stopped when it did. When the music started again he saw that no one had yet approached Hannah, so he moved quickly to take advantage of the opportunity.

Because Ike was dancing with Hannah, he didn't see Snyder return, but Hannah did, and she froze with a look of fear on her face.

"Hannah, what is it?" Ike asked, noticing the expression on her face. By then several others had also seen Snyder, including the band, and once again the music stopped.

Ike turned, and saw Snyder stepping out into the middle of the circle. This time he was carrying a pitchfork.

"Snyder, no!" Ike shouted, and before he realized what he was doing, he had pushed his way through the crowd to confront the angry young man.

"Get away, Buford, this ain't none of your affair," Snyder growled.

"John, you don't want to do this," Ike said easily.

"I said get away, damn you! I'm goin' to kill that Swede."

"No, you aren't. You are going to go back and sleep it off, just like Mr. Reed said."

"Get in my way and you'll get it too," Snyder growled.

"Ike, look out!" Hannah shouted, though her warning wasn't necessary, for Ike had also seen Snyder suddenly lunge toward him.

Ike managed to lean away at the last second, just as the tines of the pitchfork slipped by. He grabbed for the handle of the pitchfork, but he wasn't able to get a good grip on it, and Snyder managed to jerk the pitchfork back, pulling it free from Ike's hands. Snyder laughed evilly and lunged again, but again Ike managed to dance lightly to one side.

"Stop them!" Hannah called. "Oh, somebody please stop them!" But even as she yelled, she knew that Ike was on his own, and she bit her lips and hung on the edge of stark terror as she watched an angry John Snyder try to kill Ike.

Snyder may have had some advantage in strength, but Ike was much more agile, and this time, instead of trying to grab the handle, Ike hit Snyder in the face with his fist. He caught him squarely on the nose.

Snyder let out a bellow of pain, and a small trickle of blood began oozing from his nose. Ike had felt the nose go under his fist and he knew he had broken it. And yet, amazingly, Snyder didn't go down. Instead, with a roar which exposed his teeth, now stained red with the blood which ran across his mouth, Snyder made still another lunge.

"Knock him down, Ike!" one of the young herdsmen shouted with a lusty cheer, and Ike, wondering just what it would take to knock him down, caught Snyder with another solid blow, this time aimed for the Adam's apple. That one did the trick and Snyder dropped the pitchfork, then grabbed his neck and fell to his knees, gagging and choking and trying to breathe.

"You've got 'im now, Ike," someone shouted. "Finish 'im off!"

Ike stepped up to Snyder and drew back his fist for one more blow, then held it for a moment, and finally let his arms drop to his side.

"I don't want to fight you anymore, Snyder," he said quietly. "Go away. You are disturbing folks who just want to have a good time."

Snyder stood up, still clutching his neck. He looked at Ike with a face that was red, both from the struggle and his anger. Finally, he turned and stalked off into the darkness without so much as another word.

"Hoorah for Ike!" someone shouted, and the crowd responded with three lusty cheers.

"Pat, get the music started again!" Ike shouted.

"You heard the lad, me buckos," Pat said to the other musicians as he started sawing on his fiddle.

The music started again, and Ike managed to finish his

dance with Hannah. When the dance was over, however, Hannah asked if he would walk her to her tent.

"Oh. You mean you don't want to dance anymore?" Ike asked, disappointed that Hannah was ready to quit.

Hannah smiled. "I like Mr. Stanton and all the others," she said. "But I don't wish to dance with them anymore. If you would walk me to my tent, I wouldn't have to. Instead, we could have a pleasant walk and a nice conversation."

Ike smiled broadly. "Yes," he said. "I didn't think about it like that."

As they walked away from the music and the laughter and the golden bubble of light put out by the dozen or more lanterns, Hannah shivered.

"Are you cold?" Ike asked.

"The evenings are brisk," she said. She moved closer to him as if inviting him to put his arm around her, and when he did, she didn't resist.

The moon was in the quarter phase, which made the stars even more brilliant. Hannah looked up at them.

"I do not believe I have ever seen such beautiful stars," she said.

"You must have the same stars back in Boston."

"No, I think not," Hannah said. "They were but pale imitations of these. See how these stars glisten? It is almost as if the taller trees are holding them in place, they seem that close."

"I must confess that out here we do seem closer to the stars," Ike said.

They passed by some wagons and heard the snoring of sleepers inside.

"That was a nice thing you did back there at the dance," Hannah said. "Other, lesser men would've beaten him while he was down."

"He was drunk," Ike said, and chuckled. "He probably won't even remember this tomorrow."

"I hope he doesn't," Hannah said. "He frightens me. Oh,

here is my tent already," she said. "Thank you for walking me home."

"Must you go in yet? Can't we talk some?"

"It is not talk you want, Isaac Buford," Hannah said boldly, leaning toward him.

Ike put his arms around her and kissed her. He did it so quickly and easily that they were both in the middle of it before either one of them even realized what was going on. Finally he pulled his lips from hers, though he continued to hold her and look into her eyes. His lips were less than a breath's distance away.

"We shouldn't have done that," Hannah said.

"I'm sorry," Ike replied. Then he smiled. "That is, I'm sorry if I offended you," he added. "I'm not sorry I kissed you."

"I'm not either," Hannah admitted.

They kissed again, and Hannah met his lips with her own, not retreating, but moving into the kiss, testing to see how far it could carry her. She closed her eyes and drifted with the sensations evoked by the kiss. Suddenly she realized what she was doing and, abruptly, pulled back. She looked at him with an expression of surprise on her face. Then, shyly, she smiled.

"Oh, Mr. Buford, how forward you must think I am," she said.

"I could never think that about you," he replied, leaning toward her again, but this time she put her fingers up to his lips to stop him.

"No," she said. "Not again, please. Both kisses went straight to my heart. There is no room now for another."

Ike was thrilled by her words. Rather than condemnation, they seemed to be acquiescent. "Hannah, could it be—" he began, but she interrupted him.

"Good night, Ike," she said. Turning quickly, she stooped down, then disappeared into her tent.

Ike had Twilleth in hand for Hannah to milk the next morning, and when he saw her approaching, he walked the cow over to her.

"Good morning," he said, smiling broadly. He had spent a sleepless night, waiting for the moment when he would see her again. He couldn't help but wonder, though, how she would feel about it all this morning. He could only hope that she wasn't so embarrassed that she would be unable to speak. Then, when she reached for the cow without so much as a word, his fear intensified.

"Hannah, what is it?" Ike asked. "Is something wrong?"

"Grandmother Keyes died during the night," she said.

Then she is not angry with me! he thought thankfully. Then, almost as soon as he had the thought, he was embarrassed by it, for she had just told him of the death of her grandmother.

"Oh, I didn't know. I'm so sorry," he said, recovering quickly.

"I . . . I should have been with her, Ike," Hannah said. "I should have gone to see about her. Instead I was with you. We were . . ." She couldn't go on, and Ike saw tears coming down her cheeks.

"Hannah, one thing doesn't relate to the other," Ike said. He saw that she was feeling guilty about last night, and that the guilt was magnified by what had happened to her grandmother.

"Don't you see, Ike? I should have gone directly to check on her," she insisted.

"Hannah, if you had gone to her, what could you have done? Could you have kept her alive?"

"No," Hannah said. "But I could have been with her."

"Did she die alone?"

"No. Aunt Margaret and the girls were with her when she passed," Hannah said.

"Then you have nothing to be ashamed for, and nothing to feel guilty about."

"I know, I know," Hannah admitted. "It's just that, well, I was brought here to take care of her and when I was needed most, I wasn't there."

"Did Mrs. Reed say that?"

"No, no," Hannah replied quickly. "Uncle James and Aunt Margaret have been very sweet."

"Of course they have. They know how good you were to her. Why, if it hadn't been for you there's no doubt she would have died long ago."

"I suppose so," Hannah agreed.

"When will she be buried?"

"Today, I believe," Hannah said. "Uncle James said he is going to pay Jim Smith and William Herron to dig a grave at the foot of the great oak tree."

"I'll get a coffin made for her," Ike offered.

All work stopped on the raft as the train prepared for the funeral. The death of Grandmother Keyes wasn't unexpected, but it was the first death since the group had left Springfield, and everyone felt it keenly. James Reed paid an Englishman named John Denton to cut a stone for her. Ike worked on the coffin. Hannah and Tamsen Donner took care of preparing the body. They dressed her in her finest dress, and Tamsen combed her hair.

"She looks just like she was sleeping," young Virginia said. She looked at the bed where Grandmother Keyes was lying. "It is going to be very sad to come into the Prairie Palace Wagon and not see her lying there as she has every day since we left."

"Perhaps she will still be there in spirit," Hannah suggested.

The funeral took place at two o'clock that afternoon. The Reverend Mr. Cornwall prayed and delivered a funeral sermon in which he told everyone that Grandmother Keyes had reached her final destination before all of them.

"I am not talking about California, my friends," he said. "I'm talking about that glorious place that is the ultimate destination of us all . . . Paradise."

When the Reverend Cornwall was through, they lowered her into the grave. After that a hymn was sung. Then the grave was closed with prairie sod, still intact even to the wildflowers. One hour later, only Virginia and Patty stood under the tree, contemplating the bank of flowers over the grave. Patty held her doll over her grandmother's grave, as if allowing Penelope her own final good-bye.

At daybreak the next morning, the raft, which had been christened the *Blue River Rover,* was dragged to the river and made ready. Lines were attached to trees on either side of the river. Once the lines were secure, the ferrying began. The process took the entire day, with the final wagon crossing at nine o'clock that evening.

Camp was made that night just one mile beyond where they had camped the night before. There was some nervous discussion around the wagons about the fact that they had lost so much time in the crossing.

"If we don't get through the mountains before the snows, we'll be stuck," someone said, giving voice to what everyone already knew.

"George, I've been giving this a lot of thought," Reed said, walking over to a blazing campfire and lighting a stick to use to light his pipe. He took several puffs before he spoke again. "I think we should take the Hastings Cutoff. It's our only chance to make up for lost time."

This was not the first time the subject had been brought up. Reed was convinced that the cutoff was the way to go and he had already tried, unsuccessfully, to persuade Colonel Russell to commit the entire company to that route.

George was sitting on a blanket on the ground with his knees up and his arms folded around them. As usual, his brother Jacob was at his side.

"You heard what Colonel Russell said, Jim," George replied. "He doesn't want to try the new route."

"Then I say Russell be damned," Reed said. "We'll go without him."

"Hold on there. We just joined up with this company. Are you saying we should strike out on our own?"

"No," Reed answered. "At least not yet. But when we get

to the point where we must make our decision as to whether we will go the old way or the new, then I think we should go the new."

"I don't know," George said. "I'm not all that anxious to try something that's never been tried before."

"We don't know that it has never been tried before, and neither does Russell. He admitted as much. I just can't believe Hastings would put such a thing in a book if it were false."

"What is this cutoff?" a German man asked. He had been one of those of the Russell company who had moved his wagon over to the Donner column. His name was Lewis Keseberg and he and his wife, who was expecting, had quickly become good friends with George and Tamsen Donner.

Reed told Keseberg about the Hastings Cutoff. "According to the book, it will save four hundred fifty miles," he concluded.

"Then, I agree. We should take this cutoff," Keseberg said.

"I'd also like to give this cutoff a try, George," Pat Breen said.

A couple of the others said that they would be willing to go along as well.

"What do you think, George?" Reed asked, smiling broadly. "We've almost got enough right here to make up a company."

"Let me think about it a while longer," Donner answered. "We don't have to decide this night, do we?"

"No," Reed agreed. "But we do need to start thinking about it." He laughed. "Wouldn't you like to already be in California when the others arrive? Whoever gets there first will get the choice land."

"That's a fact, George," Jacob said.

"Jacob, are you in favor of this as well?"

"Maybe," Jacob replied. "I'm just sayin' let's not say no to it just yet. Let's think on it a bit more."

"I'll tell you what. When we get to Fort Laramie, there is

bound to be someone who knows a little more about it," Reed said. "We could ask them."

"All right," George agreed. "We'll look into it more when we reach Ford Laramie."

FIVE |||

A DAY ON THE TRAIL
by
Isaac Buford

Perhaps the readers of this journal would be interested in learning exactly what a typical day is like on the Oregon trail. I cannot, with any great accuracy, claim that the following description is correct for all companies on the trail. I can, however, speak for the Russell company.

Our day begins approximately one hour before dawn. Nearly all are sleeping at this time and the wagons are in one huge circle, for this has proven to be the most convenient method of encampment. Suddenly and rudely interrupting the repose of the peaceful travelers is the loud bang of discharged rifles. This is the sentinels' signal that our time of rest is over. Within seconds after this rude awakening, men and women begin emerging from their night quarters, on board the wagons in some cases, under them in others, while many more have pitched tents alongside the wagons.

For those of us who are tending cattle, and this reporter is among that number, our first job is to move the livestock from their night corral, which is inside the circle of wagons. Also included within this herd are the many milk cows which provide us with milk, butter, and cheese. They must be milked, so the women and children who have that responsibility are next to appear.

Other women prepare the breakfast meal, which is eaten between the hours of six and seven. During that time, too, the teams are yoked to the wagons, the tents are struck, and all is made ready to get under way. We begin our day's journey at the stroke of seven o'clock when the trumpeter sounds his clarion call from the wagon master's position at the front.

We are now eighty wagons in number and we have been divided into four columns of twenty for purposes of travel and control. Colonel Russell alternates who shall lead out so that one is not always required to "eat the alkali dust" of the others.

Some ride in the wagons, though most walk alongside, not only for the exercise, but also to lighten the wagons and thus ease the burden on the oxen. The wagons are followed by the livestock. There is no difficulty with the horses, for even those which are not being ridden will follow the wagons without prodding. The cattle and the spare oxen, however, are a different story. They are very difficult to move, and those of us who have that task must attend to it very diligently.

At noon we stop for a meal. The teams are cut loose from the wagons to allow them to graze, but they are not unyoked, thus making it easier to get under way again when the nooning is over. It is often at noon when the business of the train is brought before the council. As this is truly a city on the move, the council disposes of all disputes with the authority of a high court, from which no appeals are made.

By evening, humans and animals are tired. We have been on the move since before dawn and, as the sun is sinking slowly before us, we look for a suitable place to spend the night. Colonel Russell will have found such a place and he sends a pilot ahead to mark it for us. The pilot sits in his saddle with a flag held aloft, and the lead wagon turns the train toward him, then starts into the large circle. By now our wagon drivers are so proficient in this exercise that the end wagon perfectly closes the gate of a one-hundred-yard-diameter circle, with no further maneuvering required.

Fires are laid and tents are pitched for the evening. Over the next hour the stragglers come in, wagons which have been delayed by some mechanical problem. Most keep an anxious eye for them, relaxing visibly when they see them approaching.

Sometimes in the evening there is music. Whether it is a band, or a solitary instrument, or merely singing depends upon the difficulty of the day and the tiredness of the music-makers. Finally the evening watch is set and the last campfire burns down. The children, so active during the daytime, are the first to go to sleep. The women follow. The leaders of the train, however, must make final plans for the next day's activity before they can finally turn in.

Ike had no sooner finished his article when the camp was interrupted by a loud, enthusiastic shout.

"Buffalo!"

When Ike looked up, he saw that the bearer of the news was one of the young herdsmen he rode with while driving the cattle. The young man was galloping across the open area enclosed by the circled wagons, waving his hat over his head.

"We have spotted a herd of buffalo!" he shouted.

"Ladies, get ready for a feast!" one of the men said. "There will be meat tonight!"

Colonel Russell called a meeting of the men to discuss the news of the buffalo, and more than twenty men showed up, armed with various types of weapons and talking excitedly among themselves. Russell climbed up onto one of the wagons so he could be seen by everyone, then held his arms up to get their attention.

"Colonel, this ain't no time to be makin' a speech,"

someone shouted. "This is a time to get movin'. If we don't hurry, them critters may get plumb away from us."

"Hold on," Russell said. "If a bunch of you go off half-cocked, you are going to spook them for sure and we won't get anything. You can't all go buffalo huntin'. Some of you have to stay behind."

"Wait a minute! Are you sayin' some of us can't get in on this? You got no right to say that! We got families to feed," someone else shouted, and his protest was echoed by the others.

"No, that's not what I'm saying. What I'm saying is that there is a right way and a wrong way to go about this. The wrong way is what you folks are settin' off on now."

"All right, what do you propose? Only whatever it is, let's get it done before them critters get wind of us and leave."

Russell nodded. "Probably the best way to hunt them is to ride right into the middle of them, pick out the one you want, then bring him down with a well-placed pistol ball. But in order to do that, you must have good horses and skilled riders."

"I have good horses," Reed replied. "And I am as skilled a rider as any man in this company."

No one contradicted him, because though it may have been an immodest statement, it was also true.

"All right, Mr. Reed, you shall surely be one of the hunters," Russell said.

"What about those of us who don't have horses?" Keseberg asked.

"I can answer that," Reed said. "You will all get a share."

"*Ja,* but the biggest share will go to you who hunt, will it not?" Keseberg asked.

"You will get a share, Mr. Keseberg," Reed said again. "But I will not lie to you. If it is my horses, my powder, and my shot that brings the animal down, then I shall certainly take the choice pieces for myself."

"So much for sharing," Keseberg growled as he walked away.

"I have a good horse," Governor Boggs said. "And powder and ball," he added. "I should like to be one of the hunters."

"And so you shall," Russell declared.

"Colonel Russell, I am too old for a buffalo hunt," George Donner said. "But I do have some horses I can furnish."

"Very well, Mr. Donner. Gentlemen, those of you who will be a part of the hunt meet back here in fifteen minutes, mounted and ready to go. The rest of you, make preparations to butcher and cook some of the meat." He smiled. "If our hunters are as good as they seem to think they are, we will have a feast tonight."

The meeting broke up with a loud cheer as the men hurried to their assigned tasks.

Ike was chosen as one of the hunters, and as he rode out with the others he was aware that all were watching them. It was a proud and exciting moment for him, but it was a little frightening too. Suppose they failed. Suppose the buffalo got away from them, and they had to return to the camp empty-handed. It would be awfully embarrassing to disappoint everyone like that. Ike made a vow to himself that he would not fail. He would kill a buffalo, no matter what it took.

The hunters approached from downwind with James Reed in the lead. No one had appointed Reed as the leader. He had merely assumed the position, doing it with such authority that no one dared to challenge him.

They could smell the herd before they heard it, and they could hear it before they saw it. It was a wild, tangy smell, not only from their droppings, but from the animals themselves. There was no mistaking what the smell was. It filled the nostrils and excited the senses of the hunters as they approached.

Then they heard them, bawling and coughing, grunting and squeaking, rumbling and clacking as they moved.

And then they saw them.

When the six hunters crested the last little hill, they saw the buffalo in the valley below. There were thousands of them, stretching in an unbroken carpet of brown from horizon to horizon. Ike felt his heart in his throat, for never in his life had he seen a sight so exciting.

"All right," Reed said. "We'll ride toward them. If they start to run, pick one of them out and stay with him. Watch out for yourselves, don't get unseated. If you do, you'll be ground beneath their hooves and there won't be anything anyone can do for you."

"I'm ready," Ike said. Despite his assurance, however, the palms of his hands were sweating, and he wiped them on the leg of his trousers to dry them before he pulled his pistol.

"Let's go," Reed ordered, and moving as he spoke, he started toward the herd. The others followed.

As they approached the herd they began to spread out so that by the time they reached the buffalo they were separated from each other by several yards. At first the buffalo just stood there. Then one of them saw the hunters approaching and started running. That started the others, so that the entire herd was quickly set in motion. From Ike's perspective, it looked like the flowing of a great, heaving brown river.

Ike saw the buffalo that he wanted, and holding the reins in his left hand, guided his horse toward the creature. He put the horse into a full gallop, but the buffalo was much faster than he thought it would be. It was taking some effort to catch up with it.

One of the bulls suddenly thrust his great shaggy-maned head toward Ike, trying to hook Ike's horse with a horn, but Ike managed to pull away at the last minute. His horse seemed to show no particular fear of the creatures, but it was drawing its courage from its rider. That was generally the way of it, Ike knew. Horses would do things with their riders that they would never do on their own.

Finally Ike managed to get close up to the buffalo he had chosen and, raising his pistol, put the barrel right behind the bull's ear with the end of his pistol no more than six inches away. When he pulled the trigger he saw the flash of fire, then the impact of the bullet as hair and a little spray of blood flew up from the point of entry.

The buffalo continued to run for a few more steps as if it hadn't even been hit. Then Ike saw it jerk its head, wobble slightly, then fall. The stampeding buffalo behind it veered to the right, opening up a little space around it. Ike stopped his horse, jerked it around sharply, then approached the fallen bull, ready, if need be, to finish him off.

No final coup was required, however. The buffalo was dead.

There were four buffalo killed during the hunt, enough for one per column. By nightfall all four had been butchered and distributed. Four pits were cut into the prairie sod approximately six feet long, three feet wide, and eight to ten inches deep. The bottom of the pits were lined with dry grass, over which was placed an ample supply of buffalo chips. The fires were then started, and soon every pit was filled with glowing red coals. Skillets and pots were laid right on the coals while ovens were stuck down in them. But the buffalo meat itself was put on green-willow skewers, then held just over the fire by two forked sticks. The aroma of the meat cooking in such a fashion gave voracious appetites to everyone in the camp, so most went to sleep with full stomachs and satisfied spirits.

Most, but not all.

The exception was Lewis Keseberg and his family. The German had protested his portion of the buffalo so loudly that Reed grew angry and told him to take it or leave it, but be damned either way.

Keseberg threw the meat back and stormed off. Keseberg's wife, however, was pregnant and about to deliver, so several of the women in the party took pity on her. They attempted to take some meat to her. Keseberg swore at them and angrily threw the meat back in their faces. As the women left, they heard him speaking to his wife in low, growling German. They didn't know what he was saying, but they could hear her crying.

* * *

On the 26th of June, the wagon train reached Fort Laramie. This was their first encounter with civilization since leaving Independence, and though it was no more than a few mean buildings and a corral, it was as welcome as a booming city to the weary travelers. At Fort Laramie there were some major changes made in the makeup of the wagon train. Colonel Russell resigned as wagon master, and was replaced by Governor Boggs. Colonel Russell and Ed Bryant abandoned the wagon train at this point, deciding to go on alone, trading in their wagons for horses and mules.

George Donner tried to talk Russell out of it.

"You can't abandon us now. We need a man with your experience to get us through," Donner insisted.

Russell said, "Donner, when you left Springfield, you didn't even know I existed."

"Maybe not," George agreed. "But we figured we would find someone on the trail."

"Ah, you won't have any trouble," Russell said. "You are an experienced company now. You'll be able to elect someone new to lead. The trail is clear before you."

"And we can't talk you into changing your mind?"

"No," Russell said. "I've had enough of worrying about other people's problems. I want to worry about my own for a while. And I've had enough of people like Lewis Keseberg."

"Keseberg is all right," George said. "He's a foreigner and rather set in his ways. But you can deal with him."

"No, *you* can deal with him," Russell declared. "After today, I won't have to deal with him anymore. Good luck, Mr. Donner. Oh, and by the way, I wouldn't recommend your taking that cutoff that Reed is so anxious to try."

"I know. You have been against it from the beginning. But I have to tell you, it is awfully hard to turn your back on saving four hundred fifty miles."

"There is no saving. Hastings is taking all you fellas in," Russell said, shaking his head. He sighed. "Well, no matter. It's none of my worry anymore."

*   *   *

Among the people who were at Fort Laramie was an old friend of James Reed's. His name was James Clyman, and he had fought alongside Reed in the Black Hawk War. Clyman had also traveled extensively throughout the West, and now he was on his way back East.

"Reed! Reed, can this really be you?" Clyman said when he saw his old friend. The two of them embraced happily.

Reed introduced Clyman to the others in his party. Then he sent one of his hands back to the provisions wagon with instructions to bring out a bottle of his finest whiskey so he could celebrate the reunion with his old friend.

While they were waiting, Clyman looked at the wagons, clucking in awe and shaking his head in astonishment at the sight of the Prairie Palace Wagon.

"My God, Jim, you've brought that thing this far?" he asked.

"It's been a struggle a few times," Reed admitted, patting the wagon on the side. "But we've made it this far."

"Surely you don't think you are going to make it all the way with that?"

"Why not? I know it's heavy, but I have eight oxen to draw it. It is easily keeping up with the others." At that moment his man returned with the whiskey, and Reed poured a tin cup for himself and for his friend.

"Ahh," Clyman said, smacking his lips in pleasure after his first drink. "It has been a long time since I tasted whiskey that good." He smiled. "Well, you always have been one for fine living," he said. "I must confess, though, I am surprised to see you here. I thought you were doing well back in Illinois."

"I owned my own cabinetmaking shop," Reed said proudly. "You might say I was doing very well."

"Then why leave? Most men come out here to start over."

"I intend to do just that," Reed said. "If I can make one fortune, I can make another. That is the challenge of it, don't you see?"

"Lord, protect me from ambition," Clyman said. "You remind me of a man I know named Hastings."

Reed was about to take another swallow, but he brought the cup down sharply.

"Hastings? Would that be Lansford Hastings?"

Clyman was surprised that Reed recognized the name. "Yes," he answered. "Do you know him?"

"I know his book," Reed said. "In it he claims that the most direct route for California emigrants would be to leave the Oregon trail about two hundred miles east from Fort Hall, then bear west southward to the Salt Lake, and from there down to the Bay of San Francisco."

"I had hoped that damnfool book wasn't being read by the emigrants," Clyman said, taking another swallow.

"What do you mean? That cutoff will save several hundred miles."

Clyman shook his head. "You don't want to take that route, Jim. It's too dangerous."

"How do you know?"

Clyman finished his whiskey, then wiped the back of his hand across his mouth. "'Cause I just come through it, that's how I know."

"Well, hell, Clyman, if you can make it, I can," Reed said.

"I was on horseback," Reed explained. "You're in . . ." He looked at the Prairie Palace and screwed up his face. "You're in a rolling boardinghouse."

"Oh, I think we can make it, all right," Reed insisted.

"Take the regular wagon track and never leave it," Clyman insisted. "It's barely possible to get through if you follow it . . . and it may be impossible if you don't."

Reed shook his head. "There's a shorter route and I'm going to take it," he said. "Seems to me it's of no use to take so much of a roundabout course."

"Jim, I've always known you to be a stubborn man," Clyman said. "But I never thought you were foolhardy. Listen to what I'm tellin' you. Take the established wagon route."

Reed poured Clyman another cup of whiskey and shook his

head. "Hastings says this cutoff is the way to go. Now, I'm not meanin' to question your judgment, Clyman, but I have to tell you, I can't imagine a man of Hastings's reputation signing his name to a book that is full of misinformation."

"What the hell does Hastings know about it? He just come over it the first time last month. With me."

"What?" Reed asked. "I can't believe that."

"It's true, Reed. I ain't makin' this stuff up."

"All right, maybe what you're sayin' is true. But I still want to try."

"Don't do it."

"I'll at least talk to Hastings before I make up my mind."

"Bullshit, Reed, you done made up your mind," Clyman insisted.

The wagons pulled out of Fort Laramie before noon the next day with Governor Boggs now in charge. They saw several Indians shortly after they left, but they had no trouble with them. Two days after they left, Mrs. Keseberg gave birth. The baby was a boy. Because it was so close to Independence Day, several men tried to talk Keseberg into naming it George Washington, or Constitution, or even Independence. Keseberg reminded them that he was German, and Independence Day meant nothing to him. They replied that he might be German, but the baby was American and should have an American name. Keseberg said the name *was* American. He was calling it Lewis Sutter. Sutter was the colonel of the California fort which was their ultimate destination.

Four days after the Keseberg baby was born, the wagon train celebrated the 4th of July. Keseberg and the other Germans wanted to continue on the trail, but Governor Boggs insisted that they take a day off to celebrate the nation's independence. The day began with someone playing "The Star-Spangled Banner" on the bugle. George Donner protested that, saying that there were several other songs just as patriotic as that one, songs with an easier tune, and with more familiar words.

"If we're going to have patriotic music we should have something we could all sing," he said. Then, scoffing at the choice, he added, "There probably aren't any more than a dozen or so people in the camp who've ever heard of that song anyway."

After breakfast, Governor Boggs was prevailed upon to make a speech. A speaker's platform was constructed for him and he climbed up to address the crowd.

After the speech the men shot off their guns in lieu of fireworks, while the women prepared pies and cakes in celebration. There was an ample supply of whiskey to go around for all the men, while the women and children enjoyed lemonade.

Whereas the Irish and the English joined in happily, the Kesebergs and the other Germans were conspicuous by their lack of celebration.

They reached Independence Rock on the 12th of July. Independence Rock was so named because most emigrants reached it on or around Independence Day. It was also called the "Great Record of the Desert," because thousands of travelers had carved their names and dates of arrival on it, leaving their mark for all who followed.

The company stayed there just long enough to visit the rock and eat their noon meal. Just before they pulled out again, a lone rider came from the west, bearing a letter from Lansford Hastings addressed to all trains and companies still on the trail. In it Hastings said that he would be waiting at Little Sandy Creek, where he would offer his services as a guide to any train that wished to use his cutoff.

"All right, boys, here it is!" Reed said happily, holding the letter in his right hand and striking it with his left. "We've been discussin' the cutoff all along. Is there any doubt now? Hastings himself will be there to take us through."

"I'm convinced," George Donner said. "When we get to the cutoff point, I'm ready to go."

Several others agreed, and when the wagons pulled out after the nooning, Reed was singing happily.

Crossing the Great Divide was a significant event for everyone. Up until this point they could have turned and gone back. Now they were committed to the rest of the journey, for from this point on it was closer to the end of the trip than it was to the beginning. The next day they happened upon a very large wagon train that was encamped on the bottoms of Little Sandy Creek. The presence of the train in front of them wasn't a surprise, for they had heard about it at Fort Laramie and had been seeing many signs since. They were somewhat surprised to have overtaken it, though.

The wagon master of the lead train explained that they were merely allowing the livestock to be "recruited," which meant to regain their strength by rest, water, and grass.

"Is there a Mr. Hastings with you?" Reed asked.

The wagon master, a man named Will Bond, shook his head. "No, I know no one by that name."

"Surely you know of him," Reed insisted. "He is a well-known man. He wrote a guidebook telling of a cutoff that will save hundreds of miles. In fact, he sent a letter back offering his services in leading us through the cutoff. He said he would wait here for us."

Bond smiled and shook his head. "Oh, yes," he said. "I have heard of the fellow. And I have heard of his so-called cutoff. But he is not here."

"It is not so-called, Mr. Bond, I assure you. I know someone who actually took it, a man named Clyman."

"You believe him?"

"I have the utmost faith and confidence in James Clyman," Reed said, and Tamsen Donner looked at him in surprise, for she had clearly heard Clyman telling Reed *not* to take the cutoff.

"Well, be that as it may, I have no intention of trying it,"

Bond said. "I have too many wagons in my care to risk them so foolishly. I intend to take the tried-and-true route, and if I were you, especially this late in the season, I would do the same thing."

Reed shook his head. "Don't you understand?" he asked. "It is precisely because of the lateness in the season that we must take the cutoff."

"Governor Boggs, are you plannin' on takin' all your wagons through that cutoff?" Bond asked.

Boggs shook his head. "No, sir," he said. "That cutoff is an idea that Reed and the Donners have been turning over in their head ever since they joined up with us. If they want to go, I'm not going to try and stop them. But I don't intend to go with them."

"If you do not go with us, then we will go on our own," Reed said resolutely.

After James Reed's solid declaration, many began questioning whether they wanted to take the cutoff or continue on the proven trail. Hannah confided to Ike that she would feel much better about it if Hastings had been there as he'd promised.

Later, in a conversation with Tamsen Donner, Hannah learned that Tamsen felt the same way.

"I am sick at heart that the men are bent on following someone who is no more than a crude adventurer," she said. "I must confess that I was much taken with the testimony of Mr. Clyman. I believe we should listen to him."

"Then you should talk to Mr. Donner and to my uncle James," Hannah insisted. "They will listen to you."

Tamsen shook her head and smiled sadly. "No," she said. "I'm sure they would not." She sighed. "There is nothing for it now but to follow my husband. But I cannot help but have the most foreboding feeling about the path we are about to take."

SIX

July 28th, 1846

BLAZING A NEW TRAIL
by
Isaac Buford

It has been eight days now since our wagon train separated into two parties. One party continued west by northwest, the other south by southwest. All who left Springfield are in the latter group.

We are camped now at Fort Bridger. Fort Bridger is as crude a camp as was Fort Laramie, consisting of no more than two log cabins and a rude corral.

Fort Bridger is run by a man named Jim Bridger. Jim Bridger is a famous mountain man who is well known throughout the West. He is also a trader, dealing in furs supplied by the Indians, with whom he is on very friendly terms, and dealing with the emigrants who have passed here before us.

We had thought we would meet Lansford Hastings here. Mr. Hastings is the author of the book which first made us aware of the Hastings Cutoff, which we are about to take. In a letter he sent to all wagons on the trail, he invited us to join him at Little Sandy Creek, where he promised to guide us through this new route. When he wasn't there, we were told he that he would be waiting for us at Fort

Bridger. Now we learn that he has already departed Fort Bridger, leading the Harlan party, a train of sixty wagons that was here before us.

It would have been good to be a part of that sixty-wagon train, but we are not deterred. We are in good spirits and determined to take the cutoff alone, if need be.

As a result of our new route, this will probably be my last dispatch until such time as we arrive in California. It is not that I will be derelict in my writing duties, but after today, there will be no more opportunities to send an article back. Up until now, we have periodically met travelers on the trail heading East. These travelers have willingly carried the mail for us, and it was by them that we have maintained contact. Now, however, we are to be going down a trail so new that there is very little likelihood of meeting any returning travelers.

As I mentioned earlier, the trail we are taking is called the Hastings Cutoff. According to Mr. Lansford Hastings, author of *The Emigrants' Guide to Oregon and California,* this new route will save many miles. There is said to be one forty-mile stretch without water, but Hastings is supposed to be ahead of us on this very trail now, searching for water. If he finds it, he will leave a letter alongside the trail informing us.

According to Jim Bridger, the route ahead is a fine, level road with plenty of water and grass, with the exception of the forty-mile stretch mentioned. There was much discussion in the train about the cutoff before the decision was finally made. Those who believed in the new route formed what was referred to as the Hastings Cutoff group.

There are twenty wagons in the Hastings Cutoff group. They are as follows:

George Donner and his wife, Tamsen, with five children.

Jacob Donner and his wife, Elizabeth, with seven children.

James Reed and his wife, Margaret, with four children.

Hannah Price, a niece of James and Margaret Reed.

Will Eddy and his wife, Eleanor, with two children.

Pat Breen and his wife, Margaret, with seven children. One of the children is but a nursing infant.

Breen's son-in-law, Bill Foster, and his wife, Sarah, with one child.

Breen's son-in-law, Bill Pike, and his wife, Harriet, with two children.

Lavina Murphy, a widow, with five children.

Lewis Keseberg and his wife, Phillipine, with two children, one just born and nursing.

Karl Wolfinger and his wife, Magda.

Baylis Williams.

Eliza Williams, sister to Baylis.

Charles Stanton.

Pat Dolan.

Luke Halloran.

Mr. Hardkoop.

Dutch Charlie Burger.

James Smith.

John Denton.

Antoine. (His last name is unknown to us.)

The Donner teamsters: Joseph Reinhardt, August Spitzer, Noah James, Sam Shoemaker, Hiram Miller, and John Snyder.

The Reed teamsters: Milt Elliot, William Herron, and Isaac Buford.

At the morning camp before we started down the new trail, we elected a new captain. George Donner recommended James Reed as our captain, and there were many who thought Reed would be a good choice. There were more, however, who wished to have George Donner resume the position he held from Springfield until we joined the Russell company. Accordingly, George Donner is now our captain and we are, officially, the Donner party.

The Donner party spent two days at Fort Bridger, during which time the women caught up with their washing and the men worked hard to get the wagons in the best repair. Ike was helping George Donner grease the wheels on his wagon.

"Well, what do you think now, Ike?" George asked. "Do you have more confidence in the trail ahead? Jim Bridger seemed to think we would have no real problems with it."

Ike stuck his hand down into a bucket of grease. There was no shortage of grease, for twice they had passed by springs that were so clogged with it that the water was stinking of sulphur.

"I must confess he has put my mind somewhat at ease," Ike admitted. "Although I am at a loss as to why both the mountain men back in Independence and Mr. Reed's friend, Mr. Clyman, were so dead set against it."

"Maybe they don't know the trail as well as Bridger," George suggested.

"How can that be? They have both come through it."

"Maybe there is a right way and a wrong way to go through it," George said. "After all, Bridger has been out here a long time. If anyone should know it, it would be him."

"There's truth in that," Ike agreed.

"Mr. Donner?" a voice called.

George and Ike looked toward the rear of the wagon and saw a man standing there. He was a very large man, half a foot over six feet tall, with broad shoulders and powerful arms.

"Yes?" George answered.

"Mr. Donner, my name is McCutcheon. Will McCutcheon," the big man said. "I'm here at Bridger with a good team and a good wagon, my wife Peggy, and our baby daughter. We was travelin' with the Harlan party when I took sick with the recurrin' fever. I had to stay behind till I got it licked. Well, sir, I got it licked now, an' I'd like to join up with your group if you'll take us on."

"Where are you from, Mr. McCutcheon?" George asked.

"Missouri," McCutcheon replied. "'Afore that, I lived in Kentucky."

"Well, Mr. McCutcheon, I reckon you heard that we're

aimin' on takin' the Hastings Cutoff," George said. "We're leavin' tomorrow. Do you have any worry on that account?"

"I never worry about tomorrow," McCutcheon replied. "'Tomorrow, tomorrow, and tomorrow creeps in this petty pace from day to day, and all our yesteryears are but candles, lighting fools their way to dusty death.'"

"What's that?" George asked, confused by the man's response.

Ike laughed. "Mr. McCutcheon was quoting Shakespeare, Mr. Donner," he said. "Are you a learned man, Mr. McCutcheon?"

"I can read," McCutcheon replied. "And I enjoy reading Shakespeare."

"Is that a fact?" Donner asked. "Well, sir, I figure you're big enough to read 'bout anything you want to read." He stuck out his hand. "Welcome to the train, Mr. McCutcheon."

"Thanks," McCutcheon said, smiling broadly. "If you don't mind, then, I'll just move my wagon over in line with the rest of you folks."

"Go right ahead," Donner said.

The Donner party picked up one more member before leaving Fort Bridger. His name was Jean-Baptiste Trubode, and he was half French and half Mexican. He was going to work as a teamster. He claimed to know the way along the trail, and his presence offered the added benefit of having a way to communicate with the Indians.

On July 31st, with water kegs full, the stock well recruited, and the wagons in good repair, the Donner party left Fort Bridger. The first day of travel was one of the easiest days they had had since leaving Independence, and when they camped that night, they were in very high spirits.

Travel was much more difficult the next day, but no one worried about it. "After all," they said to each other, "we're goin' to have some hard days as well as the good."

The third day was even more difficult than the second day had been, and some were beginning to get disheartened. A few even suggested that maybe they would have been better off going the other way.

"We can put up with some hard traveling if it saves four hundred miles," Reed assured them, and the others agreed.

On August 3rd they reached a valley that was lush with grass and had an excellent source of water. Their spirits brightened again.

Late in the morning of August 4th, the wagon train followed the creek into a canyon. The walls of the canyon were a foreboding red and they loomed three hundred feet or more over the canyon floor. Because the wagons were closed in on either side, the canyon was filled with echoes, and the fall of every hoof, the creak of every wheel, the whistle of every teamster bounced back from the walls in an avalanche of sound.

Travel would have been very difficult through this part, had it not been for the fact that the heavy undergrowth had been cut away by the Harlan party, which had gone before them. Every man and woman breathed a small prayer of thanks as they rolled along the creek bank, following the cut trail.

Two days later, after leaving the echoing canyon, they came upon a campsite which had been used by the wagons they were following. There was a forked stick poking up from the middle of a cleared area, and in the fork was a letter from Hastings addressed to whoever might be following.

"There's a letter!" Reed shouted, pointing to it. He rode over to retrieve it, then came back, holding it over his head, smiling broadly. "I told you Hastings wouldn't let us down. Maybe he's not here to lead us in person, but he's leavin' us directions."

"What's it say, Jim?" Jacob asked.

"Wait," George called. "Get the others here. We may as well all listen to it together."

When the others were gathered around, Reed opened the letter, then cleared his throat and began to read.

" 'To all who follow I send greetings,' " he began. " 'You

have come this far with no trouble, but from this point forward, you should not attempt to take the same route we have taken. It will be too dangerous for you. Send someone forward to fetch me and I will return to guide you by a better route that I know.' "

Reed looked up.

"Is that it?" George asked.

"That's all there is."

"What the hell? If he knows a better route, why didn't he take it in the first place?" Snyder asked.

"That's what I'd like to know," Stanton added.

"Reed, what have you got us into?" Keseberg asked.

"Keseberg, nobody made you come with us," Reed replied.

"Well, what are we going to do now?" Jacob asked.

"I'm going ahead to find him," Reed said. He stroked his full black beard. "The only thing you can do is wait here till I get back."

"How long you think that'll take?" George asked.

"I don't have any idea. Maybe a couple of days or more. I would like a couple of volunteers to go with me."

"I'll go with you, Mr. Reed," Ike said.

"So will I," McCutcheon said. Then he added sheepishly, "That is, if someone will give me the loan of a horse."

"Ike, pick out a horse for him from my stock," Reed suggested.

"Yes, sir, Mr. Reed," Ike said. "Come on, Will. Let's get saddled up."

Just before the men left, Hannah came over to see Ike. He took her hands in his, and though they were in the open, she made no effort to pull away from him.

"Ike, be careful."

"Don't worry about me. I'm coming back," he promised.

"And please hurry," she added. "Already the nights are getting cold and we are the last train on the trail. I don't mind telling you that it is causing me some concern."

"If truth be told, it is causing everyone some concern," Ike said. Ike looked over at the other two men who were going with him. He saw Jim Reed kiss Margaret good-bye, and Will McCutcheon kiss his wife good-bye. Then without comment, he put his arms around Hannah and kissed her. She made no effort to resist him.

Ike was leading the little party of horsemen. By now it was easy to see why Hastings had left word that they shouldn't attempt to follow the Harlan party. The trail had squeezed down to the point that it was barely passable by men on horseback, let alone by wagons. In fact they saw several wagons that hadn't made it, including one that had fallen over a cliff, killing the oxen. Wolves had already visited the site, and they and the buzzards had picked the oxen so clean that only their bones remained, shining brightly in the sun.

The men stopped for a moment to look down at the wreckage, taking a drink of water as they rested.

"I've made a terrible mistake, Ike," Reed said. "I should have never insisted that we take the cutoff."

"You weren't the only one wanting to take it, Mr. Reed," Ike replied.

"But I was the one who forced the issue," Reed said. "I was the one they listened to."

"Yes, sir, but when you get right down to it, Mr. Donner is the leader."

"You and I both know that he is the leader in name only," Reed said. "I am the one who exercises the most influence."

"Yes, sir, I reckon that's right," Ike agreed.

Reed stroked his beard. "Which means I'm the one who could have prevented all this."

"You're not planning on turning back, are you?"

"No," Reed said. "It's too late now. Believe me, if it were earlier in the season I would. But we can't turn back now. We must go on, we have no choice."

The men corked their canteens, then wearily continued on.

It was two days of hard travel before they managed to overtake the Harlan party. When they arrived they saw a camp that was full of exhausted men and women.

"You're comin' up behind us?" Colonel Harlan asked.

"Yes," Reed replied.

Harlan shook his head. "I'm real sorry to hear that. I'm sorry to hear that anyone else was took in by Hastings."

"Then you don't believe you have saved any time by taking the cutoff?" Reed asked.

Colonel Harlan spit out a wad of tobacco, then wiped his mouth with his sleeve. "Saved time?" he replied. "I figure that by now the party we separated from is two or three weeks in front of us."

"Yes, that's about what I figure as well."

"How far behind us are you?"

"It took us two days of hard riding to get here."

"And you were on horseback. By wagon I'd make that near a week," Harlan said. "I don't want to scare you folks none, but you'd best hurry along and not take no more breaks. It's gettin' real late in the season. You don't want to get caught on this side of the mountains when the snows start."

"We'll make sure that doesn't happen," Reed said. He looked around the camp and into the faces of the tired and sullen travelers. "Where's Hastings? I'm going to take him back with us so he can lead us by that better route he claims to know about."

"Ha," Harlan snorted. "You don't really think he'll go back with you, do you?"

"He said he would in the letter he left us," Reed said.

"Yeah? Seems to me you ought to know better now than to believe anythin' that man writes."

"Does he really know a better route?" Reed asked.

"I don't know if he does or not, Mr. Reed, but if there's any other route in the whole country, it's bound to be better 'n this one."

A smallish man, clean-shaven, with bushy eyebrows and penetrating eyes, came over to join them then.

"This here is your man," Harlan said to Reed and the others. "This is Hastings."

"You?" Reed said. "You're the man who has caused so much misery in our party?"

"I didn't say the route was easier. I said it was shorter," Hastings replied defensively.

"Mister, somebody should put a pistol ball in your brain," Reed said angrily. "And I might just be the man to do it."

"Hold on now," Hastings said fearfully. He held his hands out in front of him. "I may have erred in not telling you just how difficult the trail would be for wagons. But it is the shortest route, and I'm convinced that there is a better route out of the Wasatch then the one we just took."

"Good, 'cause you're comin' back with us to show us that route," Reed said.

"No," Hastings replied, shaking his head. "I'm not comin' back with you."

"What do you mean you're not comin' back? You said you would."

"How many wagons are in your party?" Hastings asked.

"Twenty," Reed said. "And over seventy people."

"There are sixty wagons in this party," Hastings said. "Can't you see that I'm honor-bound to serve the greater number?"

"You're full of shit, Hastings. You've got no honor, period," Ike growled.

"Who is this?"

"He is one of my employees," Reed said.

"And you allow your men to speak in such a fashion?"

"He isn't saying anything that the rest of us don't think," Reed said. "You've led us on a wild-goose chase. Now you're willing to abandon us. I ought to break every bone in your body."

"Wait!" Hastings said. "I'll tell you what I'll do. I'll ride back part of the way with you, and I'll point out the way you should come. That's the best I can do."

"Mr. Reed, our horses aren't strong enough to go back right now," Ike said.

"Mr. Reed, I don't have enough horses for your whole

party, but I'll loan you one long enough to ride back with Hastings," Harlan offered. "The others can wait here for you and you can leave your horse here to recruit."

"Thanks," Reed replied.

Half an hour later, fed and mounted on a fresh horse, Reed followed Hastings back into the Wasatch range. Hastings rode up to the top of a high peak, then got off and walked out to the end of a flat rock. From this point, high above the Wasatch Valley, Reed could see all the way back to the Weber River, where he had left his own party, though he couldn't actually see the wagons.

"That's the way we came," Hastings pointed out. Then he knelt down and traced the route in the dirt with a stick. "But if you'll turn up this canyon, coming off the Weber River here, you'll find the going a lot easier." Hastings smiled. "We're stuck with the route we chose so it's too late for us. But if you'll go this way, you'll probably get ahead of us."

"Hastings, I hope you aren't just handin' us a line," Reed said. "We've got lots of women and children in that train and they've already suffered more than they should. I wouldn't want to put them through anything any worse."

"Believe me," Hastings said. "It will be a lot easier from here on out."

Reed took another look at the map Hastings had drawn in the dirt, then at the view the elevated terrain afforded him. When he felt he had it committed to memory, he walked over to his horse. Just before he mounted, he looked over at Hastings.

"Hastings, if any of my people suffer for this, I'm going to come settle accounts with you," he said menacingly.

Back at the Weber River camp, Hannah waited with the others for the men to return from their meeting with Hastings. As the days passed with no sight of them, they all began to grow more and more concerned. On the evening of the sixth day, George Donner called a meeting.

"I have been hearing a lot of talk around the camp about

the men who left to meet with Hastings," Donner said. "I know you are worried. I confess that I am a little worried myself, but there's no sense in letting panic set in."

"Mr. Donner, those men ain't comin' back," Snyder said. "They've done deserted us."

"No, you're wrong!" Margaret Reed said.

"Don't like bein' the one to make you face up to it, Mrs. Reed," Snyder said, "but even you have to know it by now. They've deserted, pure and simple."

"Deserted?" Hannah asked. "What do you mean?"

Snyder snorted. "Well, figure it out, Miss Price," he said. "Three men on horseback. The chances are a lot better for them makin' it through on their own than comin' back for us, don't you think?"

"You are talking about my husband . . . and the father of our children," Margaret said. "You will never make me believe that he would do such a thing as to desert his family."

"Well, if he hasn't deserted us, then the others have killed him and gone ahead on their own. It's as simple as that," Snyder retorted. "And one way or the other, we got no business hangin' aroun' here any longer. Already the nights are beginnin' to get cooler. We waste too much time, we're goin' to get caught by the winter."

"We'll wait here for them," Donner said.

"Yeah? Well just how long are we goin' to wait?" Snyder demanded.

"We are going to wait until I say otherwise," Donner said.

"Donner," Keseberg said, "I think Snyder is right. Maybe it would be better if we go on now. We can leave a note, saying that we have gone."

"But where would we go?" Pat Breen asked. He pointed up the river. "If we go that way, we're going the way Hastings said don't go. And without any word on what's the best way, we could just wander around until we get lost. I think we should stay here."

Suddenly Cash started barking. Then he started running around excitedly, wagging his tail.

"Miss, can't you shut that dog up?" Snyder said to Virginia Reed.

"I'm sorry," Virginia replied. "I don't know what's gotten into him. He normally only does that when Pa . . ." Virginia stopped in mid-sentence, then smiled broadly. "Pa!" she said. "Ma, Pa must be coming back! Cash! Cash, go find Pa!"

Cash darted off into the darkness. A moment later, they heard Reed's voice.

"Hello, Cash," he said. "Did you come to greet me?"

"They're back! Pa and the others are back!" Virginia shouted happily.

The entire camp stared into the dark toward the sound of the dog and the voices. They heard horses' hooves striking on stone, and a moment later saw three riders approaching. The men were sitting slumped in their saddles, and when the others rushed out to greet them, they allowed themselves to be helped down.

"Have you got anything to eat?" Reed asked. "We haven't had a thing but wild onions for two days."

"We've some antelope steak," Margaret said, crying in happiness. She rushed into her husband's arms as Will McCutcheon embraced his own wife. Hannah didn't wait for Ike to come to her. She went to him.

The new route was no easier than the old had been. In fact, as they progressed up the canyon, the route became more and more difficult. They had to make their own way, cutting timber and moving rocks, working until the blisters broke and bled. The women and children joined in as well, so that by each evening everyone in camp would be so exhausted that they would fall asleep immediately.

There were times when the going was so difficult that roads couldn't even be made. They were following nothing but a small Indian trail, and the wagons had to be hauled up to the top of the ridge by windlasses and doubled teams, then lowered down the other side of the obstruction.

They moved out of one canyon and into another, where

they encountered a creek called Bossman Creek. It was worse than the previous canyon had been. Its bottoms were crowded with boulders and wild growth. By now they were making no more than a mile or two per day, and some of the poorer families discovered that their provisions, so carefully laid in, were running dangerously low.

Eight days after resuming their journey, they left Bossman Creek Canyon and started up a side canyon. So far no part of their route had improved, though they were following the guidelines Hastings had given Reed.

Then, late in the afternoon of the ninth day, three wagons descended to the canyon floor to join up with the Donner Party. Their arrival was totally unexpected, and as they approached, the Donner people stood around looking on with as much surprise as if the new arrivals had come down from a cloud.

"What in the hell?" Donner asked as he saw the wagons approaching. "Would you look at this?"

"Hello the camp," the lead man called. "May we join up with you?"

"Yes, yes, by all means," Donner replied. "Where on earth did you come from?"

"From Vermont originally," the man said. He looked to be nearly sixty, with gray hair and a full gray beard. He smiled. "Though more recently from Illinois. My name is Franklin Ward Graves, but most folks just call me Uncle Billy."

There were a number of people with "Uncle Billy" Graves, including his wife and eight unmarried children. The children ranged from a nursing infant all the way up to twenty-year-old Mary Graves. An older daughter was married to a man named Jay Fosdick. In addition to Jay, there was an eighteen-year-old boy named Billy Graves.

"You are mighty welcome," George Donner said. He smiled. This gave them three more men to help cut the roads.

Over the next several days, despite the harshness of the travel, Hannah and Mary became very good friends. No doubt it was because they were both young, pretty, and unmarried.

They talked about their plans for the future, and wondered what California had in store for them. Hannah said that when she reached California a school would be built for her.

"But is that what you want to do forever?" Mary asked.

"It is my chosen profession," Hannah replied.

"Don't you ever want to get married?"

"Yes, I suppose I do," Hannah agreed. "If the right man comes along."

Mary smiled. "It looks to me as if the right man has already come along," she said. "I have seen the way you and Mr. Buford look at each other."

Hannah blushed. "Mary, you must not say anything to anyone about it," she said.

Mary laughed. "Why, Hannah Price, do you think the entire train doesn't know? Everyone is speaking about it."

If Mary and Hannah were getting along well, their relationship was rapidly becoming the exception, for nearly all the others in the train were becoming less and less friendly with each other. The more difficult the travel became, the more arguments there were among the travelers.

Though a few men blamed Hastings for their predicament, many more blamed James Reed, and he bore the brunt of most of the animosity. Everyone quit speaking to him, and frequently he would feel a tingling sensation in the back of his neck, only to turn around to find someone glaring angrily at him.

The oxen were suffering terribly. Not only was their work hard, but there was very little for them to eat. As a result, they were getting weaker and their ribs were beginning to show through the skin.

One of the bachelors, Luke Halloran, got sick. Because he had no one to tend to him, Tamsen moved him into their wagon and looked out for him. Despite her best efforts, though, he began to hemorrhage and started choking. At about four o'clock one afternoon he died, drowning in his own blood.

At eight that evening, the wagons stopped for the night. George Donner, discovering in Halloran's effects that he was a Master Mason, gathered together the other Masons in the party, and they convened a lodge to bury Luke Halloran.

Two days later they came upon a message left for them by Hastings. When the message was read aloud to the others, it was met with angered curses and threats of bodily harm to Hastings should God allow them to live long enough to ever meet him. Although he had said in his book that there would not be anyplace on the cutoff where they would go more than one day without water, he was now telling them something entirely different.

"Two days, two nights, hard driving, cross desert, reach water," the message read.

The note was old, which meant that Hastings had known about this even before he'd informed the parties of his cutoff. He'd known about it, but he had said nothing about it.

The men prepared for the ordeal ahead by filling every container they could find with water, and by cutting as much grass as they could carry for the oxen.

"What gets me," Hannah heard Reed saying to Margaret, "is that Hastings already knew about this. Did you see that note? It was old. There's no telling when he put it there. He knew we were going to have two days without water, but he never said a word about it."

"Cousin Hannah," Virginia asked later that night, as she sat petting Cash's head, "do you think there is a God?"

"Is there a God? Yes, of course there is."

"Will He let us die out here?"

"I don't know," Hannah admitted.

"Surely, if there is a God, He isn't so cruel," Virginia said. "And yet He is letting us suffer so. Why is that?"

"Perhaps He is testing us."

"Testing us for what?" Virginia asked.

"I don't know," Hannah answered, clearly uncomfortable

with the subject. "Testing us to see if we are worthy, I suppose."

"Tonight I will pray that we are all worthy," Virginia replied.

PART TWO

Descended Into Hell

Sacramento, California, July 4th, 1931

The shrill ring of a telephone interrupted the old lady's story. The interjection of a twentieth-century instrument into this nineteenth-century tale seemed so incongruous that, for a moment, John wondered what it was doing here.

Alice Reed excused herself to answer the phone.

"Hello? Yes, this is Alice Reed. Yes, my great-great-aunt Patty is here. Who is asking? Oh, my. Are you serious? Yes, of course, just a moment, please. I'll get her for you!"

Cupping her hand over the mouthpiece of the phone, Alice spoke excitedly to her great-great-aunt.

"Aunt Patty, this is Herbert Hoover," she said.

"Herbert Hoover has called here?" John asked. "Why would he call here?"

"He met my aunt when he was attending college at Stanford University," Alice explained. "He was doing a college paper on the westward migration and he came to talk to her."

"Have you met him?"

"No, but ever since that day he has been very faithful in sending birthday cards every year. This is the first time he has ever called her, though."

Aunt Patty walked over to take the phone from Alice.

"Hello, Herbert," she said. "How are you doing? You've called to wish me a happy Independence Day, have you? Well, that is very sweet of you, but it costs a lot of money to make a long-distance telephone call. You could have sent me a card, just

111

as you do on my birthdays. Yes, well, it is good to hear your voice too after all these years. Happy Independence Day to you. You must stop by and see me again sometime. It has been a long time since we visited. I'll have Alice make some lemonade for us. Yes, thank you. Good-bye." She hung up the phone, then returned to her rocking chair.

"So, you know Herbert Hoover?" John asked, impressed by the conversation he had just overheard.

"Oh, yes, I met him once, many years ago. Alice, wasn't it good of Mr. Hoover to call me after all these years? I wonder what he is doing now. Teaching school somewhere, no doubt. He is a very bright young man."

"Why, Aunt Patty," Alice said. "Don't you know? Herbert Hoover is President of the United States."

"Oh, my, what year is this?" Aunt Patty asked.

"It is 1931, Aunt Patty," Alice explained.

Aunt Patty was silent for a long moment. Then she sighed.

"Yes, yes, of course it is," she said. "What you must think of me, Mr. Buford," she said to John, shaking her head. "I know that Mr. Hoover is the President, I even know that Mr. Curtis is the Vice-President, but somehow it all slipped my mind. I guess I was just thinking so much about the story I was telling that I sort of lost track of time. It didn't seem like 1931 to me at all. It seemed like 1846. I apologize for that."

John reached out to put his hand on hers. "Please don't apologize for anything," he said. "You are making that time come alive for me as well. Please, go on with your story."

Aunt Patty was quiet for a moment longer. Then she took a deep breath.

"Until we separated from Governor Boggs's train," she said, "the trip West had been glorious fun. I remember that my sister Virginia told me that it was almost like a Sunday school picnic with no end. But almost from the very day we separated from the other wagons, things began to go wrong. But that was nothing compared to what was about to happen to us. You see, the next part of the journey was when we crossed the great desert."

SEVEN |||

August 29th, 1846
When Ike reached the top of the pass the next day, he was overwhelmed by what he saw in front of him. The sun glared brightly from the white surface of a desert that stretched unbroken from where he stood to the shadowy suggestion of a mountain range on the distant shimmering horizon. Not only was there no water, there was not one tree, shrub, or blade of grass to be seen. The desert was at least seventy miles wide. It looked impassable, but they had no choice. They had to go across.

As the others reached the top of the pass, their reaction was the same as Ike's had been. The wagons stopped, and every man, woman, and child just stood there for a long moment, looking ahead, shielding their eyes with their hands and trying to imagine what it was going to be like.

"It looks like we are going into the bowels of Hell itself," Uncle Billy Graves said.

"We'll never make it across," Snyder added.

"We ain't got no choice," McCutcheon said. "We've got to go."

"We're wasting time," Reed growled. "Let's move 'em out."

Many of the women, exhausted by what they had already been through, began to cry when they saw what was still before them. But as Will McCutcheon said, they had no choice other than to continue. With many mouthing a prayer, and gathering what strength they had remaining, the little party started out into the desert.

As the oxen plodded and the wagons rolled, the wheels lifted a fine, powdery dust from the ground. The dust hung in the air to clog the nostrils and burn the skin. With red-rimmed eyes, chapped lips, and a grim, determined expression, the emigrants continued their trek out into the yawning wasteland, putting one weary foot in front of the other.

They camped the first night on the desert, building fires from the greasewood to help push back the cold. It was a quiet camp, not so much from exhaustion as from a sense of profound despair. They ate little and drank less, then turned in for a few hours of fretful sleep. Before dawn they were up and going again.

As they moved farther out into the desert, the sand became deeper and harder to move through. The hooves of the oxen sank into the sand, and the wagon wheels cut grooves almost halfway up to the hubs, making the pulling much, much harder. The merciless sun continued its transit across the bright blue sky, punishing everyone with its heat and glare. Despite their best efforts to conserve what they had, parched throats and chapped lips demanded water, and they went to their containers time and time again. Often as not, when the water vessel was empty it would be cast aside so that, soon, the train could be traced by the empty canteens, jugs, bottles, and barrels that littered the route.

When they stopped for the second night they realized a grim truth. Hastings had lied again. In his book he had said only one day of desert travel. The note he left them said two. But here they were, after two hard days of travel, and the mountains on the distant horizon looked as far away now as they did when they entered the desert.

There was no water left for the animals by the third day. There was no grass either. There was only the great salt flat reaching out before them in a blazing white that glistened in the distance, giving the tantalizing but false impression of water.

By the end of the third day the wagon train had lost its integrity. Instead of one cohesive unit, it was now stretched out into a very long line, so that the lead wagon was several miles ahead of the last wagon. And because of their great weight, the wagons which were bringing up the rear were those which belonged to James Reed.

Ike was riding herd on the cattle and spare oxen. They had no weight to pull so they were moving ahead, but Ike was worried about Hannah. He kept twisting around in his saddle, looking back over his shoulder to keep an eye on the Reed wagon. Every time he looked around, it seemed as if they had fallen farther back.

"Jim," Ike said to Jim Smith, one of the others driving the cattle. "I'm going back to help the Reeds. You and the others can handle the cattle without me, can't you?"

"Sure, go ahead," Jim said. "Do what you have to do."

Ike turned and road back into the desert, finding the three Reed wagons far to the rear. He stayed with them for the rest of the day, helping Reed and his teamsters, Milt Elliot, William Herron, and Baylis Williams, urge the teams on, getting behind the wagon and pushing when there was a particularly difficult place for the wagons to negotiate. He had planned to just offer a little hand, but he was still there when they stopped for the night.

"Why did you come back?" Reed asked as they sat around the campfire that night.

"I figured you could use the help," Ike said.

Reed poked at the fire with a long stick. "I appreciate it," he finally said.

Ike stood up and looked out into the darkness toward their destination.

"How many more fires can you see?" Reed asked.

"Two," Ike answered. "No, three."

"We're scattered from here to kingdom come," Reed said. "I wouldn't be that surprised if the lead wagon wasn't already out."

"No, I don't think so," Ike said. "I was with the herd at

least five miles ahead of you and I was still a long way from the other side."

"Damn, I don't know that I wanted to hear that. They are all blaming me for this, aren't they?"

Ike didn't answer. He had heard a lot of grumbling and complaining from the others, especially from Snyder. And it was Reed, not Hastings, who was taking the brunt of everyone's hard feelings.

"That's all right, you don't have to say anything," Reed said when Ike didn't answer. "I know they are blaming me and they should." He stood up and kicked the sand. "I curse the day I ever saw that damned book!"

"We'll get through this, Mr. Reed," Ike said.

Reed walked over and put his hand on Ike's shoulder. He squeezed it. "You're a good man, Ike Buford," he said. "About the only intelligent thing I've done for this entire trip was to hire you. Hannah Price is a lucky woman."

"What do you mean?" Ike asked.

Reed smiled. It was the first smile he had enjoyed in some time. "Come on, Ike, you don't think I believe for one minute that you came back just for me, do you?" He nodded toward Hannah, who was then talking quietly with the children. "You came back for her."

Ike rubbed the back of his hand across his cheek and returned the smile. "I reckon you've called me on that one, Mr. Reed."

Reed reached over to shake his hand. "Whatever the reason, I'm glad you're here."

They sat around the fire for a while longer, watching the sparks ride a rising heat column high into the night sky until, finally, the fire burned down. By then the other teamsters and the children were asleep. Then, with a nod to each other, Reed and Margaret crawled into one of the two remaining wagons. That meant that only Hannah and Ike had not gone to bed.

"Where . . . where will you be sleeping tonight?" Hannah asked.

"I don't know," Ike answered. "I guess I'll just throw my

roll out there with the teamsters." He nodded toward the area where the oxen were hobbled, for it was there that the teamsters had chosen to bed down.

"There's a nice level place over here behind the last wagon," Hannah said.

Without another word, Ike stood up, got his bedroll, then walked over behind the wagon Hannah had mentioned. Hannah's bedroll was already there and he laid his beside hers. When he turned around he saw that she was standing there behind him. Her large eyes were shining softly in the moonlight.

Ike sat down, then held his arm out by way of invitation.

"I'm frightened," Hannah said as she sat beside him.

"Don't be. We're going to make it across this desert all right. I promise you."

"No," Hannah said, turning to look at him. "I don't mean that. I mean I'm frightened of us. I am afraid of what is going to happen tonight."

"What do you want to happen?"

"I . . . I don't know. I only know that I am frightened."

Ike raised his hand and brushed a fall of hair back from Hannah's forehead.

"Hannah, you must know that I would never force myself on you."

"You won't have to force yourself, Ike Buford, for I've no strength to resist you. But it wouldn't be right."

"It would be right," Ike said resolutely. He moved his hands to her shoulders, then lightly, with the tips of his fingers, traced a path from her shoulders up to her neck. She tensed.

"Ike, you're making it so very hard for me," she said. Her breathing became audibly more labored.

"Will you marry me, Hannah Price?"

"Will I marry you?" she gasped, surprised by the question.

Ike smiled. "I asked first. Will you marry me?"

"Yes! Yes, Ike, I will marry you," Hannah answered happily.

"And if there were a preacher here right now, this very minute, would you marry me tonight?"

"Yes."

"Then what need have we of a mere mortal to validate what God has already consecrated in our hearts?" Ike insisted. He pulled her face toward his, and she surrendered easily to his kiss. As they kissed they lay down on the blankets, and his lips traveled from her mouth down along her throat to the top button of her dress. She allowed him to do what he wished, totally submissive to his will and bending to his bidding like a slender reed in the desert wind.

Ike's fingers opened the buttons that fastened her dress, and when he folded it back her breasts shone white in the moonlight. He couldn't keep himself from moving his hand across her skin, cupping her breast, tenderly stroking the nipple with his thumb. Then he stopped and looked down at her.

"Hannah, if you've no wish for this, stop me now," he said in a husky voice. "For if I go further, I fear I cannot stop."

"No, Ike, please, don't stop now," Hannah said. "I want to! I want to!"

Inflamed by desire and emboldened by her invitation, Ike slipped out of his clothes, then dropped to one knee beside her, raised the hem of her dress, and placed a hand lightly on the inside of her thigh. He hesitated for a moment, but she reached for him and pulled her toward him. He moved his body over hers and she rose up to meet him.

"Oh, Ike!" she whispered sharply. "Oh, Ike, it's wonderful! I never knew it could be so wonderful!"

If the teamsters, or anyone in the Reed family, knew what happened between Ike and Hannah during the night, they gave no indication of it the next morning. Indeed, as Ike helped them to chain up for the brutality of a fourth day in the desert, he couldn't help but wonder himself if it really did happen. It might have been a dream. Then, when he was able to exchange a quick glance with Hannah, he knew that it was real. Her face showed neither shame, nor guilt, nor remorse for what they had done. Her face showed clearly that she was a woman in love . . . and the thrill he felt over being the recipient of that love reduced to nothingness all the obstacles he had thus far encountered, or would be asked to encounter.

That feeling of transcendency over all obstacles was put to a test that very afternoon when they crossed over a great saltwater sink, covered by a thin veneer of sand. The hooves of the oxen and the wheels of the wagon cut through the crust easily, bringing saltwater to the surface. The wagon that suffered most was James Reed's Prairie Palace Wagon. It broke through all the way to its axles, and as the oxen struggled in vain to pull it, Reed came to the realization that this was the end of his grand wagon. It had been admired by hundreds from Springfield to Independence to Fort Laramie. But here, in the middle of the great salt desert, it was coming to an inglorious end, for he could take it no farther.

"All right," Reed said, sighing. "Unyoke the team and bring up the other two wagons."

With Ike's assistance, the teamsters cut the oxen loose.

"Pa, are we going to leave our Palace Wagon here?" Patty asked.

"I'm afraid we have to," Reed replied. "There's nothing to do for it now."

"You want us to unload anything Mr. Reed?" one of the teamsters asked.

"No," Reed said. "Just leave it as it is."

"Oh, Jim," Margaret said. "Can't we take a few things? Our beautiful clock? Can't we at least take it?"

Reed shook his head. "That's what got us into trouble in the first place," he said. "We'll take food only. Let's go," he told his teamsters. "We can't wait here any longer."

"Pa, wait! Penelope is in that wagon!" Patty said.

"Leave it. It's just a doll, I'll get you another one when we reach California."

"No! I want Penelope!"

"Mr. Reed, my printing press is in one of the other wagons. We can leave it here," Ike offered.

"No," Reed said. "Part of our agreement was that I take the press in one of my wagons. That's your future, Ike. We won't leave it behind." He smiled at his eight-year-old. "But a doll doesn't add much weight. All right, honey," he said. "You can get Penelope."

Thanking him, Patty crawled into the wagon, then, an instant later, reappeared with the doll clutched tightly to her chest.

"Let's go," Reed ordered.

With the oxen from the big wagon hooked to the other two wagons, they began to trudge on. Behind them, as if crying out over its ignoble treatment, the grandfather clock began to chime.

The oxen and cattle, without water now for thirty-six hours, were going mad. Some of the oxen could travel no farther, and when they collapsed there was nothing to do but cut them loose and let them lie where they fell. As Ike and the Reeds brought up the rear, they began to pass more and more dead oxen and cattle.

The children weren't faring much better than the oxen. Margaret gave them rocks to suck on to fight the thirst, and they rubbed their eyes which were nearly blinded by the sun and irritated by blowing salt.

"Ike," Reed said, finally coming to a decision, "I'd like you to ride ahead to find water. As soon as you do find some, bring some back to us. Take Glaucus. He is the strongest and has the best chance of getting through."

"All right, Mr. Reed."

"What about the oxen, Mr. Reed?" Milt Elliot asked. "Ike can't bring back enough water for them too, and if we keep on drivin' 'em like this, we're goin' to kill 'em."

Reed rubbed his chin. "All right," he said. "I guess the only thing we can do now is cut them loose and take them on ahead. When you find water for them, you can bring them back for the wagons."

Leaving the Reeds behind, Ike rode on ahead, fighting the heat and the sun throughout the rest of the day. At about dusk Glaucus smelled water and, without Ike's urging, broke into a gallop. Ike hung on until, finally, he saw grass and trees and a gathering of other wagons. He knew this was the end of the desert, and that the others had found a spring.

When he reached the spring he leaped from the saddle and ran to the water, then lay on his stomach and stuck his head under, sucking up water in such long draughts that he got stomach cramps and had to get up and walk away from it, only to begin retching. Snyder, seeing him, began laughing.

"You ever tasted anything better 'n that?" Snyder asked.

Ike grinned. "Never," he admitted. He looked around at the others. "How many have made it out?"

"I think everyone is here now but the Breens and the Reeds," Will Eddy said.

Ike took the water jugs from the saddle of the horse and, while the animal was still drinking, began to fill them.

"What are you doin'?" Will asked.

"I'm filling these jugs to take some water back to the Reeds," Ike explained.

"To hell with 'em," Snyder snarled. "Reed is so damn rich, let him drink some of that gold he's carrying."

Ike glared at Snyder, but he didn't respond to the comment. Instead he just continued filling the water jugs.

"I've got no obligation to the Breens, but I s'pose the Christian thing to do would be to take them some water too," Will Eddy said. "I think I'll just fill a few jugs of my own and join you."

"Thanks," Ike said. "I'm sure the Breens will appreciate that."

Ike started back, continuing all through the night, until he finally reached the Reed wagons just before dawn. With Milt, William, and Baylis gone, there were now just James, Margaret, Hannah, and the children: Virginia, Patty, Jimmy, and Tommy. Reed and his family were waiting patiently by the inert wagons. Ike gave them all water to drink, then, because he had not slept in over twenty-four hours, crawled into the wagon to go to sleep. There would be nothing else to do until Milt and the others brought the refreshed oxen back for the wagons.

When Ike woke up it was mid-afternoon and he was sweating in the terrible heat.

"Mr. Reed?" he said, sitting up.

"We're right here," Reed answered.

"What is it? What's going on? Where is everyone?"

"We're all here," Margaret said. "Hannah and the children are sitting in the shade of the wagon."

Reed crawled out of the wagon and looked around. They could have been on the surface of the moon, they were so alone. The mountains rose in the distance and a hot, dry wind moaned across the desert.

"But the others," Ike said. "I would've thought Milt and the others would be back by now."

"I think it's about time we faced the fact that they won't be comin' back," Reed said.

"Then they'll be waiting at the spring," Ike said. He looked around at the children, one of whom was as young as three. "I hate to say this but . . ."

"You're figurin' we need to go on," Reed said.

"Yes, sir. But the children . . ."

"Don't worry about them. They'll make it," Reed said. He reached down and scooped up Tommy, the youngest. "Gather them up, Margaret," he said. "We can't stay here any longer."

Ike, Hannah, and the Reed family walked all through the night, finally reaching the spring the next morning. The other wagons were still there, including the Breens. They were all too exhausted and too dehydrated to go on. Reed looked around for his teamsters, planning to berate them for not coming back for him as they were supposed to, but they were nowhere to be found. What's more, no one had even seen them. Eliza Williams, Baylis's sister, was beside herself with worry.

Finally, at mid-morning, they came dragging into camp barely alive. With faces blackened and lips cracked open by the sun, they threw themselves in the water. They had with them one ox and one cow.

"Where are the rest of the animals?" Reed asked in shock.

"Gone," Milt said in a scratchy voice.

"Gone? Gone where?"

"They run off, Mr. Reed. They just went plumb loco for lack of water and they run off into the desert," William said. "There wasn't nothin' we could do to stop 'em. We searched for 'em for one whole day, but them two critters there is all we could come up with. We figured if we didn't come on in with 'em now, they, or we, was goin' to die."

Reed's face went white. "They're all gone? Do you mean to tell me I don't have any way to pull my wagons?"

"You got one ox and one cow left," Milt said. "That's all."

"Well, now, the rich Mr. Reed ain't so rich anymore, is he?" John Snyder suddenly said, laughing evilly.

Reed glared at him, but he said nothing.

"Mr. Reed, I'll lend you an ox," Lavina Murphy said.

"Aye, and I'll do the same," Pat Breen offered.

"Bless you for that," Reed said.

Milt stood up. "Now that we got water, me an' William and Baylis will go back for your wagons."

"No, you've been out there longer than anyone," Reed said. "I'll go."

"You can't bring 'em back by yourself."

"I'll go with him," Ike offered.

"I'll help," Charlie Stanton volunteered.

It was five days before all the wagons were recovered and the travelers and livestock were sufficiently rested from their ordeal in the desert to continue. Two more days of hard travel brought them to a small lake with green grass and several springs. It was such an inviting place and the oxen were so exhausted that they rested again.

Some, however, were for going on immediately. They were

beginning to grow more and more concerned over the lateness of the season, and they were so vocal about their fears that George Donner called a meeting of all the men.

The men gathered around Donner's lead wagon with gaunt faces, sore bodies, and diminished spirits. How different this meeting was, Ike thought, from the ones they used to have early in the journey. At those earlier meetings there had been jokes and good-natured ribbing. They had exchanged pleasantries and invited one another over to their wagons for supper. Now there was no friendly conversation and there were no neighborly get-togethers.

"Folks," Donner started, "I don't have to tell you that we're in a bad fix here. We've lost more 'n half our animals, we've abandoned several of the wagons, and we're beginning to run low on provisions. If we don't get some help soon, we're going to perish out here on the trail."

"What do you propose, George?" someone asked.

"I propose that we send someone ahead to Sutter's Fort," Donner said. "It galls me . . . and I know it galls you . . . to have to confess that we aren't able to do for ourselves, but the truth is, we aren't. We're goin' to have to ask Colonel Sutter to organize a relief party."

"I'll go," Charlie Stanton offered.

"You'll go?" Keseberg snorted. "You're a bachelor, Stanton. You got nobody in this train. What makes you think we believe you'd come back?"

"You have my word," Stanton offered.

"Ha. Your word, you say, like you was givin' a bond in gold."

"If I say I'll come back, I'll come back," Stanton said angrily.

"I accept your offer. But I'd feel better if there were two of you," Donner said. "I think the chances would be better for you getting through."

Will McCutcheon unwound his six-foot-six-inch frame.

" 'When in disgrace with fortune and men's eyes, I all alone beweep my outcast state, and trouble deaf heaven with my bootless cries, and look upon myself and curse my fate.'"

"Those are real pretty words," George Donner said. "What do they mean?"

Will smiled. "They're not my words. They're Shakespeare's words. And it means I'll go, if you folks'll look after my wife and baby."

"You got my word for it, Will," George Donner said. "We'll look after 'em."

"All right, let's go, Charlie," McCutcheon said. "The sooner we get started, the sooner we'll get back."

"I'm not goin' to have to listen to that Shakespeare stuff all the way, am I?" Stanton asked.

"Fear not, Charles of Stanton. I shall not cast pearls before swine," Will quipped.

The company looked on in prayerful silence as the two men saddled up, taking the two best horses remaining except for Glaucus. As Donner had said, it was a shameful thing to get this far, then have to send for help. But then, they all told themselves, it was Hastings who had brought the shame upon them.

"Will!" Uncle Billy Graves called just as the two men were riding out of the camp.

McCutcheon stopped and twisted around in his saddle. "Yes?"

"If you see Hastings, save just a little bit of that pissant for me," Graves said.

Everyone laughed uproariously. It wasn't really all that funny, but it was the first thing they had had to laugh about in a long time.

EIGHT |||

The company moved out the next day. Once again they were traveling as a unit, though there had been a definite shift. James Reed, who was perhaps the wealthiest man in the train in terms of money, was now, for all practical purposes, one of the poorest. He not only had to depend upon the others for oxen to draw his wagons, he also had to parcel out his food because he could no longer carry it all. Others agreed to carry his food for him, but they asked a dear price for their help.

By now the party was seeing occasional Indians, and though the Indians showed no outward signs of hostility, they were troublesome. They began shooting small arrows at the cattle and unyoked oxen. The arrows didn't kill the animals, but they did weaken them to the point that they could no longer keep up with the train. When the animals fell behind, the Indians took them.

The nights began growing colder, and the emigrants could see snow in the mountains. By now, they said to one another, they should have been at Sutter's Fort. And they would have been had they not taken the cutoff. They talked about it at night, mentioning that the ones who'd stayed with Governor Boggs's train, the smart ones, were probably already building their cabins. Come first snow, they'd be warm and cozy in their new homes.

"There's no tellin' where we'll be when the snow starts to fly," someone said.

On the 5th of October the wagon train started up a long

126

sandy hill. The traverse was difficult, and it required double-teaming the oxen to get the wagons over. Ike unchained one of the teams from Reed's wagon and moved it up to help with one of the others. It got fouled up with a team being driven by John Snyder and Snyder, who was about at the end of his patience, got very angry.

"Buford, you dumb son of a bitch!" Snyder shouted. "What the hell do you think you are doing?" He began whipping the team Ike was driving.

"Hold it," Ike said. "As bad a shape as these animals are in, you're going to kill them. There's no cause for that. Just ease up. I'll get them untangled."

"I'll get them untangled all right," Snyder replied, whipping the oxen. "I'll open their hides until they bleed."

"Snyder!" Reed boomed, coming back quickly. "Leave that team alone! There's no need to be cruel to dumb animals."

Snyder looked at Reed and grinned evilly. "You don't give a damn about those dumb animals, or any other dumb animals," he said. "The only thing you are worried about is your own precious hide. If this team goes, you'll be stranded out here, won't you, Mr. Rich Man Reed?"

"Just leave them alone," Reed said again.

"Leave them alone, you say? I'll leave them alone," Snyder said. He turned the whip around handle-first. "I'll just take it out on you."

"John, you're getting carried away there," Ike said.

"You stay out of this, Buford," Snyder growled. "Everybody knows we're in this fix because of Mr. Rich Man Reed. I'm going to beat Mr. Rich Man Reed's goddamn brains out."

"Just try it," Reed growled, "and I'll jam that whip handle down your throat."

"Try it, hell. Don't you understand, you dumb bastard? *I'm going to do it!*"

Snyder moved toward Reed so quickly that it caught everyone, including Reed, by surprise. There had been a lot of loose talk before, but this was the first time anyone had

ever carried it as far as an actual attack. Snyder brought the
whip down across Reed's head so hard that it made a loud
pop. Reed went down to one knee and blood began running
down his forehead.

"No!" Margaret screamed, running toward them. "Leave
him alone!"

Snyder turned his whip on her.

"You're in it with him!" he growled, and he rapped her
across the head hard enough to start it bleeding.

"Aunt Margaret!" Hannah screamed, and she ran to her
aunt and put her arms around her, putting herself between the
wild-eyed Snyder and the injured woman.

"You want some of this too?" Snyder growled. "I've got
enough to go around!"

"Reed!" Ike shouted, tossing his knife handle-first to Reed.
Very few people saw that happen, including Snyder. Not
realizing that Reed was now armed, Snyder turned back
toward Reed and raised his arm high over his head.

"Here's another one, Mr. Rich Man Reed," he said,
bringing his arm down.

As Snyder came down with the whip handle, Reed came up
with the knife. He stuck it deep in Snyder's chest, but that
didn't stop Snyder from hitting Reed a second time. It did,
however, ameliorate the blow somewhat, because this time
Reed didn't go down.

Snyder took a step back and raised his arm a third time. It
wasn't until that moment that he realized that a knife was
buried hilt-deep in his chest. The expression on his face
turned from one of anger to one of surprise, and he looked at
Reed as if unable to believe this had happened.

"Reed?" he said in a choked voice. "My God, you've killed
me!" Blood began bubbling from his mouth, and he grabbed
the knife with both hands and pulled it out. He held it in front
of him for a moment, and looked at it as if he were trying to
figure out what it was and how it got there. The blade was red
with blood, and blood began spilling down the front of
Snyder's chest. Snyder dropped the knife, then took a couple

of steps forward, holding both his hands out in front of him as if he were going to grab Reed by the neck and strangle him. Then he stumbled and fell facedown in the sand.

Keseberg dropped down on one knee beside him and put his hand to Snyder's neck.

"He is dead," Keseberg said, looking up at the others.

"Virginia," Hannah said calmly. "Wet two cloths and bring them to me. You tend to your mother's wound, I'll see to your father."

"Yes, Cousin Hannah," Virginia answered, just as calmly.

By now both James and Margaret Reed were sitting down, holding their hands over their wounds.

"What are we going to do about this?" Keseberg asked the others.

"What do you mean?" Ike replied.

"Well, by God, there has been a murder," Keseberg said. "We can't just stand by and do nothing."

"It wasn't murder. It was self-defense."

"Reed could have fought him like a man," one of the others growled. "He didn't have to use a knife. When one man is armed with a knife and the other isn't, that isn't self-defense, that is murder."

"Snyder had a weapon," Ike insisted.

"Snyder had a whip, not a weapon. He could not have killed Reed with a whip."

"Donner, you are in charge here. I say we have a trial," Keseberg insisted.

"Oh, I don't think a trial is necessary," Donner replied.

"Have it your way. We can have a trial, or we will take care of him without a trial," Keseberg said.

"All right," Donner replied. "All right, we'll do something. Get all the men together. Have them come to my wagon for a meeting."

Reed stood up to go.

"Not you, Jim," Donner said. "I think you had better stay here."

"George?" Reed said. "George, do you hear yourself? Do

you hear what you are saying? We have been friends for years, you and I. We are the ones who put this train together."

"I'm sorry," George said. "I have no choice now. This matter must be taken care of properly."

Keseberg raised the tongue of his wagon, then got out a rope. "There is only one proper way to handle it," he said. "I say we hang the murdering bastard right now."

"And I say we have a meeting to talk it over," Donner replied.

"Suppose we don't want to talk?" Keseberg demanded.

"You have no choice," Ike said to Keseberg menacingly. "You'll talk, or you'll answer to me."

"All right, all right, I'll talk," Keseberg said. "Then we'll hang him."

Ike joined the men of the train for the discussion as to how they should deal with Reed. George Donner put himself out of the picture immediately, saying that he would have to be the impartial judge. Jacob Donner, claiming a longtime friendship with Reed, did the same thing. That left the others to decide the case.

Ike, Milt Elliot, Baylis Williams, William Heron, and Will Eddy took up for Reed, saying that Snyder had provoked the argument and started the fight. But Keseberg, Graves, Breen, Dolan, and everyone else argued against Reed. They wanted him hanged.

"Breen, this has nothing to do with what just happened and you know it," Ike said. "You're blaming him for all our troubles."

"Well, by God, do you know of anyone who is more to blame for all that we have been through?" Breen asked.

"One doesn't relate to the other. If you want to blame him for taking the cutoff, then blame yourselves too. You're all grown men. You could have stayed with the main party . . . you didn't have to come this way. None of you did."

"Reed is an arrogant, bossy bastard," Uncle Billy said. "Hell, Ike, you know that."

"He may be that, but he isn't a murderer. We will be, however, if we hang him."

"We can't let him just get away with it," Keseberg said.

"Take depositions. When we get to California we'll find a judge to hear the case," Eddy proposed.

"Bullshit. What makes you think we'll even make it to California?" Keseberg asked.

"If we don't, then what difference does it make?"

"I have a compromise proposal," George Donner suggested, holding up his hands to call for quiet. When the others looked at him Donner continued. "I suggest we banish him from the camp."

"That's not good enough," Uncle Billy Graves spat.

"Well, that's the only decision you're going to get from me."

While the others were still arguing over what should be done, Ike started back to talk to Reed. He signaled for Eddy and Elliot to come with him, and after they were a few steps away from the others, Ike whispered to them.

"I think you men had better get your guns and come over to guard Reed," he said. "I'm afraid some of the hotter heads are going to try something."

"Yeah, you're right," Eddy said. "All right, I'll get the others and we'll meet you there in a minute."

Ike hurried on over to the Reed wagon. "Get your weapons out, Mr. Reed," he said. "Will, Milt, William, and Baylis are coming over to help out."

"Oh, Ike, is it that bad?" Hannah asked.

"I'm afraid so."

"Let the bastards come," Reed said through gritted teeth. A bandage was tied around his head and the front of it was spotted with blood from the wound. As Margaret's wound had not been as deep, she had no bandage. The others came shortly afterward, trotting through the night, each of them armed.

"Are you all right?" Eddy asked.

"Yes, thank you," Reed replied. "And I thank you fellas for sticking up for me as well."

"Yeah, well, let's hope it don't get no worse," Eddy said.

A few minutes later they heard angry voices as the rest of the men of the train came toward them. Keseberg was in the lead.

"Hold it right there, Keseberg!" Ike shouted.

Keseberg and the others stopped.

"Who is there? Is that you, Buford?"

"Yeah, it's me," Ike said.

"And me, Milt, Baylis, and William are here too," Eddy added.

"You men, don't be fools," Keseberg said. "Turn Reed over to us."

"So you can do what?" Eddy asked.

"So we can hang the bastard," Keseberg answered angrily.

"Yeah. Hang him!" Graves shouted.

"Hangin's too good for the son of a bitch," Bill Pike said. "Don't none of you fellas forget. He's the reason we're in this pickle in the first place."

"Pa!" Patty said in a frightened voice.

"Margaret, you, Hannah, and the children get away from here," Reed ordered.

"We're not leaving you," Margaret replied.

"You can't hide behind the women's skirts all night," Breen shouted.

"I've got two six-shooters here," Eddy said. "And the others are as well armed as I am. I don't call that hidin' behind a woman's skirts."

"You wouldn't shoot us," Bill Foster dared.

"We wouldn't, huh? You want to try us?" Ike growled.

"What are we goin' to do, Keseberg? I ain't goin' to get myself shot for this," Foster said.

"They can't guard him forever," Keseberg said. Then he yelled to the men protecting Reed, as if just stumbling upon a tactic, "You can't guard him forever!"

"We can try."

"And what happens when you get tired?" Keseberg asked triumphantly.

"That's easy, Keseberg," Ike answered. "When we get tired of guarding him, we'll just start shooting you bastards."

"You think we won't get guns and shoot back?"

"That's probably better 'n dyin' in the desert or starvin' in the mountains," Milt said. "Why don't we just start shootin' now?" Milt cocked both his guns, and the metallic click of the hammers being pulled back could be heard loudly in the dark.

"Yeah, I'm for that," Bayliss added, cocking his guns as well.

"No, wait, we don't have no guns with us!" Dolan shouted.

"I guess that puts us one up, doesn't it?" Ike said.

"Maybe . . . maybe we can work something out," Breen suggested.

"What would that be?"

"Same thing as Donner said. We'll banish Reed from the camp."

"Mr. Buford, no!" Margaret said. "Don't let them banish him."

"Banishin' ain't no punishment at all," Uncle Billy retorted. "Not unless we send him out without food or water."

"You send me out without food or water, that would be the same as hanging me," Reed said.

"Yeah, well, we could hang you and get it over with," Keseberg suggested.

"Go ahead. I'm not leaving my wife and family behind for a bunch of bloodthirsty devils like you."

"Mr. Reed, if they kill you, you *will* be leaving your family behind," Ike said. "Don't worry, we'll look after them for you."

"We all will," Will Eddy added.

"You want me to leave too, Will?"

"Looks to me like that's the only choice we've got," Eddy answered. "But we're giving him plenty of food and water," he added in a loud voice for the benefit of Keseberg and the others.

"All right, food and water, but no gun and powder."

"No. We can't turn him out in Indian country without some way to defend himself," Ike said. "He gets food, water, and he gets a gun and powder. Either that, or we settle it here and now among us." This time Ike cocked his pistol, and again the night was disturbed by the deadly metallic sound of a hammer being pulled back.

There was a long moment of silence. Then Keseberg started swearing, though as he was swearing in German, it meant nothing to Ike or the others.

"All right," Keseberg finally said. "Give him what he needs, but get him out of camp tonight."

"Oh, Jim!" Margaret cried, and Reed took her in his arms.

"Don't cry," he said. "Don't let the bastards see you cry. It will be all right. I'll just get to California before you, that's all. And I'll have our cabin raised for us by the time you arrive."

One by one, Reed kissed his children. Then he shook hands with his friends, thanking them for their support. He looked at Ike and Hannah, and he reached out for Ike's hand.

"Ike. It will be a privilege to have you in our family," he said.

"Take care, Mr. Reed," Ike replied. "And don't worry about your family. I will make them my personal responsibility from here on."

"I know you will," Reed said. "That's the only reason I can go. Otherwise I would stay here and shoot it out with these fools."

Reed saddled his horse while Margaret fixed a bundle of food and Virginia and Patty filled two canteens. A few moments later, with the men still standing in two groups, those who had supported Reed and those who were opposed, Reed clutched at his horse and rode out of camp. He disappeared into the darkness without once looking back.

When the wagon train came to a stop the next night, Hardkoop was missing. Hardkoop was an old man, a Belgian, who had paid Keseberg for the right to travel with him. As he had been growing progressively weaker, Tamsen Donner had been paying particular attention to him. When she looked into the back of Keseberg's wagon to check on him, she saw that the place where he always rode was empty. She looked in the front of the wagon, then underneath, but she couldn't find him.

"Mr. Keseberg, I'm looking for Mr. Hardkoop," Tamsen said. "Do you know where he might be?"

"Why do you ask me?" Keseberg growled as he unchained his oxen. "I don't know where he is."

"But he has been riding in your wagon all this time," she said.

"Yes, and taking up room and weight."

"Where is he now?"

"Maybe he fell out," Keseberg replied. "How should I know where he is? I am not his keeper."

"But you are. You were paid to be."

"I do not know where he is," Keseberg insisted.

"Phillipine, have you seen him?"

"Woman, you do not ask my wife," Keseberg growled. "In my country the wife does not say one thing after her husband has said another. I told you, I do not know where he is."

"But he is old and weak, Mr. Keseberg," Tamsen insisted. "I'm going to tell Mr. Donner to send someone back and look for him."

"If he is old and weak, he has no place with us," Keseberg said. "He will slow us down."

"How can you talk about him like that?" Uncle Billy Graves asked. "He is your own countryman."

"My own countryman?" Keseberg replied in amazement. "He is not my own countryman! He is from Belgium. Are all Americans so dumb that they do not know the difference between Belgium and Germany?"

"I'll saddle a horse and go back to look for him," young Billy Graves said.

"Oh, Billy, would you?" Tamsen asked. "Thank you, that would be so dear of you."

"Don't go too far," Uncle Billy said. "I wouldn't want to lose you after all this."

"I'll be careful," Billy promised.

As Billy rode out, the others tended to their evening camp. For the last few days water had been plentiful and hunting had been good, so it was not a mean camp. Soon the entire area was permeated by the smell of cooking meat and simmering stews and the travelers fell to their meal eagerly.

It was well after dark when they heard someone hail the camp.

"Hello the camp!" a voice called, and they looked out into the darkness to see Billy returning. There were two men on the horse. Young Billy was in front and Mr. Hardkoop was riding behind him, holding on to Billy.

"Where did you find him?" Ike asked as he helped the old man down.

"He was about five miles back," Billy explained. "I found him sitting on a rock."

Hardkoop was in terrible shape. The sides of his shoes had been split to accommodate his swollen feet and there was blood on his shoes and on his hands and face from the many times he had fallen.

"Mr. Hardkoop, what were you doing back there?" Tamsen asked.

Hardkoop looked over at Keseberg, who with a growl turned away. Hardkoop pointed at him with a gnarled, shaky finger.

"He put me off the wagon," Hardkoop said. "He told me I must walk or die. I am an old man. I could not keep up."

Milt looked up at Keseberg. "You worthless son of a bitch, you did that?"

"I did not do it," Keseberg said.

"You did do it. You told me I must walk or die," Hardkoop said again.

"All right, I did tell you to walk for a little while,"

Keseberg said. "But I was only thinking of my oxen and my family."

"Get some food and some rest, Mr. Hardkoop," Eddy said. "You'll feel better tomorrow."

When they started the next morning, the oxen would not pull the one remaining Reed wagon. They were about done in. Their ribs were poking through the skin so that they looked like the bows which supported the canvas covers over the wagons.

"Oh, Ike, what are we going to do?" Hannah asked.

"We'll have to cache as much here as we can," Ike said. "We'll get rid of everything but the food."

"Oh, Ike, not your printing press."

"Yes," Ike said. "That too. But even that won't help unless we can borrow a lighter wagon from one of the others. I think Uncle Billy Graves is about ready to abandon one of his . . . he'd probably be glad to let us have it."

Ike and the other teamsters unloaded the wagon, including the Washington Hand Press that Ike had so resolutely transported this far. He stood beside it for a long moment, rubbing his hand across it. The newspapers it would have printed! Maybe he could come back for it.

"Ike," Milt said, coming up to him. "Uncle Billy will loan Mrs. Reed his lightest wagon, but he wants her to sign an I.O.U. for it."

"How much of an I.O.U.?"

Milt sighed. "Three hundred dollars," he said.

"Three hundred dollars? That's six times what that wagon is worth."

"Where else are we going to get one out here?" Margaret asked, coming upon them in time to overhear the conversation. "Tell Mr. Graves I accept his offer," she said to Milt.

"Yes, ma'am," Milt said. He looked over at Ike. "I don't mind tellin' you, Ike, there's goin' to be some settlin' of accounts when this is all over. And I'm keepin' book."

Even with the lighter wagon it was all the oxen could do to

pull it. Margaret and the children, including three-year-old Tommy, had to walk alongside. Then, just before they left, Hardkoop came up to ask if he could ride.

"Mr. Hardkoop, I honestly don't think the oxen could pull the extra weight," Ike replied.

"But you must let me ride," Hardkoop insisted. "Keseberg has turned me out again. I . . . I cannot walk the distance."

Ike looked at the old man and saw that he could barely stand.

"I'll tell you what," Ike said. "If you can make it across this stretch of sand in front of us . . . I figure that's no more than five or six miles . . . then you can ride. It'll be a little easier for the oxen to pull the wagon then."

Hardkoop swallowed hard, and looked at the ground. "I will try," he said quietly.

It was a very difficult day. Even with the lighter wagon the team could barely move, and Ike had to coax and work them the whole day long. Because of that, he forgot all about Hardkoop until they made camp that night. It wasn't until Tamsen Donner came around looking for him again that Ike remembered.

"Damn!" he said, looking back into the darkness. "I told him he could ride in the wagon once we got through the deep sand. But I'll be honest with you. Once we got through, I forgot all about him."

"I will ask Mr. Keseberg to go back to look for him," Tamsen said.

"No," Keseberg replied to her request. "I will not go back for him. If he cannot keep up, he can die. He is not my responsibility."

When Ike heard that Keseberg wouldn't go back for him, he asked Pat Breen if he could borrow a horse to go back and look for him.

"There is no need for that," Breen said.

"What do you mean there is no need?"

"Hardkoop is dead."

"How do you know?"

"I saw him beside the trail," Breen said. "He was lying in the shade of a sagebrush. When I went over to look at him, I saw that he was dead."

"Why didn't you bring him in?"

"Why should I?" Breen asked. "He was dead. There was no need to take up the weight and space in my wagon for a dead foreigner."

"Do you really believe he is dead, Mr. Buford?" Tamsen asked as they walked away from Breen.

"From the way he looked this morning, yes, ma'am, I do," Ike answered. In truth, though, he didn't know if he really believed that, or if he was just trying to convince himself that it was true.

Four days later another disaster struck the party. Early one morning, Indians sneaked in and killed twenty-one cattle and oxen. Will Eddy lost all but one ox, leaving him no choice but to abandon his wagon. That meant that he and his family would have to walk to keep up with the others. His children were too young, so he proposed to carry little Jimmy, while his wife, Ellie, would carry their baby daughter, Margaret.

Eddy could take nothing from his wagon but a little sugar, some bullets, and his powder horn. Even his rifle was left behind because of a broken lock. They weren't the only ones walking, of course. By now the oxen were so weak that everyone except the infants were walking alongside their wagons. They had forty miles to go, and they made twenty of them the first day. When they reached the campsite that night, Tamsen Donner took pity on the Eddy family and gave them coffee. Not only was that all they had for supper, it was the only thing they'd had for the entire day.

By the end of the second day Will Eddy and his family had gone for two days without food and without water, except for the small amount of coffee Tamsen Donner had given them the night before. At sunset, Will asked Breen for a cup of water for his wife and for each of his children, reminding

Breen that he had brought water to them when they were still out in the desert.

"I didn't ask you to bring me any water," Breen replied.

"You took it."

"But I didn't ask for it," Breen said again.

"All right, then I'm not asking for any for myself," Eddy said. "I just want a little for my wife and children."

"I can't do it," Breen replied. "I don't know but what I'll be needin' it for my own family."

"Breen, you've more than enough water there and you know it," Will said. "'Tis only a simple kindness I'm askin' for."

"Askin'? Beggin' is more the word," Breen said derisively.

"You son of a bitch!" Will swore. "I ought to carve out your goddamned heart!" He pulled his knife and started toward Breen. Breen, frightened by the sudden outburst, retreated.

Will stopped, then turned and stomped angrily over to the water keg. Defiantly he jerked the cup down and filled it, drinking deeply. Then he called his wife and children over and gave them water as well.

After the short stop, the train started up again. Instead of making a camp as they normally would, though, they walked through the long night. They walked as if they were already dead, moving one mechanical step after another, plodding on because they had no choice. It was either move, or die.

More oxen gave in and collapsed, and they were cut loose and left lying in the sand to die. More wagons were abandoned, and those who still had wagons began discarding their final possessions, things they had managed to hold on to until now. There were iron skillets, chests, trunks, baby beds, empty water kegs, even family bibles. Under the bright moon the desert sand became an iridescent study in silver and black.

At dawn on October 15th, they saw the tops of trees over the ridge ahead. It was the first time in several days that they had seen anything but greasewood and sagebrush. This wasn't desert scrub-growth. These were real trees, like cottonwoods and aspens. When they topped the ridge they saw real green grass beneath the trees, and through the grass and trees they could see a sweet clear-water stream, tumbling white over the polished boulders and running blue and cold in the deeper channels.

The oxen, smelling the water, broke into a lumbering trot, and the men, women, and children, who had been moving only on reflex action for so long, now found a sense of strength they didn't know they possessed. They ran alongside the oxen, laughing and shouting, giddy with happiness.

The people jumped into the creek, stunned but not put off by the cold. They drank deeply, not by scooping up the water with their hands or cups or dippers, but by sucking it up with their mouths, no different from their beasts.

This was a wide, lush valley, with a lake and a creek. The lake was called Truckee, the creek was called Alder Creek. From this valley the trail led right up to the Sierra Nevada Mountains and Truckee Pass. On the other side of the pass was California and Sutter's Fort. Sutter's Fort was less than seventy miles away.

They had fewer miles to go now than they had covered when they crossed the terrible salt flat. And these miles would be alongside a fresh-flowing river, with green, juicy grass and an ample supply of ducks, geese, deer, and elk.

They had a mountain pass to negotiate, but what was that compared to what they had already been through? They laughed, and shook hands, and congratulated each other. They had come through the worst!

The next morning, Karl Wolfinger, who had been forced to abandon his wagon, felt that his oxen had recovered enough to return for it. Two of his countrymen, Joseph Reinhardt and Augustus Spitzer, offered to go with him. The three of them left early in the morning, but only two of them, Reinhardt and Spitzer, returned.

"Augustus, Joseph, where is my Karl?" Mrs. Wolfinger asked.

The two men looked down at their shoes.

"Karl?" she asked again. She took several steps back toward the desert. "Karl?"

"He's gone, Mrs. Wolfinger," Spitzer said.

"Gone? Gone where?"

"The Indians got him," Reinhardt said.

"Yes, it was the Indians," Spitzer repeated. "They attacked us when we tried to recover the wagon. They killed Karl and they burned his wagon. We just barely got away."

"Yes, we were lucky we didn't get killed too," Reinhardt added. "We had a hell of fight with them."

"No," Mrs. Wolfinger said. She covered her hands with her face and turned away, crying. "It is not fair, after we came so far. To be killed like this."

"We are real sorry. There wasn't nothing we could do about it," Spitzer insisted.

"But . . . what will I do now?" Mrs. Wolfinger asked. "Where will I go? Mr. Keseberg. Will you take me in?"

"No, I cannot," Keseberg answered. "I barely have enough for myself and my family. I cannot take on another."

"Do not worry, Mrs. Wolfinger," Tamsen Donner said. "You can stay with us."

"Thank you, Mrs. Donner. You are very kind," Mrs. Wolfinger said.

"Ike," Hannah said under her breath. "Look at them. They don't look like they were in a fight with Indians."

"They weren't," Ike said. "They murdered him, I'm sure of that."

"Oh! But what shall we do about it?"

"I'm afraid there's nothing we can do."

"I don't understand. They were quick to judge Uncle James. Why would they not be as quick to judge these men?"

"Because we have only our suspicions. No one saw them do it. I'm afraid they are going to get away with it."

"No," Hannah said. "They will not get away with it. God will punish them for what they have done. I am sure of it."

The weary travelers rested all that day and the next. On the third day, while George Donner was repositioning his wagon, it dropped off a ledge and, with a terrible cracking sound, turned over. Four-year-old Georgia and three-year-old Eliza were inside the wagon when it happened. Tamsen screamed and hurried to the wagon, climbing inside almost before it stopped sliding, even while it was still in danger of falling farther.

"Tamsen, be careful!" George shouted.

"The children!" Tamsen replied. "I must get the children! Georgia! Eliza! Where are you?"

"Here, Mama! Here!" Georgia called.

Following the sound of Georgia's voice, Tamsen dug through the bedding and clothing until she found them. One by one she passed them back outside to her husband, then scrambled back out herself.

George hooked his team to the side of the wagon, and pulled it back a short distance from the ledge so there would be no danger of it falling farther. Then he saw that the axletree was broken. He sent his teamsters into the nearby trees, where they selected a pine tree that was just the right size to make a new one.

George and Jacob fashioned a new axle from the tree, but just before it was finished, the chisel George was working with slipped and gashed his hand. He let out a yell and held his hand up to look at it. It was badly gashed and pumping blood at a furious rate. Tamsen stopped the flow of blood, then bandaged it. Without giving his hand another thought, George went back to work.

On the 19th of October they saw a string of mules approaching them from the pass. There were three riders with the string, and when they got closer they saw that one of the riders was Charlie Stanton. He was one of the two men they had sent ahead to Sutter's Fort. Stanton had seven pack mules loaded with flour and jerked beef. He also had two Indians with him, named Luis and Salvador. The Indians were civilized, as evidenced by the fact that they were wearing white men's clothing.

After greeting everyone, Stanton told them that Will

McCutcheon had taken another attack of malaria and couldn't come back with him. He also had good news for Margaret Reed.

"Mr. Reed got through," he said. "He's back at Sutter's Fort waitin' for you. It was hard goin' for him. He allowed that one day he had to eat tallow from a tar bucket he found along the trail, but he made it." He looked at Virginia and Patty. "He also wanted me to tell you girls that Glaucus made it too, but I've got to tell you, you can count every rib bone that mare has."

The Reed women laughed and cried with happiness.

"Is California as beautiful as everyone says?" someone asked.

Stanton smiled broadly. "You got no idea how beautiful it is," he said. "Just wait until you see it. I can hardly wait to get back to it myself."

"We'll see it soon as the animals are rested up enough to take us over the pass," Donner said. "I don't know how long that'll be."

"I wouldn't wait too long if I was you, Mr. Donner," Stanton cautioned. "They say that it don't never snow here till mid-November, but I been talkin' to the two Indians, an' they both say they think snow's goin' to come early this year."

"Them Indians have some sort of crystal ball, do they?" Uncle Billy asked.

Stanton chuckled. "Don't know as they do or not, but they've been mighty helpful to me on the trail. I'd pay some mind to what they got to say if it was up to me."

"But the folks in Sutter's Fort told you it would be mid-November before the first snow?" Donner asked.

"Yes, sir, that's what they said."

"Then we'll wait."

Ike looked up at the pass. It was fairly high and steep, but there was already a road cut. It would be hard on the exhausted oxen, but he thought they should go now.

"Ike?" Hannah asked, almost as if she could read what he was thinking. "You think we should go on now, don't you?"

"Yes," Ike answered. He looked at Donner. "I think Charlie has a point, Mr. Donner. We should move on . . . if not over the pass, then surely up to the foot of it so that we are ready."

"Anyone who wants to go ahead can do so," George replied. "But I'm not moving from here until my oxen are fully recruited and my wagons are put in good shape. And a little rest won't be bad for my family either." He held up his injured hand. "Also, I would like this to heal a little more. It is still bothering me some."

"To hell with your hand, Donner. I think Buford is right," Pat Breen said. "I'm going on up to the foot of the pass. Who is going with me?"

"Me an' the Indians will be goin' with you," Stanton offered.

"I'll be goin'," Pat Dolan said.

"I will go," Keseberg said.

"So will I," Will added.

"Mrs. Reed, I think we should go as well," Ike said.

"All right, Mr. Buford. You're in charge of us now," Margaret agreed.

The Graveses and the Murphys also decided to move on. That left only the Donners—George, Jacob, and their families and teamsters—back in the meadow.

Waving good-bye, the party split into two groups, with the forward group going all the way up to the lake, to the foot of the pass itself.

NINE |||

Sacramento, California, July 4th, 1931

"Won't you take a break now?" Alice asked. She came into the parlor carrying a tray with a pitcher of lemonade and a plate of sandwiches. John knew that it must have taken Alice a few minutes to prepare the lunch, but he had been so engrossed in the story that he didn't even know she had left the room.

"Oh, I'm afraid I must decline. I didn't plan to eat with you," John said.

"Young man, you should never turn your back on a kindness," Aunt Patty said.

"I didn't mean that," John said, apologizing quickly. "It's just that it wasn't necessary to prepare food to make this day complete. I deem it a distinct enough honor just to be able to share this day with you."

"You aren't sharing it with just me," Aunt Patty said.

"Yes, of course. I meant Miss Reed as well," John said, nodding toward Alice.

"I didn't mean her either. I meant the others," Aunt Patty said.

"The others?"

"The Breens, the Eddys, the Kesebergs, the Murphys, the Graveses, the Williamses, and the Donners. They are here as well." Aunt Patty looked around the room, and the expression in her face and the wonder in her eyes told John that she was truly seeing them again.

146

"I think I see what you mean."

"Do you?" Aunt Patty asked, coming back to the present. "Because if you really do, you'll be grateful for the offer of food."

"I am grateful, and I would be truly honored to break bread with you," John said, reaching for one of the sandwiches.

For the next few minutes, while they ate lunch, they exchanged pleasantries that were unrelated to the Donner party's trek westward. John told Aunt Patty about flying to California in an airliner. Aunt Patty was amazed that a trip from St. Louis to California could be accomplished so quickly.

"It is amazing, the marvels I have lived to see," she said. "Airplanes, automobiles, telephones, radio, the motion-picture show. We had none of these things when I was a girl."

"I think the marvel is not what you have lived long enough to see, but the life you have lived," John said.

Aunt Patty smiled. "Perhaps the real marvel is that I survived," she said. "Sometimes merely surviving is miraculous."

Finishing her sandwich, Aunt Patty dabbed daintily at her lips with a napkin, then put it aside and leaned back in her chair. This was the posture she assumed while telling the story, so John moved closer to be able to hear more.

"We were very happy when we arrived at Truckee Lake," Aunt Patty began. "We had water and grass, and there seemed to be an abundance of game. I can remember that Mr. Eddy shot sixteen geese in one afternoon. When he offered to share it with the others, they accepted his invitation . . . even those who had earlier refused him food and water for his family. They were very greedy about it too, so that of the sixteen geese he shot, poor Mr. Eddy wound up with only six left for himself.

"There was also a very tragic event that happened about that time. Bill Foster and Bill Pike were brothers-in-law. They were married to Pat Breen's daughters, and they were all traveling together. Soon after we arrived in that valley,

Mr. Foster and Mr. Pike were doing some packing. Mr. Pike had a small pistol, something the men called a 'pepperbox' pistol. He handed it to Mr. Foster, telling him to be careful with it, because it could go off very easily. Well, that was just what happened. Mr. Pike turned his back to Mr. Foster, and the pistol went off and the ball hit poor Mr. Pike in the back, killing him right away. Oh, it was a very tragic thing, even more so because they were from the same family and, during that long and terrible journey, family was the most important thing there was. I don't think we would have made it had we not stuck together as a family, even though Pa was gone.

"For the next few days after that, we looked up at that pass every day. It was so close to us, and all we had to do was go over it and we would be in California. There were a good many who wanted to go ahead, but the oxen were so tired and the wagons needed repair. And, of course, we knew that the snows weren't due to come for a while. So, the men figured we could wait."

November 3rd, 1846

"Breen, we have got to go on," Ike said. "We have got to go today. Look at the sky. There's snow in those clouds."

"I don't think there's goin' to be anything in those clouds more than a little rain," Breen said. "You heard what Charlie Stanton said they told him back at Sutter's Fort. It's not likely to snow hard until mid-November."

"He also said the Indians told him they think a big snow is coming soon," Ike reminded him.

"Well, who are you going to believe? Indians or white men?"

"Indians, if they've lived here all their life and know the weather better."

"Well, I believe the white men."

"Are you willing to take that chance?" Ike asked. "We've come this far. Are you going to let everything we've been through just go for nothing because you don't think it's going to snow?"

"Ike's right," Stanton said. "I think we should go on."

"And just how do you propose that we do that? Look at the oxen," Breen said, pointing to his animals. "Do you really think they can pull a load now? We'd be lucky if they could get across by themselves, let alone pulling a wagon."

"We've got to try," Ike insisted.

By now, others had gathered around to listen to the conversation.

"Ike might be right, Pat," Uncle Billy Graves said. "We've been here a few days now and the oxen aren't getting any stronger. Could be they're not going to recruit any at all until we get on the other side of that mountain. I think we should go on."

"What about the Donners?" Dolan asked. "We shouldn't leave without them. They're still back there in the first camp."

"To hell with the Donners. If they're not here it's their problem," Uncle Billy said.

"What do you think, Ike? Should we go get them?"

"I wish they were here with us," Ike answered. "But for now at least, I think it would be best if we get as many as we can over the pass."

"All right," Breen said. "If the rest of you are going to try it, I sure ain't plannin' on stayin' here alone. What's the plan?"

"I can lead the way," Stanton offered. "Me and the Indians will go on ahead with our mules. That way we can break a path through the snow that's already there, and the rest of you should have a little easier time following."

"All right," Ike said, smiling broadly, happy that the others had seen it his way. "Let's load up and give it a try."

The men returned to their wagons to pass the news along to their families that they were going to try the pass that day. The news was met with mixed emotions. Most of the women and children were anxious to finish the journey, so they were ready to go. But when they looked at the one-thousand-foot-high pass they were expected to negotiate, the top of which was now shrouded in clouds, they cringed at the difficulty of the task that lay before them.

"We're going to try it," Ike said when he returned to the Reed wagon. He and the other teamsters began chaining up the oxen to the Reed wagon.

The oxen had had almost a week of good browse and ample water, but still they were nothing but skin and bone . . . so gaunt that they were almost too small for the yoke. Nevertheless, they stood patiently as they were connected to their burdens. Then, when all the teams were connected and the wagons were ready, Stanton gave a whistle and they started up the road toward the top of the pass.

"Why are we going up into the clouds?" Patty asked.

"Because that's where the pass is," Hannah replied.

"God lives in the clouds, doesn't He?" Patty asked.

"Yes, I suppose He does."

"I don't want to go up to where God is."

Hannah laughed. "Don't worry. He won't be in those clouds."

"How do you know He won't be?"

"I can answer that," Virginia said. "God lives in heaven and in heaven the clouds are lined with gold. Do you see any gold in those clouds?"

Patty studied the clouds carefully. They were gray and dingy. "No," she admitted.

"Then God doesn't live there."

"I guess you're right."

"Of course I'm right."

"Can I ride in the wagon, Cousin Hannah?" Patty asked. "I'm very tired of walking."

"I'm afraid not," Hannah replied. "I'm afraid the oxen couldn't pull you."

"Tommy is riding."

"Tommy is just a little boy. You're a big girl."

Patty pulled her doll out from the fold of her skirt. "You'll have to walk too, Penelope," she said. "You're a big girl, just like I am."

The wagons rolled along the north shore of the lake. The lake was not yet solid ice, though ice was beginning to form around the edges and a rather wide shelf of ice now stretched out from the shore to the lake's middle. The wagons passed under the boughs of tall, dark pine trees. As they went higher in elevation, though, the trees stopped, to be replaced by a scattering of gray rock and patches of snow.

It was a dark, dreary day, so heavily overcast that the position of the sun couldn't be made out, even by a faint glow. Individual clouds couldn't be seen, but they shrouded the towering mountains so effectively that the peaks disappeared into the slate gray sky itself.

As the trail curved upward, the patches of snow grew more numerous and deeper. Before too long the patches became even greater in number and closer together, until finally the ground was completely covered.

At first the snow was shallow enough that larger rocks and gray boulders poked up through it. But the higher they went the deeper the snow became. It eventually got so deep that the bottoms of the wagons began scraping down into the crust. This had the effect of creating a plow, so that snow piled up in front of the wagons, making the passage more and more difficult. The snow formed impenetrable walls in front of each wagon. The oxen, already weak, started losing their footing in the loose snow, and the wagons were in danger of slipping back.

"Stanton! Stanton, hold it!" Ike shouted. Stanton, who along with his Indians was way in front, stopped and came back. "What is it?" he asked.

"We're not going to be able to get these wagons through," Ike said.

"Are you tellin' me you want to go back?"

"No," Ike said. "I'm not saying that. But I do think we should disconnect the teams and load what we can onto the backs of the oxen and then go on."

"You're talkin' crazy," Breen said. "You can't put no load on an ox's back."

"How do you know?"

"It just ain't done, that's all."

"You mean you've never done it."

"All right, I ain't ever done it. And I ain't about to start now."

"Why not?"

"'Cause we'll just be wastin' our time, that's why."

"It's either try to load the oxen, or carry it ourselves," Ike said. "You can see for yourself, we can't use the wagons."

"Breen, maybe Ike's got a point," Eddy said.

"What difference does it make to you?" Breen asked. "You got no animals anyway."

"Maybe I don't have any animals, but I plan to get me and my family over this pass," Will said. "With or without you and your animals."

"All right, I guess we've got no choice but to try it," Breen growled. "Dolan, help me get these critters loose. We'll see what we can do about packin' 'em down like mules."

For the next few hours the party worked hard to unload the wagons and to construct packs that would allow them to put their belongings on the backs of the oxen. The oxen, unused to carrying that type of load, fought hard to resist it, but the men persisted until the oxen were forced to accept their fate. Finally the animals settled down and were formed into an orderly line. The line was necessary because the road was so narrow that it could only be traveled in single file. Slowly they plodded up the trail.

The footing was so treacherous that both oxen and humans slipped and fell many times. It was extremely rough going, even though Stanton and his Indians made it somewhat easier by going out front, using his pack mules to break a path through the snow. In most cases the snow was nearly up to the mules' bellies, but they didn't balk, and they managed to do a pretty good job of clearing a way for those who followed.

The wind was blowing hard and carrying before it crystals of ice which cut into the skin like a million tiny knives. It was cold and painful, and it caused all the travelers to bend their heads, or to look away, unable to face it head-on.

"I thought the desert was hard," Bill Foster said. "I was so hot I thought I would never be cold again. But this . . . this is beatin' it all!"

"Come on, keep goin', everybody," Ike shouted. "We're nearly to the top! When we get there, it's all downhill."

Despite the path that Stanton had cleared, the men were having a hard time keeping their animals going. Ox and man continued to slip and fall. Sometimes they would lose their load, and when that happened everyone would have to stop until the load was recovered and repacked. That was because they were traveling in single file and no one could pass the person in front. The day grew darker, and though they couldn't see the sun, they knew that it was about to set.

Suddenly there was a loud hurrah from the front of the column.

"We're here, boys, we're here!" Stanton shouted down at them from the peak. "We made it to the top! Come on, it's just a little way now!"

The trail was at its steepest and most difficult near the very top, and it became much, much harder to move. It seemed as if they were going back at least two steps for every three they went forward. They could see Stanton and the Indians waiting for them at the top, and yet they didn't seem to be making any real progress toward the summit. Finally, in exhaustion and frustration, Pat Breen stopped and sat down.

"That's it! I ain't goin' no farther tonight," he announced. "We ain't gettin' any closer and it's gettin' too dark to see. I'm not goin' to risk any of my animals or any of my family by lettin' them fall down the side of a mountain in the middle of the night."

Except for Charlie Stanton and the Indians, Breen was in the lead, which meant that those behind him had to stop when he did.

Bill Foster was next in line, but he made no effort to get

Breen to change his mind. "Yeah," Bill Foster agreed. "Breen has a point. Why don't we just wait here for a while?"

"Wait here awhile? What do you mean?" Eddy asked. "It's gettin' darker by the minute. We wait here any longer it'll be too dark to try."

"Yeah, well, that's just what I'm talkin' about," Breen said. "I aim to spend the night right here."

"No, no," Ike said. "Keep on going! Just until we get over the pass! We can't stop here!"

"I think Breen's right," Uncle Billy said. "We ain't gettin' nowhere this way. We could spend the night right here, and get a fresh start in the mornin'. That way we can go over the pass in the daylight."

"No!" Stanton shouted down to them. "Come on, you fools! Can't you see that I'm standing right on the peak? It's just a few yards farther! Come on, I've got the trail broken for you. We've got to get over it and down the other side before the snow starts fallin'. If we get a good storm, we'll never get out of here!"

Despite Stanton's shouts, the men began unloading their oxen and making a hasty camp right where they were.

"What's the matter with you people?" Ike shouted. "We're almost there!"

"Listen, Buford, you can't expect us to just go on and on and on," Dolan said. "We're human beings, not dumb animals."

"Damn!" Ike said, turning away in tight anger. "We may not be animals," he said to Hannah and the others. "But that doesn't mean we aren't dumb. I am afraid this may well prove to be one of the dumbest things we've ever done."

They camped where they stopped that night. Charlie Stanton, who was at the top, could have gone on, but he was unwilling to go on without the others, so he came back to join them. The Indians came back with him.

"Ike, what is wrong with these people? We should have gone on," Stanton said to Ike.

"I know," Ike agreed. He put his hand on Stanton's

shoulder. "Why did you come back down, my friend? You could have gone on. You have no one here waiting for you."

"Maybe not," Stanton said. "But I still remember that Keseberg didn't want me to go ahead to Sutter's Fort because he thought I wouldn't return. I wouldn't want to give him the satisfaction of thinking that he might be right. I may not have family with the train, but I do have honor."

"Where are you going to bed down?" Ike asked.

"I don't know. Probably up at the head of the group. If me and the Indians are going to break through the snow again tomorrow morning, the further up trail we are, the easier it will be."

"You are probably right. Well, I'll see you in the morning, then," Ike said.

Jay Fosdick and young Billy Graves selected a mid-sized tree that was standing away from the other trees, and they set fire to it. The burning tree sent out a circle of heat for several feet in every direction, so the travelers found positions close to it and threw out tarpaulins right on top of the snow. Then they put their blankets on top of the tarpaulins. Some sat up staring at the burning tree, while others lay down to look at it. Still others, exhausted by their labors, fell asleep instantly, warmed by the fire.

Ike threw out one tarpaulin for Margaret Reed and her four children, then another one for himself and Hannah. No one questioned the fact, either verbally or with a disapproving expression, that Ike and Hannah were making their bed together. It was as if the marriage vows they had taken in their own hearts were validation enough for everyone, especially Margaret.

Under the shelter of the blankets, lying on snow which glistened orange in the flickering flames, Ike and Hannah came together. Their hands groped as buttons and fastenings were opened and bare skin was found. For a while, every-thing was blotted out but their need and their desire for each other. They made love that night, oblivious to anyone else . . . oblivious to the cold . . . oblivious to the precariousness of their position . . . and oblivious to the large flakes of snow which, just after midnight, began tumbling down through the blackness.

The snow fell silently, its very silence allowing it to move in unnoticed. By now most of the travelers were asleep, and even those who were awake were staring into the firelight, so mesmerized by its dying glow that they were totally unaware of what was happening.

The next morning they were awakened by a woman's scream. When Ike sat up he was immediately aware of the change. Last night he had gone to sleep on top of the snow. This morning, he awoke under it.

"Who's screaming? What is it?" Hannah asked.

"It was Mrs. Murphy, I think," Ike said.

Lavina Murphy was walking around in the fresh snow, her hands pulling at her hair, crying uncontrollably.

"Look at this!" she said. "Look at it, you fools! We should have gone on! Do you see what has happened to us now? The snow has come, just like the Indians said it would! The snow has come and we are trapped here! We should have gone on last night!"

A pristine blanket of snow covered everything in sight. No longer was the trail that Stanton and his Indians had broken visible. No longer was the trail made by the dragging wagons visible. There were no footprints, no signs of encampment. Even the tree they had burned last night was completely covered in a mantle of white. It was as if man had never been here before.

"Ike, the pass!" Hannah said. "What does the pass look like?"

Ike looked up toward the pass. It was packed solid and piled high with snow. There was no way anyone could get through. The thing they had feared most had happened. They were trapped on the wrong side of the Sierra Nevada Mountains.

They came back down the trail then, to the side of the lake. There was nothing they could do but build a winter camp.

There was already one cabin on the shore of the lake, built and then deserted, perhaps by some earlier travelers who had suffered the same fate. Pat Breen laid claim to the cabin, and he and his family set about fixing it up. Keseberg and Charlie Burger began building a lean-to against one side of the cabin. Will Eddy and Bill Foster found a large rock with one flat side and began erecting a cabin there, using the flat side as one wall.

Ike found a depressed area. He backed the wagon over it, then cut blocks of snow and piled them up around the wagon. Using snow, canvas, and pine boughs, he was able to build quite a cozy shelter. He made two fireplaces at one end, one in the depression below the wagon and the other above, in the wagon itself. He arranged it so that both fireplaces used the same chimney. Margaret and the children would use the wagon as their quarters, while he and Hannah would use the area below. Patty and Virginia laughed at the shelter, calling it "our two-story home."

One by one the others found ways to erect shelters of their own, using wagon canvas, pine boughs, and anything else that was available.

By nightfall, nearly everyone had shelter, even the Donners in their camp some five miles back down in the valley. That information was brought to the lake camp by a couple of the Donner teamsters.

The men had a meeting late in the afternoon to discuss whether or not they would try the pass the next day. Everyone was certain that the snow wouldn't melt all the way down, but perhaps if they rested up and recovered some of their strength, they would be able to make it.

"The problem is, how are we going to recruit our animals?" Uncle Billy asked. "What grass there was has been covered over with the snow. They can't eat."

"If the snow gets no deeper, they'll be able to get down to it," Baylis Williams suggested. "I've seen animals find browse in deeper snow than this."

"I would've felt a heap better if the sun had come out today," Stanton said.

That night Margaret made a stew of the rest of the jerked beef from Stanton's relief effort. Though she tried to put a cheery face on it, the truth was they were running very low on food. Part of it was due to the fact that it had been necessary to parcel out their food when they were forced to abandon each of their wagons.

"There should be plenty of game around," Ike said. "And I know there are fish in the lake because I saw some. We'll get by just fine."

"Of course we will," Margaret said, smiling with a cheerfulness she did not feel.

"Mama, Penelope can share my food," Patty offered, and the others laughed.

After supper Margaret and the children went to bed in the wagon or the "top floor" of their house, while Ike and Hannah went into the "cellar." Ike got a fire going. At first the little dug-out room filled with smoke, and Ike thought he had made a terrible mistake somewhere. Then he was able to make an adjustment so that the chimney drew as it was supposed to draw, and soon the inside was bathed in a soft orange light and suffused with a radiant warmth.

This was the first time that Ike and Hannah had ever really been alone for an extended period of time. They were able to talk to one another, to share stories of their past. Hannah told Ike about the young man she'd thought she was going to marry, only to have him die at sea. It was to escape her grief and start a new life that she had accepted her aunt's invitation to come West.

"I'm sorry you lost your love," Ike said. "But I'm glad you came West."

"I still feel sorrow over the fact that poor Harley drowned," Hannah said. "But now I know that I must not have really loved him. For I know I did not feel about him as I do about you. You are my life and soul, Isaac Buford. I was not complete until I met you."

Ike told of some of his experiences, making her laugh at his stories of the antics of the rivermen on the flatboats. He had come West not to run away from anything, but to run toward something.

"I want to start a newspaper," he said. "I want to publish the best newspaper in California."

"Only now you can't do it, because we had to leave your printing press in the desert."

"That won't stop me," Ike said. "As soon as we are settled in California, I'll come back for it. The trip won't be nearly as long, and it should be much easier because I will have been over the route before. But even if, by chance, it is not in the cards for me to start a newspaper, it doesn't matter. Because as long as I have you, my life is complete."

They talked far into the night. Then they went to bed. They made love as comfortably as if they were already married. Then, as they lay together with Hannah's head on Ike's shoulder, she let out a long, lazy sigh.

"I feel very guilty," she said.

"Do you? I thought we had settled all that," Ike replied. "I thought we had love without guilt."

"I'm not guilty that we made love," Hannah corrected. "I am happy we made love. But Ike, here we are, trapped under circumstances that could become much more serious. I should be concerned about the fate of everyone. Instead, the only thing I can feel is a sense of joy. I look at this place you have made for us and I don't see it as a shelter against the elements. I see it as our first home. I wish we could stay here forever."

Ike laughed. "We don't have to stay here forever to stay together forever," he said. "And you just wait until you see the first home I am really going to build for you."

When everyone climbed out of their shelters the next morning, they saw that it had snowed again during the night, with at least as much falling as had fallen the night before. Instead of clearing up some, the trail up to the pass was now twice as deep. As the people moved about in their encampment the next morning, they were almost knee-deep in snow. Up in the mountains they figured the snow to be deeper yet.

"What if this snow doesn't go away?" Breen asked. "We've got to face the fact that we might be here for the whole winter."

"That's a fact," Stanton said. "You should've listened to me and Ike. We should've gone over the first night, while we had the chance."

"Yeah, well, who was to know that it was going to come up a snow like this? You said yourself, it wasn't supposed to snow hard until the middle of November."

The men talked about butchering some of the cattle and oxen.

"We may as well," someone said. "They're all goin' to die anyway."

"Don't figure there's going to be that much meat on them. They're pitiful critters."

"Maybe we should just butcher a few. I've seen 'em eatin' the bark and the needles off the trees. I figure that'll keep 'em goin' for a while. As long as we can keep them alive we'll have somethin' to fall back on. Besides, we'll need 'em to get out of here when the time comes."

When Ike returned to the Reed wagon, he passed on the gist of the conversation to the others. Then he suggested that they kill the cow.

"Kill Twilleth? No, Ike, we can't kill her," Hannah protested. "She's more like a pet than a farm animal."

"Hannah, Twilleth isn't giving milk anymore," Ike said. "She probably isn't going to survive that much longer anyway. We have no choice. Besides, we can stretch her hide over the top of the wagon. That will help keep the cold air out."

"All right," Margaret said. "Do what you must do."

Will Eddy helped Ike and the teamsters kill and butcher the cow. They didn't really need his help, but Ike knew that Will needed a share of the meat so he let him participate. For supper, Margaret found some potatoes and an onion. She also made some dumplings out of some of the flour she had left, and they had a stew that was the best-tasting meal Ike had eaten in a long time. When they went to bed that night they were almost contented.

The next day Will Eddy went hunting. He came back with a coyote, the only living creature he saw in the woods. He skinned it, and his wife, Eleanor, made a soup of it. It had a horrendous smell, and the taste was almost as bad as the smell, but as Will explained to the others, it stretched out the meat supply a bit longer.

When Will went out hunting the next day he returned empty-handed. Then he saw that one of Uncle Billy Grave's oxen had died of starvation and he offered to buy it. What he really wanted was for Graves to give it to him, but Graves took him at his word and sold it, getting as much money for it after it starved to death as he would have back in civilization had it been a healthy animal.

"Ike," Margaret said over supper that evening. "We're going to be here for the entire winter, aren't we?"

Ike sighed. "I'm afraid so," he said.

"In that case, I think I should like to move out of the wagon and into a real cabin."

"Oh, Aunt Margaret, don't you like what Ike has built for us?" Hannah asked.

Margaret smiled. "It is a very fine place for a temporary shelter," she said. "But if we are going to spend the winter, I would like a proper cabin. There are plenty of trees about. Surely one could be built?"

"I'll get one built for you," Ike promised. "What about you, Hannah?"

"I like where we are," Hannah said.

"But wouldn't you and Ike like a little more privacy?" Margaret asked.

Hannah blushed, then looked toward the ground. "I expect that would be nice," she said.

Margaret smiled broadly. "Then you can stay here and the

children and I will move out. That would be better all around, won't it?"

True to his word, Ike rounded up some help the next day and started laying out plans for a cabin. When Uncle Billy Graves learned what he was doing, he proposed that they build a cabin together. That way they could use one common wall to separate the two dwellings.

Ike accepted the proposal and they began working. In the meantime, Hannah bought a yoke of oxen from Uncle Billy and another from Pat Breen, giving each of them a promissory note to replace the animals at a rate of two healthy yoke for one once they reached California.

By November 11th the lake camp had taken on the appearance of a small village. There was a look of permanence to the structures now. Not only the cabins, but even the wagons and tents were more firmly constructed. Then, in mid-afternoon, the sun came out. It was the first time the sun had been seen in several days, and everyone came out to look up at the crystal blue sky, and at the tops of the mountains rising so majestically above them. It was the first time they had actually seen the tops of the mountains, other than from a distance as they approached the range.

They could also see the pass, and though it was still glistening with snow, it seemed close now, closer than it had ever been.

"Listen," Charlie Stanton said. "Some of us ought to try and get out of here now."

"Yeah," Jay Fosdick said. "Maybe a few of us, just carrying what we need to survive, could get through."

"What about the rest of us?" someone asked.

"You've got a nice place to wait out the winter now," Fosdick said.

"Yes, and if we make it, we can bring back a rescue party," Will Eddy added.

"How long would it be before you come back?" someone asked.

"Who knows, but what does it matter? If we are gone, then there are fewer mouths to feed here. I think we should go."

"Hannah," Ike said, putting his hands on her shoulder. "They are right. We must try."

"You go, Ike," Hannah said. She looked over at Margaret. "I can't leave Aunt Margaret and the children here alone."

Ike looked into Margaret's anxious face and realized that Hannah was right.

"Then I'll stay too."

"No!" Hannah said. "If you can get through, you must. Ike, if there is any chance for rescue, then I know you will bring it about."

"But I don't want to leave you here."

"Even if your going would hasten the day that we can be together forever?"

Ike looked at Hannah for a long moment. Then he nodded. "All right," he said. "You stay here and look after them. I'll get back with a rescue party as soon as I can."

"Hannah, while he is gone, you can move into the cabin with me," Margaret suggested.

"All right," Hannah agreed.

"We'll leave first thing in the morning," Will Eddy proposed. "What about the people down at the Donner camp? Someone should tell them."

"Hell, that's a five- or six-mile trek through the snow," Breen complained.

"I'll go tell them," Milt offered. "I'll go down tonight. If any of them want to try it, I'll bring 'em back tomorrow morning."

"All right," Stanton said. "I suggest that those of you who want to go tomorrow should get a good night's sleep. Goin' over that pass ain't goin' to be all that easy."

That night, alone in their shelter, Ike and Hannah made love. There was a melancholy sweetness to it. The false sense of contentment was missing. The pleasure they found in each other's arms was tempered by the pain of their impending separation.

Afterward, they lay together as they had every night, only tonight there was no spoken conversation. That didn't mean they didn't communicate. Words weren't necessary. They spoke with their hearts and with their thoughts. Ike would squeeze his arm more tightly around her, or lay his cheek against hers, or press his leg up against her, and she would respond in kind. In this way, they hung on to the sweet moments far into the night.

Ike finally drifted off to sleep, but he woke up once, hours later, and knew immediately, by the way she was holding herself against him, that she was not asleep. He kissed her and they made love again. Then, as if reassured by that, Hannah went to sleep. Ike stayed awake for a long time, finally drifting off just before dawn.

Early the next morning Milt Elliot brought several men back from the Donner camp. They were the Donner teamsters, and they reported that both Jacob and George Donner were doing poorly. George was suffering terribly from the wound in his hand. Tamsen, who everyone thought was the strongest one of the lot anyway, had taken over. She was the one who ordered some of the oxen and cattle slaughtered and the meat stacked up, even though George had been against it.

"She's quite a woman," Dutch Charlie Burger said.

"Yes," Keseberg agreed. "She is one very fine woman."

Fifteen hikers prepared to try to make the trip over the pass. There were thirteen men and two women. Sarah Fosdick had no children and she was young and strong, so she saw no reason not to go out with her husband. Hannah's friend, Mary Graves, decided to go as well. She was Sarah's sister, and she had no one in the camp.

Stanton and the two Indians, Luis and Salvador, were going also, of course, and they would lead the way. They had Sutter's mules with them. The mules were now nearly as bad off as the oxen had been, for like the oxen, they had been reduced to eating pine bark and needles.

With the tearful good-byes still in their ears, and prayers for their success in their hearts, the party started.

Almost immediately, they ran into difficulty. The snow, which was less than knee-deep at the camp level, grew deeper as they climbed higher. They struggled against it, flailing at it with their arms and hands as it reached waist-deep, and still they went on.

The crystal-clear air made the pass seem agonizingly close, much closer than it actually was, but in actual fact, they weren't even able to get as close to it as they had gotten on that first day with all the pack animals. One of the ironies of this attempt was that they were able to see just how close they had come on that first day.

"We should have gone on!" they said to each other.

"If we could just get that close now, I know we could make it."

But they could not get that close, and finally, as night fell, they knew they were going to fail. They turned around and started back, their spirits lower now than they had been before they tried. It was as if now they were being forced to accept the brutal truth. The nightmare which had plagued them for the entire journey had come true. They were trapped here, and were likely to be so for the entire winter.

Hannah cried when Ike, cold, hungry, and exhausted, staggered into the cabin that night just after midnight. But if anyone had asked her whether she was crying for joy at seeing him again, or in frustration over the failure of the party to get through, she would not have been able to answer.

TEN |||

"Aunt Patty, would you and Mr. Buford like to come out onto the porch? You could sit in the swing and watch the fireworks."

"Is there a fireworks display?" John asked.

"Not an official one," Alice replied. "But the neighborhood children always send up bottle-rockets and Roman candles. We find that it is quite pleasant to sit out at night and watch."

"I enjoy them," Aunt Patty said.

"Then by all means, let's go out onto the front porch and watch," John agreed. He stood, then helped Aunt Patty up from her rocking chair. She put her arm through his, and he escorted her out onto the front porch.

"It's nice out here," Aunt Patty said as John helped her sit in the swing. "Won't you sit here beside me?" she invited.

"Thank you, I would love to."

A streak of gold zoomed up into the air, then burst in a shower of colored fireballs.

"Ohh, that one was pretty, wasn't it, Aunt Patty?" Alice asked.

"Yes. And look at that."

Aunt Patty pointed out the rising balls of color from a nearby Roman candle.

"And there is something else," John said.

"Where?"

166

"Oh, it's gone now," John said sheepishly. "It must have been a lightning bug."

"There are no lightning bugs in California, Mr. Buford," Aunt Patty said. "There are none west of the Rockies."

"I didn't know that," John said.

"I remember the last summer we spent in Illinois before that awful winter," Aunt Patty said. "One night I went riding with my father, and a mile or so out of town we turned and looked out over a meadow. That's when I saw them. There were hundreds . . . no . . . thousands of lightning bugs, flashing from green to gold to bright yellow. They covered the entire meadow, and I thought the stars themselves had come down from heaven. It was the most magnificent sight I had ever seen. I remembered them often during that terrible winter, and it was like a promise from God, telling me that we would make it."

"Tell me about the winter," John said.

Aunt Patty put her hand to the bridge of her nose and held it for a long moment. When she brought it away, John saw a sheen of tears on her cheeks and he realized that she was crying! The realization startled him, and quickly he apologized.

"I'm sorry," he said. "If you would rather not."

"No!" Aunt Patty said, reaching out to put her hand on his arm. "The story needs to be told. I want the villainous acts of those who became selfish, inhuman monsters to be remembered forever. And I never want those who were compassionate and honorable to be forgotten." She patted John's hand, then looked at him with a warm smile. "Your grandfather was one of the honorable ones," she said.

"I'm very glad," John replied. "Though I must confess that, not having been there, I don't think I could pass judgment against anyone."

"I see that you have inherited some of your grandfather's wisdom, as well as his good looks," Aunt Patty said. "Now, let me see. Where was I?"

"My grandfather and the others had just returned from their try at going over the pass," John reminded her.

"Yes. How happy Cousin Hannah was to see him return. How happy we all were. Oh, I suppose that deep down we were disappointed that they were not able to make it over the pass. But the joy of our being together again seemed to overcome that.

"Of course, what none of us knew then was that Father was trying to come back to us. He and Mr. McCutcheon had borrowed several mules and pack horses from Mr. Sutter and they loaded them with provisions to bring to us. They tried, but the trail was as impassable from the west side as it was from the east. They made it almost all the way up to the summit before they were forced back, just as our party had been.

"The Donners never joined us, but we managed to establish a regular exchange of news as to what was going on in each camp. That's how we learned that Mr. Jacob Donner was doing very poorly, and Mr. George Donner's hand wasn't healing as it should. Ma was concerned about them, but the Donners still had several head of cattle and oxen, so we figured they were in better shape than we were.

"In the meantime, Mr. Buford, your grandfather, realized that our food was going to run out soon if we didn't get some fresh supply. So the next day after they returned from their try at the pass, Mr. Buford and Mr. Eddy went hunting."

The Lake Camp, November 14th, 1846
"I seen some ducks yesterday," Will Eddy said. "Only thing is, we was already halfway up the trail and there was no way I could get to them. But if they was there yesterday, like as not they'll be there today."

"If they're there, we'll get them," Ike said.

"You damned right we will," Eddy agreed. "I figure it's come right down to this. We're either men enough to feed our families, or we aren't. And I don't figure on lettin' my family starve 'cause I'm not man enough to take care of them."

The snowdrifts varied from knee-deep to waist-deep, making it very slow and very difficult to walk. At first Ike and Will walked side by side. Then they decided it would be better to let just one of them break the trail while the other followed behind. They took turns that way so that neither one of them got too tired.

"You like duck better roasted or stewed?" Eddy asked.

"I like roasted duck, with maybe some apples and a few carrots cooked with it."

"Yeah, and some gravy made from the drippin's," Eddy said. "What you do is, you take some flour and brown it in the drippin's, then you add milk . . . or water will do if you've got no milk, then you whip it together in a skillet till it thickens up. Then you spoon that over mashed potatoes."

"Irish potatoes or sweet potatoes?" Ike asked, keeping the conversation going.

"Either one. Or you could serve the gravy over biscuits. That's always good too."

"Then you want to top that off with a big piece of hot apple pie," Ike suggested.

"With cheese melted on top of the pie," Eddy added.

"Damn, Will, let's shut up. We're just punishing ourselves," Ike said. "We don't have any potatoes or carrots or apples left."

"Maybe not, but we're damned sure goin' to have us some duck," Eddy said in a low, excited voice. "Look over yonder."

Ike looked in the direction Eddy pointed and saw two ducks coming toward them, flying low and fast over the water.

"Give 'em plenty of lead," Eddy said, cocking the hammer and raising his rifle. "You take the one on the left, I'll—"

"Eddy! Forget the damn ducks! Look at that!" Ike said.

"Look at what? What are you talking about, forget the ducks?"

"There's a hell of a lot more meat over there," Ike said.

Ike pointed to the edge of a clearing where a big brown grizzly bear was rooting through the snow.

"Jesus! Look at the size of that son of a bitch!" Eddy said.

"There's enough meat there to feed both our families for a month," Ike said.

"If we can kill him," Eddy replied. "From what I hear, those things aren't all that easy to kill."

"We've got no choice. We have to try."

"All right, I'm ready if you are," Eddy said. "But if we only wound him, he's going to come after us."

"Aim for his heart," Ike instructed. "With both of us shooting, one of us is bound to hit him."

The two men raised their rifles and took aim. Eddy fired first, and out of the corner of his eye Ike saw a flash of light and a puff of smoke. The gun banged and kicked back against Eddy's shoulder.

The bear, who had his back to the two men, was hit. He fell and rolled once, flinging blood onto the snow. Though hit hard, he managed to get up and turn toward the upstart puny men. He bolted forward, nostrils flared, teeth bared, and eyes flashing. The bear roared an angry challenge as he came crashing down the mountainside toward them, dislodging snow and loose gravel during his lumbering descent.

"Shoot the son of a bitch, Ike! Shoot him!" Eddy shouted.

Ike stood his ground, peering over the gunsight, watching as the bear grew bigger and bigger. The bear was running in a loping gate, sometimes raising both front legs at the same time. Ike awaited his opportunity, timing it just right. He pulled the trigger just as the front legs cleared the gunsight, giving him the bear's underbelly as a target. The ball crashed into the bear's chest.

The grizzly fell a second time and slipped forward on his belly, all four legs stretched out and useless. A swath of pink appeared on the snow behind it as it sledded the last few feet down the side of the mountain, piling snow up in front of it. Finally, it came to a halt.

"Damn!" Eddy said, excitedly. "We got him! We killed the son of a bitch!"

Eddy's triumphant shout was a little premature, for the bear raised its head and glared at them through narrowed, yellowed eyes. It growled again and blood bubbled from its mouth.

"He's not dead yet," Ike said. He reached for his powder horn and started to re-load.

"No, wait," Eddy said, holding out his hand to stop him. "Let's don't waste any more powder or ball. Pick up a club somewhere. We can finish him off that way."

"Good idea," Ike agreed.

Ike and Eddy looked around until each of them found a club they could use. Thus armed, they moved cautiously toward the bear. Ike raised his club and the bear looked at him. For a moment Ike hesitated. He felt a sense of guilt. Like him, the bear was just trying to survive the winter. It was one thing to shoot him when he was charging . . . quite another to club him to death when he was down.

Eddy had no such reservations. While the bear was looking at Ike, Eddy hit him a blow, spattering blood into the snow. The bear jerked his head toward Eddy, and Ike, recovering from his moment of indecision, took his own swing. The bear roared again, a terrible frightening roar, but now Ike knew that this was its death knell, for there was no challenge left in its cry . . . only fear and pain.

Ike and Eddy hit him again and again, until the head was so badly battered that if someone should come across it by itself, it would be difficult to tell what sort of creature the head had came from.

Finally, exhausted and exhilarated, the two men stopped clubbing it, realizing at last that it was dead. They stood there looking down at its still form for a long moment, the vapor clouds from their gasping breaths curling around their heads.

"Look how fat he is," Eddy said.

"It's no wonder," Ike replied. "He's probably just about ready to go into hibernation."

"What do you think he'll weigh?"

"Easily five or six hundred pounds," Ike replied.

"How are we going to get him back?"

"Yes, that does present a problem."

Eddy stroked his beard for a moment, looking down at the animal.

"I guess the best way to do this is to borrow a team of oxen to drag him down. 'Course that's goin' to cost us a share."

Ike smiled. "So be it, Will," he said. "Fifteen minutes ago we would've both been happy with a duck apiece. "

Eddy laughed. "You're right about that, Ike," he said. "You're mighty right. Come on, let's go get the oxen."

On the other side of the mountains, James Reed was leading a string of mules and a rescue party back toward the valley. Whether he had been banished by the wagon party or not, he had no intention of letting his family starve to death.

"Jim, I've got to tell you, if that pass is blocked with snow, we aren't going to get through it," Will McCutcheon warned. Will McCutcheon had come through with Charlie Stanton several weeks earlier, but had been unable to return with him because he had been hit with another bout of malaria. He was over that now, and willingly joined Reed's rescue effort.

"You plannin' on givin' up without so much as a try?" Reed asked.

"No, sir, not on your life," McCutcheon said. "Don't forget, I've got a wife and baby of my own back there. But I've been over that pass and I just want you to know what you're getting into."

"I came over it same as you did," Reed said. "I figure I've got a pretty good idea of what it's like."

"I suppose you have," McCutcheon said. He twisted in his saddle to look back at the string of mules and the volunteers who had come along with them. "I have to tell you, though, I'd feel better about it if our volunteers were real volunteers, instead of men you'd paid to come."

"I don't agree," Reed replied. "I like it this way. If you pay a man, he's obligated to stick with you. A volunteer answers only to himself and when the going gets a little rough, he's just as likely to drop out on you."

"Maybe you've got a point," McCutcheon said. Flakes of white started falling, and he brushed them off his coat. "Damn," he said. "If there's anything we don't need right now, it's more snow."

The few flakes turned into many, falling heavier and faster until the snowfall built into a full-fledged winter storm. The drifts grew deeper and deeper.

"No can get through pass. I go now!" the Indian guide suddenly said. "I take horses with me." The Indian turned and started back down the trail, leading three horses behind.

"No, wait!" Reed called out. "Leave the horses here!"

"My horses!" the Indian called over his shoulder.

Reed drew his pistol and pointed it at the back of the Indian's head. "Leave the horses or I'll blow your brains out," he said angrily.

"My horses!" the Indian replied angrily.

"My supplies," Reed insisted just as adamantly.

The Indian took out his knife and rode back to his three pack horses, then began cutting ropes. The packed bundles slid off the horses and buried themselves in the snow.

"My horses," the Indian said again. "If you shoot, you shoot." He turned his back on Reed and started back down the trail, leading the animals with him. The snow continued to fall, and within seconds the bundles the Indian had cut loose were covered over.

"You son of a bitch!" Reed shouted at the Indian in anger. He aimed, but he didn't pull the trigger. Instead, with a frustrated growl of rage, he put the gun back into its holster, then dismounted.

"What are you going to do?" McCutcheon asked.

"Help me get this stuff loaded onto the other horses and mules," Reed said.

"Jim, those animals are already overloaded as it is," McCutcheon said.

"Goddamnit, Will, I don't intend to let the food my family needs just lie here in the goddamn snow!" Reed growled. "Now are you going to help me or not?"

McCutcheon got off his horse and tramped through the snow to help load the packs onto the other animals.

"All right," Reed said a few minutes later when the load was redistributed. "Let's go."

"Look at Cash," Patty said, laughing. "Cash really likes bear."

The little dog was growling and snarling as it chewed away on a bone Margaret had thrown it. There was still some meat trapped in the joint of the bone, and the dog was pulling it away with its teeth.

"I almost feel guilty about giving it to him," Margaret told Hannah as she stood over the pot cooking the bear-meat stew. "We could have made a soup from that."

"I can't believe that one little bone would make any difference," Hannah said.

"Perhaps not," Margaret agreed. "Still, when one considers our predicament, one must realize that every little bit of food may be important before this is all over."

"Ma, why doesn't Pa come for us?" Patty asked.

"He is trying to come for us," Virginia said, answering for her mother.

"Then why doesn't he do so?"

"Darling, the snow is as difficult for Pa as it is for us," Margaret said. "You saw what happened when Mr. Buford and the others tried to go over the pass."

"But Pa is in California. It doesn't snow in California," Patty insisted.

"Maybe it doesn't snow down on the plains in California. But Pa is looking at the same range of mountains we are. The only difference is, he is looking at them from the other side. And when you reach the top of the mountains, no matter which side you are looking from, there is snow."

"I wish Pa was here with us right now," Patty said.

"I'm glad he isn't," Virginia said.

"You mean you don't want Pa here?" Patty asked.

"No."

"Virginia, what a strange thing to say," Margaret said.

"It isn't strange, Mama," Virginia insisted. "With Pa on the other side of the mountain, we know someone is trying to get through to rescue us. If Pa were here, we wouldn't know that. And he would be hungry just like we are. Only with one more mouth to feed, there would be even less food."

Hannah chuckled. "Aunt Margaret, sometimes I think Virginia is actually a thirty-year-old woman just pretending to be a twelve-year-old girl."

Margaret walked over and put her arms around Virginia. "Thank God for Virginia," she said. "I don't know what we would do without her."

The door opened then and Ike came in. His face was red with cold, and he tramped over to the fire to hold his hands over it. He didn't say a word, but the glum expression on his face spoke for him.

"No luck hunting?" Hannah asked.

Ike shook his head.

"Maybe you'll have better luck tomorrow," she suggested.

"I don't know," Ike replied. He sighed. "We were just lucky to find that bear. I think now that every creature alive has gone away for the winter. We didn't see one duck, one goose, we didn't see a bird of any kind. No more bear, no elk, deer, rabbits, or squirrels. We've chopped holes in the ice for fishing, but whatever it is that those fish bite on, we don't have it."

"Don't get discouraged," Hannah said. "We still have some bear meat left."

"But it's going down much faster than I thought it would," Ike said. "We are going to have to find some more game somewhere soon."

Ike held his hand out, and Hannah leaned into him so he could put his arm around her.

"Pa is coming for us, Mr. Buford," Patty said. "Don't forget that. Pa is on the other side of the mountain bringing us food."

Ike smiled. "I know he is, Patty," he said. "But I also know that it is very difficult for him, so we are going to have to get by with what we have for as long as we can."

"Well, right now we have some stewed bear meat," Margaret said. "So why don't we all sit down to supper?"

"Mama, could I have some more salt for my bear meat?" Jimmy asked.

"I'm sorry, darling. I used as much salt as I dare. We are almost out."

"Pa is bringing salt," Patty said.

"What on earth makes you say that?" Margaret asked with a little laugh.

"Don't you think Pa knows we are out of salt?"

"I guess maybe he does," Margaret agreed. "And you are probably right. I'm sure he is bringing salt."

"Mama, before we eat, don't you think we ought to say a prayer and ask God to protect Pa?" Virginia asked.

"Why, yes, dear. I think that would be a wonderful idea," Margaret said. "You may say the prayer."

"Dear God, please watch over Pa and protect him, and watch over us and protect us," Virginia prayed. "And dear God, if we come through this, I promise You, I will become a Catholic. Amen."

Margaret gasped, and looked up from the table in surprise.

"Virginia, whatever made you promise such a thing? We have no Catholics in our family."

"Don't you think Jesus would like me to become a Catholic?"

"Why, I'm sure it doesn't matter to Jesus what church you belong to as long as you are a good Christian. You don't have to become a Catholic."

"I think Jesus wants me to be a Catholic," Virginia said.

"But how can you become a Catholic? You know nothing about the Catholic religion," Margaret protested, clearly disturbed by her daughter's pronouncement.

"I will learn," Virginia replied simply.

*   *   *

"Can you get him on his feet?" Reed asked. The subject of his concern was a horse that moments before had fallen.

"I'm afraid not," McCutcheon replied. He was kneeling beside the animal. "He's dead."

Reed slapped his hands together for warmth, but they were so cold he could barely feel them. He looked up toward the mountain pass, now within view. The road up to it, however, was so totally covered by snow that it was no longer distinguishable.

The snow continued to fall, and Reed, McCutcheon, and the three men who were still with them had flakes hanging in their eyebrows and collecting on their hats. Their breathing came in hard, vapor-clouded gasps, and even as they stood there, the moisture from their breath was adding to the ice crystals on their mustaches and in their beards.

"We are now down to one horse, Jim," McCutcheon said.

"I know we're down to one horse," Reed answered testily.

"What I'm saying is, even if we could get over that pass now, what good would it do? We've got no way of taking anything in to them. We would wind up being just more people to share what they've got, that's all."

"We'll carry the stuff on our backs." Reed reached down and picked up one particularly large bundle. There was a rope tied to the bundle and he hauled the rope over his shoulder, letting the bundle hang on his back. "Let's go," he growled. He started trudging up the mountain.

The other three men looked at McCutcheon with questions in their eyes. It was clear that they believed Reed had already lost his mind, and they wanted McCutcheon to intervene.

McCutcheon gave them no help. He just shrugged his shoulders and picked up a load. "You heard the man, boys," he said. "Let's go."

They had started out with three mules and seven pack horses. Now they were down to one horse. The Indian guide had taken three with him, and the other animals had given out and lay, already covered with snow, along the trail behind them, dead of exhaustion and the cold.

The three hired men stayed with Reed and McCutcheon. Each of them picked up a load equal to Reed's, and started up the trail behind him.

Reed was in the lead, and it was up to him to break a path for the rest of them. He was pushing out a trench that varied from waist- to chest-deep. It was backbreaking, exhausting labor, and Reed had no idea how much longer he could continue. He drew the cold air into his lungs in deep, painful gasps.

"Help!" one of the men behind them said, and Reed turned just in time to see him start sliding down the side of the trail. The man screamed in fear and flailed out with his arms as he slid down the embankment of snow. Then, about forty feet below the trail, the man managed to reach out to grab the gray shoulder of a rock that was sticking up from the snow. The rock stopped his slide, but the several snowballs his slide had created tumbled over the edge and fell down into the black, cavernous depth.

"Hold on!" McCutcheon yelled.

"Get me up!"

The one remaining packhorse had among the items of its cargo a very long coil of rope. McCutcheon got the rope, then threw the end of it down to the fallen man. The rope barely reached.

"Grab hold!" McCutcheon shouted, and when the man did, McCutcheon, assisted now by Reed and the other two, began pulling him up. They dragged him through the snow pulling the rope hand-over-hand, until finally the hired man was back up on the trail.

"How'd that happen?" Reed asked.

"I don't know," the shaken man replied. "I thought I was followin' real close behind the rest of you, but the next thing you know, I was slidin' over. I tell you the truth, I thought I was a goner."

"You had better be more careful from here on," McCutcheon cautioned. "It's about to get much worse. If you want me to, I'll take the lead and break the path for a while."

"Thanks," Reed said. Breathing heavily, he moved back in the line, allowing McCutcheon to go to the front. McCutcheon started up the trail.

"Wait, hold it! Hold it, I'm slipping!" someone else shouted, and when the one nearest him grabbed for him, they both went down. Fortunately, they only slid a short distance, and were able to get back on their feet and rejoin the climb without assistance.

"Will," Reed called a minute later.

"Yes?"

"That's it, Will," he said. "You're right. We are not going to make it through that pass, and there's no sense in killing ourselves trying. Let's head back to Sutter's Fort."

"Are you certain, Jim? Because if you want to continue, I'm willing to go on."

"I'm certain," Reed said.

McCutcheon came back and put his hand on Reed's shoulder.

"Never mind, Jim. They're safe for now. And we'll get them out of there as soon as we can."

Two days later, tired, cold, and dispirited, Reed, McCutcheon, and the three men who had stayed with them returned to the fort. Down there the snow had turned into a hard, driving rain, and for the last several miles they'd had to walk through mud which clung gumbo-like to their boots, making it almost as difficult to get around as it had been while they were up on the mountain trail.

John Sutter, the man after whom the fort was named, came over to sit at the table where Reed and McCutcheon were eating a meal of beef and beans. Sutter was carrying a tin cup of coffee, richly laced with cream and sugar.

"Listen, you've got nothing to worry about as far as your families are concerned," Sutter said reassuringly. "I figure they're going to get awfully tired of eating oxen and cattle, but they've got enough poor beef to last them until early summer. Your best bet is to just wait around here until then."

"I can't wait around and do nothing," Reed growled. "I'd go daft with worry."

"Well, sir, there is somethin' you could do," Sutter suggested.

"What's that?"

"I expect you didn't hear anything about it, bein' as you've been pretty much tied up with the wagon train and all, but we've gone to war with Mexico," Sutter said.

"Who has?"

"We," Sutter replied. "The United States of America and California. We're fightin' the Mexicans tooth and nail."

"What's the fightin' about?" Reed asked.

"I don't think anyone rightly knows," Sutter said. "All I know is the Californians is lookin' for men. I thought you might be interested."

"Why would I want to go off and fight a war when my family is still stuck in the snow on the other side of the mountains?"

Sutter smiled. "That's a good question," he said. "But I figure there's a good answer too. The California government is goin' to be givin' away some choice pieces of land to those who fight."

"I thought we were going to get land anyway, just by coming here," Reed replied.

Sutter laughed. "You've been a successful businessman, Mr. Reed. You have to know that the land California is just givin' away to all comers isn't goin' to be their best land. No, sir. For that you have to be on the inside."

"Sutter may have a point, Jim," McCutcheon said.

"Will, you mean you're willing to go off and fight in some war you don't know anything about just to get a little land?"

"If it's prime land, yes," McCutcheon said. "I'm not like you, Jim. I didn't come to California with ten thousand dollars in negotiable bank bonds. I've got to make it out here any way I can, and that means I have to accept the land

California has set aside for emigrants to settle. But if I can get some really good land by killing a few Mexicans . . . well, hell, I don't have anything against that either. I'm going to do it."

"All right," Reed said. He looked over at Sutter. "Where do we go to join this California army?"

"I can take care of swearin' you in right here," Sutter said, smiling broadly.

ELEVEN ‖

November 21st, 1846

Ten clear days, with the sun shining brightly in the sky each day, began to melt the snow in the valley. As the snow in the valley disappeared, Ike and the others started looking up toward the pass. They argued among themselves as to whether the snow was melting up there as well. Some claimed that they could see rock formations that they couldn't see earlier, proving that the snow level was falling. Others insisted that every inch of snow that was there the last time they had tried the pass was still there.

"We have to try," Ike argued. "If we don't try now, then we may as well admit that we plan to stay here until spring. Well, I don't plan to do that. I'm going, even if I have to go alone."

"I'm going with you," Will Eddy said.

After Will Eddy volunteered, several others did as well. Stanton and both Indians said they would go, so that by the time they were ready to set out, the party consisted of six women and seventeen men, counting the two Indians.

Just before they left, the twenty-three gathered in front of Pat Breen's cabin.

"Ike," Breen called. "Would you step into my cabin for a moment?"

"All right," Ike said, following Breen back into the cabin. His cabin smelled of smoke and bear fat and too many people living too close.

"You bein' a writer and all," Breen said, "I thought I'd

182

show you this." He folded back a rug and pulled out a little tablet.

"What is it?"

"It's a journal of sorts. A diary, you might say. It came to my mind that, whether we live through this ordeal or not, there ought to be some sort of record made of it. So yesterday I jotted down a few thoughts. I'd like you to read it."

"All right," Ike agreed, taking the proffered tablet.

Friday, November 20th, 1846. Came to this place on the 31st of last month that it snowed. We went on to the pass the snow so deep we were unable to find the road when within three miles of the summit then returned to this shanty on the lake. Stanton came one day after we arrive here. We again took our teams and wagons and made another unsuccessful attempt to cross in company with Stanton. We returned to the shanty it continuing to snow all the time we were here. We now have killed most part of our cattle having to stay here until next spring and live on poor beef without bread or salt. It snowed during the space of eight days with little intermission after our arrival here. The remainder of time up to this day was clear and pleasant freezing at night the snow nearly gone from the valleys.

"What do you think?" Breen asked anxiously.

"I think it's a fine journal, Mr. Breen," Ike replied, handing the tablet back to him.

Breen smiled broadly. "I appreciate that, Ike," he said.

Ike walked back out front, where the others were gathered to make the try.

"Come on, Ike, time's a wastin'," Eddy called. "If we're goin' to go over that pass, let's get started."

Hannah, Margaret, and the Reed children were gathered around with the others who would remain behind, in order to bid good-bye. Again, Hannah had decided to stay and help Margaret look after the children.

"Mr. Buford, if you see Pa, will you tell him I love him?"

Patty asked. "It's been a long time since I told him and he may have forgotten."

Ike smiled. "I don't think you have to worry about that," he said. "Your pa knows that you love him. But you can be sure I'll tell him just in case."

"We will pray for you," Virginia said. Virginia was getting very religious, but, Ike thought, this was probably a pretty good time to get religious.

"Thank you," Ike said.

First Patty, then Virginia, and then Margaret gave Ike a hug. Then it was Hannah's time. Ike kissed Hannah good-bye, then turned and started walking. The others, seeing Ike leave, took that as their own cue, so that, with a final flurry of waves and shouted good-byes, the entire party got under way.

At first the travel was much easier than it had been, due to the decreased amount of snow down in the valley. As they started up the mountain trail, however, they began to encounter deep snowdrifts once again. To their pleasant surprise, however, the sun had melted the top layer of the snow, then the snow had refrozen to form a crusty layer. That crusty layer was strong enough to support them, which meant they did not sink down into the snow as they had the first time. They were able to travel on the very top of the snow.

"Hey!" someone shouted happily. "Look at this! We can move real easy on this!"

"The mules can't," someone else said. "Look at them."

Stanton and the two Indians, who had broken the trail for the travelers on their first attempt, were now lagging behind the others. That was because the mules' narrow hooves and great weight caused them to break through the snow crust. Unlike the people, the mules were having to struggle as hard this time as they had the last.

The climbing required a great deal of exertion, made more difficult by the fact that they were in a weakened condition as a result of too little to eat. But this time, unlike the first, they could clearly mark their progress.

"Look," Ike said. "This is how far we came the last time."

"And it took us hours to get here then," Eddy answered, grinning broadly. "We're doing a lot better."

They climbed on, breathing harder from the exertion and the thin air, and speaking less. Ike, who was in the lead, could hear the gasping for air of those who were coming up the trail behind him.

"Over there!" Eddy said pointing. "Isn't that—?"

"The tree we burned that first night," Ike answered before Eddy finished the question. They were looking at a blackened tree stump.

"There's the top of the pass," Eddy said. "Damn, we were so close! Look how close it is!"

"Just a few more yards," Ike said.

It was only a matter of a few more minutes before Ike reached the top of the pass. He stepped up onto a flat, gray rock, the top of which was exposed above the snow, then turned to look back down the trail. The climbers were spread out behind him, but all seemed to be moving fairly well, except for the mules. The mules were just now even with the place where the last attempt had turned around.

Ike looked down into the valley far below. He could see the cabins of the lake camp, including the one he had built from the wagon for himself and Hannah. Smoke curled up from the chimneys of all the cabins. At the far end of the valley on Alder Creek, he could see the Donner camp as well. There, too, he could see smoke from their fires.

One by one the other climbers reached the top of the pass and, like Ike, they turned to look back.

"Lordy, that's a pretty sight," Eddy said. "You know, if a fella had a good supply of food set in so as to be able to weather the winter, why, this'd be as fine a place to raise a cabin as any."

"You don't want to stay here," Ike said. "You didn't come this far just to give up before you ever get to California, did you?" Ike asked.

"No, I reckon not. I reckon I'll go on to California along

with everyone. I was just commenting that this very valley might be a nice place to live."

"Let's go on," Ike said. "This blessed pass has stood between us and California long enough."

Buoyed by the fact that they had at long last surmounted the pass, the group went on.

Within minutes the gay mood changed. The summit had been such a barrier to them on their previous attempts that they all believed once they were over it, the rest of the trip would be easy. That wasn't the case, however. On this side of the mountain the snow was even deeper than it had been on the other side. And unlike the other side, where the snow had been warmed by the morning sun so that it could melt and then refreeze to form a crest, the snow on the west side of the summit was still loosely packed. They immediately sank up to their waists. What was worse, even that wasn't the bottom of it.

"Lordy, Ike, look how high the snow is on those trees there," Eddy said. "Why it must be thirty feet deep in some places."

"I wouldn't doubt it."

"If we can't feel a bottom to this we could get in some bad trouble," Eddy suggested.

"Yeah, I know," Ike agreed. "We could walk out onto a snow bridge over a one-thousand-foot drop-off, then fall right through the bottom."

"What are we going to do?"

"We've got to find the bottom," Ike said.

"How are we going to do that?"

"I don't know," Ike admitted.

"If you men could cut me a long pole, I could go in front," Mary Graves offered. "I could poke the pole through the snow until I find the bottom."

"Mary, you can't walk in front," Eddy said. "Whoever goes first has to break the path. That's hard work."

"Will Eddy, right now I'm about as strong as you are," Mary Graves insisted. Will didn't protest, because he knew she was right. "But I'm still lighter," she went on. "And you need someone light in front."

"She's got a point," Ike said. He looked around and saw a tall, skinny pine tree. He pointed to it.

"Let's cut that tree down," he said. "We can make her a pole from it."

Ike and Eddy cut the tree. When they had it trimmed down, they handed it to Mary, who took it without comment. With grim determination she moved to the head of the column, then started walking, poking into the snow in front of her with the long pole.

They walked until the sun went down. As the sun sank in the west, the temperature began to grow much colder. A wind came up, making it colder still, and the little party shivered in its icy blasts.

"Will," Ike finally said. "We're going to have to stay here tonight."

Will stopped and looked around. The sun was below the horizon now and the snow had taken on a blue-gray hue. "Yeah," he said. "That's pretty much what I was figurin'. Let's go," he said to the others. "Let's cut some wood and build a fire."

"I thought once we got over the top we'd pretty near be there," one of the women's voices said.

"Yeah, me too," a man's voice added. "I mean, all this time I thought that was what was keepin' us trapped."

"If we would've gotten over that first day it would've been different," Ike said.

"Charlie," Eddy called.

Stanton was back talking with the two Indians.

"Charlie, come up here. We need to talk."

Stanton picked his way past the others, who were now spreading tarps over pine boughs, preparing their bed for the night.

"What do you want?" Stanton asked.

"Listen, when we start out tomorrow, maybe you'd better lead."

"I don't know," Stanton said. "The mules are having an awful rough time of it."

"Kill the mules," Ike suggested. "We can kill them and eat them."

"I don't know," Stanton replied. "You think that's a good idea? I mean, we probably ought to have something left that we can load down with goods."

"The damn things are slowing us down," Eddy said. "Ike's right. We should kill them. Then you take the lead and show us where the hell to go from here."

"I don't know where to go from here," Stanton admitted.

Both Eddy and Ike looked at Stanton with surprise.

"What do you mean, you don't know where to go from here? You came this way, didn't you? Goddamnit, we're countin' on you," Eddy said angrily.

"Look," Stanton replied just as angrily. He swept his arm over the vast panorama of snow. "Can you see anything out there that looks like a landmark? Can you even see where there's road and where there's nothin' but steep drop-off?"

"No."

"Well, I can't either," Stanton insisted. "When I come this way there wasn't no snow on the ground. You could see the road clear and you could see where it went. But I can't pick out no trail across solid snow and ice."

"You worthless son of a bitch! Then what did you come back for?" Eddy demanded.

"Will, that's enough," Ike said. He looked at Stanton. "Are you telling us you don't have any idea where to go from here?"

"Hell, Ike, right now I don't know up from down," Stanton said.

Ike shook his head, then let out a long sigh. He looked at Eddy. "That's it," he said. "Tomorrow we start back."

"Start back? Start back where?" Eddy asked.

"Back to the camp."

"No, goddamnit!" Eddy said. "We've tried for weeks to get

over the summit. Well, goddamnit, we got over the summit.
Now you're tellin' me we have to go back over it."

"You want to wander around in these mountains with no
idea of where we are or where we're going?" Ike asked.
"Because that's just what we're going to do if we keep on."

"It's better than starving to death back there in camp," Will
replied.

"Is it? Let's face it, the way we're going now, we're going
to starve to death anyway. And you've got family back there,
Will. If you go back you'll at least be with them."

"Yeah," Eddy said. He sighed. "All right. All right, first
thing in the morning, we'll start back."

The Ranch of Long John Warner, December 5th, 1846
Weary from the long ride down from Sutter's Fort, James
Reed gratefully accepted Warner's invitation to bathe in his
hot springs. He was sitting near the edge, with the water up
to his chin, when a shadow fell across him. He looked around
to see a man standing on the bank, staring down at him.

"You would be the James Reed that Warner spoke of?" the
man asked.

"I'm Colonel James Reed," Reed replied.

The man chuckled. "Colonel, is it?" he said. "And tell me,
Colonel Reed. How came you by such rank?"

"I was appointed to that rank by Colonel John Sutter."

The man chuckled again. "Colonel John Sutter. What is it
about you Californians that you are so quick to promote
everyone to colonel? You've an entire militia of colonels, all
self-appointed."

"If you have something in your craw, mister, spit it out,"
Reed snapped. "I'm in no mood for such banter."

"I am Brigadier General Stephen Watts Kearny," the man
said. "And I hold my appointment by order of the President
of the United States. My men are five miles west of here.
We'll be camping here tonight, then moving on tomorrow."

"You must be the man Sutter told me about," Reed said.

"He said I would be able to find an army to join up with if I came here."

"Have you any military experience, Mr. Reed?"

"I fought in the Black Hawk War back in Illinois," Reed said.

"I see. Very well, Mr. Reed. I'll take you into my army. Though certainly not as a colonel."

Reed got out of the water and walked over to a log, where he picked up a towel and began drying off. After a moment he looked around at the general.

"General, right now I have a family trapped on the back side of the Sierra Nevada Mountains, waiting out the winter. I've tried to go after them, but all I succeeded in doing was killing a bunch of mules and horses. They tell me now that it would be foolish to try again before spring, so I guess I'm going to have to wait. I only pray to God that my family and the others in that wagon train survive. But come early spring I'm going after them, no matter if I have to desert. Now, knowing that, if you want me to join you, I'll join you. And as far as the rank is concerned, I don't give a damn. Make me a colonel or a private, it's all the same to me."

General Kearny laughed. "Mister, I like your spirit," he said. "All right, as of now you are a first lieutenant. Come down to the campground when the troops arrive. I'll introduce you to the other officers and find a company for you."

"All right, General, I'll be there," Reed promised.

As Reed walked through the camp that night, he was shocked at the exhausted and dispirited soldiers. The horses and mules looked little better than the animals in the Donner party when last he had seen them. Then he realized what he was seeing. He was seeing another group of travelers who were showing the effects of a lengthy deprivation of water and food, beaten down by the desert and exhausted by the rigors of the trail.

He found General Kearny and several other officers sitting around on camp stools in front of a tent. A fire blazed to one side of the tent, and a soldier tended to a stew cooking in a big pot hanging over the fire.

"Ah, Lieutenant Reed," Kearny said. "I hope you will join the officers' mess tonight. We're having a very good beef stew . . . a feast compared to the jerky we've been forced to live on for the last several weeks."

"I noticed that the men don't look to be in very good shape," Reed said.

"An accurate observation. We had a difficult march from New Mexico," General Kearny said. "But I am sure you understand very well what we have gone through. Mr. Warner has told me a little of your own story. The leader of your train—a Mr. Donner, I believe Warner said—was extremely foolish to take you through an unknown cutoff."

"It wasn't George Donner's fault," Reed said quickly. "I was the one who made the decision."

Kearny looked at Reed with a quizzical expression on his face. "I was informed that Donner was the leader of the party."

"He was the elected leader, yes," Reed said. "But for all practical purposes, I was the leader."

"How is that so?"

"I am a rather forceful man, General Kearny."

General Kearny laughed. "Yes. Well, I hope you are prepared to use that forcefulness usefully, and not to subvert the canon of military discipline."

"I am prepared to follow orders, General," Reed said.

At that moment a rider arrived at a gallop. He swung down from his horse, handed the reins to a nearby soldier, then hurried over to report to General Kearny.

"Lieutenant Gillespie reporting, sir," the rider said, saluting. He was covered with dirt from the ride.

"Yes, Lieutenant, what is it?"

"Commodore Stockton's compliments, sir," Gillespie said. "I am told to inform you that a detachment of Mexicans under General Pico is camped at the Indian village of San Pascual.

I have brought thirty-nine men and a field piece to augment your force."

"Where are these men?" Kearny asked.

"They should arrive within the hour, sir," Gillespie said. "I came ahead to render the report."

"How accurate is the information?"

"I'd say it's pretty accurate, General," Reed interjected. "I rode by them on my way here."

"And you didn't arouse any suspicion?" Captain Johnston asked. "Why is that?"

"I was no threat to them," Reed replied. "I was one man."

"How many men are there?"

"I'd say a hundred to a hundred and fifty," Reed said.

"We outnumber them two to one, General," Captain Johnston said.

"I don't know," Kearny said. "Our men are exhausted, our animals are jaded."

"General, if you ask me, what the men need is a good fight. We've come all the way from Santa Fe without firing so much as a shot," Johnston insisted.

"All right," Kearny said. "All right, tell the men to eat a good supper, then saddle up. We're going into battle."

"Yes, sir!" Johnston said, smiling broadly.

Reed watched Johnston scurry off to give the orders. Almost instantly, the camp became a beehive of activity as men shouted and whooped with excitement. When he looked in Kearny's face, however, he didn't see that same measure of excitement.

"General, you're worried about this, aren't you?" he asked.

"No battle is easy," Kearny said. "But when you have untrained troops, exhausted from a one-thousand-mile forced march, and you take them in an attack against an army that is well rested, well fed, and in a defensive position on their own homeland, it becomes much, much more difficult."

"Then why are you going to do it?"

"We are at war with the Mexicans, Lieutenant," Kearny replied. "We didn't come out here to parade around. We came out here to fight. I am going to assign you to Lieutenant Gillespie's company. Go over there and introduce yourself to him."

Reed looked over to see the lieutenant filling his mess kit with stew.

"Yes, sir," Reed replied.

A cold rain was falling when General Kearny gave the signal to saddle up and move out. It was about two o'clock in the morning, and the clouds blotted out the moon and stars so that the men moved slowly through pitch darkness. The rain dampened their powder, but not their spirits. To a man, they seemed anxious to do battle with the Mexicans.

By four A.M. the rain stopped, and just before dawn the moon came out, nearly as bright as day. Despite the fact that the rain stopped, it was still cold. The wind blowing down from the snow-covered mountains chilled Reed to his very bones. Part of the chill he was feeling was because he knew that at this very minute his wife and family were up there in those mountains somewhere, fighting cold and hunger just to stay alive.

What an unusual turn of events, he thought. There was Margaret, and there were his children, huddled in some pitiful shelter in those icy climes, no doubt watching the mountain pass every day, expecting to see him come to rescue them. But they were watching in vain, for he was here, hundreds of miles away, about to go into battle for a cause which meant nothing to him.

What if he got killed? How foolish it would be of him to waste his life in such a way. And yet, what else was he to do?

One of the advance scouts returned.

"General, they have been alerted to our presence," the scout said. "They are waiting for us."

"Then the fat is in the fire," Kearny said. "We can't turn back now. Continue the advance, men!"

Captain Johnston, the mountaineer Kit Carson—whom Reed had heard of—and a platoon of well-mounted dragoons were in the lead. General Kearny and his personal staff were next, followed by Lieutenant Gillespie's detachment. Reed was with Gillespie. They continued the advance toward the Mexican encampment.

"Bugler, sound the advance!" Kearny called.

The bugler sounded the charge.

"No! Not the charge! The advance!" Kearny yelled.

It was too late for the bugler to correct his mistake. Captain Johnston, hearing the bugle sound the charge, repeated the command to his dozen dragoons, and they went forward at a gallop.

The gallop took the small element ahead of the main body of troops. Therefore, when they arrived at the Mexican position, the attacking troops were badly outnumbered. Pico waited until Johnston was right upon them, then gave the order to fire. The Mexicans loosed a broadside, and Captain Johnston was the first to go down, with a bullet in his head.

Kearny, realizing that his advance platoon was in difficulty, ordered the main body to charge. The Mexican commander, seeing the main body, gave the command for his men to withdraw. As a result, by the time the Americans reached the redoubt, the Mexicans had already withdrawn. Finding themselves in possession of their objective, the Americans cheered.

"Hold your cheering, you idiots!" General Kearny called. "We haven't won anything yet. We haven't even engaged them."

The bugler sounded the charge again, this time at Kearny's instructions, and the troops tried to obey, but it was difficult. Some were mounted on horses, others on mules, but whether horse or mule, the animals were so badly used up by the long forced march that there was no integrity to the charge. Rather than one cohesive element, the Americans were strung out in long, straggling lines.

General Pico rallied his Mexicans and turned them back toward the Americans. Using their lances, the Mexicans charged into the Americans. The Americans tried to fire, but nearly two-thirds of the guns misfired, the result of powder made wet and useless by the early morning rain.

The Mexicans were well trained in the use of their lances, and the Americans had nothing but rifle butts to use against them. The Mexicans also had fresh, powerful horses, and when they closed on the Americans, moving at full speed, they broke the back of the American attack.

More than three dozen Americans were unseated by the Mexicans' charge. Some were only wounded, but many, Reed saw, were killed. Gillespie was one of those to go down. Reed had no idea whether Gillespie was dead or wounded, but it didn't matter. He was now in command of what was left of Gillespie's detachment.

Despite the bloody carnage wreaked upon the Americans by the Mexicans, the Americans held their ground and the Mexicans finally retreated. As before, the Americans cheered while the Mexicans left the field.

"Bugler, sound recall!"

At the call, the Americans who had chased after the retreating Mexicans returned.

"Men, you have taken the redoubt," Kearny said. "See to it that we hold it."

As the Americans began moving into defensive positions within the redoubt, Kearny called his officers together. When Reed reported to the general's tent he saw that Gillespie was not dead, but was one of the wounded.

"Gentlemen," Kearny said. "We took a bad whipping today."

"How can you say that, General? We took the redoubt," Kit Carson argued.

"Yes," Kearny answered. "But at a terrible price. We lost twenty-two killed and eighteen wounded. And as far as we know, no more than a handful of the Mexicans were wounded and none killed."

"I'd like to see them come back and take it from us," Captain Turner said.

"I don't think they can take it from us," Kearny said. "But

they won't have to. We are now more or less prisoners in here. We have very little water, no forage for our animals, and no food. If we are forced to stay here very long, we will be eating mule meat."

"General?" Gillespie said through his pain.

"Yes."

"If we could get someone through the Mexican lines, they might be able to get a message to Commodore Stockton. He could send a rescue force."

"It would take a very resourceful person to worm his way through the Mexican lines, then cover the thirty miles to Stockton," Captain Turner said.

General Kearny looked at Reed. "It just so happens, gentlemen, that we have someone who is very resourceful."

Reed realized then that Kearny was talking about him.

"What about it, Lieutenant Reed? You are already on a rescue mission, aren't you? This would just be a small side trip."

"I'd be glad to go, General," Reed said.

"Wait until after dark," Kearny ordered.

After sunset that evening, Reed took off his shoes, then discarded his canteen, powder horn, cartridge box, and pistol, not only to save weight, but also to allow him to move more silently. Keeping only his knife, he waved at the others, then slipped out of his own lines, and through the first three cordons of Mexicans. Once clear of the Mexicans, he started in the direction Gillespie had told him to go in order to find Commodore Stockton. He walked barefooted over rocks and cactus all through the night. Tired, thirsty, and with bleeding feet, he stumbled into the Stockton camp at dawn the next morning.

"Halt!" a guard shouted.

"Don't shoot! I'm Lieutenant James Reed with General Kearny's brigade. Take me to Commodore Stockton."

Reed was taken to Stockton's quarters, where the commodore was having breakfast. Stockton looked up in shock when Reed was led in.

"Commodore, I am Lieutenant James Reed. I bring a message from General Kearny."

"Quickly," Stockton said to one of his aides. "Get a chair for this officer. And bring him something to eat."

Reed accepted the chair and breakfast with gratitude. He told his story as he ate.

"You stay here and rest up," Stockton told Reed afterward. "We'll rescue your general."

"Thank you, sir," Reed said. He smiled. "I am a little tired."

It was December 11th before General Kearny and his brigade returned to Stockton's headquarters, along with the men Stockton had sent to rescue them. They marched into the settlement with bands playing and flags flying. General Kearny made a special visit to Reed to congratulate him for his service.

"If this rescue mission bodes anything about the future, Lieutenant Reed, I would say that your family is all right and you are going to get them out of there," Kearny said.

"I pray to God that you are right, General," Kearny said. "It is nigh on to Christmas now, and they have been trapped on the other side of the mountains for almost two months. How they must wonder where I am."

PART THREE

*To Judge
the Quick and
the Dead*

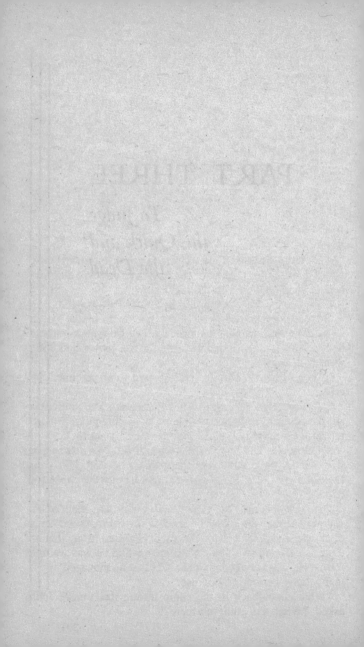

Sacramento, California, July 4th, 1931

"Aunt Patty, don't you think we should go back into the house now?" Alice asked. "Most of the fireworks are over and I do believe there is a chill in the night air."

"Yes, dear, I think you are right," Aunt Patty agreed.

John Buford helped Aunt Patty get up from the porch swing. Then he gave her his arm and they went back into the house. Aunt Patty headed straight for the parlor and John went with her.

"I hope I'm not keeping you up past your bedtime," he said.

"Nonsense, young man," Aunt Patty said. She smiled as she patted his hand lightly with hers. "I'm a big girl now. I go to bed when I want to and I get up when I want to."

John chuckled. "I don't suppose you'll get too many people who would argue with you about that," he said. "So your father fought in the Mexican War. Was he any the worse for it?"

"Oh, dear me, no," Aunt Patty said. "Why, as a result of his war service, he was given the deed to several thousand acres of choice land." Aunt Patty chuckled. "Pa used to say that he didn't sit around twiddling his fingers while he was waiting for us. He was very proud of the fact that he managed to put that waiting period to good use."

"What about back in the camp during this time?" John asked. "What was going on there?"

"We were still waiting and watching for Pa. And of course, there were still people who were trying to make it out. Everyone agreed that the problem was the deep snow, so that was when Uncle Billy Graves came up with the idea of making snowshoes from the oxbows of the wagons. He could remember using them as a boy back in New England, and he figured that anyone who was wearing snowshoes would have an easier time of it over the deep snow. Most of the others laughed at him, but Will Eddy and your grandfather thought it sounded like a pretty good idea. They encouraged Uncle Billy Graves to get busy making some. In the meantime, Cousin Hannah and Mr. Buford hiked down to the far end of the valley to visit the folks over in the Donner camp. Mr. Buford wanted to recruit some people for another try, this time wearing snowshoes."

Aunt Patty was quiet for a long moment. Then she spoke again, so softly that John had to strain to hear.

"Mr. Buford managed to get a few of the people from the Donner camp to go with him, but they would have been better off had they said no." She sighed. "The Forlorn Hope."

"I beg your pardon?"

"That's what the snowshoe party called themselves," Aunt Patty said. "The Forlorn Hope."

TWELVE ||

The Donner Camp, December 11th, 1846

The hike down the valley to the Donner camp was difficult, but not as difficult as it was going to be to go over the mountains. That was one of the reasons Hannah went with Ike. She wanted to test herself, for she had decided that this time she would go with Ike. And if she couldn't make it down the lower end of the valley, how would she ever hope to go with the snowshoe party?

Another reason she came was because she wanted to see Tamsen Donner again. Hannah had grown very fond of Tamsen during the long trip out. She had noticed that Tamsen was always the first to volunteer her assistance, and the last to complain. She had a good word for everyone and she followed that with good deeds, for she could always be counted upon to help others. From the stories Hannah was hearing about her now, Tamsen had not changed. She was easily the most dominent force in the Donner camp.

"There is where they are staying," Ike said, pointing to Tamsen's cabin. "I'm glad they finally got a cabin raised. For the first few weeks they were living in tents over here."

"I will be glad to see her again," Hannah said.

"Hello the cabin!" Ike called. "Mrs. Donner!"

The door to the cabin opened and Tamsen looked out. When she saw Hannah and Ike, she smiled broadly.

"Oh, my, how nice to have company!" she said. "Please,

come in, the two of you. Warm yourselves by the fire and have a cup of broth."

"Mrs. Donner, you'd best keep the broth," Ike said.

"Nonsense, it's little more than hot water anyway," Tamsen said. "And water is the one thing we have plenty of."

"Yes, ma'am, I'll grant you that," Ike said.

Ike and Hannah went back into the cabin. After the cold of the long walk down, the cabin seemed almost hot, but the warmth felt good to them, and they took off their coats and sat down. Tamsen handed them each a cup and when Ike tasted it, he saw that she was right in saying that it was little more than hot water. There was only the barest hint of color and aroma to the water, and even less taste. Nevertheless it was welcome.

"How are you doing, Mr. Donner?" Ike asked George. George, who had always been a robust man despite his age, was lying in bed. His arm was elevated. His hand was not bandaged, and Ike saw that gangrene had set in.

"It's the damnedest thing," George replied. "A little cut. You wouldn't think a little cut would be giving me so much trouble."

"It'll heal up," Ike said, knowing better.

"You ever see anyone beat the gangrene without cuttin' off their arm or leg?" Donner asked.

"No, sir, I don't know that I have."

"Even if I had someone who could cut it off now, I don't know that it would do any good," George said. "What a foolish thing I have done, putting my family through all this. I should have stayed in Illinois."

"Now, George Donner, you hush that kind of talk," Tamsen said. "You didn't tie us up and force us to come here. We were all just as anxious as you and you know it."

"Still," George said. He turned his head to the wall and was quiet.

"How are things over at your camp?" Tamsen asked.

"Not very good, I'm afraid. Have you heard that our

remaining animals have wandered off?" Ike asked. "Now we have nothing to fall back on."

"Yes," Tamsen said. "Milt Elliot told me that. Have you not been able to find them?"

"I'm sure they're all dead. Anyway, we've poked around in the snow for them," Ike said, "but we've had no luck. That means we have absolutely nothing to eat now, except for what little we have been able to put by from the earlier slaughterings. The Murphys have already started on the hides."

"How terrible that must be for the little ones," Tamsen said. She smiled. "But Milt also tells me that you are preparing another try to get out of here."

"Yes," Ike said. "This time we are going to use snowshoes."

"What are snowshoes?" Tamsen asked.

"It's something Uncle Billy Graves came up with," Ike said. "He said they use them back in New England. It's something that's designed to spread your weight out across the top of the snow so that you don't sink in so deep."

"Oh, how clever!" Tamsen said.

"If it works," Ike added.

"Oh, I'm sure it will work," Tamsen said. "And I believe this time you will make it through. And when you do, you'll be able to send a rescue party back for the rest of us."

"Yes," Ike said.

Tamsen got a faraway look in her eyes. "Of course, it'll be too late for poor Jacob. He died last week."

"Yes," Ike said. "I heard that he had."

"And so now you have the responsibility of all these people on your shoulders," Hannah said.

Tamsen smiled sadly. "Well, that has always been the lot of the women, hasn't it?" she asked. "But I am a firm believer that God never gives us more than we can bear."

"I wish I could believe that," Hannah said. "But I can't. How does He expect us to bear this?"

"If it becomes more than we can bear, God will simply take us up into heaven with Him," Tamsen said confidently.

Little Eliza Donner was sitting on the floor of the cabin while the adults were talking. A beam of sunlight speared down through a crack in the door and landed on the floor. Ike heard her laugh out loud, tickled by the little shaft of brightness. When he looked over at her, he saw that she was trying to pick it up. Unable to grab it with her hand, she held her apron out and caught it on the hem. Carefully, she folded her apron over it, then got up and ran to her mother.

"Ma!" she said excitedly. "Ma, look what I have!" She unfolded her apron, then gasped in surprise when she saw that the little spot of light she had so carefully captured was no longer there. Ike laughed, then told the others what she had done.

"If you want to play with the sunlight, Eliza, you'll have to stay over there where it is," Tamsen told her.

While Hannah stayed in the cabin and talked "woman-talk" with Tamsen, Ike went over to visit the teamsters. They were in bad shape, and had already started eating the hides that had once covered the roof of their cabin. A pot sat by the fireplace, its bottom covered by a hardened glue, the result of cooking a hide.

"So, you're going to try it again, are you?" Milt asked.

"Yes," Ike said. He explained about the snowshoes. "Who wants to go?"

"I'll go," Antoine said.

"Where's Shoemaker?" Ike asked, looking around. "With a name like that, he ought to be helping Uncle Billy make the shoes," he quipped, trying to get a laugh from the teamsters and thus brighten their spirits.

"Shoemaker is dead," Denton answered. "So is Jim Smith."

When they had left Springfield, Ike and Smith had been the two men in charge of herding the cattle. Often, while out on the prairie, Ike and Jim Smith had talked far into the night. Ike shared his dream of starting a newspaper, while Smith told how he wanted to become a sailor on the western ocean. Smith admitted that he had never even seen an ocean, but he was sure it was something he would want to do. Now he never would never get the opportunity.

"When do we leave?" Antoine asked, breaking Ike's reverie.

"Listen, Antoine, you don't wait for anyone to come get you," Ike replied. "The next pretty day we have, you get over to the other camp, because that's the day we'll be leaving."

"I'll be there," Antoine promised.

Ike started to leave.

"Ike?" Noah James called.

Ike turned back toward the inside of the cabin.

"We're all goin' to die here, ain't we?" Noah James asked.

"Some are," Ike admitted. "Some already have. But I tell you true, I don't plan on being one of them. I plan on getting over those damned mountains and making it to California. And I'll tell you something else. Come spring I'm going to go back and pick up my printing press. I came out here to publish a newspaper, and by God I intend to do just that."

Noah laughed, though it was a weak, hollow laugh. "By damn," he said. "What I wouldn't give for just a little of your spirit."

"It's more than spirit, Noah," Ike said. "It's conviction."

It started snowing again, even before Ike and Hannah made it back to the lake camp. Margaret had been looking anxiously for them, and she was very happy when they returned. Her obvious relief at seeing them again caused Hannah to have second thoughts about going, but Margaret insisted that she should go.

"You'll be doing us a greater favor by getting free of this place," Margaret said. "And if you carry a letter to Jim for me, then I shall feel all the closer to him. Though I imagine you shall want to travel as light as you can."

"Of course I will carry a letter to him," Hannah said.

"Now you and Ike must join us for supper," Margaret insisted. "I have made a nice soup for us."

The soup was made of oxen bones, charred until they could be ground into powder, then boiled with snow water.

"Very tasty," Ike said. "Though it could use a bit more garlic." At first Margaret looked up at him in surprise. Then when she saw that he was smiling, she laughed out loud.

"Lord, let our sense of humor be the last thing to go," she said. "For I don't know how we could make it otherwise."

"I think we do still have our sense of humor," Ike replied. "For what other reason would we call the snowshoe party The Forlorn Hope?"

"The Forlorn Hope," Margaret said. She laughed. "Aye. And it will be an even better joke if you should succeed."

Ike and Hannah returned to their own cabin after supper. It was snowing harder as they left the Reed cabin, and the snow continued all that night, and intermittently throughout the next day.

From Pat Breen's journal:

December 12th, continues to snow.

From Pat Breen's journal:

December 13th. Snowing faster than any previous day, wind NW. Buford, Stanton and Graves, with several others, making preparations to cross the mountains on snowshoes. Snow 8 feet deep on the level.

From Pat Breen's journal:

December 14th, fine morning, sunshine, cleared off last night about 12 o'clock. Wind E.S.E. don't thaw much.

"The storm is over," Ike said, coming back into the little cabin. "The sun is shining brightly."

Hannah sat up in bed.

"Will we be leaving today?" she asked.

"I don't know. I'll have to talk to the others."

"I'll get ready just in case," she said.

Hannah slipped out of her nightgown and, for a moment, stood totally nude. Ike couldn't help but notice how much smaller her breasts had become. Her ribs were showing through her sides, and the definition of her pelvic bone was easily discernible under the flare of her hips. Hannah felt him looking at her, and she blushed.

"I . . . I wish I could still be beautiful for you," she said.

"Oh, Hannah," Ike replied, taking her in his arms. "Don't you know you will always be beautiful to me?"

Hannah smiled in embarrassment, then reached for her traveling clothes. She and the other women had decided that they would covert their warmest dresses into trousers. That would make walking through the snow much easier for them.

It had already been decided that no one would carry anything except food and a blanket. Their food would be three strips of finger-sized jerky per day, for six days. They had calculated that, with the snowshoes, they could cover ten miles per day. Six days would be sixty miles. Sixty miles was surely enough to find help somewhere.

In addition to the jerky, they were taking a rifle in case they found game, a hatchet to cut wood, as well as several pistols. They were also taking some coffee and sugar.

When Ike and Hannah stepped out of the cabin a few minutes later, Hannah gasped.

"Oh, Ike, what happened? Where are all the cabins?" she asked.

It was a legitimate question, for the snow was deeper than the cabins were high, and it completely covered them all. The creek was filled with snow, and even the lake was no longer a lake, but rather a wide, flat meadow of very deep snow. The pine trees were so heavy with snow that none of their natural color or conformation could be seen. The mountains were solid white, as were the passes. It was as if all color had left the world.

"There," Ike said, pointing. "Do you see the smoke? That's from one of the cabins."

"Ike," Hannah said, with a sinking feeling inside. "Oh, Ike, there is no way we can go today. Not with the snow this deep. We must wait a little longer."

Ike put his arm around her and pulled her to him. Then he sighed.

"Yes," he said. "I'm afraid you're right."

It was two more days before The Forlorn Hope was ready to leave. The morning of their departure was marred by the fact that Baylis Williams had died the night before. Baylis had been one of those who took up for James Reed during the inquisition on the trail, so Margaret felt a particular sadness over his death. She stood by, offering what comfort she could to Baylis's sister during the improvised funeral. The funeral was short and sweet, with Will Eddy and Bill Foster burying him in the snow.

"I am sorry that he's gone," Stanton told Ike. "But in a way it's his own fault. He didn't do a thing to keep himself alive. He wouldn't eat any of the poor beef or the broth, let alone the hides."

"I know. It was almost as if he willed himself to die," Ike said. "But I'm afraid he's just the first. If we don't get through to the outside, there are going to be many more dying . . . even those who are willing to eat bone soup and roasted hide."

"All right," Uncle Billy said to the others. "Now listen up, folks. This is how you walk in snowshoes." He began tramping through the snow, demonstrating his words. "You have to lift your legs high, bending the knees like this. Don't slide the shoe forward. Have you got that?"

A few put their shoes on and began experimenting.

"Hey, it really works," someone said.

"Of course it works," Uncle Billy said. "As a boy I used them many times."

"All right," Ike called. "Is everyone ready?"

"We're ready, Ike, let's go!" Stanton called.

"I'll lead out," Ike said.

Ike started out first, followed by Hannah. Next came Will Eddy, then Uncle Billy Graves and his daughter Mary. Charlie Stanton and the two Indians, Luis and Salvador, were next, followed by Antoine. Next came Bill and Sarah Foster, then Amanda McCutcheon. She was followed by Harriet Pike, then by Sarah and Jay Fosdick. Three of the party had no snowshoes. They included the two youngest in the party, twelve-year-old Lem Murphy and his eleven-year-old brother, Billy. The big German, Dutch Charlie Burger, was also without snowshoes. They brought up the rear.

The Forlorn Hope trudged out of the lake camp, moving across the top of eight feet of dazzling white snow. They circled around the bank of the lake, more from habit than necessity, for the lake, which was solid ice and snow, offered no more impediment to their progress than did the land.

"Ike," Eddy called. "Trade places with me. I'll break trail for a while."

"Thanks," Ike said, dropping back.

Walking was extremely difficult. They not only had to lift their legs high, they also had to bend forward at the waist in order to keep their balance. They breathed hard from the effort, and the cold air hurt their lungs as they sucked it down inside. It was particularly difficult for Burger and the two Murphy boys because, without snowshoes, they were sinking nearly waist-deep into the drifts.

Because of the clear air, the unbroken whiteness, and the way distance was contorted, it seemed like they weren't going anywhere. They worked hard for two hours, and yet whenever they looked back over their shoulders, it was as if they were just barely on the edge of the camp. They felt almost as if they could shout back down to the camp and be heard.

At noon Ike called a halt, and everyone dropped into the snow to rest their throbbing leg muscles and aching backs. They ate one piece of dried beef and a few scoops of snow.

"You know what we used to do in Germany when I was a *kinder*?" Burger asked.

"Hell, Dutch, you wasn't never a *kinder*," Pat Dolan said, and the others laughed.

"*Ja,* I was a *kinder,* just like everyone else," Burger replied, not entirely sure that Dolan had been teasing him. "When I was a *kinder* and it would snow, I would take a big scoop of snow and put it in a bowl. Then I would put in milk, eggs, and honey, mix it together, and eat a snow pudding." He rolled up a snowball and took a bite. "Uhmm, *zehr gut!*" he said, smacking his lips.

"You're full of shit, making people think of food like that," Foster growled.

"Hell, Bill, you think there's anyone here who isn't thinking of food?" Eddy asked, and the others laughed.

"All right, let's go," Ike shouted, standing up and brushing the snow from his trousers.

"I can't go on no more," Billy Murphy said. "It's not fair. Everyone else has snowshoes."

"I'm sorry, Billy. You're going to have to do the best you can," Eddy said.

"It's not fair," Billy complained.

"Look at Lem. He's not complaining."

"Come on, Billy, you can do it," Lem said.

"No, I can't," Billy insisted.

Eddy sighed. "Look, Billy, we don't have time for this. You either go with us or you stay here."

"I want to go back," Billy said.

"Then go back."

"What if I can't make it by myself?"

"You'll have to."

"I take him back," Burger said, walking toward him.

"Dutch, if you take him back, we aren't waiting on you," Ike cautioned.

"I know," Burger said. "But I am like Billy. I have no snowshoes. I cannot go anymore. I am going back." He reached for Billy. "Come," he said. "We go now."

Lem looked at his brother for a moment, then resolutely turned to go with the others. Everyone began to move then, The Forlorn Hope going in one direction, Burger and Billy going in the other.

It was late afternoon by the time they reached the wagons they had abandoned on that first try across the pass, now nearly six weeks ago. The wagons were quiet and ghostly-looking, completely covered over with snow. Eddy thought they should camp there, since it was nearly dark.

"Besides, we might be able to find something from the wagons we can use," he suggested.

"Will, you know damned well there's no food in any of those wagons," Pat Dolan said. "If there was, we would've come back for it weeks ago."

"I know there's no food, but there might be something we can use. And if nothing else, we can use the wood for fire. That'll save us from having to cut down a tree."

"I agree," Ike said.

Without being asked, the two Indians, Luis and Salvador, began chopping wood away from the ghost wagons. Ike sat down in the snow, and Hannah came over to sit beside him.

"Look at the wagons just sitting there," she said. "It's so sad."

"Sad? What's sad about a few wagons?" Ike asked.

"It's like looking at an old abandoned house," Hannah said. "You've seen those old houses sitting alongside the road with the doors and shutters falling off, haven't you? You can't help but think about what it must have been like when there was someone living in the house . . . the laughter, the good times and the bad, people getting married, babies being born, people dying. Then everyone moves out and the house is alone."

"You are a romantic."

"I suppose I am," Hannah admitted. "Because now, when I see these wagons, I think of our journey across the great plains. Do you remember the buffalo? And the Fourth of July celebration? And the music and the dancing?"

"That's not all I remember about our time out on the plains," Ike said, putting his arm around her.

Hannah leaned her head against his shoulder.

"I wish . . ." she began, then stopped. "Never mind, that is very foolish of me."

"What do you wish?"

"I wish we had stopped out there on the plains. Where it was summer and the wildflowers were in bloom. Where there were wild plants to eat, and water and game, and rich land for growing."

"What good would rich farmland be for you or me?" he asked. "Neither of us are farmers. You are a schoolteacher and I am a journalist. We need people for our profession."

"I know. I said it was very foolish of me."

Ike chuckled. "No, it wasn't foolish of you. It was foolish of all the people who went right on by to California. If they had stopped there, then we could've stopped there."

"Are we going to survive this ordeal, Ike?"

"We have to," Ike said. "We owe it to Mark, Luke, John, and Anna."

Hannah looked at him in confusion. "Mark, Luke, John, and Anna? Who are they?"

"They are our children," Ike answered easily. He smiled at her. "The ones we are going to have."

Hannah raised his hand to her lips and kissed it. "I love you, Isaac Buford."

The Forlorn Hope reached the head of the pass by late afternoon of the second day. Although it took them two days to accomplish on this try what they had done in one on the previous try, they weren't discouraged. On the contrary, as they came across the top of the pass they felt a sense of elation, and despite the hunger, cold, and exhaustion, they grinned and patted each other on the back and congratulated each other on their wonderful accomplishment.

"If you will remember," Eddy said to Ike, "we made it this far the last time. It wasn't until we got over onto the other side that we began to run into trouble."

"Yes," Ike answered. "But if you will notice, the snowdrifts we just came through were as high and as bad as those we encountered on the other side in our previous attempt. So if these didn't beat us, those won't either."

The Forlorn Hope camped that night, their second night out, on top of the pass. They had come six miles in two days. Ike realized now that their hope of doing ten miles in one day really *was* forlorn. There seemed little chance that they would improve their pace any in the days ahead. What would happen to them on the sixth day, when they ran out of food?

They built a fire that night, then lay around it. For warmth they huddled together under the blankets.

The next morning they were up and moving at dawn. Although no one had spoken about it in specific terms, all had come to the realization that they were moving much slower than they had planned. And there was no one among them who could not do the simple math it required to figure out how many days' rations they had left. At this rate they were going to run out of food in the middle of nowhere.

There was another problem, one that they hadn't encountered before. The snow was so white and the sun was so bright that they couldn't keep their eyes open. They had to squint them into tiny slits, and even that did little to protect them against the painful glare of the sun.

The glare affected some more than others, and it seemed to affect Charlie Stanton the most. His eyes grew puffy and red and so painful that he could only keep them open for a few seconds at a time. He stumbled along blindly for most of the day, paying for it by frequent falls. He started dropping some distance behind the others. No one came back to help him, and as had been the case when they were coming across the desert, the little line of walkers began stretching out longer and longer.

Hannah was having a particularly difficult time of it today. Her eyes were hurting from the sun glare, her face was burned by the cold wind, and her lips were cracked and sore. Her legs and her back hurt and she was dizzy from hunger. What she wouldn't give for a piece of her mother's cherry pie!

Cherry pie.

Why had she thought of that? she wondered.

She tried to put the thought out of her mind, but it wouldn't go away. All right, good enough. If she couldn't not think about it . . . she would think about it.

First there was the smell. Whenever her mother baked a cherry pie, the entire house would be filled with such an enticing aroma that no matter where Hannah might be, she could smell it. And the smell alone would make her mouth water.

Then there was the way the pie looked. When it was brought to the table, little wisps of steam would be curling up from it. Her mother would put the pie on the table, and Hannah would look at the brownish red cherries, still bubbling hot under the golden-brown crosshatch crust.

But best of all was the taste of it. The crust was crisp and flaky and the cherry filling a delightful combination of sweet and tart. One bite, and her mouth would come alive with the most wonderful . . .

"No!" Hannah suddenly screamed.

Ike, who had been trudging along in front of her, turned when she called, the expression on his face showing concern.

"Hannah? What is it?" he asked, hurrying back to her.

Hannah was embarrassed. She had screamed out in her mind, to try to drive away the tormenting thoughts. She didn't realize until she heard herself that the scream wasn't just in her mind.

"Nothing," she said. "I'm sorry. I didn't realize I was going to do that."

"Hold on, Hannah," Ike said gently. "Just hold on. We're going to make it out of here, I promise you."

"How can you promise me that?" Hannah asked. "Look around you, Ike. Look at all these people. They are the walking dead. Do you really believe we are all going to make it?"

"No," Ike said.

Hannah looked at him in shock. It was one thing for her to say they weren't going to make it, quite another to hear it from Ike. He was her bulwark, her strength.

"No, Ike, please, don't you give up too," she pleaded quietly.

Ike put his finger to her cheek, but she was so cold that she could scarcely feel it.

"I'm not giving up on us, Hannah," he said. "You asked me if I believed we were all going to make it, and I answered no. Some . . . perhaps several of us are not going to make it. But I am going to make it out of here, and you are too. I promise you. Besides, our three sons and one daughter are counting on us."

Despite herself, Hannah managed to smile. "Mark, Luke, John, and Anna. We mustn't let them down, must we?"

"Absolutely not."

Ike moved back into his position in the line, walking in front of Hannah. Why had she cried out like that? he wondered.

Lord, he prayed, give me the strength to see this through. I made a promise to her and I know she is counting on it. Please, don't let me let her down.

Ike looked up the line at the people who were now walking in front of him. Were each of them praying now? He was sure that they were, though like him, most of them were probably turning to prayer out of a sense of desperation.

Ike had never been too religious. He could remember going to church when he was younger, but that was only because his mother made him go. He did believe in God and Jesus . . . I want you to know that, God, he prayed. I believe in you . . . I always have. It's just that I haven't been very good at expressing my belief.

Ike believed that he was basically a good man. Surely that should count for something.

Ike reviewed his life to see if there were any sins of which he should repent. He had surely cursed a great deal in his life—that was a mark against him. And during the Black Hawk War he killed an Indian. The Indian was an enemy and a heathen, and Ike was a soldier fighting a war. Still, the Indian was a human being, and Ike had taken his life.

And then there was Mr. Hardkoop. Mr. Hardkoop had come to him for help back there in the desert. He had begged to be allowed to ride in the wagon and Ike had turned him down. He hadn't turned him down out of greed, or selfishness, or for any evil reason, but he had turned him down and Hardkoop had died.

And, of course, there was also the fact that he had been with Hannah as a man is with his wife, even though he and Hannah were not married.

No, Lord, no! he prayed. I'm not counting that as a sin. I love Hannah and she loves me and surely the love we feel for each other is as binding in your eyes as the love husbands and wives feel when they have the benefit of clergy to consummate their marriage. I'm not confessing that, and I'm not asking forgiveness for it.

Ike looked up and saw that Eddy appeared to be veering off the course.

"Will!" he called. "Will, wait up! Wait a minute!"

Eddy continued on.

"Will, hold up, damn it! You're taking us off course!" Ike shouted.

Eddy stopped and waited until Ike caught up with him. Pat Dolan, Mary Graves, and Hannah were close enough to the front that they stopped too, though nearly everyone else in the group was so far back along the trail that they continued to trudge along.

"What do you mean, I'm taking us off the trail?" Will asked. "Doesn't it go that way?"

"No, hell, look at the sun. Can't you see that you're taking us to the north? We want to go west."

Eddy shielded his eyes with his hand and looked around.

"Where's Stanton?" he asked. "He's been through here. He can tell us which way to go."

"Stanton! Stanton!" Ike called back down the line. "Where is Stanton?"

"He's way back there," Dolan said.

"What's wrong with him?"

"He said he can't see."

"Hell, none of us can see," Eddy said.

"He really can't see," Dolan said. "He's gone near blind."

"Then we're just going to have to wait for him to catch up," Eddy said, dropping his pack and sitting down.

"Will, we can't keep stopping like this," Ike said. "If we're going to get out of here, we have to keep moving."

"Well, just where the hell would you have us go, Ike?" Eddy asked sharply.

"West."

"Look over there," Eddy said, pointing west. "There's nothin' but mountains over there."

"There's a way through those mountains."

"Yes, but only Stanton knows it."

"Maybe the Indians know."

"Luis! Salvador! Come here!" Eddy called.

The two Indians moved up to the front of the line.

"Which way?" Eddy asked.

The two Indians looked at each other for a moment. Then Luis answered for them both. "We don't know."

"What the hell you mean, you don't know, goddamnit? You've spent your whole lives here."

"Not in mountains," Salvador replied. "In valley."

Eddy looked at Ike. "We've got no choice," he said. "We have to wait on Stanton."

"Then we may as well spend the night here," Ike said. "Because by the time he catches up with us, it'll be too late to go on."

"Give me the hatchet," Dolan said. "I'll go cut some firewood."

THIRTEEN |||

Sacramento, California, July 5th, 1931
When the taxi let John Buford out in front of the house, he paid the driver and sent him on his way. As he stepped up onto the front porch, the window was open and the radio was playing. He could hear the well-modulated, resonant voice of a newscaster reading the news.

"The latest figures show over eight million unemployed as the Depression is deepening," the newscaster said. *"Colonel Arthur Woods, chairman of the President's Emergency Committee for Unemployment Relief, says that while unemployment is high, there is enough food being produced to feed everyone. There is no reason why anyone should starve."*

Alice came to the door even before John pulled the bell cord.

"Good morning, Mr. Buford," she said, smiling brightly. "I saw the taxi drive up."

"Good morning," John replied. "How did Aunt Patty pass the night?"

"She said it was well," Alice said. "She's listening to the morning newscast and waiting breakfast for you."

"Supper last night and breakfast this morning," John said. "I feel like I'm intruding."

"Nonsense, you know how Aunt Patty feels about such things. She is looking forward to having breakfast with you. Sharing meals with friends has always been her favorite thing, as I'm sure you might understand."

"Yes, I suppose I do," John said.

John followed Alice into the dining room, where Aunt Patty was sitting at the table, drinking a cup of coffee. She smiled broadly when she saw John.

"Alice, turn that infernal thing off," she said with an impatient wave toward the cathedral radio that sat on the buffet.

"Yes, Aunt Patty," Alice said, walking over to turn the knob. The little yellow light in the frequency window went out.

"For the life of me, I'll never understand how those things work," Aunt Patty said. Then, to John: "I am so glad you returned."

"Was there any doubt that I would return?" John asked. "I am so fascinated by your story and, I must say, by your amazing recall. It is hard to hear such detail and insight about something that happened when you were just a little girl."

"Yes, but I was a little girl thrown into extraordinary circumstances," Aunt Patty said. "I think that anyone under similar conditions would have as vivid a memory of it as I have."

"Perhaps so," John agreed. "But I doubt that anyone else could tell the story so compellingly."

Aunt Patty pointed to the radio. "I was just listening to the news about the Depression," she said.

"Yes, ma'am. It is a terrible thing. So many out of work," John said.

"And hungry," Aunt Patty said. "I feel so for those who by circumstances must be hungry. Especially in the midst of plenty. It seems to me unbelievable that farmers would actually destroy milk and wheat in one place, while people are starving somewhere else." She shook her head and sighed. "But there is no need to talk of that just now. We'll have breakfast. Then we'll withdraw to the parlor where I will finish the story."

Alice brought a stack of steaming pancakes from the kitchen.

"Oh, my, doesn't that look good?" John commented, putting his napkin in his lap.

After breakfast they went into the parlor, where Aunt Patty took her seat in her favorite rocking chair, leaned her head back, and closed her eyes. After a moment, she continued the story.

"For the first few days after The Forlorn Hope left, Virginia, Jimmy, and I looked up toward the mountains every day. We fully expected to see a relief party coming for us. We had no idea how far they had to go once they got on the other side of the pass, nor did we have any idea of what kind of difficulty they were having and would have. We were much too busy trying to stay alive ourselves."

The Lake Camp, December 21st, 1846
From Pat Breen's Journal:

Milt got back from the Donner camp last night with sad news. Jake Donner, Sam Shoemaker, Reinhardt, and Smith are all dead. The rest of them are in a low situation. Snowed all night with a strong S.W. wind. Today cloudy, wind continues, but now snowing. Thawing and shining dimly. In hopes it will clear off.

"Ma, is it nearly Christmas?" Jimmy asked.

"Yes, dear, I believe it is," Margaret answered.

"Will we see Pa at Christmas?"

"Maybe not by Christmas," Margaret said.

"Will Cousin Hannah and Mr. Buford be back by Christmas?" Patty asked.

"Oh, dear, I don't believe they will come back here at all."

"They won't? But why not? I thought they went to get help for us."

"Well, yes, of course. But they can tell the others where we are and let them come. I believe it would be too hard a trip for them to leave and then come back."

"But Mr. Stanton came back. Mr. Stanton saw Pa."

"Yes, but that was before the snows came."

"I used to like snow," Virginia said. "Now I hate it."

"Ma, are we all going to die?" Patty asked.

"Yes, someday."

"I don't mean someday. I mean now. Are we all going to die now?"

"No," Margaret answered determinedly. "Not if we keep our wits about us. We have a place to stay warm, and we have food to eat."

"We only have the hides and some bones left," Virginia said.

"We can make soup from the bones, and we can roast strips of hide," Margaret said.

"That isn't very good," Jimmy said.

"Maybe not, but it will keep us alive. We'll get something good when we get out of this," Margaret promised.

"We aren't rich anymore, are we, Ma?" Patty asked.

"Of course we are. We are as rich as we ever were," Margaret answered.

"It sure doesn't seem like we are rich," Patty said.

"It's funny, isn't it, Ma?" Virginia asked.

"What's funny, dear?"

"What makes someone rich. When we left Illinois we had gold and three wagons loaded with wonderful things. And we had lots of cattle, oxen, and horses. Then we were rich.

"Then we went through the desert and we lost our wagons and most of our cattle and we weren't as rich as we had been. Then Pa killed that mean Mr. Snyder and the others made him go, and he took the money and Glaucus with him and we got poorer. Then we came here, to this awful place, and we had no horses, no oxen, and no cattle left. The Breens were rich then, because they had lots of oxen and cattle. Now no one has any wagons, or oxen, or cattle. But people who were very poor when we started are rich now, just because they have a few cow hides to eat."

"No," Margaret said. "That's not what makes a person rich."

"What does, then?"

Margaret smiled, and put her arms around her children. "A person is rich when they have the love of their family. And we still have that, don't we?"

"Yes, Ma," Virginia replied.

Patty smiled. "Why, then, we *are* rich, aren't we?" she asked.

"Yes, dear, as rich as we ever were," Margaret insisted.

With The Forlorn Hope

"Ike," Hannah said. She was shaking him awake. "Ike," she said again.

Ike opened his eyes. "What is it," he asked. "Is anything wrong?"

"Here," Hannah said, handing Ike a small wrapped package.

Ike sat up and took the package. "What is it?"

"Shh!" Hannah said. She looked around the camp at the other sleepers. "Don't let anyone see you with it."

Ike unfolded the paper, then gasped. It was a piece of bear meat, at least half a pound in weight.

"What in the world?" he asked.

"Shhh!" Hannah said again.

"Where did you get this?" Ike whispered.

"I have had it with me ever since we left," Hannah said. "Will Eddy has a piece also."

"But how? I don't understand."

"It was Eleanor Eddy and Aunt Margaret's idea," Hannah said. "They thought it might help us."

"Bless them," Ike said. "Oh, but to think that they deprived themselves so that we could have this."

"I know. I tried to talk them out of it, but they said it was an investment," Hannah said. "They said they thought it might be the difference in our making it or not making it. And if we made it, then it would be better for them."

"We'll save it," Ike said, wrapping it up again. "We'll wait until everything else is gone before we eat it."

"Will you feel guilty eating it when there is none for anyone else?" Hannah asked.

"Yes," Ike agreed. "But when you consider the sacrifice Mrs. Reed and Mrs. Eddy made for us, then I would feel even more guilty if we didn't eat it."

"Yes," Hannah said. "Yes, that's what I think as well."

"It's nearly time to get up," Ike said. "I'll throw some wood on the fire and get it going."

"I'll help."

Ike and Hannah got the fire going, so that it was blazing merrily by the time the sun rose.

"Wake up, everybody!" Ike called. "Roll out! We have to get moving."

Groaning with aching muscles and hunger-weakened bodies, the others began to wake up one by one. They started lacing their snowshoes onto feet which were, by now, badly swollen from the cold and the effort of walking. Finally they were all ready. They chewed a piece of beef, drank some heated snow water, then formed up to leave.

Only Charlie Stanton stayed where he was. He remained sitting against a tree, smoking his pipe.

"Come on, Charlie, let's go," Ike called as he hiked his pack onto his back.

"I need another moment or two to rest up," Stanton said.

"You've had all night."

"If you remember, I didn't make it into camp until several hours after the rest of you. That means I'm owed a couple more hours of rest."

"Mr. Stanton, you can't stay here for a couple more hours. If you do that, you'll never catch up with us," Hannah warned.

Stanton drew deeply on his pipe, then blew out a cloud of smoke with a contented sigh.

"You don't worry none about me, Hannah," Stanton said.

"You ought to come on along now," Mary suggested.

"It'll be all right, Mary," Stanton said. "You and Hannah go on with the others. I'll be along soon."

"You girls come on," Eddy called. "Leave him be, if he wants to sit there."

With one last look at Stanton, Hannah turned and followed the others out of camp, leaving the still-burning campfire and the still-sitting Charlie Stanton behind them.

As the sun moved through a merciless blue sky, The Forlorn Hope trudged down the long eastern slope of the mountain. When they reached the bottom they started following a snow-filled stream canyon that was running west. Stanton had told them about this stream last night, so their spirits picked up some as they realized that they must be on the right track.

The sun continued to glare off the snow, and the wind whistled through the tops of the trees, blowing white powder before it, almost as if it was snowing. The wind-whipped snow stung the faces of the marchers. It clung to the beards of the men and hung on the wrapped scarves of the women.

The sun finally dropped below the tops of the mountains in front of them, giving them some relief from its ceaseless glare. But as they came closer to the end of the day, they realized that the canyon they had been following west was now veering to the south.

Ike, who was in the lead at that moment, stopped, and Eddy came up to him.

"The goddamned canyon is curving south," Eddy said.

"Yeah, I noticed."

"So what do we do now?"

"There's nothing we can do except continue to follow the canyon."

"Maybe if we camp here, Stanton will catch up with us again. Surely he knows."

"Stanton's not coming," Ike said.

"What do you mean?"

"Come on, Eddy, you saw him same as I did. I think he stayed back there to die."

"Damn."

"The way I see it, we've got no choice," Ike said. "We have to keep going."

"All right," Eddy agreed. "If anyone questions it, I'll side with you."

"Hell, if anyone has any other idea, I'm willing to listen to them," Ike said as he started trudging forward again.

They traveled about another mile, then camped for the night.

The Forlorn Hope went to bed on an empty stomach that night, because except for the bear meat that Eddy, Ike, and Hannah had, all food was gone. Eddy had the same-size piece of meat as Ike and Hannah, but whereas Ike and Hannah had to share, Eddy was alone. That gave him twice as much. Still, Ike and Hannah had food when no one else did, so they couldn't complain.

The next morning, before dawn, they each took one small bite, chewed, and swallowed it before the others awoke. For everyone else in The Forlorn Hope there was nothing but a cup of warm water with which to start the day. They drank that, then began walking, still following the trail.

A storm broke over them by early afternoon and travel became almost impossible, for in addition to snow, there was also a powerful, cutting wind. The men and women of The Forlorn Hope bent into the wind and cried bitter tears over their fate. Finally Luis saw a rocky ledge protruding out into the canyon from a high escarpment. He pointed to it and started in that direction. Without question, the others followed him. When they got there they found that it offered them some relief from the full effect of the wind.

They had gone no more than two miles that day, but they were too weak from cold and hunger to fight the snow and the wind any farther. When Eddy suggested that they wait the storm out there, the others readily agreed. By now it was twenty-four hours since anyone except Ike, Hannah, and Eddy had eaten. And they had eaten no more than one bite apiece.

They managed to get a fire built, but even the fire seemed

to have no warmth, and they shivered with cold for the entire night, even though they were huddled as close together as they could possibly get.

When they awoke from their fitful sleep the next morning, the snow and the wind had let up. Wearily they broke camp and, after another cup of hot water, started out again. At mid-morning they climbed up a rise that led out of the canyon and came to an overlook. From there they hoped to be able to see some sort of civilization, some reward for their efforts. Instead, from there to the distant horizon, they saw nothing but desolate, barren, lifeless white.

Bill Foster began laughing hysterically.

"What the hell are you laughin' about?" Uncle Billy asked.

"We're goners," Foster said.

"What do you mean?"

"I mean, we may as well put a gun to our heads and shoot ourselves! Look!" Foster pointed to the distant horizon. "Look, you crazy old bastard! What do you see?"

"I don't see anything."

Foster laughed again. "That's it! That's what I'm talkin' about!" he said. "There's nothing out there. We've come on a wild-goose chase! We shoulda stayed back in the camp! At least there, the folks are warm and cozy, and they've got hides to live on. Enough hides to last them through the winter and halfway into the summer, I'm bettin'. While we . . ." Foster waved his hands wildly. "We will just wander around out here until we die!"

"Get hold of yourself, Foster," Eddy said. "You ain't doin' no one any good with that kind of talk."

"Don't you understand, Will?" Foster said, pointing to the distant horizon. "They's nothing out there for as far as the eye can see. If there wasn't no snow . . . if it was flat ground from here to there, if we had a picnic hamper full of food, it would take us at least two days to get there. Only there is snow, the ground ain't flat, and we got no food. So it'll take us a week or two to get there, and then when we are there, where are we? Will we climb up on another hill and see the horizon just as far away and just as empty?" Suddenly Foster laughed again. "Only you don't have to answer that. You know why? 'Cause we ain't none of us goin' to live long enough to get over there, that's why! So why don't we just shoot ourselves now?"

"If you want to shoot yourself, do it!" Jay Fosdick said. "You'd be doin' us all a favor. We'd be rid of your bellyachin', and we could carve you up for meat."

Foster quit laughing and his eyes narrowed. He pointed at Fosdick.

"Stay away from me, you son of a bitch," he said. "You just stay the hell away from me!"

Everyone was silent for a long moment.

Then Ike spoke. "Let's go," he said. "We can't get anywhere by standing around."

Ike started first, then Hannah, then Eddy, then Mary. The others had no choice but to follow, and soon all, even Foster, were on their way, trudging down the other side of the rise and on down into the canyon.

They camped that night, again coming together to build a fire. During the night, Ike and Hannah took another small portion of the meat Margaret had sent with them, but even this did little to assuage the hunger that gnawed at them.

The next morning they drank a cup of hot water, then started again.

"What day is this?" Ike asked.

"It is the 24th of December," Eddy replied.

"Christmas Eve," Hannah said.

"This is our ninth day," Fosdick said. "We been out nine days when it was supposed to be six."

"We were fools to come," Foster said.

"We know what you think about it. You told us yesterday," Eddy said.

"And you should have listened to me yesterday," Foster insisted. "I say we go back."

"Go back? Go back to what?" Ike asked.

"Go back to the camp."

"Don't be foolish," Eddy said.

"I am not being foolish. We're crazy to be out here, can't you see that? There is nothing for us here."

"What the hell do you think there is for us back at the camp?" Ike suddenly shouted. "If it was nine days out here, that means it'll be nine days back. And when we get there, where are we? Will they have food to revive us? No! They are as hungry as we are! There will be nothing for us."

"We should go back," Foster said again.

"Mr. Foster, you are an idiot," Hannah said. "Don't you understand we can't go back?"

"And don't you understand we are going to die out here?"

"If we die, we die!" Ike screamed. "At least we'll die fighting. That's more than I can say for what's going on back there. You saw how Baylis Williams died. He just gave up. So did Shoemaker and Smith, and Jake Donner, and who knows how many more are dead now?"

"Charlie Stanton," Eddy said.

"Yeah, Charlie Stanton," Ike said. "The last time we saw him, the son of a bitch was just sitting under a tree smoking his pipe. He gave up!"

"If we're going, let's go," Eddy growled, looking up at the sky. "I'm afraid we're going to get more snow."

They moved out again with Eddy in the lead. Ike followed. He might have been too hard on Bill Foster. If so, it was necessary, not so much for Foster as for himself. Foster didn't realize how close he was coming to the thoughts that were plaguing Ike's own mind. It was to purge himself of those thoughts that he'd yelled at Foster.

It began to snow. Within minutes the snow was falling so hard and so fast that Ike could scarcely see the person in front of him. He realized almost immediately that this was not going to be an ordinary snow. This would be a snowstorm at least as heavy as the heaviest they had experienced since arriving in the mountains. They had no choice now. They had to stop. They saw a slight opening under the convergence of some trees, and Eddy led them in there. One by one they got under the branches of the tree, and there they huddled miserably.

"I want to die," Antoine said. "I want the Lord to take me now, tonight!"

Sarah Foster started crying.

"This is Christmas Eve," Hannah said. "Listen to me. This is the Lord's night!"

Bill Foster chuckled. "Well, I'm just real sorry we aren't in some big church somewhere prayin' to Jesus."

"We don't have to be in church," Pat Dolan suggested. "We could have church here."

"Who's goin' to do the preachin'?" Uncle Billy asked.

"I'll do the preachin'," Dolan offered.

"You?"

"Why not? I was an acolyte in the Episcopal church. I know all the words."

"All right, say them," Uncle Billy said.

"Do the rest of you want me to?" Dolan asked.

"Sure, why not?" Eddy replied.

"If anyone ever stood in need of God's help, it's us," Ike agreed. "Say the words."

Pat Dolan looked around at the others. Then he cleared his throat and began to speak.

"For in the night in which he was betrayed, he took bread; and when he had given thanks, he broke it and gave it to his disciples, saying, *Take, eat, this is my Body which is given for you.* Do this in remembrance of me. Likewise, after supper, he took the cup, and when he had given thanks, he gave it to them, saying, *Drink ye all of this, for this is my Blood of the New Testament, which is shed for you* and for many, for the remission of sins. Do this, as oft as ye shall drink it, in remembrance of me.

"Wherefore, O Lord and heavenly Father, according to the institution of thy dearly beloved Son our Savior Jesus Christ, we, thy humble servants, do celebrate and make here before thy Divine Majesty, with these thy holy gifts which we now offer unto thee, the memorial thy Son hath commanded us to make; having in remembrance his blessed passion and precious death, his mighty resurrection and glorious ascension; rendering unto thee most hearty thanks for the innumerable benefits procured unto us by the same.

"And we most humbly beseech thee, O merciful Father, to hear us; and of thy almighty goodness, vouchsafe to bless and sanctify, with thy Word and holy Spirit, these thy gifts and creatures of bread and wine; that we, receiving them according to thy Son our Savior Jesus Christ's holy institution, *in remembrance of his death and passion, may be partakers of his most blessed Body and Blood.*

"And we earnestly desire thy fatherly goodness, mercifully to accept his our sacrifice of praise and thanksgiving; most humbly beseeching thee to grant that, by the merits and death of thy Son Jesus Christ, and through faith in his Blood, we, and all thy whole church, may obtain remission of our sins, and all other benefits of his passion. *And here we offer and present unto thee, O Lord, our selves, our souls and bodies, to be a reasonable, holy, and living sacrifice unto thee;* humbly beseeching thee, that we, and all others who shall be partakers of this Holy Communion, *may worthily receive the most precious Body and Blood of thy Son Jesus Christ,* be filled with thy grace and heavenly benediction, and made one body with him, that he may dwell in us, and we in him. And although we are unworthy, through our manifold sins, to offer unto thee any sacrifice, yet we beseech thee to accept this our bounden duty and service, not weighing our merits, but pardoning our offenses, through Jesus Christ our Lord; by whom and with whom in the unity of the Holy Ghost, all honor and glory be unto thee, O Father Almighty, world without end.

"The Body of our Lord Jesus Christ, which was given for thee, preserve thy body and soul unto everlasting life. Take and eat this in remembrance that Christ died for thee, and *feed on him in thy heart by faith with thanksgiving.*

"The Blood of our Lord Jesus Christ, which was shed for thee, preserve thy body and soul unto everlasting life. *Drink*

this in remembrance that Christ's Blood was shed for thee,
and be thankful.

"Almighty and ever-living God, we most heartily thank
thee, for that thou dost vouchsafe to feed us who have duly
received these holy mysteries, with the spiritual *food of the*
most precious Body and Blood of thy Son our Savior Jesus
Christ; and dost assure us thereby of thy favor and goodness
towards us; and that we are very members incorporate in the
mystical Body of thy Son, which is the blessed company of
all faithful people, and are also heirs through hope of thy
everlasting kingdom, by the merits of the most precious death
and passion of thy dear Son. And we must humbly beseech
thee, O heavenly Father, so to assist us with thy grace, that we
may continue in that holy fellowship, and do all such good
works as thou has prepared for us to walk in; through Jesus
Christ our Lord, to whom, with thee and the Holy Ghost, be
all honor and glory, world without end. Amen."

Everyone was silent for a long moment. Then Uncle Billy
spoke.

"Pat, you was sayin' some of them words louder than you
was sayin' the other words. Did you mean to do that?"

"What are you talkin' about?"

"What am I talkin' about? You know what I'm talkin'
about," Uncle Billy said. "You were talkin' about eatin' the
body of Jesus."

"No, he wasn't," Fosdick said. "He wasn't talkin' about
that at all. He was talkin' about us. About how maybe if one
of us was to give up our life, like Jesus done, then the others
could *feed on him in our hearts by faith with thanksgiving.*"

"Yes," Sarah Fosdick said. "Yes, that's so, isn't it? I mean,
if one of us gave our life up for the others, then how would
that be any different from Communion?"

"Hush!" Hannah said, shocked by the way the conversation
was going. "Listen to yourselves! Do you hear what you are
saying?"

"But who would live and who would die?" someone asked.

"We can draw lots," Uncle Billy proposed. "Break up

sticks and draw them. Whoever draws the longest stick will be the one who gives up his life."

"I'll make out the lots," Foster suggested, fumbling for his knife. With shaking hands, he prepared the little sticks.

"Who'll hold them? Who can we trust?"

"Hannah. Hannah can hold them."

"No," Hannah said, shaking her head resolutely. "I don't want any part of it."

"Get Lem to hold them," Antoine suggested. "He's just a boy. We can trust him."

Foster gave the sticks to Lem and Lem arranged them in his hand, then held them out.

"Only the men shall draw," Eddy said.

"No! If it is fair, everyone should draw," Foster insisted.

"My God, man, your own wife is here," Eddy said. "If she should get the short stick, could you eat her?"

Foster looked over at his Sarah. Then he looked down at the snow. "All right," he said. "All right, only the men shall draw."

Lem held the sticks out. Antoine started to draw one, then he pulled back. Stoically, Luis drew one. It was short. Then Salvador drew one. It too was short.

"Let me draw before all the short ones are gone," Foster said. He drew then, smiling broadly, held it up. "It's short!" he said. "Look at it! It is short!"

Pat Dolan drew one and everyone gasped. It was long. To him had fallen the lot.

"Well, I guess it's me," he said.

They were quiet for a moment.

"What happens now?" Uncle Billy asked.

"You drew the straw, Pat Dolan," Foster said. "We all took our equal chance but it fell on you. Do the right thing."

"Yes, do it," Uncle Billy added.

"Do you mean kill myself?" Dolan asked.

"Yes," Foster replied.

Dolan shook his head. "No," he said. "I ain't goin' to do that."

"What do you mean? We all took our chances, equal. You're the one it come to. Now you got to kill yourself."

Dolan shook his head again. "No," he said. "I told you, I ain't goin' to do that. Killin' myself would be a sin. You want to kill me, why, I ain't goin' to fight you off. Go ahead, kill me. But I ain't goin' to kill myself."

"Well, hell, I'll do it," Foster said. He raised his pistol and pointed it at Dolan. Dolan closed his eyes and his lips began moving.

Foster pulled back the hammer and held his pistol leveled for a long moment. Finally Dolan opened his eyes and looked at him.

"Do it, damn you!" he shouted. "If you're goin' to do it, do it and be damned!"

Foster let out a long sigh, then lowered his pistol. "I can't do it," he said. "Uncle Billy?"

"Don't ask me to do your killin'," Uncle Billy said.

"Will?"

Eddy shook his head. "Leave me out of this."

"Ike?"

With a disgusted snort, Ike turned his head.

"What about one of you Indians? You'll kill him, won't you?"

The Indians stared at Foster impassively, not responding to his statement either verbally or by expression.

"Lem?"

"He's just a boy," Hannah said. "Leave him alone!" Lem had been one of her students when she was conducting the school.

"All right, someone give Mr. Dolan a gun," Harriet Pike suggested. "Mr. Dolan and Bill can shoot it out." She looked at Foster with hatred clearly visible in her eyes. "Two men shooting it out! That would be fair, wouldn't it, Bill? You killed my man with a gun. You know how to do it."

"That was an accident and you know it!" Foster said, pointing his finger at his sister-in-law. "You'd like for us to shoot it out, wouldn't you? You'd like for him to kill me!"

"It doesn't make any difference to me which one of you it is," Harriet said coldly.

"This is crazy!" Hannah said. "You're all going crazy!"

"Enough of this!" Ike said. "No more talk of eating each other."

"But he drew the long stick," Foster said.

"I said enough!" Ike roared. "I don't want to hear another word about it!"

"We'd better get a fire going," Eddy said.

There was a long beat of silence. Then the mood changed and everyone backed away from the abyss. After that, moving mechanically, the men and women of The Forlorn Hope set about making a camp. They chopped wood for a fire, then got a fire going, and gathered into a circle around it, staring morosely into the flames. No one mentioned eating anyone else again, but as Ike looked into everyone's face, he could see by the expression in their eyes that they were still thinking about it.

It had all started with Pat Dolan's church service.

Church service. Unholy service is what it was as far as Ike was concerned. It had been the service that introduced the idea of cannibalism as a very real possibility.

What greater sin could there be?

And yet, if the soul does leave the body, then what really would they be eating? Just the meat, that's all. Meat. No different from eating pork or beef or bear.

No! No, he would not think that!

Ike looked around at the others. Some had gone to sleep by now. Antoine was lying very close to the fire, with his eyes shut and his breathing coming in ragged gasps. He made a jerky movement and his hand flopped over into the fire. Amazingly, Antoine didn't pull it out. The hand began to smoke.

"Antoine!" Ike shouted. "Your hand!"

Antoine moaned, but made no move to pull out his hand. Ike got up and pulled it back. He no sooner got back to where he had been sitting than Antoine's hand fell into the fire again. This time it stayed there.

Despite the storm, Ike managed to fall into a fitful sleep. During the night he heard the fire cracking loudly, and when he opened his eyes he saw that Luis was piling on more logs. He saw too that they were running low on firewood, so he decided to take the hatchet and cut a few more.

"I don't suppose anyone wants to help me?" he asked.

He got no answer, but in truth he didn't expect one.

The snow was still falling fiercely as Ike groped his way over to one of the nearby trees. He brushed the snow away from one of the lower limbs, then started to chop away the branches. As soon as he hit the branch, though, the head flew off the hatchet. He shouted, then started searching desperately, but in the deep snow and the darkness of the night the head was nowhere to be found. Finally, with a sickening feeling, he returned to the fire. What would they do now? That had been their only hatchet. How would they get wood?

As the fire continued to burn, it melted down into the snow, creating a deep hole. Then, at about two in the morning, the fire put itself out by sinking down into the pool of icy water which it had created at the bottom of the hole.

When the fire went out, one of the women woke up and saw what happened. She cried out loud.

"The fire has gone out! The fire has gone out!"

The others awoke then. They saw that the fire was out and the storm was still raging. Some cursed, others cried, others prayed aloud.

"Everyone put your blankets together!" Eddy ordered. "Put your blankets together, that's our only chance!"

Moving slowly, the men and women of The Forlorn Hope began to come together.

"If we sit in a big circle and cover ourselves with the blankets, we'll be all right!" Eddy insisted. We'll let the snow bury us."

One by one they began to form the circle. Only Uncle Billy Graves refused to join the others.

"Pa! Pa, come on!" Sarah called. "Mary, help me with Pa!"

"No!" Uncle Billy said, waving his daughters away. "No, I ain't goin' to get in that circle with you!"

"You've got to, Pa! Otherwise you'll die!" Mary insisted.

"I been thinkin'," Uncle Billy said. "I been thinkin' about them words Pat Dolan said tonight and about what we almost did."

"What are you talkin' about?" Mary asked.

"You know what I'm talkin' about, girl."

"Uncle Billy. Mary, Sarah, get over here!" Ike called. "We've got to get this circle closed up!"

"Come on, Pa!"

"This is my body," Uncle Billy shouted. "Take, eat!"

"Leave him be!" Eddy shouted. "Get over here before we all freeze to death!"

"When I die I want you to eat me," he said. "Use my body to stay alive."

"Pa, you aren't going to die if you just come on," Mary insisted.

Uncle Billy gasped once, then fell over sideways. He was very still.

"We're closing it up!" Eddy shouted.

"He's dead, Mary," Sarah said quietly.

"I know," Mary replied. She looked at her father's body, already being covered with snow, and she wondered why she couldn't cry. Then she turned and hurried back to the blanket shelter to crawl in with the others.

The storm continued to rage, and very soon the snow covered the blankets. As they all crowded together under the blankets and the snow, it was actually pleasantly warm. In fact, it was even warmer than it had been when they were all gathered around the fire.

Outside the little shelter, two bodies lay cold and motionless in the snow. One was Antoine. The other was Franklin

Graves, "Uncle Billy," whose wagon had joined them in the Weber River valley. Uncle Billy had not only given them the idea of using snowshoes, he was the one who had supervised their manufacture.

FOURTEEN |||

Christmas Day. Began to snow yesterday about 12 o'clock. Snowed all night and snows yet rapidly. Wind about E by N. Great difficulty in getting wood. John and Edward has to get I am not able. Offered prayers to God this Christmas morning. The prospect is appalling but hope in God. Amen.

"Good mornin', Miz Reed," Milt said, coming into the Reed cabin. "I just thought I'd check to see if you needed some more wood cut."

"Merry Christmas, Milt," Margaret replied brightly.

"Merry Christmas?"

"Yes. You do know that this is Christmas, don't you? December 25th?"

"Yes'm, I reckon I knew that all right," Milt said. "But truth to tell, I can't rightly find much to be merry about."

"Well, you have to be merry on Christmas Day," Margaret said. "It just wouldn't do to be otherwise. And to celebrate this Christmas Day, I want you to take dinner with the children and me."

"Well, I, uh," Milt said, rubbing his fingers across his cheek. "I'm much obliged. But you're runnin' low on hide and bone yourself. No'm. I reckon I'll just go on back over to the teamsters' cabin an' toast up a bit of hide for myself."

"Ah, but what makes you think we're going to have hide or bone?" Margaret said. She was smiling brightly, obviously hiding a secret of some sort.

"Miz Reed, you all right?" Milt asked.

"Of course I'm all right, Milt. I told you, this is Christmas! How can you not be all right on Christmas? Now you run along and cut some wood for us. Then you come back in here and spend Christmas Day with us. We'll sing some hymns and tell stories. And I'll fix us a Christmas meal . . . a *real* Christmas meal."

"Ma, were you just teasing Mr. Elliot?" Virginia asked after Milt left for the wood.

"No, I wasn't teasing. This really is Christmas."

"I'm not talking about that."

Margaret laughed, as giddy as a child. "I know you weren't, darling," she said. "No, I wasn't teasing. I really am going to fix us a real dinner today."

"But where are you going to get the food?"

Margaret picked up a shovel and handed it to Virginia. "You and Patty and Jimmy, go around to the side of the cabin right about here," she said, pointing to a spot on the wall from the inside. "Dig down to the bottom of the snow. You'll find a wooden box. Gather it up and bring it in to me."

"What's in the box?" Patty asked.

"The Gifts of the Magi," Margaret replied.

"Gold and incense and myrrh?" Virginia asked, remembering her Christmas story.

Margaret laughed. "Actually, those are only the gifts that were written about. These are gifts they didn't write about. Now don't open the box until you get inside. Because it's magic, you see, and if you open the box before you come in, the magic will go away."

Virginia, Patty, and Jimmy went outside and began digging as their mother had instructed. In order to get down to the bottom of the cabin, they had to dig a hole eight feet deep. By the time they were finished, the rim of the hole was far above their heads.

"There it is!" Jimmy shouted excitedly. "I see the box!"

"Get it, Patty!" Virginia ordered.

Patty got down on her knees, scraped the last bit of snow away, then picked up the box.

"Open it!" Virginia urged.

"No!" Patty said, wrapping both arms protectively around the box. "You heard Ma. She said it was magic, but the magic would go away if we opened it out here."

"There's no such thing as magic," Virginia insisted.

"I don't care. That's what Ma said and that's what we're going to do," Patty said.

"All right, baby. If you're afraid the magic will go away," Virginia said. She turned and looked at the mountain of snow around them. "Now if we can only get out of here."

"Look!" Jimmy said. "I can get out!" Using his hands and feet to construct handholds and footholds in the snow, Jimmy scrambled up the side. The girls, seeing how it was done, followed after handing the box up to Jimmy. A moment later they went back into the house carrying the box with them. The kettle over the fireplace was half-full of water, and steam was just beginning to curl up.

"Did you get the box?" Margaret asked.

"Yes."

"And we didn't let any of the magic out," Patty said.

"Well, then, it should still be in there, shouldn't it?" Margaret said. She opened the box and looked inside and smiled. "And it is."

"What is it, Ma?"

Margaret tilted the box to show to her children. Inside the box were four potatoes, a little packet of beans, a little packet of rice, and some salt.

"Salt!" Jimmy said. "Ma, that's salt!"

"And beans and rice and potatoes! Where did you get all this food?" Virginia asked.

"I held it back," Margaret replied. "Just for this day."

"Oh, it's going to be wonderful," Virginia said.

"Wait," Margaret said. "That's not the best part."

"It isn't?"

"Look in the pot," Margaret suggested.

The children hurried over to the fireplace and looked into the pot. There, they saw a large chunk of meat.

"Ma! You've got meat!" Virginia said.

"It is the last of Mr. Buford and Mr. Eddy's bear," Margaret said.

"I wish Mr. Buford and Cousin Hannah could have some," Patty said.

"Oh, but they do have some," Margaret said. "You see, when they left, I cut this piece in half. I sent half of it with them, and kept the other half back, especially for our Christmas dinner."

Milt Elliot returned then, bearing a double armload of wood.

"Miz Reed?" Milt said. "Am I goin' crazy, or do I smell meat cookin'?"

"You aren't crazy, Milt," Margaret said.

"And look what else we got!" Virginia said, showing Milt the box of vegetables.

"And salt!" Jimmy added excitedly.

Milt walked over to a stool, then sat down. He looked at the smiling faces of Margaret Reed and her four children, and suddenly he was transported to another place and another time . . . his own childhood in his mother's kitchen, and he couldn't stop the tears from streaming down his cheeks.

"Mr. Elliot's crying, Ma," Patty said.

"Hush, Patty. You aren't supposed to look at adults when they cry," Virginia said.

Milt smiled through his tears. "You can look at me all you want, darlin'," he said. "I'm just cryin' 'cause I'm happy. Merry Christmas, Miz Reed. Merry Christmas, children."

"Merry Christmas, Mr. Elliot!" the children responded, laughing with pure joy over the wonderful day they were going to have.

With The Forlorn Hope, Christmas Day

During the night Pat Dolan went crazy. Because he had drawn

the long straw, he was convinced that the others were going to kill him, so he refused to stay under the blankets with them. Without the warmth provided by the blankets and the shared body heat, Dolan froze to death. When the others took their blankets down and got up to face the new day, they saw Pat Dolan's body lying in the snow.

"We have to have a fire," Hannah said.

"I will chop wood," Salvador offered.

"You can't," Ike replied. He looked at the others. "We have no hatchet."

"What? What happened to it?"

Ike explained how he had tried to cut some wood during the night, only to have the hatchet head fly off the handle.

"I looked everywhere for it," he concluded. "But I couldn't find it."

"You dumb son of a bitch! You have just killed us all!" Foster said.

"Leave him alone. It was an accident," Eddy said.

"Our lives depend upon us not having accidents," Foster said.

"The way my husband's life depended upon you not having an accident?" Harriet challenged.

"Woman, you know I did not kill your man on purpose!" Foster said. "I am tired of hearing about it."

"This talk is not getting us warm," Sarah Foster said, shivering in the early morning cold.

"Maybe you men can cut some limbs down with your knives," Sarah suggested.

"To hell with that," Foster growled. "I'll just set fire to a tree."

Foster rounded up some tinder, then found a likely tree and set it afire. Within moments the tree was blazing mightily, throwing out a huge amount of heat, and shedding burning limbs to fall and hiss in the snow.

As The Forlorn Hope stood around the tree, Ike looked over their campsite. Antoine and Uncle Billy's bodies were almost totally covered from the snow that had fallen after they died. Dolan was lying on the very top of the snow. Several footprints showed that he had wandered around almost aimlessly during the night, probably trying to stay warm. Evidently he had succeeded in staying alive until after the snow quit falling, sometime just before dawn this morning.

Jay Fosdick walked over to look down at Dolan's body. Then, without looking at anyone else, he knelt beside him, took out his knife, then cut out Dolan's heart and liver. The others watched in morbid fascination as he carried the two organs over to the fire. He then cut the heart and liver into strips and, using a green stick, held a piece over the fire, cooking it, just as they had sometimes cooked buffalo meat when they were back on the plains.

Sarah Foster was next, followed by her sister Harriet. Then, one by one, they all lined up to stand around the fire, roasting and eating their grisly meal. They were unable to look into each other's faces. Lem Murphy couldn't eat because he had fallen into a stupor and was now too far gone. Only Will Eddy, Ike, Hannah, and the two Indians refused to eat.

Once or twice Ike suggested to the others that they should go on, but his suggestion was met with stony silence. The others continued to feed on the dead. That night, for the first time in almost three months, their stomachs were not gnawing at them when they went to bed.

As they slept that night, Ike was lying with his arms around Hannah, when he felt, more than heard, her crying. He kissed her forehead and made tiny shushing sounds.

"Oh, Ike, what is going to become of us?" she asked. "All of our food is gone now. I can't . . . I can't do what the others have done."

"Yes, you can," Ike said.

"Ike, no! It's a sin! It's a terrible sin!"

"No, it isn't a sin," Ike replied. "Hannah, I have been giving this a lot of thought. And I have come to the conclusion that we must do it."

"Oh, Ike."

"Listen to me," Ike said, shushing her. "Do you believe in God?"

"Yes. Yes, of course."

"And do you believe in the survival of the soul? Do you think that, when we die, there is a life after death?"

"Yes."

"If that is so, then what is left in those bodies? Muscle, blood, fat, and bone, that's all. It is sustenance. Tell me, if we had brought a mule with us and the mule died, would you eat him?"

"Yes, of course."

"Do you normally eat mule?"

"No."

"But you would eat mule meat now if we had it?"

"Yes."

"Why?"

"To keep from starving to death," Hannah said. "It would be . . ." She stopped in mid-sentence.

"Sustenance?" Ike asked.

"Ike, no, it isn't the same thing."

"It is the same thing."

"No, it isn't. You can't compare a mule with a human being."

"Why not?"

"Because mules don't have souls."

"And humans do?"

"Yes."

"And what happens to the soul when someone dies? Is it trapped in the body?"

"No, it goes . . ." Again, Hannah stopped in mid-sentence.

"It goes on," Ike finished for her. "It leaves the body. There is nothing left but the flesh. Just like in the mule."

"Yes," Hannah agreed in a quiet, defeated voice.

"Hannah, I know that the thought of it is ghastly. But it is not immoral, certainly not in this case. If you believe that life is a gift from God, then you have the moral obligation to preserve it for as long as you can. By that logic, it would be immoral not to take advantage of any means of saving your life, no matter how ghastly it may seem."

"All right," Hannah finally said.

"Then tomorrow you'll eat something?"

"Yes. God help me, yes."

Ike wrapped his arms more tightly around her and pulled her to him.

"We will live through this, Hannah," he said. "I promise you, we will survive."

The next morning the survivors went straight to the bodies. There was a new one. Twelve-year-old Lem Murphy had died during the night.

"All right!" Ike shouted, getting everyone's attention. "Listen to me! If we are going to do this, let's do it right."

"What do you mean, right?" Foster growled.

"If we stay here and eat until everything is gone, we'll still be in the same situation," Ike said. "But if we'll butcher the . . . the meat, and cut it up into small strips, we can make it into jerky . . . no different from beef jerky. That way we can renew our food supply, and we can get a fresh start."

"Mr. Buford is making sense," Harriet said. "Let's go. We've got work to do."

"Could I . . . could I make a suggestion?" Mary asked.

"What?"

"Could we keep them separated? I mean, so that we don't have to eat our own kin?"

"You heard Uncle Billy, same as the rest of us," Foster said. "He wanted us to eat him."

"Yes, but I just, I mean, my own pa."

"How hard can it be to keep it separated?" Hannah asked. She walked over to Mary and put her arms around her. "We'll put the jerky in packets," she said. "That way we can label it so that no one will have to . . . have that problem."

"Let's get busy while we have the sun to help us," Amanda McCutcheon said.

"I think it might be easier if the men carve off the big chunks, then the women cut it up into small strips," Foster said.

"Yes," Hannah agreed. She believed she could cut small strips off what was handed to her, as long as she didn't have to look at it while it was still attached to the human form.

Ike found a limb that he was able to break off a nearby tree, and stripping it bare, he brought it over to use as a drying rack. Then The Forlorn Hope began to work. By late afternoon, the tree limb was full of finger-sized strips of meat, drying and graying in the sun.

The Lake Camp
From Pat Breen's journal, December 27th:

> Continues clear. Froze hard last night. Snow very deep, near 9 feet. Chopped down tree but it sinked in the snow and was hard to be got.

From Pat Breen's journal, December 28th:

> Snowed more last night but cleared off this morning. Then snowed a little more but now clear and pleasant.

From Pat Breen's journal, December 29th:

> Fine clear day but froze hard during the night. Charley Burger is sick. Keseberg has Wolfingers rifle gun.

From Pat Breen's journal, December 30th:

> Fine clear morning. Froze hard last night. Charley died last night about 10 o'clock. Had with him in money $1.50 two good looking silver watches one razor 3 boxes caps. Keseberg took them into his possession. Spitzer took his

coat and waistcoat Keseberg all his other effects gold pin, one shirt and tools for shaving.

From Pat Breen's journal, December 31st:

Last of year, may we with God's help spend the coming year better than the past which we propose to do if Almighty God will deliver us from our present dreadful situation which is our prayer if the will of God sees it fitting for us Amen. Morning fair now cloudy wind E by S for three days past freezing hard every night. Looks like another snow storm. Snow storms are dreadful to us. Snow very deep crust on the snow.

From Pat Breen's journal, January 1st, 1847:

We pray the God of mercy to deliver us from our present calamity if it be his Holy will Amen. Commenced snowing last night does not snow fast. Wind S.E. Sun peeps out at times provisions getting scant. Dug up a hide from under the snow yesterday for Milt. Did not take it yet.

"Children," Margaret said solemnly. "There is something I have been thinking about for a long time."

"What is it, Ma?" Virginia asked. The expression in her mother's voice frightened her.

Margaret looked over at Cash. The dog had suffered as terribly from hunger as the humans, and now it lay unmoving by the fire, its rib cage clearly visible.

"I think it is time we put Cash out of his misery," she said.

"Oh, Ma. You mean kill him?"

"Yes," Margaret said. "It is the only decent thing to do. I mean, look at him, poor thing. He is so hungry he can hardly move."

"We're hungry too, Ma. You aren't going to put us out of our misery, are you?" Patty asked.

Margaret smiled sadly, then put her arm around her daughter.

"No, of course not, dear," she said. "But we haven't even been feeding poor Cash anything at all. We can't spare it, and it has been several days since he ate anything. It is cruel to just let him suffer like this. You know it's a sin to let a poor animal suffer. You've seen Pa destroy a horse because it broke a leg."

"Yes," Virginia said.

"It's only right that we should show poor Cash the same pity, don't you think?"

"I guess so," Patty agreed.

"Now when we do this, there is a way that Cash can help us, a way to keep him with us . . . actually make him a part of us," Margaret said.

"What do you mean?" Patty asked.

"I know what you mean," Virginia said.

"What?" Jimmy asked.

"Tell them, Virginia," Margaret said. "Tell them what I'm talking about."

"You want us to eat Cash, don't you?"

"Yes."

"Eat Cash? No!" Patty said adamantly.

"We have to," Margaret said. "We have no choice, don't you see? Children, we are starving to death. If we don't eat something we are going to die."

"We've got some hide left," Jimmy said.

"I know. And we have to eat it too. But Cash could provide enough meat to keep us going for another week."

"But Ma, he's our pet," Virginia insisted.

"Virginia, do you remember the Fourth of July before we left Illinois? Do you remember Pa's cabinet factory had a picnic?"

"Yes, I remember."

"And do you remember what we had?"

"We had corn and beans and potato salad and watermelon and cherry pie," Virginia said.

"And chocolate cake and cornbread," Patty added.

"Yes," Margaret agreed. "And we cooked some meat on a spit over a fire. Do you remember what it was?"

"It was goat," Virginia said.

"It was Marsha."

"Marsha? Pa said you traded Marsha for another goat," Virginia said.

"I know. He told you that so you wouldn't be upset. But honey, we bought that goat to have for the Fourth of July picnic. We didn't know you were going to name it and make a pet of it. Then, when the time came, you were so attached to it that you wouldn't let us kill it. So Pa told you he traded it for another goat, but it was the same one."

"That wasn't fair."

"No, what you did wasn't fair. Honey, you must know that God put the beasts in the field to serve mankind."

"Cash isn't a beast in the field."

"Yes, he is. Dogs serve mankind. They serve them by herding sheep. They serve them by being watchdogs. They serve them by being pets. And now, Cash is going to be able to serve us in another way. Cash is going to help keep us alive."

"It's awful," Virginia said.

"Yes, it is," Margaret agreed. "But if Cash is going to die anyway, don't you think he would want to do this for us?"

"I think he would," Patty said.

"Yes, I do too," Virginia admitted.

"I'm glad you understand."

"I don't," Jimmy said. "I'm not going to eat Cash."

"We'll see," Margaret said. "We'll see." She walked over to the shelf and got the pistol James had left for her, slipped a cap into the firing pan, then looked over at the dog. "I'll be back in a few moments," she said. She picked up the dog, then walked out of the cabin.

"I'm sorry, Cash," she said quietly. "You know I wouldn't do this if I didn't have to."

Margaret lay the dog on the snow, then cocked the pistol

and aimed it. The dog made no effort to move, but it did look
up at her. Margaret lowered the pistol.

"Do you want me to do that for you, Miz Reed?"

Margaret turned to see Milt Elliot looking at her.

"Yes, Milt," she said. "If you would." She handed the pistol
to him.

"Turn your head," Milt ordered as he pointed the pistol at
the dog.

Margaret turned her head, but she couldn't avoid looking
back at him. She saw Cash looking up at Milt with his large
brown eyes open wide. There was a sadness in the eyes, but
there was something else as well. Margaret was almost ready
to believe that the dog understood what was happening, and
was telling them that it was all right. He would rather go this
way then linger on in slow starvation.

Milt pulled the trigger. The gun flashed, banged, and
puffed out smoke. Cash's head fell down and began spilling
dark red blood onto the snow.

"Milt, don't waste any of the blood," Margaret said
practicality once again getting control of her emotions.

Sacramento, California, July 5th, 1931

"Poor Cash. He did his part," Aunt Patty said. "We ate his
head and feet and hide and everything about him. We lived on
little Cash for a week."

Aunt Patty fell silent for a moment. When John looked
over at her, he saw that she was crying.

"Aunt Patty," he said softly. "Can I get something for you?
A glass of water perhaps?"

Aunt Patty waved her hand and shook her head no. John
realizing that she needed a little time, sat quietly. Out in the
hall he could hear the loud ticking of the grandfather clock.
He remembered that Alice told him it was James Reed's
clock. He knew now that it was the same one Reed had
abandoned in the desert, reclaimed the next summer when
Reed took a wagon back for his belongings.

"I know it must seem foolish for me to shed tears over a

dog after all these years," Aunt Patty said. "Especially when so many people suffered so . . . when so many were driven by desperation to do terrible things to survive. I don't expect you to understand."

"Oh, but I do understand," John said. "You see, it isn't really Cash you are crying over. Cash is merely the symbol of all the suffering of everyone. Baylis Williams, Charlie Stanton, Pat Dolan, Uncle Billy . . ."

"Lem," Aunt Patty said. She smiled through her tears. "Poor Lem. He used to tease me unmercifully, you know. In school he would pull my hair. Once he dropped a frog down my dress."

John smiled.

"I'm sure he would have grown into a fine young man," she said.

Aunt Patty leaned her head back and was quiet for a moment or two. Then she continued the story.

"Of course, as difficult as it was for us back in the camp, it was nothing compared with what The Forlorn Hope was going through."

With The Forlorn Hope

Strengthened by the food, The Forlorn Hope continued its journey. Each of them now had a cache of jerky, cut from the bodies of Antoine, Uncle Billy, Pat Dolan, and Lem Murphy. When they took breakfast, lunch, or supper, they did so without comment, without meeting each others' eyes, eating only because it was necessary to sustain life.

They had no real idea of where they were, or where they should be going. They knew only that they should be going west, so as much as they could do so, they moved in that direction. Their feet were swollen and sore and the snowshoes were gradually beginning to break apart. However, the snow had melted and refrozen, giving them a hard surface to travel on, thus making walking a little easier.

They trudged on, up and down hills, alongside snow-packed and ice-choked streams, until they started up one very high ridge. When they reached the top of the ridge, Eddy let out a little shout. It was the first sound anyone had made all day long.

"Look!" Eddy shouted. "Come here, all of you! Look!"

The others quickened their pace to see what had gotten him so excited.

Hannah was the first one to reach him. "Oh, my!" she gasped.

Ike was next, and when he looked in the direction they were pointing, he felt a sense of elation. There, in the distance, on the other side of another range of hills, they saw a broad green plain, shining brilliantly under a bright sun. Except for the dark green color of the snow-covered ever-green trees, this was the first green they had seen in over two months.

"What is that?" Amanda asked.

"Miz McCutcheon, that there is California!" Fosdick answered.

Ike looked over at the two Indians. For the first time since he had met them, they were smiling.

"Let's go," Ike said. "Now we know what we are looking for."

The Forlorn Hope moved along the crest of the hill, following it west. There was a bounce in their step now. They had seen the valley.

One mile later the hill they were following came to an end, sloping down into a steep canyon that ran north and south across their trail. In order to go on they would have to climb down this wall, cross the canyon, then climb up the wall on the other side. In the summertime with no snow, well-fed, and with the aid of ropes, the climb would have been difficult. Now, in ill-fitting, disintegrating snowshoes, in deep snow, weakened by hunger and other maladies, the climb would be almost impossible. And they would have to do it twice . . . once down the eastern wall to the floor of the canyon, then across the canyon, and back up the western wall.

"We're trapped!" Foster said. "There's no way to get out of this!"

"We've got to try," Ike said.

"Ike, it's goin' to be dark soon," Eddy said. "You don't want to get caught climbin' down in the dark, do you?"

"No, I guess not," Ike agreed. "All right, we'll camp up here tonight and go down at first light."

"Isaac. Isaac, you get out of bed now. Go milk the cows and gather the eggs."

"Yes, Ma," Isaac said. Isaac looked at his mother. She was wearing a light cotton dress and her forehead was bathed with a patina of perspiration. "Ma, aren't you cold, dressed like that?"

"Nonsense. Why should I be cold? It's the middle of summer and it's very hot."

"But it's wintertime," Isaac insisted. "I'm cold." Isaac got out of bed and walked down to the kitchen, where he saw the rest of his family sitting at the table. The table was filled with food, more food than he had ever seen before. There was fried chicken and whole hams, there were bowls of steaming potatoes, beans, peas, and cornbread. He started to sit down to the table.

"No," his mother scolded. "You can't eat yet. You have work to do first."

"But I'm hungry, Ma."

"Ike is hungry! Ike is hungry! There is so much food but Ike is hungry!" one of his sisters chanted.

Ike reached for a biscuit. "I'll just take this out with me," he suggested.

"No. You finish your work, then you can eat," his mother said. "And take off that coat. You can't work with that coat on."

"I'm cold," he protested.

"In the middle of summer?" Ike's father challenged. "You can't be cold in the middle of the summer. Take off your coat like your ma said."

Ike took off his coat, then stepped outside and looked toward the barn. Where the barn should be there was a mountain, huge and covered with snow. Ike started shivering and he turned to go back into the house, but when he turned back the house was gone. His family was gone too, though the table was still there, sitting in the snow. The table was laden with chicken and ham and vegetables. Ike walked back to the table and reached for a drumstick. When his fingers closed around it, however, it was no longer a drumstick. It was Lem Murphy's hand.

"No!" Ike shouted, throwing it away from him. "No!"

"Ike! Ike, wake up!"

Ike opened his eyes and saw Hannah looking at him anxiously.

"What is it?" he asked. "What's wrong? Why did you wake me?"

"You were screaming," Hannah explained. "I thought you were having a nightmare."

"A nightmare, Hannah?" Ike asked. "You woke me up because I was having a nightmare? My God, woman, I don't have to be asleep to have a nightmare. We're living a nightmare. Don't you see that?"

Hannah began to cry, and Ike softened.

"I'm sorry," he said, reaching for her. "You were right to wake me."

The others began stirring then, and Ike got up and walked over to look down into the canyon. By the time he got back to where they had camped, Eddy already had a fire going. They warmed themselves at the fire, drank warm water, ate, then got started.

Going down the east side of the canyon proved to be somewhat easier than Ike had thought it would be. In some cases they were able to sit down and slide for several feet. When such sliding was controlled, there was no problem. Sometimes, though, the slides were uncontrolled, and they would fall, picking up cuts and bruises in their tumble.

Fortunately, there seemed little real danger of falling all the way. They reached the canyon floor in less than an hour. Crossing the canyon floor wasn't all that difficult either. But it got very hard when they started back up the western wall.

The first part was so steep that they had to use their hands and arms to help climb. It didn't get any easier as the slope grew more gradual, for they found that they had to actually dig steps in the snow to work their way up. Jay Fosdick, who had been one of the stronger ones up until now, seemed to be having particular difficulty with the climb, and he started falling behind the others. The longer they climbed, and they climbed for the better part of the day, the farther back Fosdick fell.

Eddy reached the top first, followed by Mary. Next came Bill Foster, then Ike, then Hannah, then Harriet, Sarah Foster, Amanda McCutcheon, Luis, Salvador, and finally Sarah Fosdick. Sarah had tried to stay back to help her husband, but he'd insisted that she go on with the others.

When they reached the top of the canyon, they pulled themselves over the lip, then fell down, panting from exhaustion. They lay there for several minutes, recovering their breath. Finally Ike sat up and looked around. That was when he noticed that Fosdick wasn't with them.

"Sarah, where is Jay?" he asked.

"He was behind me," Sarah said, still gasping for breath. "But he began falling farther and farther back."

Ike walked over to the edge and looked down toward the canyon floor, but he didn't see anything.

"Jay!" he called. His call bounced back from the opposite wall. "Jay, are you down there?"

He got no answer, and Sarah, finally finding the strength to get to her feet, came over to stand beside him.

"Jay!" she called. "Jay, if you're alive, answer us!"

Like Ike, Sarah got no reply. Shrugging, she turned away.

"I had no strength to help him," she said. "He'll have to make it on his own."

"We can wait for him," Eddy said. "It's nearly dark and we're going to have to spend the night here anyway."

"Thank you," Sarah said. "I wouldn't want to leave him."

Ike looked across the canyon to the wall on the other side. He could see very clearly where they had camped the night before. If there had been a bridge across the canyon, they would have been able to cover the distance in less than half an hour. But there was no bridge. They'd had to climb down one side and up the other. That had taken them from early morning until dusk, though in actual distance they had come no more than half a mile.

Ike shook his head. He couldn't think like that. If he allowed such thoughts to creep in, he would lose all hope and determination. He had to hang on to hope and determination. Those were his two strongest allies if he was going to make it to California. And he planned to make it to California. Not only that, he intended to see to it that Hannah made it with him.

As darkness fell, the little group huddled around a fire on the western rim of the canyon and ate the last of their prepared flesh. Just before they went to bed they were startled to see Fosdick work his way up over the edge of the canyon wall. He looked like death . . . but then, Ike guessed, so did they all.

From Pat Breen's journal, January 2nd, 1847:

Fair and thawing. Snow got soft wind S.E. Froze pretty hard last night.

From Pat Breen's journal, January 3rd, 1847:

Continues fair in day time, freezing at night, wind about E. Mrs. Reed talks of crossing the mountains with her children. Provisions scarce.

From Pat Breen's journal, January 4th, 1847:

Fine morning looks like spring thawing now about 12 o'clock. Wind S.E. Mrs. Reed, Milt, Virginia and Eliza started about ½ hour ago with prospect of crossing the mountain. May God of Mercy help them. Left their children here. Tom with us, Patty with Keseberg and James with Graves. It was difficult for Mrs. Reed to get away from the children.

Margaret saw the abandoned wagons as they walked by. One of the wagons was half-dismantled now, and for a moment she wondered why. Then she saw the blackened remnants of a campfire and realized that the snowshoe party must've used it for firewood.

She wondered what had become of the snowshoe party. Were they all safe in California, warm and eating? Or were they all dead somewhere up ahead? It had to be one or the other, she was certain of that. There was no way they could still be alive if they hadn't made it by now. They had only taken enough food for six days. She hoped and prayed that they were safe, and yet that didn't seem possible, for if they had made it through, why hadn't any relief party come back?

Unlike The Forlorn Hope, this little group had no snowshoes. But the level of the snow had gone down some, and the top of the snow had formed enough of a crust to make walking a little easier.

There was something else this group didn't have. This group didn't have as much food as The Forlorn Hope had had when they started out. Margaret had toasted several strips of hide before they left, but even as she was doing so, she knew that it was a futile gesture. Those strips of hide had very little food value, and they simply weren't going to be enough.

And yet, what else could they do? If someone didn't get out and tell others of their plight, they were all going to die. That was the argument Milt had used when he said he was going to go. At first he was going to try it alone, but Baylis Williams's sister Eliza had said she was going with him.

Eliza had then talked Margaret and Virginia into coming along as well.

It had been difficult for Margaret to leave Patty, Jimmy, and Tommy behind, but she'd felt that she had no choice. Something had to be done.

She looked up at Milt and saw him tramping stoically through the snow. Milt was their leader, because Milt was the only man in the group. The truth was, however, that Milt was no longer the strongest. In fact, she was now much stronger than Milt. For some reason, Margaret noticed, the men seemed to be suffering the most. She would not have thought that, yet it was true.

With The Forlorn Hope

They had come nearly five miles today. Jay Fosdick was still with them, though he could barely keep up with the others. Sarah, his wife, helped support him as much as she could, but she was very weak herself and he was drawing what little strength she had away from her.

"Go on, Sarah," Jay ordered several times. "Go on, keep up with the others. Leave me be."

"No," Sarah said. "I don't aim to leave you here to die."

"If I die I die," Jay said. "There's no sense in my killin' you too."

"I'll stay with you," Sarah insisted.

"Look!" Eddy said, pointing. "Bare ground!"

The others saw it too. There wasn't much bare ground. It was just bare because a mound had protruded up from the snow. Yet it was the first bare ground they had seen in over two months . . . other than the one tantalizing glimpse they had had from the top of the mountain on the grassy plain far to the west. Ironically, instead of buoying their spirits, that one glimpse now seemed to mock them . . . as if God had shown them what they couldn't have.

"Let's stop here," Mary pleaded. "Jay needs to rest some."

Eddy looked at Jay, then at Sarah. It wasn't Jay who needed the rest, it was Sarah. But if they stopped here, they were just wasting time, time that should be spent in traveling. Still, the rest might do them all some good. Especially the two Indians. Eddy noticed that the two Indians were nearly as bad off as Jay. The feet of both of the Indians were black from frostbite, and one of them had already lost a couple of toes.

"What do you think, Ike?" Eddy asked.

Ike wanted to go on, but when he looked into the faces of the others, he knew they needed to stop. "All right," he said. "We'll stay the rest of the day and the night here. We can get a fresh start in the morning."

Hannah laughed.

"What is it?"

"The way we keep saying 'fresh start,'" she replied. "As if there really were such a thing."

"I see what you mean," Ike agreed, laughing grimly.

They used their hands and knives to break and cut off enough limbs to build a fire. Then, as they sat around the fire, Ike looked at his snowshoes.

"You know," he said. "The snow is down to about three feet or less, and it's pretty hard-packed. I don't think we'll be needing these anymore."

"I don't mind throwing them away," Foster said. "I hate these goddamned things."

"No, don't throw them away."

"What else will you do with them?"

"The lacing . . ."

"Is made out of hide!" Mary finished quickly. "We can eat them!"

They had been all day and all night without food of any kind, having exhausted their packets of dried flesh the night before. Now, with eager, fumbling hands, they ripped out the lacing of the snowshoes and began toasting them over the fire. Then they ate them.

There wasn't much to the lacing and when they were finished, Foster looked over at the two Indians.

"Where are your boots?" he asked, looking at their feet.

"No boots," Salvador answered.

"Where are they?"

"We take off our boots," Luis explained. He pointed to his feet and to Salvador's feet. They were black, swollen, and bleeding.

"Goddamnit, I can see that!" Foster said angrily. "What I'm askin' you is, what did you do with them?"

"Throw away," Luis said.

"Throw away? You threw away the boots? Why, you dumb son of a bitches! Don't you know we could have eaten them boots? You threw away a day's supply of food!"

"Sorry," Luis said.

"Sorry? Sorry, is it?" Foster said.

Luis looked at Salvador, and the two of them moved away from the others.

"Yeah, you ought to move away!" Foster called out to them. "Anyone who would throw away good food!"

"Knock it off, Foster," Ike said. "Did you see their feet? Those two boys have to be suffering more than any of us. They don't need you to be riding like that."

"I'll tell you what we ought to do. You know what we ought to do? We ought to kill those goddamned Indians," Foster said. He smiled evilly. "Yeah, that's what we ought to do. We ought to kill 'em and eat 'em."

"Shut up, Foster," Eddy said. "You're not makin' sense."

"The hell I ain't," Foster said. "The way I look at it, if someone has to die, it ought not to be white men. Not when we got us a couple of Indians right here with us. I mean, when you stop to think about it, it was Indians got us in this mess in the first place."

"Now how the hell do you figure that?"

"Who was it kilt off so many of our cattle?" Foster said. "Don't tell me you already forgot that?"

"Bill's right," Sarah Foster said. "It was Indians who kilt off all our cattle."

"And the desert, and that goddamned Hastings," Ike added.

"Yeah, but Indians got the most."

"Not these Indians," Ike said, pointing to Luis and Salvador, who were now far enough away so as not to be able to hear the conversation. "Not even the same kind of Indians these are. These are Valley Indians, from California. They are civilized. And they came to help us, for Christ's sake. Don't forget, the only reason they are here is because they brought food to us."

"They're still Indians, by God, be they civilized or uncivilized, whether they come to help us or not. And there ain't nothin' to killin' an Indian. Hell, you done it yourself, Ike, I know you did. You was in the Black Hawk War."

"That was different. There was a war on then, and it was kill or be killed."

"Yeah, well we are in a war now too. We are in a war to stay alive, and I say those two Indians are what could keep us alive."

"And I say that I don't want to talk about it anymore. Listen, we're down out of the deep snow. There's bound to be some game around here. I'll go hunting tomorrow," Eddy offered.

"You seen any game? Or even any sign of any game?" Foster challenged.

"No," Eddy said. "But if there's any around, I'll find it. I'll go out first thing in the morning." He stood up and stretched, then walked away from the camp toward the two Indians.

"Luis, Salvador," he said. He looked back toward Foster to make sure he wasn't being overheard. "We've going to stay here for the night, but I think you two had better go on ahead of us."

"Why?" Salvador asked.

"Because Foster is talking about killing you."

"Foster want to kill us because we throw away boots?" Luis asked in surprise.

Eddy shook his head. "No," he said. "It's crazier than that. Foster wants to kill you because he wants to eat you."

Luis and Salvador looked at each other for a moment, then

shook their heads in disbelief. Finally they got to their feet and without another word started off. Eddy watched them walk away, noticing that both of them were leaving bloody footprints in the snow.

FIFTEEN |||

When The Forlorn Hope awoke the next morning they built a fire, then Eddy started checking over his rifle, getting it ready to go hunting.

"What are you messin' around with that rifle for?" Foster asked.

"Why do you think?" Eddy replied, looking back across the fire at Foster. Foster's face was underlit by the fire and it glowed orange. His eyes shined red and he looked like a demon who had just stepped from Hell.

"You just wastin' your time. You ain't goin' to find nothin'," Foster said.

"I aim to try."

"You lookin' for somethin' to eat, we got it right here," he said.

Ike looked up. "What? What are you talking about, Foster? We don't have anything to eat, not even by your twisted logic. In case you haven't noticed, the Indians are gone."

"Hell, that don't matter none. We can kill one of the women. With their tits and ass, even dried up the way they are, they got to be better eatin' than a man." He pointed to Hannah. "We could kill that one there," he suggested. "She ain't got no family . . . she's got no reason to live. If we was to kill her, it would give us enough food to last another two, maybe three days."

"Foster you've gone crazy," Eddy said. "I think you'd better . . ."

"Hold it, Will, let me into this!" Ike interrupted angrily. He pulled his pistol out and pointed it at Foster, then pulled the hammer back. The metallic click of its cocking made a loud, ominous sound in the still, cold air. "Foster, I think it's about time you and I settled this," he said.

"What are you aimin' to do? Shoot me?" Foster asked. He chuckled, a hoarse, demonic laugh.

"You're goddamned right I'm going to shoot you, you sorry son of a bitch. But before you die I'm going to carve your liver out and let you watch me eat it raw for breakfast." He raised his pistol and took careful aim, tightening his finger on the trigger.

"Yes!" Harriet said. "Yes, kill the bastard! Kill him! He killed my man! You kill him!"

"Harriet!" Sarah Foster shouted to her sister. "Harriet, no!" She jumped in front of Foster, putting herself between Foster and Ike. "If you're going to shoot someone, Mr. Buford, then shoot me," she said. "Without him, I wouldn't have anything to live for anyway."

"Ike, no, please!" Hannah said. "Don't shoot anyone."

Ike held the gun level for another long moment, then, with a disgusted sigh, lowered it. He pointed at Foster with his other hand.

"If I hear you mention killing any of the women again, I mean if you just mention it once, I'll kill you without another word. Do you understand me, mister? I swear to God, I'll kill you in your tracks."

"No one has to kill anyone," Sarah Fosdick said quietly.

The others looked at her, and for a long moment there was absolute silence, except for the crackling of the fire.

"What do you mean?"

"Jay is dead," she said. "We can commence eatin' on him."

From Pat Breen's journal, January 6th:

Fine day, clear, not a cloud. Froze very hard last night wind S.E. Eliza Williams came back from the mountain yesterday evening not able to proceed. Today went to Graves. The others kept ahead.

From Pat Breen's journal, January 7th:

Continues fine, freezing hard at night very cold this morning wind S.S.E. Don't think we will have much more snow. Snow not thawing much, not much diminished in depth.

From Pat Breen's journal, January 8th:

Fine morning, wind E. froze hard last night very cold this morning. Mrs. Reed and company came back this morning. Could not find their way on the other side of the mountain. They have nothing but hides to live on. Patty is to stay here. Milt and Eliza going to Donners. Mrs. Reed and the two boys going to their own shanty and Virginia. Prospects dull may God relieve us all from this difficulty as if it is his Holy Will. Amen.

From Pat Breen's journal, January 9th:

Continues fine freezing hard at night. This is a beautiful morning. Wind about S.S.E. Mrs. Reed here. Virginia's toes frozen a little. Snow settling none to be perceived.

The Forlorn Hope was on bare ground now, having at last come down from the snow. There were, however, a few patches here and there, and on one of the patches they saw bloody fingerprints.

"Someone has been here!" Amanda said, pointing to the snow.

"It's the Indians," Eddy said.

"The goddamned Indians! They're still crawlin' around here somewhere!" Foster said. He left the trail and started looking through the bushes. "Here, Indians, Indians, Indians," he called, as if calling a dog. "Here, Indians, Indians. Nice Indians. Come to Papa!" Foster had his pistol in his hand.

"Ike, Will, what's he going to do?" Hannah asked.

"If he finds them, he's going to kill them," Eddy said.

Ike took a step toward Foster, but Eddy called out to him.

"Ike, no," he said. "It's not worth it. Like as not the Indians are already dead. Come on, we'll just leave the son of a bitch here."

"Will's right, Ike," Hannah said.

Ike shrugged, then turned away from Foster and started following Eddy. Hannah, Mary Graves, Sarah Fosdick, and Amanda McCutcheon went as well. Sarah Foster and Harriet Pike stayed behind, waiting for Foster.

"I found the bastards!" Foster shouted. Almost immediately afterward there was the sound of a gunshot. "I got one of them," he said. There was another shot. "There's the other one! Get a fire goin'! We've got food!"

The Lake Camp

Keseberg was sorry when Margaret Reed returned for Patty. Patty was such a sweet little girl. She was bright, inquisitive, and always talking about her pa. She had tried to learn German while she was there and Keseberg had enjoyed teaching it to her.

He wasn't exactly sure when he started getting disquieting thoughts about her. At first he believed the thoughts were sexual, though he had never lusted after a very young girl before. Then he suddenly understood that his thoughts weren't sexual at all, and he was stunned by the realization of what he had been thinking.

He sat down on the edge of his bed and hung his head in shame, trying hard to fight against the real lust. The little girl did not arouse him sexually. What she aroused in him was his appetite. He found himself fantasizing about eating her.

He thought of what she would look like hanging naked on the wall, her young, blemish-free skin waiting for the butcher's knife. He could see the dark red of her blood against the white skin . . . like the blood of a rabbit splashed on the surface of undisturbed snow.

The liver would be the best part of her. As small as she was, it would be no more than an ounce or two, but it would be rich in flavor and blood.

"Lewis . . . Lewis, are you all right?" Phillipine was asking.

Keseberg looked up at his wife. "What?"

"I have been calling you for the last several minutes, but you would not answer me," Phillipine said. "I was getting worried."

"Do not concern yourself with me, woman," Keseberg growled. He looked at the baby. "Concern yourself with the baby. You must nurse him more."

"I cannot nurse him anymore," Phillipine said. "That's what I was trying to tell you. I am out of milk."

"We must have some food soon," Keseberg said.

"Yes, but where shall we get it?"

"I think, soon, I will find a way," Keseberg answered.

With Half of The Forlorn Hope

Ike, Hannah, Eddy, Mary, Sarah Fosdick, and Amanda had gone on alone, leaving Foster, his wife, and sister-in-law behind to feed on the flesh of the two dead Indians.

Ike and the others with him had cannibalized when necessary, but only from those who were already dead. Now Foster had taken it to the next level by murdering the two Indians. Ike considered that wrong, even though he was ready to admit that neither of the Indians would have lived through the night.

"What scares me," Eddy told Ike, "is that if he killed the Indians, he might kill again. He's already talked about killing one of the women, and I don't know how much longer we could protect them."

Ike had agreed, and for that reason they were now staying away from Foster.

"Eddy!" Ike said suddenly. "Eddy, look!" His voice was so hoarse that he could barely make himself heard.

"Oh, my God!" Eddy said when he saw what Ike was pointing to. "A deer! That's a deer!"

"Don't spook him!" Ike said.

Quickly, Eddy loaded the rifle, then raised it to take aim. He held it for no more than a second, then let out a little cry of frustration and lowered it.

"What the hell's wrong?" Ike said. "Shoot him before he sees us!"

"I can't hold the gun up, Ike," Eddy said with tears of frustration forming in his eyes. "It's too heavy."

Ike stood in front of Eddy and put his hands on his hips.

"Put the barrel on my shoulder. Use it for support," he said.

"Yeah. Yeah, that'll do it," Eddy growled. He rested the rifle barrel on Ike's shoulder. "Yeah," he said again, more confidently this time. "Just hold steady for a moment."

Eddy pulled the trigger and the gun roared and kicked back. Ike's face was burned by the powder flash, but he saw the deer's knees buckle and he knew Eddy had hit it.

"You got him!" Ike said. "You got him!"

The six of them moved quickly toward the deer, which had fallen within a few yards of where it had been hit. As they approached, the deer lifted its head and looked at them through large, expressive eyes. Unlike the time with the bear, though, Ike had absolutely no second thoughts about administering the final kill. He fell upon the deer, slashing its throat with his knife. Blood began to gush from the deer's throat and all of them, the two men and the four women, got down on their knees beside the animal, scooping up the blood with hands cupped as if they were scooping up water. They drank until the blood stopped flowing. Then they fell, exhausted by their effort and by the excitement. Finally Ike spoke.

"Get a fire going," he said. "For the first time in a long time, we're going to eat like civilized human beings."

From Pat Breen's journal, January 10th:

Began to snow last night. Still continues. Wind W.N.W.

From Pat Breen's journal, January 11th:

Still continues to snow fast, looks gloomy. Mrs. Reed at Kesebergs. Virginia with us. Wood scarce. Difficult to get any more. Wind W. Not one living thing, without it has wings, can move about.

From Pat Breen's journal, January 12th:

Snows fast yet. New snow about three feet deep. Wind S.W. No sign of clearing off.

From Pat Breen's journal, January 13th:

Snowing fast. Wind N.W. Snow higher than the shanty. Must be thirteen feet deep. Don't know how to get wood this morning. It is dreadful to look at.

From Pat Breen's journal, January 14th:

New moon. Cleared off yesterday evening. Snowed a little during first part of night. Calm but a little air from the north. Very pleasant today. Sun shining brilliantly renovates our spirits. Praise be to God. Amen.

From Pat Breen's journal, January 15th:

Fine clear day. Wind N.W. Mrs. Murphy blind. John Landrum not able to get wood. Has but one ax betwixt him and Keseberg. He moved to Murphys yesterday. Looks like another storm. Expecting some account from Sutters soon.

From Pat Breen's journal, January 16th:

Wind blew hard all night from the W. abated a little. Did not freeze much. This is clear and pleasant. Wind a little S. of W. No telling what the weather will do.

From Pat Breen's journal, January 17th:

Fine morning. Sun shining clear. Wind S.S.E. Eliza came here this morning, sent her back again to Graves. John Landrum crazy last night so Billy says. Keseberg sent Billy to get hides off his shanty and carry them home this morning. Provisions scarce. Hides are the only article we depend on. We have a little meat yet. May God send us help.

With Half of The Forlorn Hope

Ike, Eddy, Hannah, and the other three women were down out of the mountains. They had eaten most of the deer on the same day they killed it, but their systems couldn't handle that much rich food so quickly, so most of it came back up. They ate more slowly the next day and were able to keep their food down. But they had run out of the last of it two days ago, so that they were, once again, on the verge of starvation.

"I can't go on," Mary said, sitting down on the side of the trail. "I'm going to die right here."

"No, you're not," Ike said. "We've come this far. We're going on."

"You go on," Sarah Fosdick said. She sat beside Mary and began crying. "I should have died back there with my husband. I should have died when he did."

"Ike, look," Eddy said. "Look, isn't that smoke up ahead?"

"Don't do that, Eddy," Ike said. "Don't act as if you see something that you don't. It's even worse to get our spirits built up and then have nothing."

"I'm not lyin', damn it! I do see smoke!" Eddy said.

Ike looked ahead, then felt his heart leap.

"It is!" he said. "It is smoke! Hannah! It's a house! It's civilization! We've made it!"

"No, we haven't," Hannah said weakly. She pointed to the other women. "They can't go another step and neither can I."

"I'll go on ahead," Eddy said. "Ike, you stay here with the women. I'll go ahead and send someone back for you."

Ike started to protest, to tell Eddy that Eddy was just as tired as they were and there was no sense in him having to go on alone. Then he realized, perhaps for the first time, just how exhausted he really was. The thoughts of sitting down for a rest sounded good to him. "All right," he said. "We'll wait right here."

Ike sat down with the others, but like the women, soon discovered that he was too weak to sit. He lay back, just to close his eyes, just to rest for a moment.

Only for a moment.

Ike felt something hot on his lips, and he woke up coughing and spitting, trying to brush it away.

"Easy, fella, easy," someone said. "It's just coffee. We've got some bread here too."

Ike opened his eyes wide and saw at least half a dozen men standing around, looking down at them with eyes full of shock and pity. He had never seen people so strong and well fed. He began to cry.

"It's all right," one of the men said. Ike discovered then that the man was holding his head in his lap, almost as one would hold a child. "We're going to get your strength up a little here. Then we're going to take you back to Johnson's ranch."

"Johnson's ranch?"

"It's just a little ways from here. It's where your friend came for help."

"Hannah?" Ike called. He tried to raise up. "Hannah?"

"I'm here, Ike," Hannah replied.

Ike tried to go to her, but he couldn't move.

"Just lie still."

"Take me to her!" Ike demanded. "Please, take me to her!"

"Put them together in the wagon," someone suggested

gently. "We'll go get the others. There's supposed to be two women and a man just up the trail a piece."

Ike felt himself being lifted, then laid carefully on a pile of fresh, clean straw. Hannah was put beside him. He tried to put his arms around her, but he could not because he was too weak to even raise one arm. All he could do was hold her hand.

"I told you, Hannah," he said, tears streaming down his face. "I told you we would get through."

"Say, mister, the fella that came in this morning—Eddy. I think he said his name was—told me that there were several more back on the other side of Truckee Pass."

"Yes," Ike said. "We're part of the Donner party."

"How many more are there?"

"I'm not sure," Ike replied. "Fifty or better."

"God in heaven," one of the other men said. "We've got to get them out of there."

"Yes, I know. I'll be going with you," Ike said, just before he went to sleep again.

From Pat Breen's journal, January 18th:

Wind W. Thawing in the sun. Mrs. Murphy here today. Very hard to get wood.

From Pat Breen's journal, January 19th:

Clear and Pleasant. Thawing a little in the sun. Wind S.W. Peggy and Edward sick last night by eating some meat that Dolan threw his tobacco on. Pretty well today, praise God for his blessings. John Landrum very low. In danger if relief don't soon come. Hides are all we have. Not much of any other in camp.

From Pat Breen's journal, January 20th:

Fine morning. Wind N. Froze hard last night. Expecting some person across the mountain this week.

From Pat Breen's journal, January 21st:

Fine morning. Wind W. Did not freeze quite so hard last night as it has done. Jean Baptiste and Denton came this morning with Eliza. She won't eat hides. Mrs. Reed sent her back to live or die on them. Milt got his toes froze. The Donners are all well.

From Pat Breen's journal, January 22nd:

Began to snow a little after sunrise. Likely to snow a good deal. Wind W. came up very suddenly. Now 10 o'clock.

From Pat Breen's journal, January 23rd:

Blew hard and snowed all night. The most severe storm we experienced this winter. Wind W. Sun now 12 o'clock peeps out.

From Pat Breen's journal, January 24th:

Some cloudy this morning. Ceased snowing yesterday about 2 in the afternoon. Wind about S.E. All in good health thanks be to God for his mercies endureth for ever. Heard nothing from Murphys camp since the storm. Expect to hear they suffered some.

From Pat Breen's journal, January 25th:

Began to snow yesterday evening and still continues. Wind W.

From Pat Breen's journal, January 26th:

Cleared up yesterday. Today fine and pleasant. Wind S. In hopes we are done with snow storms. Those that went over the mountain not yet returned. Provisions getting very scant. People getting weak living on short allowance of hides.

From Pat Breen's journal, January 27th:

Began to snow yesterday and still continues to sleet, thawing a little. Wind W. Mrs. Keseberg here this morning. The baby, Lewis, died three days ago. Keseberg sick and John Landrum lying in bed the whole of his time. Don't have fire enough to cook their hides. Billy and Simon Murphy sick.

From Pat Breen's journal, January 28th:

Cleared off last night and froze some today. Fine and warm. Wind S.E. Looks some like spring weather. Birds chirping quite lively. Full moon today.

From Pat Breen's journal, January 29th:

Fine morning. Began to thaw in the sun early. Wind S.W. Froze hard last night. There will be a crust soon. God send. Amen.

From Pat Breen's journal, January 30th:

John and Edward went to Graves this morning. The Graves seized on Mrs. Reed's goods until they would be paid. Also took the hides that she and family had to live on. She got two pieces of hides from there and the balance they have taken. You may know from these proceedings what our fare is in camp. There is nothing to be got by hunting, yet perhaps there soon will. God send it. Amen.

From Pat Breen's journal, January 31st:

The sun don't shine out brilliant this morning. Froze pretty hard last night. Wind N.W. John Landrum Murphy died last night about one o'clock. Mrs. Reed and John went to Graves this morning to look after her goods.

From Pat Breen's journal, February 1st:

Froze very hard last night. Cold today and cloudy. Wind N.W. Sun shines dimly. The snow has not settled much. John is unwell today. With the help of God he will be well by night. Amen.

From Pat Breen's journal, February 2nd:

Began to snow this morning and continued to snow until night. Now clear. Wind during the storm S.W.

From Pat Breen's journal, February 3rd:

Cloudy. Looks like more snow. Now cold, froze a little last night. Wind S.S.W. It was clear all last night. Sun shines out at times.

From Pat Breen's journal, February 4th:

Snowed hard all night and still continues with a strong S.W. wind. Snowed about two feet.

At the Johnson Ranch

With most of her strength now recovered, Mrs. Isaac Buford—for Hannah and Ike were legally married now—stood in the window of the little cabin and looked out at the cold rain. Behind her, her husband, also nearly recovered, was sitting on the edge of the bed, pulling wool socks over feet that were still sore from the ordeal.

Outside the cabin, working in the rain, members of the relief party were loading the pack animals with jerked beef.

They had spent the last two days and nights working around the clock, slaughtering cows, drying the beef, then packing it for the trip back over the mountains.

"Ike, you know you don't have to go," Hannah said.

Fully dressed now, Ike walked over to put his arms around her. "Yes," he said. "I do have to go. You know that, Hannah."

"It's just that I am so frightened for you. After all we've been through, I couldn't bear to lose you now."

Ike smiled. "Nothing is going to happen to me now. We made it through once, didn't we? And we had no idea of where we were going and we had no supplies. This time we've got enough food to feed an army. And we know exactly where we're going."

"They've already got Eddy and Foster going with them. They know where to go. And Eddy and Foster both have families back there."

Ike smiled. "So do I," he said. "Mrs. Reed is now my aunt Reed. What kind of new nephew would I be if the first thing I did was run out on her? That wouldn't be a very honorable thing to do now, would it?"

"No, I guess not. I know you have to go," Hannah finally admitted. "And I love you for your sense of honor. But please, be careful."

There was a knock on the door.

"Ike? Ike, you in there?" It was Eddy. "We got to get going. Every hour we spent down here, someone up there could be dyin'."

Ike reached for his coat. "I'm coming right out, Will," he called back.

When Ike stepped outside, Foster brought him his horse. Ike looked at Foster, and Foster cut his glance away. He had come to Ike a few days ago, begging his and Hannah's forgiveness for the way he had acted out on the trail. He told them he had gone mad, there was no other way to explain it. He had gone mad, but he was all right now and he was begging for forgiveness. He was going back because he still had family in the mountains and he owed it to them. He also felt that he needed to go back as an act of contrition for his sins.

Ike took the reins, then put his left hand on Foster's shoulder.

"I'm glad to have you with us," he said.

Foster smiled gratefully. "Thanks, Ike," he replied.

Ike swung into the saddle, then moved up to the front. He didn't know how long they would be able to ride horses. Rain down here meant more snow up in the mountains, and more snow meant that the horses would founder. But they were going to use the horses for as long as they could.

"Let's go!" Eddy shouted to the others, and he urged his horse forward without even waiting to see if the others came.

"Poor bastard," one of the rescue party said. "His wife and both children are still back there."

From Pat Breen's journal, February 5th:

> Snowed hard all yesterday until midnight. Wind still continued to blow hard from the S.W. Today pretty clear, a few clouds only. Peggy very uneasy for fear we shall all perish with hunger. We have but a little meat left and only part of three hides to support Mrs. Reed. She has nothing left but one hide and it is on Graves shanty. Milt is living there and likely will keep that hide. Eddy's daughter died last night.

Yerba Buena, California, February 6th

James Reed waited in Governor Hull's outer office until the governor's secretary asked him to please come in. The governor came around from behind a big desk with his hand extended, smiling broadly as he greeted Reed.

"So, Colonel Reed," he said. "Welcome to Yerba Buena. I am proud to meet the hero of the Battle of San Pascual."

"General Kearny and Commodore Stockton were the heroes, Governor," Reed said. "Not I."

"That's not the way I heard it," Governor Hull said. "I heard that you covered thirty miles in bare feet to carry the message to Stockton. If there is anything California can do for you, all you have to do is ask."

"As a matter of fact there is something California can do, Governor. I need some assistance. I need it now, and I need it very badly."

"Yes, yes, I have been informed of your situation. You have some people trapped on the other side of the mountains, I believe?"

"A good many people," Reed replied. "They have been there for the entire winter, having to slaughter their horses, mules, and oxen in order to survive. However, by my calculations, they only had enough livestock to last them until the first of March, and that on a starvation diet. The first of March is just a few weeks away. After they run out of their animals, I don't know how they will survive."

"Well, you don't worry about them anymore, Colonel Reed," the governor said expansively. "I am making it my personal responsibility to see to it that we get a rescue party put together posthaste. There is no way I am going to let down the family and friends of one of California's genuine heroes. No, sir. The citizens of San Francisco will come to your aid, I promise you."

"San Francisco?"

"Yes, well, some people still insist upon calling it Yerba Buena," Governor Hull explained. "But the editor of the newspaper has proposed that we change the name of our community to San Francisco. And I must confess, the name San Francisco does have a certain appeal, especially if my supporting the newspaper editor's suggestion means that the newspaper will, in turn, support me in the next election." Governor Hull laughed.

"Yes, I see what you mean," Reed replied.

"Well, never mind all that. I'm sure you are much more interested in the fate of your people than in California politics. Let me assure you, Colonel Reed, my interest in getting them safely out of there is genuine. I intend to put the entire weight of my office behind the rescue efforts."

"Thank you, Governor," Reed said, thankful that at long last people's attention could be turned away from the war and onto saving the lives of those who were still trapped with the Donner party. Thank God for the livestock. He knew they were probably getting pretty sick of stringy, coarse meat by now. But at least they had something to sustain them.

From Pat Breen's journal, February 6th:

> It snowed faster last night and today than it has done this winter and still continues without intermission. Wind S.W. Murphys folks or Kesebergs say they can't eat hides. I wish we had enough of them. Mrs. Eddy very weak.

"Mrs. Eddy, try and eat some of this hide," Margaret Reed begged.

Eleanor turned her head away when Margaret held the piece of crisped hide out to her.

"Will has gone for help," Margaret said. "What is he going to think when he comes back and learns that you aren't even trying?"

"Will is dead," Eleanor said in a flat voice. "Will is dead and so is the baby. Soon we'll all be dead."

"No, you mustn't think that. You must live for little James. And you must hold on to the belief that Will is alive and coming for you. I know my Jim is alive."

"Then where is he?" Margaret asked. "Where is Will? Where is Jim? Where is Ike? Where are they all? I'll tell you where they are. They are somewhere out in the mountains, lying under twenty or thirty or God only knows how many feet of snow. And they are dead! Dead like my baby girl. Dead like we all are going to be. Only why is God so cruel as to make it take so long to die? Why doesn't he take me now?"

"I wish I could get you over to the Donner camp," Margaret said.

"They don't have any more to eat than we do."

"No. But they do have Tamsen Donner," Margaret said. "She is amazing. She is the strongest of us all. If you were there, she could be strong for both of you. She would make you pull through."

"No one can help me," Eleanor said flatly. "Go away. Go away and leave me alone. Please, just let me die in peace."

"But what about little James? What will happen to him?" Margaret asked.

"He will die," Eleanor said without passion.

"Just get some rest," Margaret insisted. "You'll be all right. Milt is out now, trying to round up something for us to eat."

Margaret put her hand on Eleanor's forehead. How she wished Eleanor had just a little more strength. She remembered that it had been Eleanor's idea to give Will, Ike, and Hannah the extra supply of bear meat when they left. If only she could show some of that same spirit and determination now.

Margaret wondered where her Jim was now. Was he trying to get back across the mountains? Did he have any idea how bad off they were? Did Ike and Hannah and the others get through?

She prayed that they had. She was praying more now than she had ever prayed before. She wondered if God thought she was hypocritical for praying so little before, and so much now that she needed Him.

She looked over toward the fire and saw Virginia sitting there, just staring morosely at the flames. Virginia had been praying a lot too. Virginia was still insistent that she would become a Catholic, though why she was choosing Catholicism, Margaret had no idea.

Where was Milt? Milt was staying with the Murphys, but he had been coming over at least every other day. He should've been here by now. Margaret was worried about Milt. She and the children had depended on him so much since first Jim and then Ike had left. He had been a good and faithful servant, and if they ever got out of this mess, she intended for Jim to reward Milt well. But more and more, she was beginning to wonder if Milt was going to survive. He had gotten so weak now that he could scarcely move, and every time he made the trip over, she worried that he wouldn't have the strength to make it back.

From Pat Breen's journal, February 7th:

Ceased to snow last night after one of the most severe storms we have experienced this winter. The snow fell about 4 feet deep. I had to shovel the snow off our shanty this morning. It thawed so fast and thawed during the whole storm. Today it is quite pleasant. Wind S.W.

From Pat Breen's journal, February 8th:

Fine clear morning, wind S.W. Froze hard last night. Spitzer died last night about 3 o'clock. Today we will bury him in the snow.

From Pat Breen's journal, February 9th:

Mrs. Eddy died during the night. Mrs. Murphy here this morning. She says Pikes child all but dead and Milt not even able to get out of bed. Keseberg never gets out of bed now. Says he is not able. John went down today to bury Mrs. Eddy and child. Heard nothing from Graves for 2 or 3 days. Mrs. Murphy just now going to Graves. Fine morning.

From Pat Breen's journal, February 10th:

Milt Elliot died last night at Murphys shanty about 9 P.M. Mrs Reed went there this morning to see after his effects. John Denton trying to borrow meat from Graves. Had none to give. They have nothing but hides. All are entirely out of meat but a little we have. Our hides are nearly all eat up. With Gods help spring will soon smile on us.

When Margaret heard someone coming into the cabin, she turned, smiling, hoping that it was Milt. Instead, she saw young Billy Murphy. Since Milt was staying with the Murphys now, she didn't think seeing Billy was a good sign.

"Billy," Margaret said. "Billy, how is Milt?"

"That's what I come to tell you, Miz Reed," Billy replied. "About Milt, I mean. He's dead."

"Oh," Margaret said. She felt a profound sadness, though she no longer had tears to spare.

"He didn't eat nothin' at all for the last two or three days," Billy said. "He didn't eat nothin' an' he didn' ask for nothin'."

"Of course not," Margaret replied. "Anything Milt would have eaten would only deprive others. He would never do that."

"Ma wants to know what you goin' to do with him?" Billy asked.

"Bury him in the snow like the others, I suppose," Margaret said. "I'm afraid there's nothin else we can do with him."

From Pat Breen's journal, February 11th:

Fine morning, wind W. Froze hard last night. Some clouds lying in the E. Looks like thaw. John Denton here last night very delicate. John and Mrs. Reed went to Graves this morning.

From Pat Breen's journal, February 12th:

We hope with the assistance of Almighty God to be able to live long enough to see the bare surface of the earth once more. Oh God of Mercy grant it if it be thy holy will. Amen.

From Pat Breen's journal, February 13th:

Fine morning. Snowed a little and continued cloudy all night. Cleared off about daylight. Wind about S.W. Mrs. Reed has headache, the rest in health.

From Pat Breen's journal, February 14th:

Fine morning but cold before the sun got up. Now thawing in the sun. Wind S.E. Ellen Graves here this morning. John Denton not well. Froze hard last night.

From Pat Breen's journal, February 15th:

Morning cloudy until 9 A.M. then cleared off. Warm and sunshine. Wind W. Mrs. Graves refused to give Mrs. Reed any hides. Put Sutters pack hides on her shanty. Would not let her have them.

From Pat Breen's journal, February 16th:

Commenced to rain yesterday evening turned to snow during the night and continued until after daylight this morning. It is now sunshine and light showers of hail at times. Wind N.W. by W. We all feel very weakly today. Snow not getting much less in quantity.

From Pat Breen's journal, February 17th:

Froze hard last night with heavy clouds running from the N.W. and light showers of hail at times. Today same kind of weather. Wind N.W. Very cold and cloudy. No sign of much thaw.

From Pat Breen's journal, February 18th:

Froze hard last night. Today clear and warm in the sun. Cold in the shanty or in the shade. Wind S.W. All in good health. Thanks be to Almighty God. Amen.

Ike was the first one to reach the top of the pass. He stepped up onto the same flat rock on which they had stood on their way out, the rock that had been their elusive goal on those first, abortive tries. From here they had stopped to look back at the little encampment. How long ago was that? Two months! My God, it was. It had been two months since The Forlorn Hope had left, eighteen of them trudging out on snowshoes, full of hope and totally ignorant of what lay before them. Eighteen had started out; only eight survived.

What about the lake camp? Was there anyone down there now? Was anyone left alive?

"Hell, Buford, there ain't no one down there," one of the others said, almost as if answering Ike's unasked question. "If there was anybody there, they're dead now. We've made this trip for nothin'."

"We're going down to take a look," Eddy insisted, arriving at the pass. He came up to stand beside Ike. "There is bound to be someone left alive. I'm sure of it."

Ike turned to look back at the rest of the rescue team as they struggled up the west side of the pass. Each man was laden with backpacks loaded with food. The backpacks were necessary since the packhorses had foundered in the snow several days earlier. They wound up having to stash most of the food, bringing in only what they could carry on their backs. That meant that the total they could bring in was much less than would actually be needed. However little it was, though, Ike knew that it would be welcome in camp.

"What do you think? Should we go down?" one of the other men asked.

Instead of answering, Ike just glared. Then he started down the east side of the pass, over the same route they had tried so many times, unsuccessfully, to conquer in those first days after they arrived in the valley. They trudged past the

burned-out tree and Ike felt a tug at his heart. He knew that
many of those who had gathered around the burning tree that
night were dead now. He looked over at Eddy and saw that he
was thinking the same thing.

Is Eddy's family still alive? Ike prayed that they were, but
he didn't dare say anything aloud because he didn't want to
add to Eddy's worry.

They passed by the abandoned wagons where The Forlorn
Hope had camped on their first night out. Then they were at
the edge of the lake. Ike could see several little mounds
ahead, and he knew that the mounds were cabins, buried
under the snow. Would they find anyone alive?

"Hello!" Ike called. "Hello! Is anyone here?"

A woman suddenly popped up from a hole in the snow. Ike
believed it was Peggy Breen, though she had changed so that
Ike almost didn't recognize her.

"Mrs. Breen?" he asked.

"Who are you?" Peggy Breen asked. "Are you men from
California, or do you come from heaven?"

"Mrs. Breen, it's me, Ike," Ike said. "We've come back for
you."

"Ike!" another voice shouted, and Ike saw Margaret Reed
appear. Ike was moved to immediate tears by her gaunt
appearance. "You've come for us," she said. "I knew you
would come back."

From Pat Breen's journal, February 19th:

Froze hard last night. 7 men arrived from California
yesterday evening with some provisions but left the greater
part on the way. Today clear and warm for this region.
Some of the men are gone today to Donners camp. Will
start back on Monday.

Of Eddy's family, only young Jimmy remained, and he was
very weak. Will cried for his Ellie and the baby Margaret, but
he hoped he would be able to keep Jimmy alive. Because of

that, he stayed at the lake camp to feed him broth and try to get him ready for the trip back, while Ike and the others went over to the Donner camp.

Tamsen Donner came out to greet the men when they arrived, smiling at them, not as if they were saving her life but as if they had arrived for a social call.

"Mr. Buford, it is good to see you again," she said. "How about Mr. Eddy? Did he make it out all right?"

"Yes, ma'am," Ike replied. "He's over in the other camp tending to young Jimmy."

"I heard that Ellie and the baby died. It's very distressful."

"Mrs. Donner," one of the men said, taking off his backpack. "We'd like to come in and start cooking, if you don't mind. You have to get some food in you."

"Yes, yes, that would be nice," Tamsen said. "But feed the children first. I can wait."

Ike followed Tamsen into the shanty, then was struck by the smell that assailed him. It was more than the smell of bodies too close together. It was the smell of putrefied flesh. When he looked over on the bed and saw George Donner, he knew where the smell was coming from. Donner's entire arm was black and swollen.

"Hello, Mr. Donner," Ike said.

"I see you made it back," Donner replied. "Well, you are a good man, but then I knew that from the moment we left Illinois."

Illinois. How long ago that all seemed now.

"What about the others? How many of you made it?" Donner asked.

"All of the women made it across, Mr. Donner," Ike said. "Only three of the men."

Donner shook his head. "It's a terrible thing."

They talked for several minutes while the inside of the cabin began to fill with the aroma of cooking beef. Finally Tamsen came over to the bed, carrying a steaming bowl.

"George, look what I have for you," Tamsen said, sitting on

the bed beside him. "I have some stew that these nice men made for us. Here, you must eat."

"You are wasting good food on me, Tamsen," Donner said, trying to wave her away with his good hand. "Eat it yourself."

"I will eat when everyone else has eaten," Tamsen replied, holding a spoon to his mouth.

As Tamsen fed her husband and the children, the men of the rescue party went outside to lay in a supply of wood. Ike went over to Jacob Donner's cabin to see who among them would be going back with the rescue party.

"I will go," Noah James said.

"Me, too," Solomon Hook said. Solomon's twelve-year-old brother, William, also wanted to go.

There were some who wanted to go, but agreed to stay and help look after those who would be forced to remain behind. They knew that the amount of food the first relief team brought was quite limited and, once it ran out, they would be right back in the same situation. They were promised that a second relief team was on the way.

Tamsen was one of those who stayed behind. Ike tried to talk her into coming out with the relief party.

"I know your intentions are good, Mr. Buford," Tamsen said. "But as you can clearly see, my husband is in no condition to travel, and I will not abandon him."

"Tamsen," Donner said. "Don't be a fool. I'm going to die, and you know it. You go on out with them now."

"And if I do, who will look after you?"

"What's there to look after?" Donner replied. "I told you, I'm going to die."

"All right, then you're going to die," Tamsen agreed. "But you are not going to die alone. I intend to be here with you."

Ike tried one last, desperate tactic. "Mrs. Donner, we are telling everyone that a second relief party is on the way . . . and I am sure it is. But as you have no doubt learned by now, you can never tell about the weather. If another huge storm blocks the pass, it could be a couple of months before we get back."

"I understand what you are saying, Mr. Buford, and I appreciate your concern," Tamsen replied. "But I am not going to let my husband die alone."

Ike sighed. "Then God be with you, Mrs. Donner," he said. "If we meet the next relief party, I will send them on as quickly as I can."

"Thank you, Mr. Buford," Tamsen said.

Ike hiked back over to the lake camp, taking with him those who would be going from the Donner camp. In all there were five going.

Bill Foster's mother-in-law was too weak to travel, as was Foster's son, George. He hated leaving George behind, but he was glad George's grandmother would be there to look after him.

Margaret Reed, Virginia, and young Jimmy Reed were leaving with the rescue party, but Tommy was not well enough to travel, so Patty volunteered to stay behind with him. Despite Will Eddy's efforts, his son, Jimmy, was also unable to make the trip. Keseberg told Margaret that since Phillipine would be leaving with the rescue party, he would have the cabin all alone. Patty and Tommy Reed and Jimmy Eddy could stay with him.

"That is very nice of you, Mr. Keseberg," Margaret said.

"Patty is a sweet girl," Keseberg said, looking at her. "We had a fine time when she was here before."

"Patty, I will send someone back for you as quickly as I can," Margaret promised.

"Ma," Patty said. "If you never see me again, do the best that you can."

Margaret embraced her youngest daughter, squeezing her tightly. Then, with tears in her eyes, she turned to Ike to tell him that she was ready.

From Pat Breen's journal, February 22nd:

The Californians started this morning 24 in number some in a very weak state. Fine morning, wind S.W. for the last 3 days. Mrs. Keseberg started and left Keseberg here unable to go. I buried Pikes child this morning in the snow. It died 2 days ago.

The children who were going back with the rescue party were too small and two weak to follow easily in the tracks put down by the adults. Young Jimmy Reed had to fight his way through snow that came to his waist, and though he fell several times, and crawled through the snow nearly as much as he walked through it, he didn't complain.

"Jimmy," Virginia called to her youngest brother, concerned about him. "Jimmy, are you all right?"

"I'm all right," Jimmy replied.

"This is very hard for you, I know. If you need to stop, say so. Maybe the men will let us rest."

"No," Jimmy replied resolutely. "I'm not going to stop. Don't you know? Every step I take is one step nigher Pa, and somethin' to eat."

Though he was larger than the children, the Englishman, John Denton, seemed to be having even more difficulty than they were. Ike saw the way he was struggling, and remembering how Jay Fosdick had suddenly given up and died, couldn't help but believe that the same fate was in store for Denton. He said nothing about it, though. Maybe he was wrong. Maybe Denton would make it all the way. Maybe he had a reservoir in strength that Ike couldn't see. He prayed that he did.

From Pat Breen's journal, February 23rd:

Froze hard last night. Today fine and thawey, has the appearance of spring all but the deep snow. Wind S.S.E. Shot Towser today and dressed his flesh. Mrs. Graves came here this morning to borrow meat, dog or ox. They think I have meat to spare but I know to the contrary. They have plenty hides. I live principally on the same.

The food was gone over in the Donner camp. The rescue party had been able to bring in very little, and of course they had to have enough to feed themselves and the people they were taking back with them, so they were able to leave very little of what they did bring. Tamsen was the first to realize what must be done, so she called Jean-Baptiste over to talk to him.

"It is very frustrating," she said. "There are cattle buried under the snow, but we can't find them."

"I have looked, Mrs. Donner," Jean-Baptiste said. "I have used a long pole to prod through the snow. I've looked hard."

Tamsen put her hand on his shoulder. "I know you have, Jean-Baptiste. And I'm not blaming you. But we do have to have something to eat."

"Yes, ma'am, I know that."

"And there are no hides left."

"No, ma'am, there are no hides left."

"Do you have any suggestions on what we can do?"

"No, ma'am. I reckon I'm about at my wit's end."

Tamsen looked at Jean-Baptiste with cool, unflinching eyes. "Think about it, Jean-Baptiste," she said. "If we were wolves, we wouldn't be going hungry now, would we?"

"Don't know what the wolves could find that we can't," Jean-Baptiste said.

"Don't you?"

Suddenly Jean-Baptiste knew what Tamsen was saying.

"Um, Mrs. Donner, are you talking about what I think you are talking about?"

"Food is food, Jean-Baptiste," she said. "Now you go do what you have to do. I'll get the water boiling."

"Yes, ma'am."

From Pat Breen's journal, February 24th:

Froze hard last night. Today cloudy, looks like a storm. Wind blows hard from the W. Commenced thawing. There has not any returned from those who started to cross the mountains.

From Pat Breen's journal, February 25th:

Froze hard last night. Fine and sunshiny day. Wind W.

With the Rescue Party
Ike sat gazing into the fire. It was The Forlorn Hope all over again. Their first two food caches had been discovered and eaten by wild animals, and now they were out of food. He had eaten rawhide yesterday. It wasn't the first time for him, nor for those who were being taken out. But it was for the others, the ones who had volunteered in a fit of heroic compassion to make this journey. Unlike Ike, Eddy, and Foster, they had no idea of what they were letting themselves in for.

Everyone sprawled around the fire, the rescued and the rescuers, now in the same boat. They were hungry and cold, but Ike saw in their eyes the same sense of determination he had carried with him when he came out with The Forlorn Hope. And if he had made it then, they could make it now. In fact he was going to draw some of his strength from them.

They had one big advantage over the snowshoe party. This time Ike, Eddy, and Foster knew where they were going. It would be a hard, cold, and hungry trip, but at least they wouldn't be lost.

SIXTEEN |||

From Pat Breen's journal, February 26th:

> Froze hard last night. Today clear and warm. Wind S.W.
> blowing briskly. Patty's jaw swelled with the toothache.
> Hungry times in camp, plenty hides but the folks will not
> eat them. We eat them with a tolerable good appetite.
> Thanks be to Almighty God. Amen. Mrs. Murphy said here
> yesterday that thought she would commence on Milt and
> eat him. I don't know that she has done so yet. It is
> distressing. The Donners told the California folks that they
> would commence to eat the dead people 4 days ago, if they
> did not succeed that day or then next in finding their cattle
> then under ten or twelve feet of snow and did not know the
> spot or near it. I suppose they have done so ere this time.

Keseberg sat on the bed watching young Patty entertain her
baby brother. Patty had fared well, better than most. Of
course the Breens were feeding her. Not out of any sense of
Christian brotherhood. They would be getting paid plenty for
their charity.

It wasn't fair. Keseberg was looking out for them, yet he
got none of the Breens' meat. And they could deny it all
wanted, but Keseberg knew that they still had plenty of meat
left. How else could Patty still look as healthy as she was?
That didn't come from hides.

"Patty," Keseberg called.

Patty, who was sitting on the fire hearth, looked over at him. "Yes, Mr. Keseberg?"

"No, no, that is not how you answer me. Remember?" Keseberg asked, waving his finger.

"Oh, I forgot," Patty said. She smiled. *"Ja, Herr Keseberg?"*

"Zehr gut, liebchen," Keseberg said. "Come over here to me, will you?"

Patty got up, then turned to Tommy. "You stay right there," she cautioned. "Don't go away and don't get into the fire."

Tommy shook his head. "I won't," he said.

While Patty's attention was diverted, Keseberg reached into the folds of the bedclothing and found his knife. He held it behind him until Patty got there. He could feel his heart pounding and the blood racing in his veins. He would strike quickly, before she knew what happened. He didn't want to frighten the poor girl. He just wanted to kill and eat her.

Just before Patty reached him, Tommy knocked over a stack of firewood, causing her to stop and look back at him.

"Oh, Tommy, you are always doing something," she scolded, going back to take care of him.

Keseberg got up from the bed and started toward her, holding the knife behind his back.

"You don't have to help me, Herr Keseberg," Patty said. "I know you aren't feeling well. I'll take care of everything myself."

Keseberg stopped and smiled at her, though the smile didn't reach his eyes. His eyes were large and glazed. There were beads of perspiration on his forehead.

"Patty," Peggy Breen called, sticking her head through the door of Keseberg's shanty. "Patty, you get Tommy and bring him on over now."

"Yes, ma'am, Miz Breen," Patty said, standing and reaching down for Tommy. "Good-bye, Herr Keseberg. I'll see you later," Patty called over her shoulder.

By now Keseberg's hands were sweating so profusely that he could scarcely hold on to his knife. He returned to his bed, put the knife down, then wiped the palms of his hands on the bed cover. He waited until his heart quit pounding, then got up and went outside into the snow, where he walked directly over to Milt Elliot's body. Then he bent over and cut off a leg with all the skill of a surgeon, an art he had once studied as a young man in Westphalia.

From Pat Breen's journal, February 27th:

> Beautiful morning sun shining brilliantly, wind about S.W. The snow has fell in depth about 5 feet but no thaw but in the sun in day time, it freezing hard every night. Heard some geese fly over last night. Saw none.

True to his word, Governor Hull had outfitted a rescue party for James Reed. Well-equipped and with plenty of manpower, Reed rounded up Will McCutcheon and off they went. As yet McCutcheon didn't know that his wife had made it out of the camp, for neither he nor Reed knew anything about The Forlorn Hope or the first rescue party, which had already gotten through ahead of them. And because they thought there was a goodly supply of cattle left, they knew nothing about the actual conditions of the people who were still up on the mountain. As a result, though they were hurrying, they were making no special effort at speed.

On the night of the 26th, however, they met two men coming back down from the first rescue party, sent ahead by Ike to look for more food from their cached supply. The two men told a harrowing tale to Reed and McCutcheon, not only about the ones who were still trapped on the mountain, but about the people, rescuers and rescued, who were just ahead.

Reed learned that while his wife, daughter, and one son were with the rescue party, his other daughter and other son were back at the lake camp. McCutcheon learned that, though his wife was now safe, his daughter had died. He didn't know whether to cry tears of joy or sorrow.

"Them folks down in the valley is pure starvin' to death,

Mr. Reed," the messenger said. "If you don't get somethin' to them in a hurry, I'm afraid it's goin' to be too late. They're all goin' to be goners. And the rescue party is nigh on as bad."

Jim looked around at the others in his party. "Get a fire started," he said. "And get busy. We're going to bake bread all night and take it to the rescue party at first light. Then we're goin' on to the lake for the others."

"Yes, sir," one of Reed's men said, and within a few minutes a roaring fire was going. Shortly thereafter the smell of baking bread filled the cold night air.

Reed didn't sleep a wink through the entire night. By first light he had several biscuits baked and ready to go, and as soon as he could, he rushed forward. The second rescue party and the first rescue party met about an hour later.

"Mr. Reed!" Ike shouted. "Mr. Reed! What a sight for sore eyes!"

"Ike!" Reed replied, returning the greeting. "Ike, where is Mrs. Reed! Is she with you?"

"Yes," Ike replied. "She and Virginia."

"And Hannah? Where is she?"

"My wife is back at Johnson's ranch with Mrs. McCutcheon," Ike said, smiling broadly.

"Your wife?" McCutcheon asked.

Ike smiled. "Hannah and I got married," he said.

McCutcheon pumped Ike's hand. "Well, congratulations," he offered.

Reed left Ike, then moved up the trail, searching for his family.

"Margaret! Margaret, where are you?" he shouted.

Margaret Reed recognized her husband's voice. It was the first time she had heard it in nearly six months, and she was so overcome with joy that she fainted dead away.

Virginia also heard her father's voice, and she started running toward him. "Pa!" Virginia called, "Pa."

Reed ran to his daughter, then swept her up into his arms. He had always been a strong man and she had always been small, but never, he believed, had she been this small. Virginia was as light as a feather.

"Where is your ma, girl?" Reed asked. "Where is your ma?"

"She's back there, Pa," Virginia said. "She fainted when she heard you talkin'."

With another embrace and kiss, Reed put Virginia down, then hurried back to his wife. Margaret was just getting up again when he reached her, and they embraced and cried in each other's arms. While still holding her, he saw young Jimmy standing behind her.

"Jimmy!" Reed said, kneeling down to his young son's level. "Jimmy, are you too big a boy to give your pa a kiss?"

Jimmy smiled happily, then wrapped his arms around his father's neck.

"Here," Reed said, taking out a handful of biscuits and passing them around. "Here, take these. There's more up ahead. I left someone in the camp, cooking more food."

"Jim," Margaret said. "Patty and Tommy. They are still in the camp. You've got to get to them. Bring them out of there."

"I will, Margaret," Jim said. "Don't you worry about that. I will."

From Pat Breen's journal, February 28th:

Froze hard last night. Today fair and sunshine. Wind S.E. 1 solitary Indian passed by yesterday. Come from the lake. Had a heavy pack on his back. Gave me 5 or 6 roots resembling onions in shape. Taste some like a sweet potato, all full of tough little fibers.

Leaving the members of the first rescue party behind him, Reed continued on toward the lake camp. They made fourteen miles that day, camped that night, then got started before dawn. They reached the lake camp at about mid-morning. Patty was sitting outside Breen's cabin. The moment she recognized him she ran to Reed, babbling happily.

"I knew you would come, Pa! I knew you would come!" she shouted, holding her arms open wide.

As he had with her sister the day before, Reed scooped up Patty and squeezed her tight.

"Where's Tommy? Is he all right?"

"He's all right, Pa," Patty said. "He's staying in the Breens' cabin."

Reed went into the cabin to see his son. The Breens were sitting there watching, almost as if they were totally disinterested parties. Finally Reed spoke.

"What happened to the cattle, man? I thought you would have food until March."

"All the animals wandered off after the first big snowstorm," Breen said. "We've been without them since November."

"God in heaven, how have you survived?"

"Have you been over to the Murphys' cabin yet?" Breen asked.

"No."

"Thought not. You wouldn't of asked the question if you had."

"Why? What are you talking about?"

"I reckon I'd better prepare you before you go over," Breen said.

"Prepare me? Prepare me for what?"

"The Murphys and the Donners done started eatin' their dead," Breen said matter-of-factly. "Keseberg's moved in with the Murphys now, and he's the worst of the lot."

"God forgive me for not coming before now," Reed said, not mentioning that he had tried, only to be turned back.

Leaving some food for the Breens, Reed walked through the snow to the Murphys' cabin. On the way, he passed by a body that was already three-quarters butchered. The head was still attached, so he was able to recognize it as Milt Elliot. His stomach turned.

Inside the cabin, Reed saw that McCutcheon was already there. He was trying to clean up, though the smell was so bad it was difficult for him to even stay there.

Keseberg was sitting on the bed, eating something from a bowl.

"You fed him before you fed the others?" Reed asked.

"The son of a bitch was already eating when I got here," McCutcheon said.

"Eating what?"

"You don't want to know."

Reed was across the cabin in two long strides. He slapped the bowl out of Keseberg's hands, and it flew across the cabin, then clattered against the door.

"There was no call for you to do that," Keseberg complained.

"The hell there wasn't," Reed said. "What do you think we're doing here? We've brought food. You don't have to do that anymore."

"No need in wasting it," Keseberg said.

From Pat Breen's journal, March 1st:

> There has been 10 men arrived this morning from Bear Valley with provisions. We are to start in two or three days and cache our goods here. There is amongst them some old mountainers. They say the snow will be here until June.

The next day Reed and three men hiked down to the lower end of the lake to the Donner camp. One of the rescuers, a man named Potter, had gone over the day before, and now he met them just outside the camp.

"You ain't ready for what you're about to see in this here camp," Potter told them.

Reed thought of the partially butchered body of Milt Elliot, and he nodded.

"Maybe we're more ready than you think," he said. "What is it?"

"They ain't one body over here but what ain't been et on," Potter said. "All except the heads." He shivered. "The heads are just settin' about here an' there in the snow. Some of 'em have their eyes open, like as if they're starin' at you. I tell you the truth, Hell can't be no worse than this place."

"Only God can judge the quick and the dead," Reed said. He pulled himself together. "I'm going in."

When Reed reached the camp, he went immediately to George Donner's cabin to see his old friend. He was appalled at George's condition.

"Jim," Donner said. He chuckled weakly. "I guess runnin' you out of camp was the best favor I ever done for you."

"I guess so, George," Reed answered.

Donner nodded toward his grotesque arm. "Who would've ever thought that a little cut would do somethin' like this?" he asked. "And then, once it set in, to take so long to kill me. There's been folks that's starved to death since all this started that was in twice the health I was."

"You have had a good nurse," Reed said.

Tamsen just nodded.

"You mighty damned right about that," Donner replied. "Ain't never been a man nowhere had him a woman like my Tamsen. She's kept us alive . . . Lord knows how she's done it, but she has."

Reed studied his friend's face. At first he was ready to believe that Donner didn't know how they had survived. Then he realized that Donner did know. He was just playing the game of not admitting that he knew.

"I have done what had to be done, that's all," Tamsen said.

"God knows what you have, Mrs. Donner," Reed said. "You'll get no contempt from me."

"You are very kind."

"Mrs. Donner, it's time for you to get out of here," Reed said. "I want you to come with me."

"Thank you, Mr. Reed, but I cannot," Tamsen replied. "I must stay with my husband."

"It is urgent that you leave now."

"There's no sense in you arguin' with her, Jim," Donner said. "I've been after her from the first to go with the others, but she wouldn't do it."

"Take care of the others, Mr. Reed. Your children and mine," Tamsen said. "I'll be all right here until the next relief party comes."

"God be with you, Mrs. Donner," Reed said.

They got under way at noon the next day. The Graveses left, as did the Breens. Patty and Tommy also went, though Keseberg stayed. So did Mrs. Murphy. There were still children who were too weak to travel—her grandson, George Foster, along with Eddy's son Jimmy, and Jacob Donner's two young children, Samuel and Lewis—so she agreed to stay with them.

Within two weeks after the second rescue party left, the food they had brought with them ran out. Keseberg lay in his bed, dreaming of the days when his stomach was full. He could remember hard rolls, and sauerkraut, and *wurst. Blutwurst.* Blood sausage. He wished he had some right now.

Keseberg thought of young Patty Reed, and began thinking about eating her. He should have taken advantage of the situation whenever he had had the chance. It was too late now. She was gone.

He turned onto his side and looked over into the shadows in the corner, where four-year-old George Foster and three-year-old Jimmy Eddy lay. They were beginning to come around now, and Mrs. Murphy had already lamented the fact that they hadn't been this healthy when Reed was here. If they had been, they could have gone with them, and she too.

Keseberg got up and walked over to the bed. He picked up George and carried him back with him. He did not intend to let a second chance get away.

When Lavina Murphy awakened the next morning, she rolled over in her bed and looked at the wall on the opposite side of the room. At first she was confused by what she saw. Then suddenly, the horror of it struck her and she screamed. It was her grandson, hanging from a hook, his head lolling to one side, his eyes open and opaque.

Mrs. Murphy's scream startled the other children awake, and Keseberg sat up quickly.

"What is it?" he asked. "Why are you screaming?"

Unable to speak, Mrs. Murphy just pointed with a shaking, bony finger.

"The boy?" Keseberg challenged. "You scream because of the boy? He is dead. He died from starvation like the others."

Mrs. Murphy looked at Keseberg with fear and disbelief in her eyes.

"You think maybe I killed the boy?" Keseberg asked.

"I . . . I didn't say that," Mrs. Murphy replied.

"*Ja,* it is good you didn't say that, for it is not true." Keseberg got out of bed and walked over to take the boy's body down from the hook. "We will not let his death be in vain," he said. He laid the body down on the floor near the fireplace, then took out his knife and began, very precisely, to cut him up.

Over in the Donner camp, Jean-Baptiste had a little bit of luck. He shot a bear cub. The cub wasn't very big, but it was a godsend right now, and with so few people left in the camp, it could feed them for a few days at least. He would take it back to Tamsen Donner to divide and cook. Thank God for Mrs. Donner. She was the strongest of them all, physically, mentally, and morally. If Tamsen had not had the moral strength to do what had to be done to keep them all alive, Jean-Baptiste did not think he would have survived.

It would be better for Tamsen if Mr. Donner would go ahead and die. Forgive me, Lord, he prayed quickly. But it is true, and you know it is true.

When Reed tried to get the second rescue party moving the next morning, the Breens and the Graveses refused to go.

"Why should we go on?" Pat Breen asked. "We've got a nice warm windbreak here. There's plenty of firewood. It won't hurt none to stay here until we're good rested."

"By God, Breen, you should've stayed in the camp," Reed said angrily. "All these good folks risked their lives to bring you out and what do you do? You squat here."

"There's more relief comin'," Breen replied. "I see no need in hikin' through the snow."

"God will look out for us," Peggy Breen insisted.

"God looks out for those who look out for themselves," Reed replied. "If you stay here and die, you've no one but yourself to blame."

"Aye," Peggy said. "And we're accountable only to ourselves, Mr. Reed, not to you."

"You're responsible for your children too," Reed said.

"They are our children. Go on now. Leave us be," Breen said.

"Let's go," Reed said disgustedly to the others.

The party trudged on while, behind them, the Breens and the Graveses stayed put. Reed could understand the Graveses. Elizabeth Graves was in such bad shape now that she could scarcely go another step, and two of the children weren't far behind. But the Breens were just out-and-out lazy.

When Reed's party camped that night, everyone complained of feet that were numb with cold. When they got the fire going, their feet throbbed with pain as the heat began to restore the circulation, and Reed realized they were all very close to getting a severe case of frostbite. He made them all take off their shoes and socks and rub their feet with snow, warning them that if they didn't, they could wind up losing their toes.

"I am glad you came for us, Pa," Patty said as Reed rubbed her feet. "I knew you would all along."

Reed looked at his daughter and thought of what she had been through. The thought brought tears to his eyes and he held her close to him. When they slept that night, he rolled Patty and Tommy up in the blankets with him. It wasn't until then that he realized Patty was still clutching her Penelope. Once, during the night, the doll fell out into the snow and Reed saw it. He reached down, picked it up, blew the snow off, then put it back into Patty's arms. Without even waking fully, she pulled it to her.

Reed felt his eyes fill with tears.

When Peggy Breen awakened the next morning, she walked over to the opposite side of the campfire to check on the Graveses. She found two bodies: Elizabeth Graves and her one-year-old son, Franklin. She noticed also that the fire had melted all the way through the snow. There was a patch of dry ground around the fire . . . the first time any of them had seen the ground since before Christmas. She moved her family, and what was left of the Graves family, off the snow and onto the ground. Now dry, and with a fire going, they were warm and comfortable, even if they were hungry.

By mid-afternoon of the next day, the Reed–McCutcheon party on the way down encountered Ike, Eddy, and Foster on the way back to the lake camp. The three men had taken their first group to safety, and now they were returning for the others. For Eddy and Foster, it was a personal quest, for each of them had a son in the camp who had been too weak to come out the first time. They were going to bring them out this time if they had to carry them every step of the way.

There was a happy reunion, made more so by the fact that it took place around a cache of food which had survived the animals. Everyone got to eat a hearty meal.

"There are fourteen people camped out on the trail behind us, Will," Reed said. "That is in addition to the people who are still back at the lake camp."

"The people at the lake camp are the most important," Potter said. "Those bastards back on the trail are there of their own accord. They could've come on with us, but they wouldn't."

"The Breens could've come on," McCutcheon agreed.

"But Mrs. Graves was in no shape to travel and neither were any of her children. Ike, we had been two days without food then, and it's been another two days since. There's not much telling what you'll find when you reach them."

"We'll get there as quickly as we can, Mr. Reed," Ike promised. "You get these folks on down. The rest of your family is waiting for you."

"God bless you men for what you have done for us," Reed said. "God bless you."

The two parties went on their separate ways then, Reed and his group going west, Ike and the others going east.

They discovered the Breens' trail encampment the next afternoon. The Breens had a merry fire going and a pot simmering over the fire. Lying on the ground near the pot was a woman's body, both breasts cut away and her heart and liver removed. Sitting on the ground next to the woman was one-year-old Elizabeth. "Ma," she was crying, as she held on to what was left of her mother's mutilated body. "Ma."

For the volunteers, this was a scene beyond belief. Some turned away in shock and began throwing up. For Ike, Eddy, and Foster, it was a vivid reminder of something they had hoped they would never have to see or even think about again.

"Pour that out," Eddy said, pointing to the kettle. "Let's get a real stew going."

They spent the night at the campsite. The next morning, the Breens, fortified with food, decided they were ready to go on.

"You fellas take them on down to Johnson's ranch," Ike said to the volunteers who had come with them. "Mr. Eddy, Mr. Foster, and I will go on to the lake camp."

"Yeah," one of the volunteers said. "Yeah, it would probably be better if we didn't go on with you, wouldn't it?"

Ike knew that the volunteers were anxious to go back with the Breens so that they wouldn't have to go on to the camp. They were beginning to suspect that what they had seen at the trail camp was but a tiny sample of what would be waiting for them at the lake camp. For Ike, Eddy, and Foster, it was more than a suspicion. They knew for a fact what they would find.

Back at the lake, in the Donner camp, Tamsen sat beside the bed of her husband. She had been revived somewhat by the bear meat, and she was buoyed by the knowledge that the outside world now knew of their plight and had already sent two relief parties after them.

"If two have come there will be more," she told her husband when he berated her for not leaving when she had the opportunity. "You don't worry about me. You just lie there and get well."

"Get well," Donner said. He raised his good hand to Tamsen's cheek. "You have nursed me until I am well in spirit, woman," he said. "That is what is important."

Jean-Baptiste came into the cabin carrying an armload of firewood. He dropped it on the hearth, then tossed a few sticks into the flames and held his hands out over the fire.

"How are you gettin' along, Mr. Donner?" he asked.

"Fine, Jean-Baptiste. Fine," Donner replied. "I thought maybe I'd go out and chop down a tree or two today."

Jean-Baptiste laughed, then turned to Tamsen. "Miz Donner, you don't mind, I think I'll hike on up to the other camp and see how things are goin' over there."

"All right, Jean-Baptiste," Tamsen said. "You go ahead. Mr. Donner and I will be fine."

Jean-Baptiste left at about nine, and reached the lake camp by noon. When he saw a couple of half-butchered bodies lying by the entrance of the Murphy cabin, he knew that the camp here had found it necessary to return to cannibalism. So far the bear he had killed had spared the other camp.

"Hello!" Jean-Baptiste called. "Hello! Is anyone there?"

Mrs. Murphy came out of the cabin to meet him. Her eyes were wide with horror, and she looked around, obviously disappointed that he was alone.

"I was thinkin' maybe you were one of them Californians with more food," she said.

"No, ma'am, I'm sorry to say it's only me. Who is left here?"

"There is only me, Keseberg, and the one child he has not yet murdered."

"Murdered?"

"Yes, murdered," Mrs. Murphy invited. "If you don't believe me, go in and have a look."

When Jean-Baptiste stepped into the cabin he saw Keseberg kneeling over the body of a dead child. Keseberg was carving it as precisely as a first-class butcher would cut up a side of beef. He didn't even bother to look around at Jean-Baptiste.

Jean-Baptiste could not stay around anymore. He decided not to return to the Donner camp. There was only Mr. and Mrs. Donner now, and Mr. Donner would be dead within two or three more days. Without Mr. Donner and Jean-Baptiste eating, the bear meat that was left could feed Mrs. Donner for several more days, perhaps until the next rescue party arrived. Anyway, she'd had her chance to leave and she hadn't taken it. Whatever happened to her now was her own fault. It was time for Jean-Baptiste to leave.

When Ike, Eddy, and Foster reached the lake camp they were stunned by what they saw. The snow was littered with corpses. The bodies had been selectively mutilated, as if only the choicest parts were being taken from each. The three men had been through it themselves, but even they were not quite prepared to see it on such a large scale.

"Look, over there," Foster said, pointing. "Do you see where the snow has melted down? There are whole legs of beef exposed now."

"Then why all this?" Eddy asked, taking in the mutilated bodies with a sweep of his hand. "Have these people gone stark raving mad?"

"I don't know," Ike said. "Let's find out. Keseberg! Keseberg, are you here?" he shouted.

"There, over there!" Foster said, pointing.

Ike saw something, a shadowlike movement.

"Keseberg, is that you?"

A filthy scarecrow of a man came out from behind one of the cabins. His hair and beard were long, stringy, and matted with dry blood. His eyes were dark and beady. Except for the filth, and the wild look in his face and eyes, he was amazingly healthy looking. He was not skin-and-bones thin as the others had been.

"So, you have come back," Keseberg said.

"Where are the others?"

"Others? There are no others."

"The children," Eddy said. "Where is my son?"

"And mine?" Foster asked.

"I have consumed them. Both of them," Keseberg replied matter-of-factly.

"What?" Eddy asked in a weak voice.

"They died, and I ate them," Keseberg said. "I have eaten many others as well. Sam and Lewis Donner. Milt Elliot. John Landrum Murphy, Lavina Murphy, and others. It was necessary. It was all necessary."

"Man, what are you talking about?" Ike asked. "Don't you know the beef is exposed now? You didn't have to do all this. You could've been eating beef."

Keseberg waved his hand. "The beef is stringy and too dry for eating. Human liver and lungs taste much better. And human brains make a good soup."

"My God," Foster said. "You have gone mad."

"Let's go over to the other camp," Ike said. "We'll get Tamsen Donner and get out of here."

"You cannot get her, I am afraid," Keseberg said.

"If she's still staying because of her husband, I'll take care of that," Ike said.

"Her husband is dead."

"Then she has no reason to stay."

"She is also dead," Keseberg added.

"What? How?"

Keseberg shrugged his shoulders. "Many have died," he said. "It is not surprising that one more should."

"But she was the healthiest of anyone," Ike insisted.

"I do not know why she died. But she died."

"Where is the body? I want to see it."

"What remains of her is in there," Keseberg said, pointing to a large black kettle.

"You ate her, too?"

"Yes. She was the best of them all," Keseberg said. "She had several pounds of fat."

"Ike, look. Look what I found," Eddy said, opening a bundle that had been lying on the snow just outside the cabin. The bundle held silk, jewelry, a brace of pistols, and several gold coins. "You ever see any of this before?"

"The pistols are George Donner's," Ike said.

"I thought so. The jewelry and silk belonged to Tamsen. Like as not the gold did too."

"It is mine now," Keseberg insisted. "Mrs. Donner gave it all to me as payment for letting her stay with me until she died."

"You mean she paid you to kill her?" Eddy growled.

"Kill her? I did not kill her. I ate her, yes, but I did not kill her. Just as I did not kill any of the children."

With a shout of rage, Eddy swung at Keseberg, catching him on the point of his chin and dropping him. Keseberg rolled into a ball and began to whimper.

"I did nothing wrong!" he shouted. "I am not the only one who ate the dead!"

Eddy had already raised his foot to stomp Keseberg, but he paused, then turned away with tears stinging his eyes. Keseberg was right, he was not the only one who had eaten the dead. Eddy had as well, as had Ike and Foster.

Ike, seeing the change in Eddy's expression, knew what he was thinking. He put his hand out to Eddy's shoulder.

Keseberg realized then that he wasn't going to be beaten anymore, so he got up, rubbing his chin and glaring at the men.

"Who are you to judge me?" he asked.

"Shut your mouth, Keseberg," Ike said.

"I was only saying . . ."

"I said shut up!" Ike yelled, doubling his own fist.

Keseberg cowered back, then watched the three men, his rodentlike eyes darting fearfully from one to the other. He glanced over at the pistols, but they were worthless to him. Not only were they too far away, they weren't even loaded.

"Come on," Ike said, regaining his composure. "Let's get out of here."

"Ja, ja, I will just get my things together," Keseberg replied, turning to go into the cabin.

"I wasn't talking to you, you son of a bitch," Ike said. "You aren't going with us."

"What? But you must take me with you. I am the only one left."

"You're staying here."

"I will not stay here any longer. If you go, I will follow you," Keseberg said.

"No!" Foster said angrily. "If you try to follow us, so help me I'll kill you and eat you myself."

"Do you think such talk frightens me? You are just talking so because you are angry now," Keseberg said. "What you have seen here has disgusted you. That is why I know you wouldn't really do such a thing."

Foster smiled, and for a moment Ike recognized the same demonic expression in Foster's face that he had seen just before Foster had killed the two Indians.

"Do you want to try the experiment?" he asked almost benignly.

"Keseberg, I would believe him if I were you," Ike said flatly.

Keseberg, with a look of fear on his face, took several steps back. Then, with a shaking finger, he pointed. "All right, go then," he said. "Go away from here and leave me be."

Eddy gathered up the little bundle that had belonged to Tamsen Donner. Though none of the Donner adults had survived, six of the Donner children had. This would be theirs.

"No, you cannot take that! That is mine!" Keseberg insisted.

No one even answered him. Instead, with one final look of disgust, the three men turned and walked away. They were nearly fifty yards away when Keseberg came running out of his cabin and started yelling at them. At first he cursed them in German, then in English. Then he stopped cursing and began pleading.

"Don't leave me here!" Keseberg shouted, and his shout bounced back from the mountain. *"Don't leave me here . . . here . . . here!"*

"You cannot do this!" He shouted. *"You cannot do this . . . this . . . this!"*

"I will live!"

"I will live . . . live . . . live!" the echo returned.

"I will eat the bodies who are left here! I will eat your children! I will eat your friends! I will eat them all!"

"I will eat them all . . . eat them all . . . eat them all!"

Keseberg continued to shout for several more minutes, even after they were too far to be able to hear what he was saying.

They reached the top of the pass just before nightfall. As Ike stepped upon the flat, gray rock that had become symbolic of the pass, he turned and looked back. From there he could see the remnants of the wagons, now beginning to emerge from the snow. In a way those dead, gray wagon shells were as grotesque as the mutilated bodies that lay scattered about the lake camp. He studied them, and the camp, for one long moment, then turned and stepped over the rock. Soon it would all be behind him.

July 6th, 1931
As the airliner flew east across the Sierra Nevadas, John Buford looked down on the mountains below. The peaks were snow-covered, but the slopes and passes were green with the

thick growth of evergreen trees. It was quite possible that he
was now looking down upon the very trees Aunt Patty, his
grandfather, and the others had used for shelter, or to provide
wood for their life-saving fires.

He saw a road winding through the pass, and on the road
there were at least a dozen or more cars and trucks. He
thought of how routinely they were taking the pass today, and
he wondered if any of them had any idea of how easily they
were traversing a route that had been difficult in his grandfather's day.

A sun glare flashed off something ahead, and he reposi-
tioned himself in the seat so he could look beyond the
spinning propeller at the lake. This was Truckee Lake, now
called Donner Lake, and it was the same lake alongside
which his grandfather and the others had camped. As John
stared at it, he could almost see the snow, the cabins, the bear
Will Eddy and his grandfather had killed, and the maniacal
Lewis Keseberg, raving madly as he strolled along its shores,
going about his grisly business.

Aunt Patty had told him that Keseberg had managed to
come out, and, in a final bit of irony, had even opened a
restaurant. The entire Reed family had survived, and James
Reed had made a fortune in California real estate.

John's grandfather Ike did start his newspaper, and though
the paper was never as large or as prominent as some of the
other California newspapers, it did manage to support him
and his family until his later years, when he sold it and moved
back to St. Louis.

"I see you are looking at Donner Lake, sir!" the stewardess
shouted over the sound of the engines.

John turned to see her leaning over his seat, looking
through the window with him.

"Yes," he said.

"Have you ever been there?"

"No."

"I haven't either, but I am told it is a beautiful place to go
camping. In the wintertime people cut holes in the ice and go

fishing." The stewardess chuckled. "They say that such fishing is marvelous, though I can't believe it is something I would want to do. Have you ever been ice-fishing?"

"No."

"My cousin took his family camping and ice-fishing at that very lake last winter, and they caught enough fish to feed them for an entire week. Isn't that something?"

"Yes," John answered. "Yes, it is."

"But of course, I don't suppose winter camping is for everyone. Would you like a stick of gum?" She held out the little tray.

"Yes, thank you," John said. He put the gum in his mouth, then turned to look at the lake again. They were already passing over it. Soon it would be behind him.